NORA ROBERTS

Gabriel's Angel

Harlequin Mills & Boon

First Published 1989
First Australian Paperback Edition 2004
ISBN 0 733 55162 9

Published by
Harlequin Mills & Boon
3 Gibbes Street
CHATSWOOD NSW 2067
AUSTRALIA

Printed and bound in Australia by
McPherson's Printing Group

To Tom and Ky and Larry,
for having the good sense to marry well.

Chapter 1

Damn snow. Gabe downshifted to second gear, slowed the Jeep to fifteen miles an hour, swore and strained his eyes. Through the frantic swing of the wipers on the windshield all that could be seen was a wall of white. No winter wonderland. Snow pelted down in flakes that looked as big and as mean as a man's fist.

There would be no waiting out this storm, he thought as he took the next curve at a crawl. He considered himself lucky that after six months he knew the narrow, winding road from town so well. He could drive almost by feel, but a newcomer wouldn't stand a chance. Even with that advantage, his shoulders and the back of his neck were tight with tension. Colorado snows could be as vicious in spring as they were in the dead of winter, and they could last for an hour or a day. Apparently this one had been a surprise to everyone—residents, tourists and the National Weather Service.

He had only five miles to go. Then he could unload his supplies, stoke his fire and enjoy the April blizzard from the comfort of his cabin, with a hot cup of coffee or an ice cold beer.

The Jeep chugged up the incline like a tank, and he was grateful for its sturdy perseverance. The unexpected snowfall might force him to take three times as long to make the twenty-mile trip from town to home, but at least he'd get there.

The wipers worked furiously to clear the windshield. There were seconds of white vision followed by seconds of white blindness. At this rate there would be better than two feet by nightfall. Gabe comforted himself with the thought that he'd be home long before that, even as the air in the Jeep turned blue from his cursing. If he hadn't lost track of the time the day before, he'd have had his supplies and been able to laugh at the weather.

The road went into a lazy S and Gabe took it cautiously. It was difficult for him to move slowly under any circumstances, but over the winter he had gained a healthy respect for the mountains and the roads that had been blasted through them. The guardrail was sturdy enough, but beneath it the cliffs were unforgiving. He wasn't worried so much about making a mistake himself—the Jeep was solid as a rock—but he thought of others who might be traveling north or south on the pass, pulling over to the side or stopping dead in the middle of the road.

He wanted a cigarette. His hands gripping the wheel

hard, he all but lusted for a cigarette. But it was a luxury that would have to wait. Three miles to go.

The tension in his shoulders began to ease. He hadn't seen another car in more than twenty minutes, and he wasn't likely to now. Anyone with any sense would have taken shelter. From this point on he could almost feel his way home. A good thing. Beside him the radio was squawking about roads closed and activities canceled. It always amazed Gabe that people planned so many meetings, luncheons, recitals and rehearsals on any given day.

But that was human nature, he supposed. Always planning on drawing together, if only to sell a bunch of cakes and cookies. He preferred to be alone. At least for now. Otherwise he wouldn't have bought the cabin and buried himself in it for the last six months.

The solitude gave him freedom, to think, to work, to heal. He'd done some of all three.

He nearly sighed when he saw—or rather felt—the road slant upward again. This was the final rise before his turnoff. Only a mile now. His face, which had been hard and tight with concentration, relaxed. It wasn't a smooth or particularly handsome face. It was too thin and angular to be merely pleasant, and the nose was out of alignment due to a heated disagreement with his younger brother during their teens. Gabe hadn't held it against him.

Because he'd forgotten to wear a hat, his dark blond hair fell untidily around his face. It was long and a bit shaggy over the collar of his parka and had been styled hastily with his fingers hours before. His eyes, a dark, clear green, were starting to burn from staring at the snow.

While his tires swished over the cushioned asphalt he

glanced down at his odometer, saw that there was only a quarter mile left, then looked back to the road. That was when he saw a car coming at him out of control.

He didn't even have time to swear. He jerked the Jeep to the right just as the oncoming car seemed to come out of its spin. The Jeep skimmed over the snow piled on the shoulder, swaying dangerously before the tires chewed down to the road surface for traction. He had a bad moment when he thought the Jeep was going to roll over like a turtle. Then all he could do was sit and watch and hope the other driver was as lucky.

The oncoming car was barreling down the road sideways. Though only seconds had passed, Gabe had time to think of how nasty the impact would be when the car slammed into him. Then the driver managed to straighten out. With only feet between them the car fishtailed and swerved to avoid the collision, then began to slide helplessly toward the guardrail. Gabe set his emergency brake and was out of the Jeep when the car rammed into the metal.

He nearly fell on his face, but his boots held as he raced across the road. It was a compact—a bit more compact now, with its right side shoved in and its hood sprung like an accordion, also on the passenger side. He had another moment to think, and he grimaced at the thought of what would have happened if the car had hit on the driver's side.

Fighting his way through the snow, he managed to make it to the wrecked car. He saw a figure slumped over the wheel, and he yanked at the door. It was locked. With his heart in his throat, he began to pound against the window.

The figure moved. A woman, he saw from the thick wave

of wheat-blond hair that spilled onto the shoulders of a dark coat. He watched her reach up and drag a ski cap from her head. Then she turned her face to the window and stared at him.

She was white, marble white. Even her lips were colorless. Her eyes were huge and dark, the irises almost black with shock. And she was beautiful, stunningly breathtakingly beautiful. The artist in him saw the possibilities in the diamond-shaped face, the prominent cheekbones, the full lower lip. The man in him rejected them and banged on the glass again.

She blinked and shook her head as if to clear it. As the shock passed out of them, he saw that her eyes were blue, a midnight blue. They filled now with a rush of concern. In a quick movement she rolled down the window.

"Are you hurt?" she demanded before he could speak. "Did I hit you?"

"No, you hit the guardrail."

"Thank God." She let her head slump back on the seat for a moment. Her mouth was as dry as dust. And her heart, though she was already fighting to control it, was thudding in her throat. "I started to skid coming down the incline. I thought—I hoped—I might be able to ride it out. Then I saw you and I was sure I was going to hit you."

"You would have if you hadn't swerved away toward the rail." He glanced at the front of her car again. The damage could have been worse, much worse. If she'd been going any faster… There was no use speculating. He turned to her again, studying her face for signs of shock or concussion. "Are you all right?"

"Yes. I think so." She opened her eyes again and tried

to smile at him. "I'm sorry. I must have given you quite a scare."

"At least." But the scare was over now. He was less than a quarter of a mile from hearth and home, and stuck in the snow with a strange woman whose car wasn't going anywhere for several days. "What the hell are you doing out here?"

She took the furiously bitten-off words in stride as she unhooked her seat belt. The long, deep breaths she'd been taking had gone a long way toward steadying her. "I must have gotten turned around in the storm. I was trying to get down to Lonesome Ridge to wait it out, find a place for the night. That's the closest town, according to the map, and I was afraid to pull over on the shoulder." She glanced over at the guardrail and shuddered. "What there is of it. I don't suppose there's any way I'm going to get my car out of here."

"Not tonight."

Frowning, Gabe stuck his hands in his pockets. The snow was still falling, and the road was deserted. If he turned around and walked back to his Jeep, leaving her to fend for herself, she might very well freeze to death before an emergency vehicle or a snowplow came along. However much he'd have liked to shrug off the obligation, he couldn't leave a woman stranded in this storm.

"The best I can do is take you with me." There wasn't an ounce of graciousness in his tone. She hadn't expected any. If he was angry and impatient about nearly being plowed into, and inconvenienced on top of it, he was entitled.

"I'm sorry."

He moved his shoulders, aware that he'd been rude. ''The turnoff for my cabin's at the top of the hill. You'll have to leave your car and ride in the Jeep.''

''I'd appreciate it.'' With the engine off and the window open, the cold was beginning to seep through her clothes. ''I'm sorry for the imposition, Mr.—?''

''Bradley. Gabe Bradley.''

''I'm Laura.'' She slipped out of the safety harness that had undoubtedly saved her from injury. ''I have a suitcase in the trunk, if you wouldn't mind giving me a hand with it.''

Gabe took the keys and stomped back toward the trunk, thinking that if he'd only left an hour earlier that afternoon he'd be home—alone—at this moment.

The case wasn't large, and it was far from new. The lady with only one name traveled light, he thought. He muttered to himself as he hefted it out of the trunk. There was no use being angry with her, or being snotty. If she hadn't managed to skid quite so well, if she hadn't avoided him, they might have been needing a doctor now instead of a cup of coffee and dry feet.

Deciding to be more civil, Gabe turned to tell her to go across to the Jeep. She was standing, watching him, with the snow falling on her uncovered hair. That was when he saw she was not only beautiful, she was very, very pregnant.

''Oh, God'' was all he could manage.

''I'm really sorry to be so much trouble,'' Laura began. ''And I want to thank you in advance for the lift. If I could call from your cabin and find a tow truck, maybe we could clear this whole thing up quickly.''

He hadn't heard a word she'd said. Not one. All he could do was stare at the ripe slope beneath her dark coat. "Are you sure you're all right? You didn't tell me you were—Are you going to need a doctor?"

"I'm fine." This time she smiled, fully. The cold had brought the color back into her face. "Really. The baby wasn't hurt. He's annoyed a bit, I'd say from the way he's kicking me, but we hardly felt the impact. We didn't ram the guardrail, we sort of slid into it."

"You might have..." What? he wondered. "Jarred something."

"I'm fine," she said again. "I was strapped in, and the snow, though it started it all, cushioned the hit." Noting that he still seemed unconvinced, she tossed back her snow-covered hair. Her fingers, though they were tucked into subtle, silk-lined leather, were going numb. "I promise, I'm not going to give birth in the middle of the road—unless you plan on standing here for a few more weeks."

She was all right...he hoped. And the way she was smiling at him made him feel like an idiot. Deciding to take her word for it, he offered her a hand. "Let me help you."

The words, such simple words, went straight to her heart. She could have counted on her hands the number of times she had heard them.

He didn't know how to deal with pregnant women. Were they fragile? It had always seemed to him that the opposite must be true, given what they had to go through, but now, faced with one, he was afraid she'd shatter at a touch.

Mindful of the slippery road, Laura took a firm grip on his arm as they started across. "It's beautiful here," she said when they reached the Jeep. "But I have to admit, I'm going to appreciate the snow more from inside.'' She glanced at the high step below the door of the Jeep. ''I think you're going to have to give me a bit of a boost. I'm not as agile as I used to be.''

Gabe stowed her case, wondering exactly where to grab her. Mumbling, he put a hand under her elbow and another on her hip. Laura slid into the seat with less fuss than he'd expected.

''Thanks.''

He grunted a response as he slammed the door. He skirted the hood, then took his place behind the wheel. It took a little maneuvering, but with a minimum of effort they inched back onto the road.

The dependable Jeep started up the hill. Laura uncurled her hands as they moved along at a steady pace. They'd finally stopped shaking. ''I wasn't sure anyone lived along here. If I'd known, I'd have begged a roof long before this. I wasn't expecting a snowstorm in April.''

''We get them later than this.'' He said nothing for a moment. He respected other people's privacy as zealously as his own. But these were unusual circumstances. ''You're traveling alone?''

''Yes.''

''Isn't that a little risky in your condition?''

''I'd planned on being in Denver in a couple of days.'' She laid a hand lightly on her belly. ''I'm not due for six weeks.'' Laura took a deep breath. It was a risk to trust him, but she really had no other option. ''Do you live alone, Mr. Bradley?''

''Yes.''

She shifted her gaze just enough to study him as he

turned down a narrow, snow-covered lane. At least she assumed a lane was buried somewhere under all the white. There was something tough and hard about his face. Not rugged, she thought. It was too lean and fine-boned for that. It was coldly sculpted, as she imagined a mythic warrior chief's might be.

But she remembered the stunned male helplessness in his eyes when he'd seen she was pregnant. She believed she'd be safe with him. She had to believe that.

He felt her gaze and read her thoughts easily enough. "I'm not a maniac," he said mildly.

"I appreciate that." She smiled a little, then turned to look out the windshield again.

The cabin could barely be seen through the snow, even when he stopped in front of it. But what Laura could see, she loved. It was a squat rectangle of wood with a covered porch and square-paned windows. Smoke puffed from the chimney.

Though it was buried under snow, there was a path of flat rocks leading from the lane to the front steps. Evergreens mantled with white trooped around the corners. Nothing had ever looked as safe and warm as this snow-decked little cabin in the mountains.

"It's lovely. You must be happy here."

"It does the job." Gabe came around to help her down. She smelled like the snow, he thought, or perhaps more like water, the pure, virginal water that poured down the mountain in the spring. "I'll take you in," he told her, knowing both his reaction and his comparison were ridiculous. "You can warm up by the fire." Gabe opened the front door and waved her in. "Go ahead. I'll bring in the rest."

He left her alone, snow dripping wet from her coat onto the woven mat inside the door.

The paintings. Laura stood just where she was and stared openmouthed at the paintings. They covered the walls, they were stacked in corners, they were piled on tables. Only a few were framed. They didn't need the ornamentation. Some where half finished, as though the artist had lost interest or motivation. There were oils, in colors vivid and harsh, and watercolors in soft, misty hues that might have sprung from dreams. Shrugging out of her coat, Laura moved in for a closer look.

There was a scene from Paris, the Bois de Boulogne. She remembered it from her honeymoon. Looking at it made her eyes swim and her muscles tense. Breathing deeply, she forced herself to look at it until her emotions settled.

An easel was set near the window, where the light would come in and fall on the canvas. She resisted the temptation to go over and steal a look. She already had the sensation that she was trespassing.

What was she going to do? Laura gripped her hands together tightly as she let the despair come. She was stranded, her car wrecked, her money dwindling. And the baby— The baby wasn't going to wait until she made things right.

If they found her now…

They weren't going to find her. Deliberately she unlaced her hands. She'd come this far. No one was going to take her baby, now or ever.

She turned as the door to the cabin opened. Gabe shifted

the bags he'd carried inside, leaving them jumbled together in a pile. He, too, shrugged out of his coat and hung it on a hook by the door.

He was as lean as his face had indicated. Though he might have been a bit under six feet, the spare toughness of his build gave the illusion of more height, more power. More like a boxer than an artist, Laura thought as she watched him kick the clinging snow from his boots. More like a man of the outdoors than one who came from graceful mansions and gentle blood.

Despite what she knew of his aristocratic background, he wore flannel and corduroy and looked perfectly suited to the rustic cabin. Laura, who came from humbler stock, felt fussy and out of place in her bulky Irish knit sweater and tailored wool.

''Gabriel Bradley,'' she said, and gestured widely toward the walls. ''My brain must have been scrambled before. I didn't put it together. I love your work.''

''Thanks.'' Bending, he hefted two of the bags.

''Let me help—''

''No.'' He strode off into the kitchen, leaving Laura biting her lip.

He wasn't thrilled to have her company, she thought. Then she shrugged. It couldn't be helped. As soon as it was reasonably safe for her to leave, she would leave. Until then… Until then Gabriel Bradley, artist of the decade, would have to make do.

It was tempting just to take a seat and passively stay out of his way. Once she would have done just that, but circumstances had changed her. She followed him into the adjoining kitchen. Counting the baby she carried, there were three of them in the little room, and it was filled to capacity.

"At least let me make you something hot to drink." The ancient two-burner stove looked tricky, but she was determined.

He turned, brushed against her belly and was amazed at the wave of discomfort he felt. And the tug of fascination. "Here's the coffee," he mumbled, handing her a fresh can.

"Got a pot?"

It was in the sink, which was filled with water that had once been sudsy. He had been trying to soak out the stains from the last time he'd used it. He moved to get it, bumped her again and stepped back.

"Why don't you let me take care of it?" she suggested. "I'll put this stuff away and start the coffee, and you can call a tow truck."

"Fine. There's milk. Fresh."

She smiled. "I don't suppose you have any tea."

"No."

"Milk's fine, then. Thank you."

When he left, Laura busied herself in the kitchen. It was too small for it to be complicated. She used her own system in storing the goods since it appeared Gabe had none. She'd only emptied the first bag when he reappeared in the doorway.

"Phone's out."

"Out?"

"Dead. We lose service a lot when there's a storm."

"Oh." Laura stood holding a can of soup. "Is it usually out for long?"

"Depends. Sometimes a couple hours, sometimes a week."

She lifted a brow. Then she realized that he was perfectly serious. "I guess that puts me in your hands, Mr. Bradley."

He hooked his thumbs in his front pockets. "In that case, you better call me Gabe."

Laura frowned down at the can in her hand. When things got bad, you made the best of them. "Want some soup?"

"Yeah. I'll, ah...put your things in the bedroom."

Laura simply nodded, then began to search for a can opener.

She was a piece of work, all right, Gabe decided as he carried Laura's suitcase into his room. Not that he was an expert when it came to women, but he wasn't what anyone would have called a novice, either. She hadn't batted an eye when he'd told her that the phone was dead and they were effectively cut off from the outside world. Or, to put it more precisely, that she was cut off from everyone but him.

Gabe glanced into the streaked mirror over his battered dresser. As far as he knew, no one had ever considered him harmless before. A quick, cocky smile flashed over his face. He hadn't always been harmless, when it came right down to it.

This, of course, was an entirely different situation.

Under other circumstances he might have entertained some healthy fantasies about his unexpected guest. That face. There was something haunting, something indefinable, about that kind of beauty. When a man looked at it, he automatically began to wonder and imagine. Even if she hadn't been carrying a child, the fantasies would have remained only that. Fantasies. He'd never been enthusiastic about flings and one-night stands, and he certainly wasn't in any shape for a relationship. Celibacy had been the order of the day for the last few months. The desire to paint had finally seduced him again. Gabe needed no other love affair.

But as for more practical matters, he did have a guest, a lone woman who was very pregnant—and very secretive. He hadn't missed the fact that she'd told him only her first name and hadn't volunteered any information about who she was and where and why she was traveling. Since it was unlikely that she'd robbed a bank or stolen secrets for the Russians, he wouldn't press too hard right now.

But, given the strength of the storm and the seclusion of the cabin, they were likely to be together for a few days. He was going to find out more about the calm and mysterious Laura.

What was she going to do? Laura stared at the empty plate in her hand and saw a hint of her reflection. How could she get to Denver or Los Angeles or Seattle—or any huge, swallowing city that was far enough away from Boston—when she was trapped here? If only she hadn't felt that urgent need to move on this morning. If she'd stayed in that quiet little motel room another day she might still have had some control over what was happening.

Instead, she was here with a stranger. Not just any stranger, Laura reminded herself. Gabriel Bradley, artist—wealthy, respected artist from a wealthy, respected family. But he hadn't recognized her. Laura was certain of that. At least he had yet to recognize her. What would happen when he did, when he found out who she was running from? For all she knew, the Eagletons might be close family friends of the Bradleys. The gesture of her hand over the mound of her stomach was automatic and protective.

They wouldn't take her baby. No matter how much money and how much power they wielded, they wouldn't take her baby. And if she could manage it they would never find her or the child.

Setting down the plate, she turned her attention to the window. How odd it was to look out and see nothing. It gave her a nice, settled feeling to know that no one could see in, either. She was effectively curtained off from everyone. Or nearly everyone, she corrected, thinking again of Gabe.

Perhaps the storm had been a blessing. When there was no choice, she found it best to look on the bright side. No one could follow her trail in this kind of weather. And who would think of looking for her in some tiny, out-of-the-way cabin in the mountains? It felt safe. She would cling to that.

She heard him moving around in the next room, heard the sound of his boots on the hardwood, the thud of a log being added to the fire. After so many months alone she found even the sound of another human being a comfort.

''Mr. Bradley...Gabe?'' She stepped through the doorway to see him adjusting the screen in front of the fire. ''Could you clear off a table?''

''Clear off a table?''

''So we could eat...sitting down.''

''Yeah.''

She disappeared again while he tried to figure out what to do with the paints, brushes, canvas stretchers and general disorder on the picnic table that had once served as a dining area. Annoyed at having his space compromised, he spread his equipment throughout the room.

"I made some sandwiches, too." Using a bent cookie sheet as a makeshift tray, she carried in bowls and plates and cups. Embarrassed and edgy, Gabe snatched it from her.

"You shouldn't be carrying heavy things."

Her brows lifted. Surprise came first. No one had ever pampered her. And certainly her life, which had rarely been easy, had been hardest over the last seven months. Then gratitude came, and she smiled. "Thanks, but I'm careful."

"If you were careful, you'd be in your own bed with your feet up and not snowbound with me."

"Exercise is important." But she sat and let him set out the dishes. "And so's food." With her eyes closed, she breathed in the scents. Hot, simple, fortifying. "I hope I didn't put too much of a dent in your supplies, but once I got started I couldn't stop."

Gabe picked up half a sandwich that was thick with cheese, crisp bacon and sliced hothouse tomatoes. "I'm not complaining." The truth was, he'd gotten into the habit of eating right out of the pan over the kitchen sink. Hot food made with more care than hurry tasted one hell of a lot better from a plate.

"I'd like to pay you back, for the bed and the food."

"Don't worry about it." He scooped up clam chowder while he studied her. She had a way of sticking out her chin that made him think of pride and will. It made an interesting contrast with the creamy skin and the slender neck.

"That's kind of you, but I prefer paying my own way."

"This isn't the Hilton." She wore no jewelry, he noted, not even a plain gold band on her finger. "You cooked the meal, so we'll call it even."

She wanted to argue—her pride wanted to argue—but the simple truth was, she had very little cash, except for the baby fund she'd scrupulously set aside in the lining of her suitcase. "I'm very grateful." She sipped at the milk, though she detested it. The scent of his coffee was rich and forbidden. "Have you been here long, in Colorado?"

"Six months, seven, I guess."

That gave her hope. The timing was good, almost too good. From the looks of the cabin, he didn't spend much time poring over the newspapers, and she hadn't noticed a television. "It must be a wonderful place to paint."

"So far."

"I couldn't believe it when I walked in. I recognized your work right away. I've always admired it. In fact, my—someone I knew bought a couple of your pieces. One of them was a painting of a huge, deep forest. It seemed as though you could step right into it and be completely alone."

He knew the work, and, oddly enough, he'd had the same feeling about it. He couldn't be sure, but he thought it had been sold back east. New York, Boston, perhaps Washington, D.C. If his curiosity about her persisted, it would only take a phone call to his agent to refresh his memory.

"You didn't say where you were traveling from."

"No." She continued to eat, though her appetite had fled. How could she have been foolish enough to describe the painting? Tony had bought it, or rather had snapped his fingers and arranged for his lawyers to buy it on his behalf because Laura had admired it. "I've been in Dallas for a while."

She'd been there almost two months before she'd discovered that the Eagletons' detectives were making discreet inquiries about her.

"You don't sound like a Texan."

"No, I suppose I don't. That's probably because I've lived all over the country." That was true enough, and she was able to smile again. "You're not from Colorado."

"San Francisco."

"Yes, I remember reading that in an article about you and your work." She would talk about him. From her experience men were easily distracted when the conversation centered on themselves. "I've always wanted to see San Francisco. It seems like a lovely place, the hills, the bay, the beautiful old houses." She gave a quick gasp and pressed a hand to her stomach.

"What is it?"

"The baby's just restless." She smiled, but he noted that her eyes were shadowed with fatigue and her complexion was pale again.

"Look, I don't know anything about what you're going through, but common sense tells me you should be lying down."

"Actually, I am tired. If you wouldn't mind, I'd like to rest for a few minutes."

"The bed's through here." He rose and, not certain she could get up and down on her own, offered her a hand.

"I'll take care of the dishes later if…" Her words trailed off as her knees buckled.

"Hold on." Gabe put his arms around her and had the odd, rather humbling sensation of having the baby move against him.

"I'm sorry. It's been a long day, and I guess I pushed it further than I should have." She knew she should move away, pull back on her own, but there was something exquisite about leaning against the hard, sturdy body of a man. "I'll be fine after a nap."

She didn't shatter as he'd once thought she might, but now she seemed so soft, so delicate, that he imagined her dissolving in his hands. He would have liked to comfort her, would have liked to go on holding her like that while she leaned into him, trusting, depending. Needing him. Calling himself a fool, he picked her up.

Laura started to protest, but it felt so good to be off her feet. "I must weigh a ton."

"That's what I was expecting, but you don't."

She found she could laugh, even though the fatigue was smothering her. "You're a real charmer, Gabe."

His own awkwardness began to fade as he moved through the door to the bedroom. "I haven't had many opportunities to flirt with pregnant ladies."

"That's all right. You redeemed yourself by rescuing this one from a snowstorm." With her eyes half closed, she felt herself being lowered onto a bed. It might be nothing more than a mattress and a rumpled sheet, but it felt like heaven. "I want to thank you."

"You've been doing that on an average of every five minutes." He pulled a slightly ragged comforter over her. "If you really want to thank me, get some sleep and don't go into labor."

"Fair enough. Gabe?"

"Yeah."

"Will you keep trying the phone?"

"All right." She was nearly asleep. He had a moment's attack of guilt for wanting to press her while she was vulnerable. Right now, she didn't look as though she had the strength to brush away a fly. "Do you want me to call anyone for you? Your husband?"

She opened her eyes at that. Though they were clouded with fatigue, they met his levelly, and he saw that she wasn't down for the count yet.

"I'm not married," she said, very clearly. "There's no one to call."

Chapter 2

In the dream she was alone. That didn't frighten her. Laura had spent a large portion of her life alone, so she was more comfortable in solitude than in a crowd. There was a soft, misty quality to the dream—like the seascape she had seen on the wall of Gabe's cabin.

Oddly, she could even hear the ocean, purring and lapping off in the distance, though a part of her knew she was in the mountains. She walked through a pearl-colored fog, listening to the waves. Under her feet sand shifted, warm and soft. She felt safe and strong and strangely unencumbered. It had been a long, long time since she had felt so free, so at ease.

She knew she was dreaming. That was the best part. If she could have managed it, she would have stayed there, in the soft-focused fantasy of it, forever. It would be so easy to keep her eyes closed and cling to the utter peace of the dream.

Then the baby was crying. Screaming. A pulse began to beat in her temple as she listened to the high, keening wails. She started to sweat, and the clean white fog changed to a dark, threatening gray. No longer warm, the air took on a chill that whipped straight to the bone.

The cries seemed to come from everywhere and nowhere, echoing and rebounding as she searched. Sobbing for breath, she fought her way through the mist as it circled and thickened. The cries became louder, more urgent. Her heart was beating in her throat, and her breath rasped and her hands shook.

Then she saw the bassinet, with its pretty white skirt and its lacy pink and blue ruffles. The relief was so great that her knees sagged.

''It's all right,'' she murmured as she gathered the child in her arms. ''It's all right. I'm here now.'' She could feel the baby's warm breath against her cheek, could feel the weight in her arms as she rocked and soothed. The fine scent of powder surrounded her. Gently she cradled the child, murmuring and comforting as she began to lift the concealing blanket from its face.

And there was nothing, nothing in her arms but an empty blanket.

Gabe was sitting at the picnic table, sketching her face, thinking of her, when he heard her cry out. The moan was so long, so desperate, that he snapped the pencil in two before he jumped up and raced to the bedroom.

''Hey, come on.'' Feeling awkward, he took her by the shoulders. She jerked so hard that he had to fight back his own panic, as well as hers, to hold on to her. "Laura, take it easy. Are you in pain? Is it the baby? Laura, tell me what's going on."

"They took my baby!" There was hysteria in her voice, but it was a hysteria that was laced with fury. "Help me! They took my baby!"

"No one took your baby." She was still fighting him, with a strength that awed him. Moving on instinct, he wrapped his arms around her. "You're having a dream. No one took your baby. Here." He clamped a hand around her wrist, where her pulse was beating like a jackhammer, and dragged her hand to her belly. "You're safe, both of you. Relax before you hurt yourself."

When she felt the life beneath her palms, she slumped against him. Her baby was safe, still inside her, where no one could touch him. "I'm sorry. It was a dream."

"It's okay." Without being aware of it, he was stroking her hair, cradling her as she had cradled the baby of her imagination, rocking her gently in an age-old comforting motion. "Do us both a favor and relax."

She nodded, feeling protected and sheltered. Those were two sensations she had experienced very rarely in her twenty-five years. "I'm all right, really. It must have been the shock from the accident catching up with me."

He drew her away, angry with himself because he wanted to go on holding her, shielding her. When she had asked him for help, he had known, without understanding why, that he would do anything to protect her. It was almost as though he had been dreaming himself, or had been caught up in her dream.

The snow was still falling in sheets outside the window

and the only light was what came slanting through the bedroom door from the main cabin. It was dim and slightly yellow, but he could see her clearly, and he wanted to be certain that she saw him, as well. He wanted answers, and he wanted them now.

"Don't lie to me. Under normal circumstances you'd be entitled to your privacy, but right now you're under my roof for God knows how long."

"I'm not lying to you." Her voice was so calm, so even, that he nearly believed her. "I'm sorry if I upset you."

"Who are you running from, Laura?"

She said nothing, just stared at him with those dark blue eyes. He swore at her, but she didn't flinch. He sprang up to pace the room, but she didn't shudder. Abruptly he dropped down on the bed again and caught her chin in his hand. She went absolutely still. Gabe would have sworn that for an instant she stopped breathing. Though it was ridiculous, he had the odd sensation that she was bracing for a blow.

"I know you're in trouble. What I want to know is how big. Who's after you, and why?"

Again she said nothing, but her hand moved instinctively to protect the child she carried.

Since the baby was obviously the core of the problem, they would begin there. "The baby's got a father," he said slowly. "You running from him?"

She shook her head.

"Then who?"

"It's complicated."

He lifted a brow as he jerked his head toward the window. ''We've got nothing but time here. This keeps up, it could be a week before the main roads are open.''

''When they do, I'll go. The less you know, the better off we'll both be.''

''That won't wash.'' He was silent a moment, trying to organize his thoughts. ''It seems to me that the baby is very important to you.''

''Nothing is or can be more important.''

''Do you figure the strain you're carrying around is good for it?''

He saw the regret in her eyes instantly, saw the concern, the almost imperceptible folding into herself. ''There are some things that can't be changed.'' She took a long breath. ''You have a right to ask questions.''

''But you don't intend to answer them.''

''I don't know you. I have to trust you, to a point, because I have no choice. I can only ask you to do the same.''

He moved his hand away from her face. ''Why should I?''

She pressed her lips together. She knew he was right. But sometimes right wasn't enough. ''I haven't committed a crime, I'm not wanted by the law. I have no family, no husband looking for me. Is that enough?''

''No. I'll take that much tonight because you need to sleep, but we'll talk in the morning.''

It was a reprieve—a short one, but she'd learned to be grateful for small things. With a nod, she waited for him to walk to the door. When it shut and the darkness was full again, she lay down. But it was a long, long time before she slept.

* * *

It was silent, absolutely silent, when Laura woke. She opened her eyes and waited for memory to return. There had been so many rooms, so many places where she'd slept, that she was used to this confusion upon waking.

She remembered it all…Gabriel Bradley, the storm, the cabin, the nightmare. And the sensation of waking in fear to find herself safe, in his arms. Of course, the safety was only temporary, and his arms weren't for her. Sighing, she turned her head to look out the window.

The snow was still falling. It was almost impossible to believe, but she lay and watched it, thinner now, slower, but still steady. There would be no leaving today.

Tucking her hand under her cheek, she continued to watch. It was easy to wish that the snow would never stop and that time would. She could stay here, cocooned, isolated, safe. But time, as the child she carried attested, never stopped. Rising, she opened her suitcase. She would put herself in order before she faced Gabe.

The cabin was empty. She should have felt relieved at that. Instead, the cozy fire and polished wood made her feel lonely. She wanted him there, even if it was just the sound of his movements in another room. Wherever he had gone, she reminded herself, he would be back. She started to walk into the kitchen to see what could be done about breakfast.

She saw the sketches, a half dozen of them, spread out on the picnic table. His talent, though raw in pencil or charcoal drawing, was undeniable. Still, it made her both uneasy and curious to see how someone else—no, how Gabriel Bradley—perceived her.

Her eyes seemed too big, too haunted. Her mouth was too soft, too vulnerable. She rubbed a finger over it as she frowned at the drawing. She'd seen her face countless times, in glossy photographs, posed for the best angle. She'd been draped in silks and furs, drenched in jewels. Her face and form had sold gallons of perfume, hawked fortunes in clothes and gems.

Laura Malone. She'd nearly forgotten that woman, the woman they'd said would be the face of the nineties. The woman who had, briefly, held her own destiny in her hands. She was gone, erased.

The woman in the sketches was softer, rounder and infinitely more fragile. And yet she seemed stronger. Laura lifted a sketch and studied it. Or did she just want to see the strength, need to see it?

When the front door opened, she turned, still holding the pencil sketch. Gabe, covered with snow, kicked the door shut again. His arms were loaded with wood.

"Good morning. Been busy?"

He grunted and stomped the worst of the snow from his boots, then walked, leaving a wet trail, to the firebox to dump his wood. "I thought you might sleep longer."

"I would have." She patted her belly. "He wouldn't. Can I fix you some breakfast?"

Drawing off his gloves, he tossed them down on the hearth. "Already had some. You go ahead."

Laura waited until he'd stripped off his coat. Apparently they were back on friendly terms again. Cautiously friendly. "It seems to be letting up a little."

He sat on the hearth to drag his boots off. Snow was caked in the laces. "We've got three feet now, and I wouldn't look for it to stop before afternoon." He drew out a cigarette. "Might as well make yourself at home."

"I seem to be." She held up the sketch. "I'm flattered."

"You're beautiful," He said offhandedly as he set his boots on the hearth to dry. "I can rarely resist drawing beautiful things."

"You're fortunate." She dropped the sketch back on the table. "It's so much more rewarding to be able to depict beauty than it is to be beautiful." Gabe lifted a brow. There was a trace, only a trace, of bitterness in her tone. "Things," she explained. "It's strange, but once people see you as beautiful, they almost always see you as a thing."

Turning, she slipped into the kitchen, leaving him frowning after her.

She brewed him fresh coffee, then idled away the morning tidying the kitchen. Gabe gave her room. Before night fell again, he would have some answers, but for now he was content to have her puttering around while he worked.

She seemed to need to be busy. He had thought a woman in her condition would be content to sleep or rest or simply sit and knit for most of the day. He decided it was either nervous energy or her way of avoiding the confrontation he'd promised her the night before.

She didn't ask questions or stand over his shoulder, so they rubbed along through the morning without incident. Once he glanced over to see her tucked into a corner of the sagging sofa reading a book on childbirth. Later she threw some things together in the kitchen and produced a thick, aromatic stew.

She said little. He knew she was waiting, biding her time until he pushed open the door he'd unlocked the night before. He, too, was waiting, biding his time. By midafternoon he decided she looked rested. Taking up his sketch pad and a piece of charcoal, he began to work while she sat across from him peeling apples.

"Why Denver?"

The only sign of her surprise was a quick jerk of the paring knife. She didn't look up or stop peeling. "Because I've never been there."

"Under the circumstances, wouldn't you be better off in some place that's familiar?"

"No."

"Why did you leave Dallas?"

She set the apple down and picked up another. "Because it was time."

"Where's the baby's father, Laura?"

"Dead." There wasn't even a shadow of emotion in her voice.

"Look at me."

Her hands stilled as she lifted her gaze, and he saw that that much, at least, was true.

"You don't have any family who could help you?"

"No."

"Didn't he?"

Her hand jerked again. This time the blade nicked her finger. The blood welled up as Gabe dropped his pad to take her hand. Once again she saw her face in the sweeping charcoal lines.

"I'll get you a bandage."

"It's only a scratch," she began, but he was already up and gone. When he returned he dabbed at the wound with antiseptic. Again Laura was baffled by the care he displayed. The sting came and went; his touch remained gentle.

He was kneeling in front of her, his brows drawn together as he studied the thin slice in her finger. "Keep this up and I'll think you're accident-prone."

"And I'll think you're the original Good Samaritan." She smiled when he looked up. "We'd both be wrong."

Gabe merely slipped a bandage over the cut and took his seat again. "Turn your head a little, to the left." When she complied, he picked up his pad and turned over a fresh sheet. "Why do they want the baby?"

Her head jerked around, but he continued to sketch.

"I'd like the profile, Laura." His voice was mild, but the demand in it was very clear. "Turn your head again, and try to keep your chin up. Yes, like that." He was silent as he formed her mouth with the charcoal. "The father's family wants the baby. I want to know why."

"I never said that."

"Yes, you did." He had to hurry if he was going to capture that flare of anger in her eyes. "Let's not beat that point into the ground. Just tell me why."

Her hands were gripped tightly together, but there was as much fear as fury in her voice. "I don't have to tell you any-thing."

"No." He felt a thrill of excitement—and, incredibly, one of desire—as he stroked the charcoal over the pad. The desire puzzled him. More, it worried him. Pushing it aside, he concentrated on prying answers from her. "But since I'm not going to let it drop, you may as well."

Because he knew how to look, and to see, he caught the subtle play of emotions over her face. Fear, fury, frustration. It was the fear that continued to pull him over the line.

"Do you think I'd bundle you and your baby off to them, whoever the hell they are? Use your head. I haven't got any reason to."

He'd thought he would shout at her. He'd have sworn he was on the verge of doing so. Then, in a move that surprised them both, he reached out to take her hand. He was more surprised than she to feel her fingers curl instinctively into his. When she looked at him, emotions he'd thought unavailable to him turned over in his chest.

"You asked me to help you last night."

Her eyes softened with gratitude, but her voice was firm. "You can't."

"Maybe I can't, and maybe I won't." But as much as it went against the grain of what he considered his character, he wanted to. "I'm not a Samaritan, Laura, good or otherwise, and I don't like to add someone else's problems to my own. But the fact is, you're here, and I don't like playing in the dark."

She was tired, tired of running, tired of hiding, tired of trying to cope entirely on her own. She needed someone. When his hand was covering hers and his eyes were calm and steady on hers, she could almost believe it was him she needed.

"The baby's father is dead," she began, picking her way carefully. She would tell him enough to satisfy him, she hoped, but not all. "His parents want the baby. They want…I don't know, to replace, to take back, something that they've lost. To…to ensure the lineage. I'm sorry for them, but the baby isn't their child." There was that look again, fierce, protective. A mother tiger shielding her cub. "The baby's mine."

"No one would argue with that. Why should you have to run?"

"They have a lot of money, a lot of power."

"So?"

"So?" Angry again, she pushed away. The contact that had been so soothing for both of them was broken. "It's easy to say that when you come from the same world. You've always had. You've never had to want and to wonder. No one takes from people like you, Gabe. They wouldn't dare. You don't know what it's like to have your life depend on the whims of others."

That she had was becoming painfully obvious. "Having money doesn't mean you can take whatever you want."

"Doesn't it?" She turned to him, her face set and cold. "You wanted a place to paint, somewhere you could be alone and be left alone. Did you have to think twice about how to arrange it? Did you have to plan or save or make compromises, or did you just write a check and move in?"

His eyes were narrowed as he rose to face her. "Buying a cabin is a far cry from taking a baby from its mother."

"Not to some. Property is property, after all."

"You're being ridiculous."

"And you're being naive."

His temper wavered, vying with amusement. "That's a first. Sit down, Laura, you make me nervous when you swing around."

"I'm not going to break," she muttered, but she eased into a chair. "I'm strong, I take care of myself. I had an examination just before I left Dallas, and the baby and I are fine. Better than fine. In a few weeks I'm going to check into a hospital in Denver and have my baby. Then we're going to disappear."

He thought about it. He almost believed the woman sitting across from him could accomplish it. Then he remembered how lost and frightened she'd been the night before. There was no use pointing out the strain she'd been under and its consequences for her. But he knew now what button to push.

"Do you think it's fair to the baby to keep running?"

"No, it's horribly, horribly unfair. But it would be worse to stop and let them take him."

"Why are you so damn sure they would, or could?"

"Because they told me. They explained what they thought was best for me and the child, and they offered to pay me." The venom came into her voice at that, black and bitter. "They offered to give me money for my baby, and when I refused they threatened to simply take him." She didn't want to relive that dreadful, terrifying scene. With an effort she cleared it from her mind.

He felt a swift and dark disgust for these people he didn't even know. He buried it with a shake of his head and tried to reason with her. "Laura, whatever they want, or intend, they couldn't just take what isn't theirs. No court would just take an infant from its mother without good cause."

"I can't win on my own." She closed her eyes for a moment because she wanted badly to lay her head down and weep out all the fear and anguish. "I can't fight them on their own ground, Gabe, and I won't put my child through the misery of custody suits and court battles, the publicity, the gossip and speculation. A child needs a home, and love and security. I'm going to see to it that mine has all of those things. Whatever I have to do, wherever I have to go."

"I won't argue with you about what's right for you and the baby, but sooner or later you're going to have to face this."

"When the time comes, I will."

He rose and paced over to the fire to light another cigarette. He should drop it, just leave it—her—alone and let her follow her own path. It was none of his business. Not his problem. He swore, because somehow, the moment she'd taken his arm to cross the road, she'd become his business.

"Got any money?"

"Some. Enough to pay a doctor, and a bit more."

He was asking for trouble. He knew it. But for the first time in almost a year he felt as though something really mattered. Sitting on the edge of the hearth, he blew out smoke and studied her.

"I want to paint you," he said abruptly. "I'll pay you the standard model's fee, plus room and board."

"I can't take your money."

"Why not? You seem to think I have too much for my own good, anyway."

Shame brought color flooding into her cheeks. "I didn't mean it—not like that."

He brushed her words aside. "Whatever you meant, the fact remains that I want to paint you. I work at my own pace, so you'll have to be patient. I'm not good at compromise, but owing to your condition I'm willing to make some concessions and stop when you're tired or uncomfortable.''

It was tempting, very tempting. She tried to forget that she'd traded on her looks before and concentrate on what the extra money would mean to the baby. ''I'd like to agree, but the fact is, your work is well-known. If the portrait was shown, they'd recognize me.''

''True enough, but that doesn't mean I'd be obliged to tell anyone where we'd met or when. You have my word that no one will ever trace you through me.''

She was silent for a moment, warring with herself. ''Would you come here?''

Hesitating only a moment, he tossed his cigarette into the fire. He rose, walked over, then crouched in front of her chair. She, too, had learned how to read a face. ''Your word?''

''Yes.''

Some risks were worth taking. She held both hands out to his, putting her trust into them.

With the continuing fall of snow, it was a day without a sunrise, a sunset, a twilight. The day stayed dim from morning on, and then night closed in without fanfare. And the snow stopped.

Laura might not have noticed if she hadn't been standing by the window. The flakes didn't appear to have tapered off, but to have stopped as if someone had thrown a switch. There was a vague sense of disappointment, the same she remembered feeling as a young girl when a storm had ended. On impulse, she bundled herself in her boots and coat and stepped out onto the porch.

Though Gabe had shoveled it off twice during the day, the snow came almost to her knees. Her boots sank in and disappeared. She had the sensation of being swallowed up by a soft, benign cloud. She wrapped her arms around her chest and breathed in the thin, cold air.

There were no stars. There was no moon. The porch light tossed its glow only a few feet. All she could see was white. All she could hear was silence. To some the high blanket of snow might have been a prison, something to chafe against. To Laura it was a fortress.

She'd decided to trust someone other than herself again. Standing there, soaking up the pure dark, the pure quiet, she knew that the decision had been the right one.

He wasn't a gentle man, or even a contented man, but he was a kind one, and, she was certain, a man of his word. If they were using each other, her for sanctuary, him for art, it was a fair exchange. She needed to rest. God knew she needed whatever time she could steal to rest and recover.

She hadn't told him how tired she was, how much effort it took for her just to keep on her feet for most of the day. Physically the pregnancy had been an easy one. She was strong, she was healthy. Otherwise she would have crumpled long before this. But the last few months had drained every ounce of her emotional and mental reserves. The cabin, the mountains, the man, were going to give her time to build those reserves back up again.

She was going to need them.

He didn't understand what the Eagletons could do, what they could accomplish with their money and their power. She'd already seen what they were capable of. Hadn't they paid and maneuvered to have their son's mistakes glossed over? Hadn't they managed, with a few phone calls and few favors called in, to have his death, and the death of the woman with him, turned from the grisly waste it had been into a tragic accident?

There had never been any mention in the press about alcohol and adultery. As far as the public was concerned, Anthony Eagleton, heir to the Eagleton fortune, had died as a result of a slippery road and faulty steering, and not his criminally careless drunk driving. The woman who had died with him had been turned from his mistress into his secretary.

The divorce proceedings that Laura had started had been erased, shredded, negated. No shadow of scandal would fall over the memory of Anthony Eagleton or over the family name. She'd been pressured into playing the shocked and grieving widow.

She had been shocked. She had grieved. Not for what had been lost—not on a lonely stretch of road outside of Boston—but for what had been lost so soon after her wedding night.

There was no use looking back, Laura reminded herself. Now, especially now, she had to look forward. Whatever had happened between her and Tony, they had created a life. And that life was hers to protect and to cherish.

With the spring snow glistening and untouched as far as she could see, she could believe that everything would work out for the best.

"What are you thinking?"

Startled, she turned toward Gabe with a little laugh. "I didn't hear you."

''You weren't listening.'' He pulled the door closed behind him. ''It's cold out here.''

''It feels wonderful. How much is there, do you think?''

''Three and a half, maybe four feet.''

''I've never seen so much snow before. I can't imagine it ever melting and letting the grass grow.''

His hands were bare. He tucked them in the pockets of his jacket. ''I came here in November and there was already snow. I've never seen it any other way.''

She tried to imagine that, living in a place where the snow never melted. No, she thought, she would need the spring, the buds, the green, the promise. ''How long will you stay?''

''I don't know. I haven't thought about it.''

She turned to smile at him, though she felt a touch of envy at his being so unfettered. ''All those paintings. You'll need to have a show.''

''Sooner or later.'' He moved his shoulders, suddenly restless. San Francisco, his family, his memories, seemed very far away. ''No hurry.''

''Art needs to be seen and appreciated,'' she murmured, thinking out loud. ''It shouldn't be hidden up here.''

''And people should?''

''Do you mean me, or is that what you're doing, too? Hiding?''

''I'm working,'' he said evenly.

''A man like you could work anywhere, I think. You'd just elbow people aside and go to it.''

He had to grin. ''Maybe, but now and again I like to have some space. Once you make a name, people tend to look over your shoulder.''

"Well, I, for one, am glad you came here, for whatever reason." She brushed the hair away from her face. "I should go back in, but I don't want to." She was smiling as she leaned back against the post.

His eyes narrowed. When he cupped her face in his hands, his fingers were cold and firm. "There's something about your eyes," he murmured, turning her face fully into the light. "They say everything a man wants a woman to say, and a great deal he doesn't. You have old eyes, Laura. Old, sad eyes."

She said nothing, not because her mind was empty, but because it was suddenly filled with so many things, so many thoughts, so many wishes. She hadn't thought she could feel anything like this again, and certainly not this longing for a man. Her skin warmed with it, even though his touch was cool, almost disinterested.

The sexual tug surprised her, even embarrassed her a little. But it was the emotional pull, the slow, hard drag of it, that kept her silent.

"I wonder what you've seen in your life."

As if of their own volition, his fingers stroked her cheek. They were long, slender, artistic, but hard and strong. Even so, he might merely have been familiarizing himself with the shape of her face, with the texture of her skin. An artist with his subject.

The longing leaped inside her, the foolish, impossible longing to be loved, held, desired, not for her face, not for the image a man could see, but for the woman inside.

"I'm getting tired," she said, managing to keep her voice steady. "I think I'll go to bed now."

He didn't move out of her way immediately. And his

hand lingered. He couldn't have said what kept him there, staring at her, searching the eyes he found so fascinating. Then he stepped back quickly and shoved the door open for her.

"Good night, Gabe."

"Good night."

He stayed out in the cold, wondering what was wrong with him. For a moment, damn it, for a great deal longer than a moment, he'd found himself wanting her. Filled with self-disgust, he pulled out a cigarette. A man had to be sinking low to think about making love to a woman who was more than seven months along with another man's child.

But it was a long time before he could convince himself he'd imagined it.

Chapter 3

He wondered what she was thinking. She looked so serene, so quietly content. The pale pink sweater she wore fell into a soft cowl at her throat. Her hair shimmered to her shoulders. Again she wore no jewelry, nothing to draw attention away from her, nothing to draw attention to her.

Gabe rarely used models in his work, because even if they managed to hold the pose for as long as he demanded they began to look bored and restless. Laura, on the other hand, looked as though she could sit endlessly with that same soft smile on her face.

That was part of what he wanted to capture in the portrait. That inner patience, that…well, he supposed he could call it a gracious acceptance of time—what had come before, and what was up ahead. He'd never had much patience, not with people, not with his work, not with himself.

It was a trait he could admire in her without having the urge to develop it himself.

Yet there was something more, something beyond the utterly feminine beauty and the Madonna-like calm. From time to time he saw a fierceness in her, a warriorlike determination. He could see that she was a woman who would do whatever was necessary to protect what was hers. Judging from her story, all that was hers was the child she carried.

She had more to tell, he mused as he ran the pencil over the pad. The bits and pieces she'd offered had only been given to keep him from asking more. He hadn't asked for more. It wasn't his usual style, once he'd decided an explanation was called for, to accept a partial one. He couldn't quite make himself push for the whole when even the portion she'd given him had plainly cost her so much.

There was still time. The radio continued to squawk about the roads that were closed and the snow that was yet to come. The Rockies could be treacherous in the spring. Gabe estimated it would be two weeks, perhaps three, before a trip could be managed with real safety.

It was odd, but he would have thought the enforced company would annoy him. Instead, he found himself pleased to have had his self-imposed solitude broken. It had been a long time since he'd done a portrait. Maybe too long. But he hadn't been able to face flesh and blood, not since Michael.

In the cabin, cut off from memories and reminders, he'd begun the healing process. In San Francisco he hadn't been able to pick up a brush. Grief had done more than make him weak. For a time it had made him…blank.

But here, secluded, solitary, he'd painted landscapes, still lifes, half-remembered dreams and seascapes from old sketches. It had been enough. Not until Laura had he felt the need to paint the human face again.

Once he'd believed in destiny, in a pattern of life that was meant to be even before birth. Michael's death had changed that. From that point, Gabe had had to blame something, someone. It had been easiest, and most painful, to blame himself. Now, sketching Laura, thinking over the odd set of circumstances that had brought her into his life, he began to wonder again.

And what, he asked himself yet again, was she thinking?

"Are you tired?"

"No." She answered, but she didn't move. He'd stationed a chair by the window, angling it so that she was facing him but still able to look out. The light fell over her, bringing no shadows. "I like to look at the snow. There are tracks in it now, and I wonder what animals might have passed by without us seeing. And I can see the mountains. They look so old and angry. Back east they're more tame, more good-natured."

He absently murmured his agreement as he studied his sketch. It was good, but it wasn't right, and he wanted to begin working on canvas soon. He set the pad aside and frowned at her. She stared back, patient and—if he wasn't reading her incorrectly—amused. "Do you have anything else to wear? Something off-the-shoulder, maybe?"

The amusement was even more evident now. "Sorry, my wardrobe's a bit limited at the moment."

He rose and began to pace, to the fire, to the window, back to the table. When he strode over to take her face in his hand and turn it this way and that, she sat obligingly. After three days of posing, she was used to it. She might have been an arrangement of flowers, Laura thought, or a bowl of fruit. It was as if that one moment of awareness on the snow-covered porch had never happened. She'd already convinced herself that she'd imagined that look in his eyes—and, more, her response to it.

He was the artist. She was the clay. And she'd been there before.

"You have a completely feminine face," he began, talking more to himself than to her. "Alluring and yet composed, and soft, even with the angular shape and those cheekbones. It's not threatening, and yet, it's utterly distracting. This—" his thumb brushed casually over her full lower lip "—says sex, even while your eyes promise love and devotion. And the fact that you're ripe—"

"Ripe?" She laughed, and the hands that had clenched in her lap relaxed again.

"Isn't that what pregnancy is? It only adds to the fascination. There's a promise and a fulfillment and—despite education and progress—a compelling mystery to a woman with child. Like an angel."

"How?"

As he spoke, he began to fuss with her hair, drawing it back, piling it up, letting it fall again. "We see angels as ethereal creatures, mystic, above human desires and flaws, but the fact is, they were human once."

His words appealed to her, made her smile. "Do you believe in angels?"

His hand was still in her hair, but he'd forgotten, totally forgotten, the practical reason for it. "Life wouldn't be worth much if you didn't.'' She had the hair of an angel, shimmery-blond, cloud-soft. Feeling suddenly awkward, he drew his hand away and tucked it in the pocket of his baggy corduroys.

''Would you like to take a break?'' she asked him. Her hands were balled in her lap again.

''Yeah. Rest for an hour. I need to think this through.'' He stepped back automatically when she rose. When he wasn't working, he took great care not to come into physical contact with her. It was disturbing how much he wanted to touch her. ''Put your feet up.'' When she lifted a brow at that, he shifted uncomfortably. ''It recommended it in that book you leave lying around. I figured it wouldn't hurt for me to glance through it, under the circumstances.''

''You're very kind.''

''Self-preservation.'' Things happened to him when she smiled like that. Things he recognized but didn't want to acknowledge. ''The more I make sure you take care of yourself, the less chance there is of you going into labor before the roads are clear.''

''I've got more than a month,'' she reminded him. ''But I appreciate you worrying about me—about us.''

''Put your feet up,'' he repeated. ''I'll get you some milk.''

''But I—''

''You've only had one glass today.'' With an impatient gesture, he motioned her to the sofa before he walked into the kitchen.

With a little sigh of relief, Laura settled back against the cushions. Putting her feet up wasn't as easy as it once had been, but she managed to prop them on the edge of the coffee table. The heat from the fire radiated toward her, making her wish she could curl up in front of it. If she did, she thought wryly, it would take a crane to haul her back up again.

He was being so kind, Laura thought as she turned her head toward the sound of Gabe rummaging in the kitchen. He didn't like her to remind him of it, but he was. No one had ever treated her quite like this—as an equal, yet as someone to be protected. As a friend, she thought, without tallying a list of obligations, a list of debts that had to be paid. Whether he listed them or not, someday, when she was able, she'd find a way to pay him back. Someday.

She could see the future if she closed her eyes and thought calm thoughts. She'd have a little apartment somewhere in the city. Any city. There would be a room for the baby, something in sunny yellows and glossy whites, with fairy-tale prints on the walls. She'd have a rocking chair she could sit in with the baby during the long, quiet nights, when the rest of the world was asleep.

And she wouldn't be alone anymore.

Opening her eyes, she saw Gabe standing over her. She wanted, badly, to reach up, to take his hands and draw in some of the strength and confidence she felt radiating from him. She wanted, more, for him to run his thumb along her lip again, slowly, gently, as though she were a woman, rather than a thing to be painted.

Instead, she reached up to take the glass of milk he held. "After the baby's born and I finish nursing, I'm never going to drink a drop of milk again."

"This is the last of the fresh," he told her. "Tomorrow you go on powdered and canned."

"Oh, joy." Grimacing, she downed half the contents of the glass. "I pretend it's coffee, you know. Strong, black coffee." She sipped again. "Or, if I'm feeling reckless, champagne. French, in fluted crystal."

"It's too bad I don't have any wineglasses handy. It would help the illusion. Are you hungry?"

"It's a myth about eating for two, and if I gain much more weight I'll begin to moo." Content, she settled back again. "That painting of Paris…did you do it here?"

He glanced over at the work. So she'd been there, he thought. It was a moody, almost surreal study of the Bois de Boulogne. "Yes, from old sketches and memory. When were you there?"

"I didn't say I'd been to Paris."

"You wouldn't have recognized it otherwise." He took the empty glass out of her hand and set it aside. "The more secretive you are, Laura, the more it makes me want to dig."

"A year ago," she said stiffly. "I spent two weeks there."

"How did you like it?"

"Paris?" She ordered herself to relax. It had been a lifetime ago, almost long enough that she could imagine it had all happened to someone else. "It's a beautiful city, like an old, old woman who still knows how to flirt. The flowers were blooming, and the smells were incredible. It rained and rained, for three days, and you could sit and watch the black umbrellas hurrying by and the blossoms opening up."

Instinctively he put a hand over hers to calm the agitated movement of her fingers. "You weren't happy there."

''Paris in the spring?'' She concentrated on making her hands go limp. ''Only a fool wouldn't be happy there.''

''The baby's father...was he with you there?''

''Why does it matter?''

It shouldn't have mattered. But now, whenever he looked at the painting, he would think of her. And he had to know. ''Did you love him?''

Had she? Laura looked back at the fire, but the only answers were within herself. Had she loved Tony? Her lips curved a little. Yes, she had, she had loved the Tony she'd imagined him to be. ''Very much. I loved him very much.''

''How long have you been alone?''

''I'm not.'' She laid a hand on her stomach. When she felt the answering movement, her smile widened. Taking Gabe's hand, she pressed it against her. ''Feel that? Incredible, isn't it? Someone's in there.''

He felt the stirring beneath his hand, gentle at first, then with a punch that surprised him. Without thinking, he moved closer. ''That felt like a left jab. Makes you feel as though it's fighting to get out.'' He knew the feeling, the impatience, the frustration at being trapped in one world while you longed for another. ''How does it feel from the other side?''

''Alive.'' Laughing, she left her hand over his. ''In Dallas they put a monitor on, and I could hear the baby's heartbeat. It was so fast, so impatient. Nothing in the world ever sounded so wonderful. And I think...''

But he was looking at her now, deeply, intently. Their hands were still joined, their bodies just brushing. Even as the life inside her quickened, so did her pulse. The warmth, the intimacy, of the moment washed over her, leaving her breathless and full of needs.

He wanted to hold her, badly. The urge to gather her close and just hold on was so sharp, so intense that he hurt. He dreamed of her every night when he struggled for sleep on the floor of the spare room. In his dreams they were curled in bed together, with her breath warm on his cheek and her hair tangled in his hands. And when he woke from the dreams he told himself he was mad. He told himself that again now and moved aside.

Though they were no longer touching, he could feel, as well as hear, her long, quiet sigh.

"I'd like to work some more, if you're up to it."

"Of course." She wanted to weep. That was natural, she told herself. Pregnant women wept easily. Their emotions ran on the surface, to be bruised and battered without effort, and often without cause.

"I've got something in mind. Hold on a minute."

She waited, still sitting, while he went into the spare room. Moments later he came back holding a navy blue shirt.

"Put this on. I think the contrast between the man's shirt and your face might be the answer."

"All right." Laura went into the bedroom and stripped off the big pink sweater. She started to draw an arm through the sleeve and then she caught his scent. It was there, clinging to the heavy cotton. Tough, and unapologetically sexual. Man. Unable to resist, she rubbed her cheek over it. The material was soft. The scent was not, but somehow even the scent of him made her feel safe. And yet, foolish as it seemed, it made her feel a dull, deep tremor of desire.

Wasn't it wrong to want as a woman, to want Gabe as a man, when she carried such a responsibility? But it didn't seem wrong when she felt so close to him. He had sorrows, too. She could see them, sense them. Perhaps it was that common ground, and their isolation, that made her feel as though she'd known him, cared about him, for so long.

With a sigh, she slipped into the shirt. What did she know about her own feelings? The first, the only, time she'd trusted them completely had brought misery. Whatever emotions Gabe stirred in her, she would be wise to keep gratitude in the forefront.

When she stepped back into the main cabin, he was going through his sketches, rejecting, considering, accepting. He glanced up and realized that his conception of Laura fell far, far short of the mark.

She looked like the angel he'd spoken of, illusory, golden, yet tied now to the earth. He preferred to think of her as an illusion rather than as a woman, one who stirred him.

"That's more of the look I want," he said, managing to keep his voice steady. "The color's good on you, and the straight-line masculine style is a nice contrast."

"You may not get it back anytime soon. It's wonderfully comfortable."

"Consider it a loan."

He walked over to the chair as she sat and shifted into the precise pose she'd been in before the break. Not for the first time, Gabe wondered if she'd modeled before. That was another question, for another time.

"Let's try something else." He shifted her, mere inches,

muttering to himself. Laura nearly smiled. She was back to being a bowl of fruit.

''Damn, I wish we had some flowers. A rose. Just one rose.''

''You could imagine one.''

''I may.'' He tilted her head a fraction to the left before he stood back. ''This feels right, so I'm going to draw it on canvas. I've wasted enough time on rough sketches.''

''Three whole days.''

''I've completed paintings in half that time when things clicked.''

She could see it, him sitting on a tall stool at an easel, working feverishly, brows lowered, eyes narrowed, those long, narrow hands creating. ''There are some in here you haven't finished at all.''

''Mood changed.'' He was already making broad strokes on canvas with his pencil. ''Do you finish everything you start?''

She thought about that. ''I suppose not, but people are always saying you should.''

''When something's not right, why drag it out to the bitter end?''

''Sometimes you promise,'' she murmured, thinking of her marriage vows.

Because he was watching her closely, he saw the swift look of regret. As always, though he tried to block it, her emotions touched a chord in him. ''Sometimes promises can't be kept.''

''No. But they should be,'' she said quietly. Then she fell silent.

He worked for nearly an hour, defining, refining, perfecting. She was giving him the mood he wanted. Pensive, patient, sensuous. He already knew, even before the first brush stroke, that this would be one of his best. Perhaps his very best. And he knew he would have to paint her again, in other moods, in other poses.

But that was for tomorrow. Today, now, he needed to capture the tone of her, the feel, the simplicity. That was pencil lines and curves. Black against white, and a few shades of gray. Tomorrow he would begin filling in, adding the color, the complexities. When he had finished he would have the whole of her on canvas, and he would know her fully, as no one had ever before or would ever again.

"Will you let me see it as you go along?"

"What?"

"The painting." Laura kept her head still but shifted her eyes from the window to him. "I know artists are supposed to be temperamental about showing their work before it's finished."

"I'm not temperamental." He lifted his gaze to hers, as if inviting her to disagree.

"Anyone could see that." Though she kept her expression sober, he could hear the amusement in her voice. "So will you let me see it?"

"Doesn't matter to me. As long as you realize that if you see something you don't like I won't change it."

This time she did laugh, more freely, more richly than before. His fingers tightened on the pencil. "You mean if I see something that wounds my vanity? You don't have to worry about that. I'm not vain."

"All beautiful women are vain. They're entitled."

"People are only vain if their looks matter to them."

This time he laughed, but cynically. He set down his pencil. "And yours don't matter to you?"

"I didn't do anything to earn them, did I? An accident of fate, or a stroke of luck. If I were terribly smart or talented somehow I'd probably be annoyed with my looks, because people look at them and nothing else." She shrugged, then settled with perfect ease into the pose again. "But since I'm neither of those, I've learned to accept that looking a certain way is…I don't know, a gift that makes up for a lack of other things."

"What would you trade your beauty for?"

"Any number of things. But then, a trade isn't earning, either, so it wouldn't count. Will you tell me something?"

"Probably." He took a rag out of his back pocket and dusted off his hands.

"Which are you more vain about, your looks or your work?"

He tossed the rag aside. It was odd that she could look so sad, so serious, and still make him laugh. "No one's ever accused me of being beautiful, so there's no contest." He started to turn the easel. When she began to rise, he motioned her back. "No, relax. Look from there and tell me what you think."

Laura settled back and studied. It was only a sketch, less detailed than many of the others he'd done. It was her face and torso, her right hand resting lightly just below her left shoulder. For some reason it seemed a protective pose, not defensive, but cautious.

He'd been right about the shirt, she realized. It made her seem more of a woman than any amount of lace or silks could have. Her hair was long and loose, falling in heavy, disordered curls that contradicted the pose. She hadn't expected to find any surprises in her face, but as she studied his conception of it, she shifted uncomfortably in her chair.

"I'm not as sad as you make me look."

"I've already warned you I wouldn't change anything."

"You're free to paint as you please. I'm simply telling you that you have a misconception."

There was a huffiness in her voice that amused him. He turned the easel around again but didn't bother to look at his work. "I don't think so."

"I'm hardly tragic."

"Tragic?" He rocked back on his heels as he studied her. "There's nothing tragic about the woman in the painting. *Valiant* is the word."

She smiled at that and pushed herself out of the chair. "I'm not valiant, either, but it's your painting."

"We agree on that."

"Gabe!"

She flung out a hand. The urgency in her voice had him crossing to her quickly and gripping her hand. "What is it?"

"Look, look out there." She turned to him, using her free hand to point.

Not urgency, Gabe realized. He was tempted to strangle her. Excitement. The excitement of seeing a solitary buck less than two yards from the window. It stood deep in snow, its head lifted, scenting the air. Arrogantly, and without a trace of fear, it stared at them through the glass.

"Oh, he's wonderful. I've never seen one so big before, or so close."

It was easy to share the pleasure. A deer, a fox, a hawk

circling overhead...those were some of the things that had helped him over his own grief.

"A few weeks ago I hiked down to a stream about a mile south of here. I came across a whole family. I was downwind, and I managed three sketches before the doe spotted me."

"This whole place belongs to him. Can you imagine it? Acres and acres. He must know it, even enjoy it, or else he wouldn't look so sure of himself." She laughed again, and pressed her free hand to the frosted glass. "You know, it's as if we were exhibits and he'd come to take a quick look around the zoo."

The deer nosed down in the snow, perhaps looking for the grass that was buried far beneath, perhaps scenting another animal. He moved slowly, confident in his solitude. Around him the trees dripped with ice and snow.

Abruptly he raised his head, his crown of antlers plunging high in the air. In bounds and leaps he raced across the snow and disappeared into the woods beyond.

Laughing, Laura turned, then instantly forgot everything.

She hadn't realized they had moved so close together. Nor had he. Their hands were still linked. Beside them the sun streamed in, losing power as the afternoon moved toward evening. And the cabin, like the woods beyond, was absolutely silent.

He touched her. He hadn't known he would, but the moment his fingers grazed her cheek he knew he needed to. She didn't move away. Perhaps he would have accepted it if she had. He wanted to believe he would have accepted it. But she didn't move.

There were nerves. He felt them in the hand that trembled in his. He had them, too. Another new experience. How did he approach her, when he knew he had no business approaching her? How did he resist what common sense told him he had to resist?

Yet her skin was warm under his touch. Real. Not a portrait, but a woman. Whatever had happened in her life, whatever had made her into the woman she was, that was yesterday. This was now. Her eyes, wide and more than a little frightened, were on his. She didn't move. She waited.

He swore at himself even as he slowly, ever so slowly, lowered his lips to hers.

It was madness to allow it. It was more than madness to want it. But even before his lips touched hers she felt herself give in to him. As she gave, she braced herself, not knowing what to expect for herself, or for him.

It might have been the first. That was her one and only thought as his mouth closed over hers. Not just the first with him but the first with anyone. No one had ever kissed her like this. She had known passion, the quick, almost painful desire that came from heat and frenzy. She had known demands, some that she could answer, some that she could not. She had known the anger and the hunger a man could have for a woman, but she had never known, had never imagined, this kind of reverence.

And yet, even with that, there were hints of darker needs, needs held down by chains, that made the embrace more exciting, more involving, than any other. His hands were in her hair, searching, exploring, while his lips moved endlessly over hers. She felt the world tip and knew instinctively that he would be there to right it again.

He had to stop. He couldn't stop. One taste, just one

taste, and he craved more. It seemed he'd been empty, without knowing it, and now—incredibly, swiftly, terrifyingly—he was filled.

Her hands, hesitant, somehow innocent, slipped over his arms to his shoulders. When she parted her lips, there was that same curious shyness in the invitation. He could smell the spring, though it was still buried beneath the snow, could smell it in her hair, on her skin. Even the woodsmoke that always tinted the air in the cabin couldn't overwhelm it. Logs shifted in the grate, and the wind that came up with evening began to moan against the window. And Laura, her mouth warm and giving under his, sighed.

He wanted to play out the fantasy, to draw her up into his arms and take her to bed. To lie with her, to slip his shirt from her and feel her skin against his own. To have her touch him, hold on to him. Trust him.

The war inside him raged on. She wasn't merely a woman, she was a woman who was carrying a child. And growing inside her was not merely a child, but the child of another man, one she had loved.

She wasn't his to love. He wasn't hers to trust. Still, she pulled at him, her secrets, her eyes, eyes that said much, much more than her words, and her beauty, which she didn't seem to understand went far beyond the shape and texture of her face.

So he had to stop, until he resolved within himself exactly what he wanted—and until she trusted him enough to tell him the whole truth.

He would have drawn her away from him, but she pressed her face into his shoulder. "Please don't say anything, just for a minute."

There were tears in her voice, and they left him more shaken than the kiss had. The tug-of-war increased, and finally he lifted a hand to stroke her hair. The baby turned, moving inside her, against him, and he wondered what in God's name he was going to do.

"I'm sorry." Her voice was under control again, but she didn't let go. How could she have known how badly she needed to be held, when there had been so few times in her life when anyone had bothered? "I don't mean to cling."

"You're not."

"Well." Drawing herself up straight, she stepped back. There were no tears, but her eyes glimmered with the effort it took to hold them in. "You were going to say that you didn't mean for that to happen, but it's all right."

"I didn't mean for that to happen," he said evenly. "But that's not an apology."

"Oh." A little nonplussed, she braced a hand on the back of the chair. "I suppose what I meant is that I don't want you to feel—I don't want you to think that I— Hell." With that, she gave in and sat. "I'm trying to say that I'm not upset that you kissed me and that I understand."

"Good." He felt better, much better than he'd thought he would. Casually he dragged over another chair and straddled it. "What do you understand, Laura?"

She'd thought he would let it go at that, take the easy way out. She struggled to say what she felt without saying too much. "That you felt a little sorry for me, and involved a bit, because of the situation, and the painting, too." Why couldn't she relax again? And why was he looking at her that way? "I don't want you to think that I misunderstood.

I would hardly expect you to be…'' The ground was getting shakier by the minute. She was ready to shut up entirely, but he quirked a brow and gestured with his hands, inviting her, almost challenging her, to finish.

''I realize you wouldn't be attracted to me—physically, that is—under the circumstances. And I don't want to think that I interpreted what just happened as anything other than a—a sort of kindness.''

''That's funny.'' As if he were considering the idea, Gabe reached up and scratched his chin. ''You don't look stupid. I'm attracted to you, Laura, and there's a part of that attraction that's very, very physical. Making love with you may not be possible under the circumstances, but that doesn't mean that the desire to do so isn't there.''

She opened her mouth as if to speak, but ended up just lifting her hands and then letting them fall again.

''The fact that you're carrying a child is only part of the reason I can't make love with you. The other, though not as obvious, is just as important. I need the story, Laura, your story. All of it.''

''I can't.''

''Afraid?''

She shook her head. Her eyes glimmered, but her chin lifted. ''Ashamed.''

He would have expected almost any other reason than that. ''Why? Because you weren't married to the baby's father?''

''No. Please don't ask me.''

He wanted to argue, but he bit the words back. She was looking pale and tired and just too fragile. ''All right, for now. But think about this. I have feelings for you, and they're growing much faster than either of us might like. Right now I'm damned if I know what to do about it.''

When he rose, she reached up and touched his arm. ''Gabe, there's nothing to do. I can't tell you how much I wish it were otherwise.''

''Life's what you make it, angel.'' He touched her hair then stepped away. ''We need more wood.''

Laura sat in the empty cabin and wished more than she had ever wished for anything that she had made a better job of hers.

Chapter 4

More snow had fallen during the night. It was, compared to what had come before, hardly more than a dusting. The fresh inches lay in mounds and drifts over the rest, where the wind had blown them. In places the snow was as high as a man. Miniature mountains of it lay cozily against the windowpanes, shifting constantly in the wind.

Already the sun was melting the fresh fall, and if Laura listened she could hear the water sliding down the gutters from the roof like rain. It was a friendly sound, and it made her think of hot tea by a sizzling fire, a good book read on a lazy afternoon, a nap on the sofa in early evening.

But this was morning, only an hour or two past dawn. As usual, she had the cabin to herself.

Gabe was chopping wood. From the kitchen, where she was optimistically heating milk and a chocolate bar in a pan, she could hear the steady thud of the ax. She knew the woodbox was full, and the stack of logs outside the rear door was still high. Even if the snow lasted into June, they would still have an ample supply. Artist or not, he was a physical man, and she understood his need to do something manual and tiring.

It seemed so…normal, she thought. Her cooking in the kitchen, Gabe splitting logs, icicles growing long and shiny on the eaves outside the window. Their little world was so well tuned, so self-contained. It was like this every morning. She would rise to find him already outdoors, shoveling, chopping, hauling. She would make fresh coffee or warm what he'd left in the pot. The portable radio would bring her news from the outside, but it never seemed terribly important. After a little while he would come in, shake and stomp the snow off, then accept the cup of coffee she offered him. The routine would continue with him taking his place in behind the easel and Laura taking hers by the window.

Sometimes they would talk. Sometimes they would not.

Beneath the routine, she sensed some kind of hurry in him that she couldn't understand. Though he might paint for hours, his movements controlled and measured, he still seemed impatient to finish. The fact was, the portrait was coming along faster than she could ever have imagined. She was taking shape on canvas—or rather the woman he saw when he looked at her was taking shape. Laura couldn't understand why he had chosen to make her look so otherworldly, so dreamy. She was very much a part of the world. The child she carried grounded her to it.

But she'd learned not to complain, because he didn't listen.

He'd done other sketches, as well, some full-length, some just of her face. She told herself he was entitled, particularly if that was all the payment she could give him for the roof over her head. A few of the sketches made her uneasy, like the one he'd drawn when she'd fallen asleep on the sofa late one afternoon. She'd looked so…defenseless. And she'd felt defenseless when she'd realized that he'd watched her and drawn her while she was unaware of it.

Not that she was afraid of him. Laura poked halfheartedly at the mixture of powdered milk, water and chocolate. He'd been kinder to her than she'd had any right to expect. And, though he could be terse and brusque, he was the gentlest man she'd ever known.

Perhaps he was attracted to her. Men had often been attracted to her face. But whether he was or not he treated her with respect and care. She'd learned not to expect those things when there was attraction.

With a shrug, she poured the liquid into a mug. Now wasn't the time to focus on the feeling Gabe might or might not have. She was on her own. Fixing a mental image of creamy hot chocolate in her mind, Laura downed half the contents of the mug. She made a face, sighed, then lifted the mug again. In a matter of days she would be on her way to Denver again.

A sudden pain had her gripping the side of the counter for support. She held on, fighting back the instinctive need to call for Gabe. It was nothing, she told herself as it began to ease. Moving carefully, she started into the living room. Gabe's chopping stopped. It was in that silence that she heard the other sound. An engine? The panic came instantly, and almost as quickly was pushed down. They hadn't found her. It was ridiculous to even think it. But she walked quickly, quietly, to the front window to look out.

A snowmobile. The sight of it, shiny and toylike, might have amused and pleased her if she hadn't seen the uniformed state trooper on it. Preparing to stand her ground if it came to that, Laura moved to the door and opened it a crack.

Gabe had worked up a warm, healthy sweat. He appreciated being outdoors, appreciated the crisp air, the rhythm of his work. He couldn't say that it kept his mind off Laura. Nothing did. But it helped him put the situation into perspective.

She needed help. He was going to help her.

There were some who knew him who would have been more than a little surprised by his decision. It wasn't that anyone would have accused him of being unfeeling. The sensitivity in his paintings was proof of his capacity for emotion, passion, compassion. But few would have thought him capable of unconditional generosity.

It was Michael who had been generous.

Gabe had always been self-absorbed—or, more accurately, absorbed in his art, driven to depict life, with all its joys and pains. Michael had simply embraced life.

Now he was gone. Gabe brought the ax down, his breath whistling through his teeth and puffing white in the thin air. And Michael's leaving had left a hole so big, so great, that Gabe wasn't certain it could ever be filled.

He heard the engine when his ax was at the apex of his swing. Distracted, he let it fall so that the blade was buried in wood. Splinters popped out to join others on the trampled snow. With a quick glance toward the kitchen window, Gabe started around the cabin to meet the visitor.

He didn't make a conscious decision to protect the woman inside. He didn't have to. It was the most natural thing in the world.

"How ya doing?" The cop, his full cheeks reddened by wind and cold, shut off the engine and he nodded to Gabe.

"Well enough." He judged the trooper to be about twenty-five and half frozen. "How's the road?"

Giving a short laugh, the trooper stepped off the snowmobile. "Let's just say I hope you got no appointments to keep."

"Nothing pressing."

"Good thing." He offered a gloved hand. "Scott Beecham."

"Gabe Bradley."

"I heard somebody bought the old McCampbell place." With his hands on his hips, Beecham studied the cabin. "A hell of a winter to pick for moving in. We're swinging by to check on everybody on the ridge, seeing if they need supplies or if anyone's sick."

"I stocked up the day of the storm."

"Good for you." He gestured toward the Jeep. "At least you've got a fighting chance in a four-wheel drive. Could've filled a used car lot with some of the vehicles towed in. We're checking around on a compact, an '84 Chevy that took a spin into the guardrail about a quarter mile from here. Abandoned. Driver might have wandered out and got lost in the blizzard."

"My wife," Gabe said. In the doorway, Laura opened her eyes wide. "She was worried that something had happened to me and got the idea of driving into town.'' Gabe grinned and drew out a cigarette. ''Damn near ran into me. At the rate things were going, I figured it was best to leave the car where it was and get us back here. Haven't been able to get back out to check on the damage.''

''Not as bad as some I've seen the last few days. Was she hurt?''

''No. Scared ten years off both of us, though.''

''I'll bet. Afraid we're going to have to tow the vehicle in, Mr. Bradley.'' He glanced toward the house. His voice was casual, but Gabe sensed that he was alert. ''Your wife, you say?''

''That's right.''

''Name on the registration was Malone, Laura Malone.''

''My wife's maiden name,'' Gabe said easily.

On impulse, Laura pushed open the door. ''Gabe?''

Both men turned to look at her. The trooper pulled off his hat. Gabe merely scowled.

''I'm sorry to interrupt—'' she smiled ''—but I thought the officer might like some hot coffee.''

The trooper replaced his hat. ''That's mighty tempting, ma'am, and I appreciate it, but I have to get along. Sorry about your car.''

''My own fault. Can you tell us when the road will be open?''

''Your husband ought to be able to manage a trip into town in a day or two,'' Beecham said. ''I wouldn't recommend the drive for you, ma'am, for the time being.''

''No.'' She smiled at him and hugged her elbows. ''I don't think I'll be going anywhere for a little while yet.''

''I'll just be on my way.'' Beecham straddled the snowmobile again. ''You got a shortwave, Mr. Bradley?''

''No.''

''Might not be a bad idea to pick one up next time you're in town. More dependable than the phones. When's your baby due?''

Gabe just stared for a moment. The pronoun had stunned him. ''Four or five weeks.''

''You got yourself plenty of time, then.'' With a grin, Beecham started the engine. ''This your first?''

''Yes,'' Gabe murmured. ''It is.''

''Nothing quite like it. Got myself two girls. Last one decided to be born on Thanksgiving. Hardly had two bites of pumpkin pie when I had to drive into the hospital. My wife still says it was my mother's sausage stuffing that started her off.'' He raised a hand and his voice. ''Take care, Mrs. Bradley.''

They watched, Gabe from the yard, Laura from the doorway, as the snowmobile scooted up the lane. And then they were alone.

Clearing his throat, Gabe started up the stairs. Laura said nothing, but she stepped out of the way and closed the door behind him. She waited until he was sitting on the low stone hearth, unlacing his boots.

''Thank you.''

''For what?''

''You told the trooper that I was your wife.''

Still frowning, he pried off a boot. ''It seemed less complicated that way.''

''For me,'' Laura agreed. ''Not for you.''

He shrugged his shoulders and then rose to go into the kitchen. ‘‘Any coffee?’’

‘‘Yes.’’ She heard the glass pot chink against the mug, heard the liquid pour into the stoneware. He’d lied for her, protected her, and all she had done was take from him. ‘‘Gabe.’’ Praying that her instincts and her conscience were right, she walked to the doorway.

‘‘What the hell is this?’’ He had the pan she’d used to heat the milk in his hand.

For a moment the tension fled. ‘‘If you’re desperate enough, it’s hot chocolate.’’

‘‘It looks like… Well, never mind what it looks like.’’ He set it back on the stove. ‘‘That powdered stuff tastes filthy, doesn’t it?’’

‘‘It’s hard to argue with the truth.’’

‘‘I’ll try to make it into town tomorrow.’’

‘‘If you do, could you…’’ Embarrassed, she let her words trail off.

‘‘What do you want?’’

‘‘Nothing. It’s stupid. Listen, could we sit down a minute?’’

He took her hand before she could back away. ‘‘What do you want from town, Laura?’’

‘‘Marshmallows, to toast in the fireplace. I told you it was stupid,’’ she murmured, and tried to tug her hand away.

He wanted, God, he wanted just to fold her into his arms. ‘‘Is that a craving or just a whim?’’

‘‘I don’t know. It’s just that I look at the fireplace and think about marshmallows.’’ Because he wasn’t laughing at her, it was easy to smile. "Sometimes I can almost smell them."

"Marshmallows. You don't want anything to go with them? Like horseradish?"

She made a face at him. "Another myth."

"You're spoiling all my preconceptions." He wasn't sure when he'd lifted her hand to his lips, but after the faintest taste of her skin he dropped it again. "And you're not wearing the shirt."

Though he was no longer touching it, her hand felt warm, warm and impossibly soft. "Oh." She took a long breath. He was thinking of the painting, not of her. He was the artist with his subject again. "I'll change."

"Fine." More than a little shaken by the extent of his desire for her, he turned back to the counter and his coffee.

The decision came quickly, or perhaps it had been made the moment she'd heard him lie for her, protect her. "Gabe, I know you want to work right away, but I'd like…I feel like I should…I want to tell you everything, if you still want to hear it."

He turned back, his eyes were utterly clear and intent. "Why?"

"Because it's wrong not to trust you." Again the breath seemed to sigh out of her. "And because I need someone. We need someone."

"Sit down," he said simply, leading her to the couch.

"I don't know where to start."

It would probably be easier for her to start further back, he thought as he tossed another log in the fire. "Where do you come from?" he asked when he joined her on the couch.

"I've lived a lot of places. New York, Pennsylvania, Maryland. My aunt had a little farm on the Eastern Shore. I lived with her the longest."

"Your parents?"

"My mother was very young when I was born. Unmarried. She…I went to live with my aunt until…until things became difficult for her, financially. There were foster homes after that. That isn't really the point."

"Isn't it?"

She took a steadying breath. "I don't want you to feel sorry for me. I'm not telling you this so that you'll feel sorry for me."

The pride was evident in the tilt of her head, in the tone of her voice—the same quiet pride he was trying to capture on canvas. His fingers itched for his sketchpad, even as they itched to touch her face. "All right, I won't."

With a nod, she continued. "From what I can gather, things were very hard on my mother. Even without the little I was told, it's easy enough to imagine. She was only a child. It's possible that she wanted to keep me, but it didn't work out. My aunt was older, but she had children of her own. I was essentially another mouth to feed, and when it became difficult to do so, I went into foster care."

"How old were you?"

"Six the first time. For some reason it just never seemed to work out. I would stay in one place for a year, in another for two. I hated not belonging, never being a real part of what everyone else had. When I was about twelve I went back with my aunt for a short time, but her husband had problems of his own, and it didn't last."

He caught something in her voice, something that made him tense. "What sort of problems?"

"They don't matter." She shook her head and started to rise, but Gabe put his hand firmly on hers.

"You started this, Laura, now finish it."

"He drank," she said quickly. "When he drank he got mean."

"Mean? Do you mean violent?"

"Yes. When he was sober, he was discontented and critical. Drunk, he was—could be—vicious." She rubbed a hand over her shoulder, as if she were soothing an old wound. "My aunt was his usual target, but he often went after the children."

"Did he hit you?"

"Unless I was quick enough to get out of his way." She managed a ghost of a smile. "And I learned to be quick. It sounds worse than it was."

He doubted it. "Go on."

"The social services took me away again and placed me in another home. It was like being put on hold. I remember when I was sixteen, counting the days until I'd be of age and able to at least fend for myself. Make…I don't know, make some of my own decisions. Then I was. I moved to Pennsylvania and got a job. I was working as a clerk in a department store in Philadelphia. I had a customer, a woman, who used to come in regularly. We got friendly, and one day she came in with a man. He was short and balding—looked like a bulldog. He nodded to the woman and told her she'd been absolutely right. Then he handed me a business card and told me to come to his studio the next day. Of course, I had no intention of going. I thought…that is, I'd gotten used to men…''

''I imagine you did,'' Gabe said dryly.

It still embarrassed her, but since he seemed to take it in stride she didn't dwell on it. ''In any case, I set the card aside and would have forgotten about it, but one of the girls who worked with me picked it up later and went wild. She told me who he was. You might know the name. Geoffrey Wright.''

Gabe lifted a brow. Wright was one of the most respected fashion photographers in the business—no, *the* most. Gabe might not know much about the fashion business, but a name like Geoffrey Wright's crossed boundaries. ''It rings a bell.''

''When I found out he was a professional, a well-known photographer, I decided to take a chance and go to see him. Everything happened at once. He was very gruff and had me in makeup and under the lights before I could babble an excuse. I was terribly embarrassed, but he didn't seem to notice. He barked out orders, telling me to stand, sit, lean, turn. He had a fur in his vault—a full-length sable. He took it out and tossed it around my shoulders. I thought I was dreaming. I must have said so aloud, because while he was shooting he laughed and told me that in a year I could wear sable to breakfast.''

Saying nothing, Gabe settled back. With his eyes narrowed, he could see her, enveloped in furs. There was a twist in his stomach as he thought about her becoming one of Wright's young and casually disposable mistresses.

''Within a month I had done a layout for *Mode* magazine. Then I did another for *Her*, and one for *Charm*. It was incredible. One day I was selling linens and the next I was having dinner with designers."

"And Wright?"

"No one in my life had ever been as good to me as Geoffrey. Oh, I knew he saw me as a commodity half the time, but he set himself up as, I don't know, a watchdog. He had plans, he'd tell me. Not too much exposure too quickly. Then, in another two years, there wouldn't be a person in the Western world who wouldn't recognize my face. It sounded exciting. Most of my life I'd been essentially anonymous. He liked that, the fact that I'd come from nothing, from nowhere. I know some of his other models saw him as cold. He often was. But he was the closest thing I'd ever had to a father."

"Is that how you saw him?"

"I suppose. And then, after all he'd done for me, after all the time he'd invested, I let him down." She started to rise again, and again Gabe stopped her.

"Where are you going?"

"I need some water."

"Sit. I'll get it."

She used the time to compose herself. Her story was only half done, and the worst part, the most painful part, was yet to come. He brought her a clear glass with ice swimming in it. Laura took two long sips, then continued.

"We went to Paris. It was like being Cinderella and being told midnight never had to come. We were scheduled to be there for a month, and because Geoffrey wanted a very French flavor to the pictures we went all over Paris for the shoot. We went to a party one night. It was one of those gorgeous spring nights when all the women are beautiful and the men handsome. And I met Tony.''

He caught the slight break in her voice, the shadow of pain in her eyes, and knew without being told that she was speaking now of her baby's father.

''He was so gallant, so charming. The prince to my Cinderella. For the next two weeks, whenever I wasn't working, I was with Tony. We went dancing, we ate in little cafés and walked in the parks. He was everything I'd thought I'd wanted and knew I could never have. He treated me as though I were something rare and valuable, like a diamond necklace. There was a time when I thought that was love.''

She fell silent for a moment, brooding. That had been her mistake, her sin, her vanity. Even now, a year later, it cut at her.

''Geoffrey grumbled and talked about rich young pups sowing wild oats, but I wouldn't listen. I wanted to be loved, I wanted so terribly for someone to care, to want me. When Tony asked me to marry him, I didn't think twice.''

''You married him?''

''Yes.'' She looked at him again. ''I know I led you to believe that I hadn't married the baby's father. It seemed easiest.''

''You don't wear a ring.''

Color washed into her face. The shame of it. ''I sold them.''

''I see.'' There was no condemnation in the two words, but she felt it nonetheless.

''We stayed in Paris for our honeymoon. I wanted to go

back to the States and meet his family, but he said we should stay where we were happy. It seemed right. Geoffrey was furious with me, lectured and shouted about me wasting myself. At the time I thought he meant my career, and I ignored him. It was only later that I realized he meant my life.''

She jumped when a log fell apart in the fire. It was easier to continue if she looked at the flames, she discovered. ''I thought I'd found everything I'd ever wanted. When I look back I realize that those weeks we spent in Paris were like a kind of magic, something that's not quite real but that you believe because you aren't clever enough to see the illusion. Then it was time to come home.''

She linked her hands together and began to fidget. He had come to recognize it as a sign of inner turmoil. Though the urge was there, he didn't take them in his to calm her. ''The night before we were to leave, Tony went out. He said he had some business to tie up. I waited for him, feeling a little sorry for myself that my new husband would leave me alone on our last night in Paris. Then, as it got later and later, I stopped feeling sorry for myself and started feeling frightened. By the time he got back, it was after three and I was angry and upset.''

She fell silent again. Gabe pulled the afghan from the back of the couch and spread it over her lap. ''You had a fight.''

''Yes. He was very drunk and belligerent. I'd never seen him like that before, but I was to see him like that again. I asked him where he'd been and he said—essentially he told me it was none of my business. We started shouting at each other, and he told me he'd been with another woman. At first I thought he said that just to hurt me, but then I saw that it was true. I started to cry.''

That was the worst of it, Laura thought. Looking back on the way she'd crumbled and wept. ''That only made him angrier. He tossed things around the suite, like a little boy having a tantrum. He said things, but the gist of it was that I'd have to get used to the way he lived, and that I hardly had a right to be upset when I'd been Geoffrey's whore.''

Her voice broke on the last word, so she lifted the glass and cooled her throat with the water. ''That hurt the most,'' she managed. ''Geoffrey was almost like a father to me, never, never anything else. And Tony knew, he knew that I'd never been with anyone before our wedding night. I was so angry then, I stood up and began to shout at him. I don't even know what I said, but he went into a rage. And he—''

Gabe saw her fingers tighten like wires on the soft folds of the afghan. Then he saw how she deliberately, and with great care, relaxed them again. With an effort, he kept his voice calm. ''Did he hit you, Laura?''

She didn't answer, couldn't seem to push the next words out. Then he touched a hand to her cheek and turned her face to his. Her eyes were brimming over.

''It was so much worse than with my uncle, because I couldn't get away. He was so much stronger and faster. With my uncle, he'd simply struck out at anyone who didn't get out of the way in time. With Tony, there was something viciously deliberate in the way he tried to hurt me. Then he—'' But she couldn't bring herself to speak of what had happened next.

It was a moment before she went on, and Gabe sat in silence as the rage built and built inside him until he thought he'd explode. He understood temper, he had a hair-trigger one of his own, but he could never understand, never forgive, anyone who inflicted pain on someone smaller, weaker.

"When it was over," she continued, calmer now, "he just went to sleep. I lay there, not knowing what to do. It's funny, but later, when I talked with other women who had had some of the same experiences, I found out that it's fairly common to believe you had it coming somehow.

"The next morning, he wept and he apologized, promised that it would never happen again. That became the pattern for the time we were together."

"You stayed with him?"

The color came and went in her face, and part of that, too, was shame. "We were married, and I thought I could make it work. Then we went back to his parents' home. They hated me right from the start. Their son, the heir to the throne, had gone behind their back and married a commoner. We lived with them, and though there was talk about getting our own house, nothing was ever done about it. You could sit at the same table, hold a conversation with them, and be totally ignored. They were amazing. Tony got worse. He began to see other women, almost flaunting them. They knew what he was doing, and they knew what was happening to me. The cycle got uglier and uglier, until I knew I had to get out. I told him I wanted a divorce.

"That seemed to snap him out of it for a while. He made promises, swore he'd go into therapy, see a marriage counselor, anything I wanted. We even began to look at houses.

I have to admit that I'd stopped loving him by this time, and that it was wrong, very wrong, for me to stay with him, to make promises myself. What I didn't realize was that his parents were pulling on the other end. They held the financial strings and were making it difficult for him to move out. Then I discovered I was pregnant.''

She laid a hand over her belly, her fingers spread. ''Tony was, well, at best ambivalent about the idea of having a child. His parents were thrilled. His mother immediately started redecorating a nursery. She bought antique cribs and cradles, silver spoons, Irish linen. Though it made me nervous, the way she was taking over, I thought that the baby might be the way to help us come together. But they weren't looking at me as the baby's mother, any more than they'd looked at me as Tony's wife. It was *their* grandchild, *their* legacy, *their* immortality. We stopped looking for houses, and Tony began to drink again. I left the night he came home drunk and hit me.''

She drew a careful breath and continued to stare at the fire. ''It wasn't just me he was hitting now, but the child. That made all the difference. In fact, it made it incredibly easy to walk out. I called Geoffrey, buried my pride and asked for a loan. He wired me two thousand dollars. I got an apartment of my own, found a job and started divorce proceedings. Ten days later, Tony was dead.''

The pain came, dull and low. Laura shut her eyes and rode it out. ''His mother came to see me, begged me to bury the divorce papers, to come to the funeral as Tony's widow. His reputation, his memory, were all that was important now. I did what she asked, because—because I could still remember those first days in Paris. After the funeral I went back to their house. They'd told me there were things we needed to talk about. That was when they told me what they wanted, what they intended to have. They said they would pay all my medical expenses, that I would have the best possible care. And that after the baby was born they would give me a hundred thousand dollars to step aside. When I refused, when I had the nerve to be angry at what they were suggesting, they explained that if I didn't cooperate they would simply take the baby. Tony's baby. They made it very clear that they had enough money and influence to win a custody suit. They would bring out the 'fact' that I had been Geoffrey's mistress, that I had taken money from him. They'd checked my background and would show that due to my upbringing I would be an unstable influence on a child. That they, as the child's grandparents, could provide a better environment. They gave me twenty-four hours to think it over. And I ran."

He didn't speak for several minutes. What she had told him had left a bitter taste in his mouth. He had asked for her story, had all but demanded it. Now that he had it, he wasn't at all sure he could handle it.

"Laura, no matter what you were told, how you were threatened, I don't believe they could take the child."

"That isn't enough? Don't you see? As long as there's a chance, I can't risk it. I'd never be able to fight them on their terms. I don't have the money, the connections."

"Who are they?" When she hesitated, he took her hand again. "You've trusted me with this much."

"Their name is Eagleton," she said. "Thomas and Lorraine Eagleton of Boston."

His brows drew together. He knew the name. Who

didn't? But because of his family's position, it was more than a name, more than an image. "You were married to Anthony Eagleton?"

"Yes." She turned to him then. "You knew him, didn't you?"

"Not well. Barely. He was more—" More Michael's age, he'd started to say. "He was younger. I met him once or twice when he came to the Coast." And what he had seen hadn't impressed him enough to have him form any opinion. "I read that he had been killed in a car accident, and I suppose a wife was mentioned, but this past year has been a little difficult, and I didn't pay attention. My family has socialized with the Eagletons occasionally, but they aren't well acquainted."

"Then you know they're an old, well-established family with old, well-established money. They consider this child a part of their...holdings. They've had me followed all across the country. Every time I would settle in a place and begin to relax I'd discover that detectives were making inquiries about me. I can't—I won't—let them find me."

He rose, to pace, to light a cigarette, to try to organize his thoughts and, more, his feelings. "I'd like to ask you something."

She sighed tiredly. "All right."

"Once before, when I asked you if you were afraid, you said no, that you were ashamed. I want to know why."

"I didn't fight back, and I didn't try hard enough to fix what was wrong. I just let it happen to me. You have no idea how difficult it is to sit here and admit that I let myself be used, that I let myself be beaten, that I let myself be driven down so low that I accepted it all."

''Do you still feel that way?''

''No.'' Her chin lifted. ''No one's ever going to take control of my life again.''

''Good.'' He sat on the hearth. The smoke from his cigarette disappeared up the draft. ''I think you've had a hell of a time, angel, worse than anyone deserves. Whether you brought some of it on yourself, as you choose to think, or if it was just a matter of circumstances, doesn't really matter at this point. It's over.''

''It's not as easy as that, Gabe. I don't just have myself to worry about now.''

''How far are you willing to go to fight them?''

''I've told you I can't—''

He interrupted her with a wave of his hand. ''If you had the means. How far?''

''All the way. As far and as long as it takes. But that isn't the point, because I don't have the means.''

He drew on his cigarette, studied it with apparent interest, then tossed it into the fire. ''You would, if you were married to me.''

Chapter 5

She said nothing, could say nothing. He sat on the hearth, his legs folded up, his eyes very cool, very calm, on her face. Part of the enormity of his talent was his ability to focus on an expression and draw the underlying emotions out of it. Perhaps because he did it so well, he also knew how to mask emotions when they were his own.

She could hear the logs sizzling behind him. The mid-morning sunlight sparkled through the frost on the window-panes and landed at his feet. He seemed totally at ease, as though he'd just suggested that they have soup for lunch. If her life had depended upon it, Laura couldn't have said whether it meant any more to him than that.

Using the table for leverage, she rose.

"I'm tired. I'm going in to lie down."

"All right. We can talk about this later."

She whirled around, and it wasn't anguish or fear he saw

on her face now, it was fury, livid and clear. "How could you sit there and say something like that to me after everything I've told you?"

"You might consider that I said it because of everything you've told me."

"Oh, the Good Samaritan again." She detested the bitterness in her voice, but she could do nothing to stop it. "The white knight, riding in full of chivalry and good intentions to save the bumbling, inept female. Do you think I should fall on my knees and be grateful? That I would blindly let myself be taken over again, fall back into the same pitiful, destructive pattern a second time, because a man offers me a way out?"

He thought about controlling his temper, then rose, deciding to let her see it. "I have no desire to control you, and I'll be damned if you're going to stand there and compare me with some weak-minded alcoholic wife-beater."

"What then—the knight on a white charger, selflessly rescuing damsels in distress?"

He laughed at that, but his anger was still on the edge. "No one's ever accused me of that. I'm very selfish, which is another reason for my suggestion. I'm moody—you've been around me long enough to know that. I have a temper and I can get angry. But I don't hit women, and I don't use them."

With an effort, she pulled her emotions back in and forced them to settle. "I didn't mean to imply that you did, or to compare you with someone else. It's the situation that's comparable."

"One has nothing to do with the other. The fact that I have money only works to your advantage."

"I didn't marry Tony for his money."

"No." His tone softened. "No, I'm sure you didn't. But in this case I'm willing to accept that you marry me for mine."

"Why?"

Something flickered in his eyes and was gone before she could read it. "That might have been the wisest question to ask first."

"Maybe you're right." She already regretted the outburst of temper and harsh words, as she invariably did. "I'm asking it now."

With a nod, he roamed the room, stopping before the nearly completed portrait. He stared at it, as he had stared at it countless times before, trying to understand, to define, not only Laura, but himself.

"I feel something for you. I'm not sure what it is, but it's very strong. Stronger than anything I've felt before." He lifted a finger to the face on canvas. He wished he could explain himself completely, to himself, to her, but he'd always expressed himself best through painting. "I'm attracted to you, Laura, and I've discovered recently that I've been alone long enough."

"That might be enough, almost enough, for marriage, but not for me, not to me. Not with what you'd be taking on."

"I have some debts to pay," he murmured, then turned to her again. "Helping you, and the child, might just clear the slate."

Whatever anger she'd felt evaporated. It only took the kindness and the grief in his eyes. "You've already helped us, more than I can ever repay."

"I don't want payment." The impatience, the edge, was back in his voice. "What I want is you. How many ways do you want me to say it?"

"I don't think I want you to say it." The nerves began to eat at her again, and she twisted her fingers together. He meant it. She had no doubt that he meant what he said. The prospect of being wanted by him both thrilled and terrified her. "Don't you see, I've already made one terrible mistake."

He crossed to her, gently drawing her hands apart and into his. "You're not indifferent to me?"

"No, but—"

"You're not afraid of me?"

Some of the tension seeped out of her. "No."

"Then let me help you."

"I'm going to have another man's child."

"No." He took her face in his hands because he wanted her eyes on his. "Marry me, and the child is ours. Privately, publicly, totally."

The tears came back. "They'll come."

"Let them. They won't touch you again, and they won't take the baby."

Safety. Could what had always eluded her really be only a promise away? She opened her mouth, knowing that agreement was on her tongue. Then her heart turned over in her chest and she lifted a hand to his cheek. "How could I do this to you?"

For an answer, he put his lips to hers. The need was there, she couldn't deny it, couldn't pretend it away. She tasted it as his mouth drew from hers. She felt it when his hand skimmed through her hair to brace, both possessive and supportive, at the back of her neck. Instinctively, wanting to give, she lifted her other hand to his face. They rested there, comforting.

She wasn't the only one who had demons, Laura thought. She wasn't the only one who needed love and understanding. Because he was strong, it was easy to forget that he, too, might have pain. Seeking to soothe, she drew him closer into her arms.

He could have sunk into her, into the softness, the generosity. This was what he wanted to capture on canvas, her warmth, her spirit. And this was what he was forced to admit he would never have the skill to translate. This part of her beauty, this most essential part, could never be painted. But it could be cherished.

"You need me," he murmured as he drew her away. "And I need you."

She nodded, then rested her head on his shoulder, because that seemed to say it all.

Due to fresh flurries, it was three days before Gabe risked a trip into town. Laura watched him as he downed a final cup of coffee before pulling on his coat.

"I'll be as quick as I can."

"I'd rather you took your time and paid attention to the roads."

"The Jeep drives like a tank." He accepted the gloves she held out to him but didn't put them on. "I don't like leaving you alone."

"Gabe, I've been taking care of myself for a long time."

"Things have changed. My lawyers have probably sent the marriage license."

Immediately she began to fuss with the breakfast dishes. "That would be quick work."

"They get paid to work fast, and it's been three days since I contacted them. If I can arrange it, I'd like to bring a justice of the peace back here with me."

A cup slipped out of her hand and plopped into the soapy water. "Today?"

"You haven't changed your mind?"

"No, but—"

"I want my name on the birth certificate." He had a moment of panic, vague and disturbing, at her hesitation. "It would be less complicated if we were married before the baby's born."

"Yes, that makes sense." It seemed so rushed. She plunged her hands into the water and began to wash. Her first wedding had been rushed, too, a whirlwind of flowers and champagne and white silk.

"I realize you might prefer something a little more festive, but under the circumstances—"

"No." She turned and managed a smile. "No, I don't care about that. If you can arrange it for today, here, that's fine."

"All right, then. Laura, I'd feel better if you rested until I got back. You didn't sleep well."

She turned back again. No, she hadn't slept well. The nightmare had come back, and she hadn't rested until Gabe had come in and finally slipped into bed with her. "I won't overdo."

"I don't think it would tax your strength for you to kiss me goodbye."

That made her smile. She turned, her hands still dripping, to lift her lips to his.

"Not even married yet and you're already kissing me as though we've been together twenty years." He changed the mood simply by nipping her lip. In seconds she was clinging to him, and there was nothing casual about the embrace.

"Better," he murmured. "Now go lie down. I'll be back in less than two hours."

"Be careful."

He closed the door. In moments she heard the sound of the Jeep's engine chugging to life. Moving into the living room, she watched Gabe drive away.

Strangely enough, even as the quiet settled over the cabin, she didn't feel alone. She felt nervous, she admitted with a little laugh. Brides were entitled to nerves. If Gabe had his way—and she'd come to believe that he nearly always did—they would be married that afternoon.

And her life, Laura realized, would change yet again.

This time it would be better. She would make it better.

As the ache in her lower back grew worse, she pressed her hand against it. Blaming the discomfort she'd been feeling all morning on the mattress and a restless night, she walked over to the portrait.

He'd finished it the day before. She knew, because he'd explained it to her, that the paint would take a few days to set and dry completely, so she didn't touch it. She sat on the stool Gabe sometimes used and studied her own face.

So this was how he saw her, she thought. Her skin was pale, with only a faint shadow of color along her cheekbones. It was partly that whiteness, that translucence, that made her appear like the angel he sometimes called her.

She looked as though she were caught in a daydream, one of the many she'd indulged in during the hours Gabe had painted. As she had told him—as she had complained—there was too much vulnerability. It was in her eyes, around her mouth. There was something strong and independent about the pose, about the way her head was tilted, but that lost, sad look in her eyes seemed to negate the strength.

She was reading too much into it, Laura decided as the pain dug, deep and dull, into her back. Rubbing at it, she rose to look around the cabin.

She would be married here, in a matter of hours. There would be no crowd of well-wishers, no pianist playing romantic songs, no trail of rose petals. Yet, with or without the trimmings, she would be a bride. She might not be able to make it look festive, but at least she could tidy up.

The pain in her back drove her to lie down. Two hours later she heard the Jeep coming down the lane. For a moment longer she lay there, working to block out the discomfort. Later, she told herself, she would soak the ache away in a hot tub. She walked into the living room just as Gabe ushered an elderly couple into the cabin.

''Laura, this is Mr. and Mrs. Witherby. Mr. Witherby is a justice of the peace.''

''Hello. It's so nice of you to come all this way.''

''Part of the job,'' Mr. Witherby said, adjusting his fogging glasses. '''Sides that, your young man here wasn't going to take no for an answer.''

''Don't you worry about this old man here.'' Mrs. Witherby patted her husband's arm and studied Laura. ''He loves to complain.''

''Can I get you something, some coffee?''

"Don't you fuss. Mr. Bradley's got a carload of supplies. You just sit down and let him take care of it." She had already walked over to lead Laura to the couch with her frail hands. "Man's nervous as a goose at Christmas," she confided. "Let him keep busy for a spell."

Though she couldn't imagine Gabe being nervous about anything, she thought the Witherbys would expect such emotion from a man about to marry. Laura listened to Gabe rattling bags and cans in the kitchen. "Maybe I should help him."

"Now, you sit right here." Mrs. Witherby motioned to her husband to sit, as well. "A woman's entitled to be waited on when she's carrying. The good Lord knows you won't have much time to sit once that baby's born."

Grateful, Laura shifted to ease the throbbing in her back. "You have children?"

"Had six of them. Now we've got twenty-two grandchildren and five great-grandchildren."

"And another on the way," Mr. Witherby stated, pulling out a pipe.

"You can just put that smelly thing away," his wife told him. "You aren't smoking up this room with this lady expecting."

"I wasn't going to light it," he said, and began to chew on the stem.

Satisfied that her husband had been put in his place, Mrs. Witherby turned back to Laura. "That's a pretty picture there." She indicated a sprawling landscape that might very well sell for an amount in six figures. "Your man's an artist fellow?"

Her man. Laura experienced a twinge of panic and a glow of pleasure at the phrase. "Yes, Gabe's an artist."

"I like pictures," she said comfortably. "Got me one of the seashore over my sofa."

Gabe walked back in carrying an armful of flowers. Feeling awkward, he cleared his throat. "They sold them at the market."

"And he bought them out, too," Mrs. Witherby cackled. Then, with a few wheezes, she heaved herself off the couch. "You got a vase? She can't be carrying all of them."

"No, at least…I don't know."

"Men." She sighed and then winked at Laura. "Give them to me and let me take care of it. You can do something useful, like putting more wood on that fire. Wouldn't want your lady to catch a chill."

"Yes, ma'am."

If he'd ever felt more of a fool, he couldn't remember when. Wanting to keep his hands busy, he moved to the fire.

"Don't let her browbeat you, boy," Mr. Witherby advised him from the comfort of his chair. "She's already spent fifty-two years nagging me."

"Somebody had to," Mrs. Witherby called out from the kitchen, and he chuckled.

"Sure you two know what you're getting into?"

Gabe dusted his hands on the thighs of his jeans and grinned. "No."

"That's the spirit." Witherby laughed and rested his head against the back of the chair. "Essie, get that bag of bones you call a body moving, will you? These two people want to get married while they're still young."

''Keep your tongue in your mouth,'' she muttered. ''Already lost his teeth.'' She came in carrying a watering can filled with flowers. She set it in the middle of the coffee table, nodded her approval, then handed Laura a single white carnation.

''Thank you. They're lovely.'' She started to rise and nearly winced at the stab of pain in her back. Then Gabe was there to take her hand and draw her to his side.

They stood in front of the fire with wood crackling and the scent of the flowers merging with that of the smoke. The words were simple and very old. Despite the countless weddings she'd been to, Mrs. Witherby dabbed at her eyes.

To love. To honor. To cherish.

For richer. For poorer.

Forsaking all others.

The ring he slipped onto her finger was very plain, just a gold band that was a size too large. Looking at it, Laura felt something grow inside her. It was warm and sweet and tremulous. Curling her hand into his, she repeated the words, and meant them, from her heart.

Let no man put asunder.

''You may kiss the bride,'' Witherby told him, but Gabe didn't hear.

It was done. It was irrevocable. And until that moment he hadn't been completely aware of how much it would mean to him.

With her hand still caught in his, he kissed her and sealed the promise.

''Congratulations.'' Mrs. Witherby brushed her dry lips over Gabe's cheek, then Laura's. ''Now you sit down, Mrs.

Bradley, and I'm going to fix you a nice cup of tea before we drag your husband off again.''

''Thank you, but we don't have any tea.''

''I bought some,'' Gabe put in.

''That and everything else he could lay his hands on. Come on, Ethan, give me a hand.''

''You ought to be able to fix a cup of tea by yourself.''

Mrs. Witherby rolled her eyes. ''You'd think the old goat would have a little more romance, seeing as he's married more'n five hundred couples in his time. In the kitchen, Ethan, and give these young people five minutes alone.''

He grumbled about wanting his supper, but he followed her.

''They're wonderful,'' Laura murmured.

''I don't think I'd have gotten him away from his TV if she hadn't shoved him out the door.''

Silence followed, awkward. ''It was nice of you to think of flowers...and the ring.''

He lifted her hand and studied it. ''They don't have a jewelry store in Lonesome Ridge. They sell these at the hardware in a little case next to sixpenny nails. It may just turn your finger green.''

She laughed and knew she'd treasure it even more now. ''You may not believe it, but you may have saved my life by buying that tea.''

''I got some marshmallows, too.''

She hated it, despised herself for not being able to control it, but she started to cry. ''I'm sorry. I can't seem to do anything about this.''

Discomfort surged through him. He was feeling edgy himself, and tears did nothing to help matters. ''Look, I know it wasn't exactly the wedding of the century. We can have some sort of party or reception back in San Francisco."

"No, no, that's not it." Though she urged her hands over her face, the tears kept coming. "It was lovely and sweet and I don't know how to thank you."

"Not crying would be a good start." He had a bandanna in his pocket, one that he used more often than not as a paint rag. He drew it out and offered it to her. "Laura, we're legally married. That means you don't have to be grateful for every bunch of daisies I hand you."

She sniffled into the cloth and tried to smile. "I think it was the marshmallows that did it."

"Keep this up and you won't get any more."

"I want you to know..." She dried her face and managed to compose herself. "I want you to know that I'm going to do everything I can to make you happy, to make you comfortable, so that you never regret what you did today."

"I'm going to regret it," he said suddenly impatient, "if you keep making it sound as though I gave someone else the last life jacket as the ship was sinking. I married you because I wanted to, not to be noble."

"Yes, but I—"

"Shut up, Laura." To make certain she did, he closed his mouth over hers. And for the first time she felt the true strength of his passion and need and desire. With a little murmur of surprise, she drew him closer.

This was what he had needed, all he had needed, to settle him. Yet even as the first layer of tension dissolved, a new layer, one built on desire, formed.

"Before too much longer," he said against her mouth, "we're going to finish this. I want to make love with you, Laura. And after I do you won't have the strength to thank me."

Before she could think of a response, Mrs. Witherby came in with her tea. "Now let the poor thing rest and drink this while it's hot." She set the cup on the table in front of Laura. "I hate to drag you out on your wedding day, Mr. Bradley, but the sooner you drive us back to town, the sooner you can get back and fix your wife that nice steak you bought for supper."

She moved over to gather up her coat. On impulse, Laura drew one of the flowers from the watering can and took it to her. "I'm never going to forget you, Mrs. Witherby."

"There now." Touched, she sniffed at the flower. "You just take care of yourself and that baby of yours. Shake a leg, Ethan."

"I should only be an hour," Gabe told her. "The roads aren't too bad. I really think you should rest, Laura. You look exhausted."

"I'm supposed to look glowing, but I promise I won't lift anything heavier than a teacup until you get back."

This time she watched the Jeep drive away, running her finger over and over her wedding ring. It took so little, she thought, to change so much. She bent, trying to ease the ache in her back, then she crossed the room to finish her tea.

Her back had never ached like this, not even after she'd worked a full day on her aunt's farm. The pain was constant and deep. She tried stretching out, then curling up, then stretching out again. Impatient with herself, she tried to ignore it, concentrating instead on roasting marshmallows and warming tea.

She'd been alone less than ten minutes when the first contraction hit.

It wasn't the vague warning pain she'd read about. It was sharp and long. Caught off guard, she had no time to breathe her way over it. Instead, she tensed, fought against it, then collapsed against the cushions when it faded.

It couldn't be labor. Her forehead broke out in sweat as she tried to dismiss the idea. It was too early, a month too early, and it had come on so suddenly. False labor, she assured herself. Brought on by nerves and by the excitement of the day.

But the back pain. Struggling to keep calm, she pushed herself into a sitting position. Was it possible she'd been having back labor all morning?

No, it had to be false labor. It had to be.

But when the second contraction hit she began to time them.

She was in bed when Gabe returned, but she couldn't call out to him, because she was riding out the latest contraction. The fear that had gripped her in a stranglehold for the past hour faded a bit. He was here, and somehow that meant that everything would be all right. She heard him toss a log on the fire, took a last cleansing breath as the pain passed and called out.

The urgency in her voice had him across the room in three strides. At the bedroom door he paused, and his heart jumped into his throat.

She was propped against the pillows, half lying, half sitting. Her face was bathed in sweat. Her eyes, always dark, were sheened with moisture and nearly black.

"I have to go back on our deal," she managed, struggling with a smile because she saw the same blank fear she felt reflected on his face. "The baby's decided to come a little early."

He didn't ask if she was sure or fumble with reasons why it wasn't a good idea. He wanted to, but he found himself beside the bed, with her hand gripped in his. "Take it easy. Just hold on and I'll phone for a doctor."

"Gabe, the phone's out." Nerves skipped in and out of her voice. "I tried it when I realized this was happening so fast."

"Okay." Fighting for calm, he brushed the damp hair away from her face. "There was an accident on the way into town. Lines must have gone down. I'll get some extra blankets and I'll take you in."

She pressed her lips together. "Gabe, it's too late. I couldn't make the trip." She tried to swallow, but fear had dried up the moisture in her mouth and throat. "I've been in labor for hours, all morning, and I didn't know it. It was back labor, and I didn't pay attention. With everything that was going on, I thought it was nerves and the restless night I'd had."

"Hours," he murmured, and eased himself down on the edge of the bed. His mind went blank, but then her fingers tightened on his. "How far apart are the pains?"

"Five minutes. I've been—" She let her head fall back and began to breathe in short, deep gasps. Gabe slipped his hand over her and felt the hardening of her abdomen.

He'd glanced through the birth and baby books she'd

brought with her. To pass the time, he'd told himself, but there had been something deep inside him that had been compelled to understand what she was going through. Perhaps it was instinct that had had him absorbing the advice, the details, the instructions. Now, seeing her in pain, everything he'd read seemed to slip away from him.

When the contraction passed, her face was shiny with fresh sweat. "Getting closer," she whispered. "There's not much time." Though she bit down on her lips, a sob escaped her. "I can't lose the baby."

"The baby's going to be fine, and so are you." He squeezed her hand once reassuringly. They would need towels, lots of them. String and scissors had to be sterilized. It was really very simple when you thought about it. He only hoped it was as simple when you put it into practice.

"Just hang on. I have to get some things." He saw the doubt flash in her eyes, and he leaned over her. "I'm not going to leave you. I'm going to take care of you, Laura. Trust me."

She nodded, and with her head slumped back on the pillow, she closed her eyes.

When he came back, her eyes were focused on the ceiling and she was panting. After setting fresh towels on the foot of the bed, he spread another blanket over her. "Are you cold?"

She shook her head. "The baby will need to be kept warm. He's not full-term."

"I've built up the fire, and there are plenty of blankets." Gently he wiped her face with a cool, damp cloth. "You've talked to doctors, you've read the books. You know what to expect."

She looked up at him, trying to swallow past a dry throat. Yes, she knew what to expect, but reading about it, imagining it, was a far cry from the experience.

"They lied." Her mouth moved into a weak smile when his brows drew together. "They try to tell you it doesn't hurt so much if you ride out the pain."

He brought her hand to his lips and held it there. "Yell all you want. Scream the roof down. Nobody's going to hear."

"I'm not screaming this baby into the world." Then she gasped, and her fingers dug into his. "I can't—"

"Yes, you can. Pant. Pant, Laura. Squeeze my hand. Harder. Concentrate on that." He kept his eyes locked on hers while she pushed air out. "You're doing fine, better than fine." When her body went lax, he moved to the foot of the bed. "The pains are closer?" As he spoke, he knelt on the mattress and shifted the blanket.

"Almost on top of each other."

"That means it's almost over. Hold on to that."

She tried to moisten her dry lips, but her tongue was thick. "If anything happens to me, promise you'll—"

"Nothing's going to happen." He bit off the words. Their eyes met again, hers glazed with pain, his dark with purpose. "Damn it, I'm not going to lose either of you now, understand? The three of us are going to pull this off. Now, you've got work to do, angel."

Each time the pains hit her, he shuddered with it. Time seemed to drag as she struggled through them, then race again as she rested. Gabe moved back and forth, to arrange her pillows, to wipe her face, then knelt again to check the progress of birth.

He could hear the fire roaring in the next room, but he still worried that the cabin would be too cold. Then he worried about the heat, because Laura's laboring body was like a furnace.

He hadn't known birth could be so hard on a woman. He knew she was close to total exhaustion, but she managed to pull herself through time after time, recharging somehow during the all-too-brief moments between contractions. Pain seemed to tear through her, impossibly hard, impossibly ruthless. His own shirt was soaked with sweat, and he swore constantly, silently, as he urged her to breathe, to pant, to concentrate. All his ambitions, his joys, his griefs, whittled down to focus on that one room, that one moment, that one woman.

It seemed to him that she should weaken, with her body being battered by the new life fighting to be born. But as the moments passed she seemed to draw on new reserves of strength. There was something fierce and valiant about her face as she pushed herself forward and braced for whatever happened next.

"Do you have a name picked out?" he asked, hoping to distract her.

"I made lists. Sometimes at night I'd try to imagine what the baby would look like and try to— Oh, God."

"Hold on. Breathe, angel. Breathe through it."

"I can't. I have to push."

"Not yet, not yet. Soon." From his position at the foot of the bed, he ran his hands over her. "Pant, Laura."

Her concentration kept slipping in and out. If she stared into his eyes, if she pulled the strength from them, she would make it. "I can't hold off much longer."

''You don't have to. I can see the head.'' There was wonder in his voice when he looked back at her. ''I can see it. Push with the next one.''

Giddy, straining with the effort, she bore down. She heard the long, deep-throated moan, but she didn't know it was her own voice. Gabe shouted at her, and in response she automatically began to pant again.

''That's good, that's wonderful.'' He barely recognized his own voice, or his own hands. Both were shaking. ''I have the head. Your baby's beautiful. The shoulders come next.''

She braced herself, desperate to see. ''Oh, God.'' Tears mixed with sweat as she steepled her hands over her mouth. ''It's so little.''

''And strong as an ox. You have to push the shoulders out.'' Sweat dripped off his forehead as he cupped the baby's head in his hand and leaned over it. ''Come on, Laura, let's have a look at the rest of it.''

Her fingers dug into the blankets, and her head fell back. And she gave birth. Over her own gasping breaths she heard the first cry.

''A boy.'' Gabe's eyes were wet as he held the squirming new life in his hands. ''You have a son.''

As the tears rolled, she began to laugh. The pain and the terror were forgotten. ''A boy. A little boy.''

''With a loud mouth, ten fingers and ten toes.'' He reached for her hand and gripped it hard. ''He's perfect, angel.''

Their fingers linked over the baby, and the cabin echoed with the high, indignant wails of the newborn.

* * *

She couldn't rest. Laura knew Gabe wanted her to sleep, but she couldn't shut her eyes. The baby, nearly an hour old now, was wrapped in blankets and tucked in the curve of her arm. He was sleeping, she thought, but she couldn't stop herself from tracing a fingertip over his face.

So tiny. Five pounds, seven ounces, on the vegetable scale that Gabe had unearthed and scrubbed down. Seventeen and a half inches tall, and with only a bit of pale blond peach fuzz covering his head. She couldn't stop looking at him.

"He's not going to disappear, you know."

Laura glanced up at the doorway and smiled. Fatigue had left her skin almost pale enough to see through. Triumph had given her eyes a rich glow. "I know." She held out a hand in invitation. "I'm glad you came in," she said as he sat on the bed. "I know you must be exhausted, but I'd like you to stay a minute."

"You did all the work," he murmured, running a finger down the baby's cheek.

"That's not true, and that's the first thing I want to say. We wouldn't have made it without you."

"Of course you would have. I was basically a cheerleader."

"No." Her hand tightened on his, demanding that he look at her. "You were as responsible for his life as I was. I know what you said about having your name on the birth certificate, about helping us, but I want you to know it's more than that. You brought him into the world. There's nothing I can ever do or say that could be enough. Don't look like that." She gave a quiet laugh and settled back among the pillows. ''I know you hate to be thanked, and that's not what I'm doing.''

''Isn't it?''

''No.'' She shifted the baby from her arm to his. It was a gesture that said more, much more, than the words that followed it. ''I'm telling you that you got more than a wife today.''

The baby went on sleeping peacefully, cupped between them.

He didn't know what to say. He touched the tiny hand and watched it curl reflexively. As an artist he'd thought he understood the full range of beauty. Until today.

''I've been reading about preemies,'' he began. ''His weight is good, and from what the book says a baby born after the thirty-fourth week is in pretty good shape, but I want to get you both into a hospital. Will you be strong enough to travel into Colorado Springs tomorrow?''

''Yes. We'll both be strong enough.''

''We'll leave in the morning, then. Do you think you could eat now?''

''Only a horse.''

He grinned, but he couldn't quite bring himself to give her back the baby. ''You may have to settle for beefsteak. Isn't he hungry?''

''I imagine he'll let us know.''

Just as Laura had been, he was compelled to trace the shape of the child's face. ''What about that name? We can't keep calling him *he*.''

''No, we can't.'' Laura stroked the soft down on his head. ''I was wondering if you'd like to pick his name.''

''Me?''

"Yes, you must have a favorite, or a name of someone who's important to you. I'd like you to choose."

"Michael," he murmured, looking down at the sleeping infant.

Chapter 6

San Francisco. It was true that Laura had always wanted to see it, but she had never expected to arrive there with a two-week-old son and a husband. And she had never expected to be shown into a tall, gracious house near the Bay.

Gabe's house. Hers, too, she thought as she rubbed her thumb nervously over her wedding ring. It was foolish to be jumpy because the house was beautiful and big. It was ridiculous to feel small and insecure because you could taste the wealth and the prominence just by breathing the air.

But she did.

She stepped into the tiled foyer and wished desperately for the comfort of the tiny cabin. It had begun to snow again the day they'd left Colorado, and though the mild spring breeze and the tiny buds here were wonderful, she found herself wishing for the cold and ferocity of the mountains.

''It's lovely,'' she managed, glancing up at the gentle curve of the stairs.

''It was my grandmother's.'' Gabe set down the luggage and took in the familiar surroundings. It was a house he'd always appreciated for its beauty and its balance. ''She held on to it after her marriage. Shall I show you around, or would you rather rest?''

She nearly winced. It was as though he were talking to a guest. ''If I rested as much as you'd like, I'd sleep my way through the rest of the year.''

''Then why don't I show you the upstairs.'' He knew he sounded polite, overly polite, but he'd been edgy ever since they'd stepped off the plane. The farther away from Colorado they'd gotten, the farther Laura had withdrawn from him. It was nothing he could put his finger on, but it was there.

Hefting two cases, he started up the stairs. He was bringing his wife, and his son, home. And he didn't know quite what to say to either of them. ''I've used this bedroom.'' He strode in and set the cases at the foot of a big oak bed. ''If there's another you'd prefer, we can arrange it.''

She nodded, thinking that though they'd shared a motel room while the baby had been in the hospital they had only shared a bed in the cabin, the night before Michael had been born. It would be different here. Everything would be different here.

''It's a beautiful room.''

Her voice was a little stiff, but she smiled, trying to soften it. The room was lovely, with its high ceilings and the glossy antiques. There was a terrace, and through the glass doors she could see a garden below, with green leaves already formed. The floors were dark with age and gleaming, just as the Oriental rug was faded with age and rich with heritage.

"The bath's through there," Gabe told her as she ran a finger down the carving in an old chifforobe. "My studio's at the end of the hall. The light's best there, but there's a room next to this that might do as a nursery."

When they spoke of the baby, things always relaxed between them. "I'd love to see it. After all those days in the incubator, Michael deserves a room of his own."

She followed Gabe out and into the next room. It was decorated in blues and grays with a stately four-poster and a many-cushioned window seat. As with the other rooms she'd seen, paintings hung on the wall, some of them Gabe's, others by artists he respected.

"It's beautiful, but what would you do with all these things?"

"They can be stored." He dismissed the furnishings with a shrug. "Michael can stay in our room until his is finished."

"You don't mind? He's bound to wake during the night for weeks yet."

"I could stick the pair of you in a hotel until it's convenient."

She started to speak, but then she recognized the look in his eyes. "Sorry. I can't get used to it."

"Get used to it." He moved over to cup her face in his hand. Whenever he did that, she was almost ready to believe that dreams came true. "I may not have the equipment to feed him, but I figure I can learn to change a diaper.'' He stroked a thumb under her jawline. ''I've been told I'm clever with my hands.''

The heat rushed into her face. She was torn between stepping into his arms and backing away. The baby woke and decided her. ''Speaking of feeding...''

''Why don't you use the bedroom, where you can be comfortable? I have some calls to make.''

She knew what was coming. ''Your family?''

''They're going to want to meet you. Are you up to it this evening?''

She wanted to snap that she wasn't an invalid, but she knew he wasn't speaking of her physical health. ''Yes, of course.''

''Fine. I'll make arrangements about the nursery. Did you have any colors in mind?''

''Well, I...'' She expected to paint the room herself. She'd wanted to. Things were different now, she reminded herself. The cabin had easily become theirs, but the house was his. ''I'd like yellow,'' she told him. ''With white trim.''

She sat in a chair by the window while Michael suckled hungrily. It was so good to have him with her all the time instead of having to go to the hospital to feed him, touch him, watch him. It had been so hard to leave him there and go back to a hotel room and wait until she could go back and see him again.

Smiling, she looked down at him. His eyes were closed, and his hand was pressed against her breast.

He was already gaining weight. Healthy, the doctor in

Colorado Springs had said. Sound as a dollar. And the tag on his little wristband had read Michael Monroe Bradley.

Who was Michael? she wondered. Gabe's Michael. She hadn't asked, but knew that the name, the person, was important.

"You're Michael now," she murmured as the baby began to doze at her breast.

Later she laid him on the bed, surrounding him with pillows though she knew he couldn't roll yet. Going to her suitcase, she took out her hairbrush. It was silly, of course, to feel compelled to leave some mark of herself on the room. But she set the brush on Gabe's bureau before she left.

She found him downstairs, in a dark-paneled library with soft gray carpet. Because he was on the phone, she started to back out, but he waved her in and continued to talk.

"The paintings should be here by the end of the week. Yes, I'm back in harness again. I haven't decided. You take a look first. No, I'm going to be tied up here for a few days, thanks anyway. I'll let you know." He hung up, then glanced at Laura. "Michael?"

"He's asleep. I know there hasn't been time, but he's going to need his own bed. I thought I could run out and buy something if you could watch him for a little while."

"Don't worry about it. My parents are coming over soon."

"Oh."

He sat on the edge of the desk and frowned at her. "They're not monsters, Laura."

"Of course not, it's just that... It seems we're so out in

the open,'' she blurted out. ''The more people who know about Michael, the more dangerous it is.''

''You can't keep him in a glass bubble. I thought you trusted me.''

''I did. I do,'' she amended quickly, but not quickly enough.

''Did,'' Gabe repeated. It wasn't anger he felt so much as pressing regret. ''You made a decision, Laura. On the day he was born, you gave him to me. Are you taking him back?''

''No. But things are different here. The cabin was—''

''An excellent place to hide. For both of us. Now it's time to deal with what happens next.''

''What does happen?''

He picked up a paperweight, an amber ball with darker gold streaks in the center. He set it down again, then crossed to her. She'd shed weight quickly. Her stomach was close to flat, her breasts were high and full, her hips were impossibly narrow. He wondered how it would feel to hold her now, now that the waiting was over.

''We might start with this.''

He kissed her, gently at first, until he felt her first nerves fade into warmth. That was what he'd been desperate for, that promise, that comfort. When he gathered her close, she fitted against him as he'd once imagined she would. Her hair, bound up, was easily set free with a sweep of his hand. She made a small sound—a murmur of surprise or acceptance—and then her arms went around him.

And the kiss was no longer gentle.

Passion, barely restrained, and hunger, far from sated, rippled from him into her. An ache, long buried, grew in her until she was straining against him, whispering his name.

Then his lips were roaming over her face, raking over her throat, searing her skin, then cooling it, then searing it again, while his hands stroked and explored with a new freedom.

Too soon. Some sane part of him knew it was too soon for anything more than a touch, a taste. But the more he indulged in her, the more his impatience grew. Taking her by the shoulders, he drew her away and fought to catch his breath.

"You may not trust me as you once did, angel, but trust this. I want you."

Giving in to the need, she held on to him, pressing her face into his shoulder. "Gabe, is it so wrong of me to wish it was just the three of us?"

"Not wrong." He stared over the top of her head as he stroked her hair. "Just not possible, and less than fair to Michael."

"You're right." Drawing a breath, she stepped back. "I want to go check on him."

Shaken by the emotions he pulled out of her, she started back up the stairs. Halfway up, she stopped, stunned.

She was in love with him. It wasn't the love she'd come to accept, the kind that came from gratitude and dependence. It wasn't even the strong, beautiful bond that had been forged when they'd brought Michael into the world. It was more basic than that, the most elemental love of woman for man. And it was terrifying.

She had loved once before, briefly, painfully. That love had kept her chained down. All her life she'd been a victim, and her marriage had both accented that and ultimately freed her. She'd learned through necessity how to be strong, how to take the right steps.

She couldn't be that woman again, she thought as her fingers gripped the banister. She wouldn't. That was what had bothered her most about the house, about the things in it. She had stepped into a house like this before, a house in which she had been out of place and continually helpless.

Not again, she told herself, and shut her eyes. Never again.

Whatever she felt for Gabe, she wouldn't allow it to change her back into that kind of woman. She had a child to protect.

The doorbell rang. Laura sent one swift look over her shoulder, then fled up the stairs.

When Gabe opened the door, he was immediately enveloped in soft fur and strong perfume. It was his mother, a woman of unwavering beauty and unwavering opinions. She didn't believe in brushing cheeks, she believed in squeezing, hard and long.

''I've missed you. I didn't know what it would take to drag you off that mountain, but I didn't think it would be a wife and a baby.''

''Hello, Mother.'' He smiled at her, giving her a quick sweeping look that took in her stubbornly blond hair and her smooth cheeks. She had Michael's eyes. They were a darker green than his own, with touches of gray. Seeing them brought a pang and a pleasure. ''You look wonderful.''

''So do you, except for the fact that you've lost about

ten pounds and can't afford to. Well, where are they?" With that, Amanda Bradley marched inside.

"Give the boy a chance, Mandy." Gabe exchanged bear hugs with his father, a tall, spare man with a hangdog expression and a razor-sharp mind. "Glad you're back. Now she'll take to rattling your cage instead of mine."

"I can handle you both." She was already slipping off her gloves with short, quick little motions. "We brought a bottle of champagne over. I thought since we missed the wedding, the birth and everything else, we should at least toast the homecoming. For heaven's sake, Gabe, don't just stand there, I'm dying to see them."

"Laura went up to check the baby. Why don't we go in and sit down?"

"This way, Mandy," Cliff Bradley said, taking his wife's arm when she started to object.

"Very well, then. You can hold me off for five minutes by telling me how your work's been going."

"Well." He watched his parents sit but couldn't relax enough to follow suit. "I've already called Marion. The paintings I finished in Colorado should be delivered to her gallery by the end of the week."

"That's wonderful. I can't wait to see them."

His hands were in his pockets as he moved around the room with a restlessness both of his parents recognized. "There's one piece in particular I'm fond of. I plan to hang it in here, over the fire."

Amanda lifted a brow and glanced at the empty space above the mantel. Gabe had always claimed that nothing suited that spot. "It must be very special."

"You'll have to judge for yourself." He drew out a cigarette, then set it down when Laura moved into the doorway.

She said nothing for a moment, just studied the couple on the couch. His parents. His mother was lovely, her smooth skin almost unlined, her hair swept back to accent her aristocratic features and fine bones. There were emeralds at her ears and at her throat. She wore a rose silk suit with a fox stole carelessly thrown over her shoulders.

His father was tall and lean, like Gabe. Laura saw a diamond wink at his pinky. He looked sad and quiet, but she saw his eyes sharpen as he studied her.

"This is my wife, Laura, and our son."

Braced for whatever was to come, holding the baby protectively against her breasts, she stepped into the room. Amanda rose first, only because she always seemed to move quicker than anyone else.

"It's so nice to meet you at last." Amanda had reservations, a chestful of them, but she offered a polite smile. "Gabe didn't mention how lovely you were."

"Thank you." She felt a little trip-hammer of fear in her throat. Laura knew formidable when she saw it. Instinctively she lifted her chin. "I'm glad you could come. Both of you."

Amanda noted the little gesture of pride and defiance and approved. "We wanted to meet you at the airport, but Gabe put us off."

"Rightly so," Cliff added in his soothing take-your-time voice. "If I'd been able to, I'd have held Mandy off another day."

"Nonsense. I want to see my grandchild. May I?"

Laura's arms had tightened automatically. Then she

looked at Gabe and relaxed her hold. ''Of course.'' With care and caution, she shifted the slight weight into Amanda's arms.

''Oh, how beautiful.'' The cool, sophisticated voice wavered. ''How precious.'' The scents, the baby scents of talc and mild soap and fragile skin, made her sigh. ''Gabe said he was premature. No problems?''

''No, he's fine.''

As if to prove it, Michael opened his eyes and stared out owlishly.

''There, he looked right at me.'' With emeralds glowing on her skin, Amanda grinned foolishly and cooed. ''Looked right at your gran, didn't you?''

''He looked at me.'' Cliff leaned closer to chuck the baby under the chin.

''Nonsense. Why should he want to look at you? Do something useful, Cliff, like opening the champagne.'' She clucked and cooed at the baby while Laura stood twisting her hands. ''I hope you don't object to the wine. I didn't ask if you were nursing.''

''Yes, I am, but I don't think a sip would hurt either of us.''

Approving a second time, Amanda started for the couch. Laura took an instinctive step forward, then made herself stop. This wasn't Lorraine Eagleton, and she wasn't the same woman who had once cowered. But as hard as she tried to dispel the image, she saw herself standing just outside the family circle.

''I'd get glasses,'' she said lamely, ''but I don't know where they are.''

Saying nothing, Gabe went to a cabinet and drew out four champagne flutes.

Cliff took Laura's arm. ''Why don't you sit down, dear? You must be tired after traveling.''

''You sound like Gabe.'' Laura found herself smiling as she eased into a chair.

Glasses were passed. Amanda lifted hers. ''We'll drink to— For goodness' sake, I don't know the child's name.''

''It's Michael,'' Laura offered. She saw the grief flash into Amanda's eyes before she closed them. When she opened them again, they were wet and brilliant.

''To Michael,'' she murmured, and after a sip she leaned down to kiss the baby's cheek. Looking up, she smiled at Gabe. ''Your father and I have something in the car for the baby. Would you get it?''

Though they didn't touch, and the glance lasted only a moment, Laura saw something pass between them. ''I'll just be a minute.''

''We won't eat her, for heaven's sake,'' Amanda muttered as her son left the room.

With a laugh, Cliff rubbed her shoulder. There was something familiar about the gesture. It was Gabe's, Laura realized. The same casual intimacy.

''Have you been to San Francisco before?'' he asked Laura, snapping her back to the present.

''No, I— No. I'd like to offer you something, but I don't know what we have.'' Or even where the kitchen is, she thought miserably.

''Don't worry about it.'' Cliff draped his arm comfortably over the back of the chair. ''We don't deserve anything after barging in on your first day home.''

"Families don't barge," Amanda put in.

"Ours does." Grinning, he leaned over and chucked the baby under the chin again. "Smiled at me."

"Grimaced, you mean." With a laugh of her own, Amanda kissed her husband's cheek. "Granddad."

"I take it the cradle's for Michael and the roses are for me." Gabe strode in, carrying a dark pine cradle heaped with frilly sheets and topped with a spray of pink roses.

"Oh, the flowers. I completely forgot. And no, they're certainly not for you, but for Laura." Amanda handed the baby to her husband and rose. Though she moved to rise, Laura saw Cliff tuck the baby easily in the crook of his arm. "We'll need some water for these," Amanda decided. "No, no, I'll get it myself."

No one argued with her as she marched out of the room, carrying the flowers.

"It's very lovely," Laura began, bending from the chair to run a finger along the smooth wood of the cradle. "We were just talking about the baby needing a bed of his own."

"The Bradley bed," Cliff stated. "Fix those sheets, Gabe, and let's see how he takes to it."

"This cradle's a family tradition." Obediently Gabe lifted out the extra sheets and smoothed on white linen. "My great-grandfather built it, and all the Bradley children have had their turn rocking in it." He took the baby from his father. "Let's see how you fit, old man."

Laura watched Gabe set the baby down and give the cradle a gentle push. Something seemed to break inside her. "Gabe, I can't."

Crouched at her feet beside the cradle, he looked up.

There was a dare in his eyes, a challenge, and, she was certain, a buried anger. ''Can't what?''

''It isn't right, it isn't fair.'' She drew the baby from the cradle into her arms. ''They have to know.'' She might have fled right then and there, but Amanda came back into the room holding a crystal vase filled with roses. Sensing tension, and intrigued by it, she continued in.

''Where would you like these, Laura?''

''I don't know, I can't— Gabe, please.''

''I think they'll look nice by the window,'' she said mildly, then moved over to arrange them to her satisfaction. ''Now, then, don't you three gentlemen think you could find something to occupy yourselves while Laura and I have a little talk?''

Panic leaping within, Laura looked from one to the other, then back at her husband. ''Gabe, you have to tell them.''

He took the baby and settled him on his shoulder. His eyes, very clear and still sparking with anger, met hers. ''I already have.'' Then he left her alone with his mother.

Amanda settled herself on the sofa again. She crossed her legs and smoothed her skirts. ''A pity there isn't a fire. It's still cool for this time of year.''

''We haven't had a chance—''

''Oh, dear, don't mind me.'' She waved a hand vaguely at a chair. ''Wouldn't you rather sit?'' When Laura did so without a word, she lifted a brow. ''Are you always so amenable? I should certainly hope not, as I liked you better when you stuck your chin out at me.''

Laura folded her hands in her lap. ''I don't know what to say. I hadn't realized Gabe had explained things to you. The way you were acting...'' She let her words trail off.

Then, when Amanda continued to wait patiently, she tried again. "I thought you believed that Michael was, well, biologically Gabe's."

"Should that make such a big difference?"

She was calm again, at least outwardly, and able to meet Amanda's eyes levelly. "I would have expected it to, especially with a family like yours."

Amanda drew her brows together as she thought that through. "Shall I tell you that I'm acquainted with Lorraine Eagleton?" She saw the instant, overwhelming fear and backed up. She wasn't often a tactful woman, but she wasn't cruel. "We'll save talk of her for another time. Right now, I think I should explain myself instead. I'm a pushy woman, Laura, but I don't mind being pushed back."

"I'm not very good at that."

"Then you'll have to learn, won't you? We may be friends, or we may not, I can't tell so soon, but I love my son. When he left all those months ago, I wasn't sure I'd ever have him back. You, for whatever reason, brought him back, and for that I'm grateful."

"He would have come when he was ready."

"But he might not have come back whole. Let's leave that." Again, the vague gesture. "And get to the point. Your son. Gabe considers the child his. Do you?"

"Yes."

"No hesitation there, I see." Amanda smiled at her, and Laura was reminded of Gabe. "If Gabe considers Michael his son, and you consider Michael his son, why should Cliff and I feel differently?"

"Bloodlines."

"Let's leave the Eagletons out of this for the time being," Amanda said. Laura merely stared, surprised that the mark had been hit so directly. "If Gabe had been unable to have children and had adopted one, I would love it and think of it as my grandchild. So, don't you think you should get past this nonsense and accept it?"

"You make it sound very simple."

"It sounds to me as though your life's been complicated enough." Amanda picked up the glass of champagne she'd discarded before. "Do you have any objections to our being Michael's grandparents?"

"I don't know."

"An honest woman." Amanda sipped.

"Do you have any objections to me being Gabe's wife?"

With the slightest of smiles, Amanda raised her glass to Laura. "I don't know. So I suppose we'll both have to wait and see. In the meantime, I'd hate to think that I'd be discouraged from seeing Gabe or Michael because we haven't made up our minds about each other."

"No, of course not. I wouldn't do that. Mrs. Bradley, no one's ever been as kind or as generous with me as Gabe. I swear to you I won't do anything to hurt him."

"Do you love him?"

Uneasy, Laura cast a look toward the doorway. "We haven't…Gabe and I haven't talked about that. I needed help, and I think he needed to give it."

Pursing her lips, Amanda studied her glass. "I don't believe that's what I asked you."

The chin came up again. "That's something I should discuss with Gabe before anyone else."

"You're tougher than you look. Thank God for that."

Finishing off the sparkling beverage, she set down the empty glass. "I might just like you at that, Laura. Or, of course, we might end up detesting each other. But whatever is between the two of us doesn't change the fact that Gabe has committed himself to you and the child. You're family." She sat back, lifting both brows, but inside she felt a faint twist of sympathy. "From the look on your face, that doesn't thrill the life out of you."

"I'm sorry. I'm not used to being in a family."

"You've had a very rough time, haven't you?" There was compassion there, but not so much that it made Laura uncomfortable. Mentally Amanda made a note to do a little digging on the Eagletons.

"I'm trying to put that behind me."

"I hope you succeed. Some things in the past need to be remembered. Others are best forgotten."

"Mrs. Bradley, may I ask you something?"

"Yes. On the condition that after this question call me Amanda or Mandy or anything—except, please God, Mother Bradley."

"All right. Who was Michael named for?"

Amanda's gaze drifted to the empty cradle and lingered there. There was a softening, a saddening, in her face that compelled Laura to touch her hand. "My son, Gabe's younger brother. He died just over a year ago." With a long sigh, she rose. "It's time we left you to settle in."

"Thank you for coming." She hesitated because she was never quite sure what people expected. Then listening to her heart, she kissed Amanda's cheek. "Thank you for the cradle. It means a great deal to me."

"And to me." She brushed her hand over it before she

left the room. "Clifton, aren't you the one who said we shouldn't stay more than a half hour?"

His voice carried, muffled, from upstairs. Clucking her tongue, Amanda pulled on her gloves. "Always poking around in Gabe's studio. The poor dear doesn't know a Monet from a Picasso, but he loves to look over Gabe's work."

"He did some beautiful things in Colorado. You must be so proud of him."

"More every day." She heard her husband coming and glanced upstairs. "Do let me know if you want any help setting up the nursery or finding a good pediatrician. I also expect you'll understand if I buy out the baby boutiques."

"I don't—"

"Not understand, then, but you'll have to tolerate. Kiss your new daughter-in-law goodbye, Cliff."

"You don't have to tell me that." Rather than the formal, meaningless kiss she was expecting, Laura received a hearty hug that left her dazed and smiling. "Welcome to the Bradleys, Laura."

"Thank you." She had an urge to hug him back, to just throw her arms around his neck and breath in that nice, spicy after-shave she'd caught on his throat. Feeling foolish, she folded her hands instead. "I hope you'll come back, maybe next week for dinner, when I've had a chance to find things."

"Cooks, too?" He pinched Laura's cheek. "Nice work, Gabe."

When they were gone, she stood in the foyer, rubbing a finger over her cheek. "They're very nice."

"Yes, I've always thought so."

The sting was still in his voice, so she steadied herself and looked at him. "I owe you an apology."

"Forget it." He started to stride back into the library, then stopped and turned around. He'd be damned if he'd forget it. "Did you think I would lie to them about Michael? That I would have to?"

She accepted his anger without flinching. "Yes."

He opened his mouth, rage boiling on his tongue. Her answer had him shutting it again. "Well, you shoot straight from the hip."

"I did think so, and I'm glad I was wrong. Your mother was very kind to me, and your father..."

"What about my father?"

He hugged me, she wanted to say, but she didn't believe he could possibly understand how much that had affected her. "He's so much like you. I'll try not to disappoint them, or you."

"You'd do better not to disappoint yourself." Gabe dragged a hand through his hair. It fell in a tumble of dark blond disorder, the way she liked it best. "Damn it, Laura, you're not on trial here. You're my wife, this is your home, and for better or worse the Bradleys are your family."

She set her teeth. "You'll have to give me time to get used to it," she said evenly. "The only families I've ever known barely tolerated me. I'm through with that." She swung away to start up the stairs, then called over her shoulder, "And I'm painting Michael's nursery myself."

Not certain whether to laugh or swear, Gabe stood at the foot of the stairs and stared after her.

Chapter 7

Laura brushed the glossy white enamel paint over the baseboard. In her other hand she held a stiff piece of cardboard as a guard against smearing any of the white over the yellow walls she'd already finished.

On the floor in the far corner was a portable radio that was tuned to a station that played bouncy rock. She'd kept the volume low so that she could hear Michael when he woke. It was the same radio Gabe had kept on the kitchen counter in the cabin.

She wasn't sure which pleased her more, the way the nursery was progressing or the ease with which she could bend and crouch. She'd even been able to use part of her hospital fund to buy a couple of pairs of slacks in her old size. They might still be a tad snug in the waist, but she was optimistic.

She wished the rest of her life would fall into order as easily.

He was still angry with her. With a shrug, Laura dipped her brush into the paint can again. Gabe had a temper, he had moods. He had certainly never attempted to deny or hide that. And the truth was, she'd been wrong not to trust him to do the right thing. So she'd apologized. She couldn't let his continuing coolness bother her. But, of course, it did.

They were strangers here, in a way that they had never been strangers in the little cabin in Colorado. It wasn't the house, though a part of her still blamed the size and the glamour of it. Before, the simple mechanics of space had required them to share, to grow close, to depend on each other. Being depended on had become important to Laura, even if it had only been to provide a cup of coffee at the right time. Now, beyond her responsibilities to Michael, there was little for her to do. She and Gabe could spend hours under the same roof and hardly know each other existed.

But it wasn't walls and floors and windows that made the difference. It was quite simply the difference—the difference between them. She was still Laura Malone, from the wrong side of the tracks, the same person who had been moved and shuffled from house to house, without ever being given the chance to really live there. The same person who had been handed from family to family without ever being given the chance to really belong.

And he was… Her laugh was a bit wistful. He was Gabriel Bradley, a man who had known his place from the moment he'd been born. A man who would never wonder if he'd have the same place tomorrow.

That was what she wanted for Michael, only that. The money, the name, the big, sprawling house with the stained-glass windows and the graceful terraces, didn't matter. Belonging did. Because she wanted it, was determined to have it for her son, she was willing to wait to belong herself. To Gabe.

The only time they were able to pull together was when Michael was involved. Her lips curved then. He loved the baby. There could be no doubt about that. It wasn't pity or obligation that had him crouching beside the cradle or walking the floor at three in the morning. He was a man capable of great love, and he had given it unhesitatingly to Michael. Gabe was attentive, interested, gentle and involved. When it came to Michael.

It was only with her, when they had to deal with each other one on one, that things became strained.

They didn't touch. Though they lived in the same house, slept in the same bed, they didn't touch, except in the most casual and impersonal of ways. As a family they had gone out to choose all the things Michael would need—the crib and other nursery furniture, blankets, a windup swing that played a lullaby, soft stuffed animals that Michael would undoubtedly ignore for months. It had been easy, even delightful, to discuss high chairs and playpens and decide together what would suit. Laura had never expected to be able to give her son so much or to be able to share in that giving.

But when they'd come home the strain had returned.

She was being a fool, Laura told herself. She'd been

given a home, protection and care, and, most of all, a kind and loving father for her son. Wishing for more was what had always led her to disappointment before.

But she wished he would smile at her again—at her, not at Michael's mother, not at the subject of his painting.

Perhaps it was best that they remained as they were, polite friends with a common interest. She wasn't entirely sure how she would manage when the time came for him to turn to her as a woman. The time would come, his desire was there, and he was too physical a man to share the bed with her without fully sharing it much longer.

Her experience with lovemaking had taught her that man demanded and woman submitted. He wouldn't have to love her, or even hold her in affection, to need her. God, no one knew better how little affection, how little caring, there could be in a marriage bed. A man like Gabe would have many demands, and loving him as she did she would give. And the cycle she'd finally managed to break would begin again.

Gabe watched her from the doorway. Something was wrong, very wrong. He could see the turmoil on her face, could see it in the set of her shoulders. It seemed that the longer they were here the less she relaxed. She pretended well, but it was only pretense.

It infuriated him, and the harder he held on to his temper the more infuriated he became. He hadn't so much as raised his voice to her since their first day in the house, and yet she seemed continually braced for an outburst.

He'd given her as much room as was humanly possible, and it was killing him. Sleeping with her, having her turn to him during the night, her skin separated from his only by the fragile cotton of a nightgown, had given new meaning to insomnia.

He'd taken to working during the middle of the night and spending his free time in the studio or at the gallery, anywhere he wouldn't be tempted to take what was his only legally.

How could he take when she was still so delicate, physically, emotionally? However selfish he'd always been, or considered himself, he couldn't justify gratifying himself at her expense—or frightening her by letting her see just how desperately, how violently, he wanted her.

Yet there was passion in her, the dark, explosive kind. He'd seen that, and other things, in her eyes. She needed him, as much as he needed her. He wasn't sure either of them understood where their need might take them.

He could be patient. He was aware that her body needed time to heal, and he could give her that. But he wasn't sure he could give her the time it might take for her mind to heal.

He wanted to cross to her, to sit down beside her and stroke his hand over her hair. He wanted to reassure her. But he had no idea what words to use. Instead, he tucked his hands into his pockets.

"Still at it?"

Laura started, splattering paint on her hand. She sat back on her heels. "I didn't hear you come in."

"Don't get up," he told her. "You make quite a picture." He stepped into the room, glancing at the sunny walls before looking down at her. She wore an old pair of jeans, obviously his, he could see the clothesline she'd used to secure the waist. One of his shirts was tented over her, its hem torn at her hip.

''Mine?''

''I thought it would be all right.'' She picked up a rag to wipe the paint from her hand. ''I could tell from the splatters on them they'd already been worked in.''

''Perhaps you don't know the difference between painting and—'' he gestured toward the wall ''—painting.''

She'd nearly fumbled out an apology before she realized he was joking. So the mood had passed. Perhaps they were friends again. ''Not at all. I thought your pants would give me artistic inspiration.''

''You could have come to the source.''

She set the brush on top of the open paint can. Relief poured through her. Though he didn't know, Gabe had found exactly the right words to reassure her. ''I would never have suggested that the celebrated Gabriel Bradley turn his genius to a lowly baseboard.''

It seemed so easy when she was like this, relaxed, with a hint of amusement in her eyes. ''Obviously afraid I'd show you up.''

She smiled, a bit hesitantly. He hadn't looked at her in quite that way for days. Then she was scrambling back up on her knees as he joined her on the floor. ''Oh, Gabe, don't. You'll get paint all over you, and you look so nice.''

He had the brush in his hand. ''Do I?''

''Yes.'' She tried to take it away from him, but he didn't give way. ''You always look so dashing when you go to the gallery.''

''Oh, God.'' The instant disgust on his face made her laugh.

"Well, you do." She checked the urge to brush at the hair on his forehead. "It's quite different from the rugged-outdoorsman look you had in Colorado, though that was nice, too."

He wasn't certain whether to smile or sneer. "Rugged outdoorsman?"

"That's right. The cords and the flannel, the untidy hair and the carelessly unshaven face. I think Geoffrey would have loved to photograph you with an ax...." She was staring at him, seeing him as he'd been and as he was. Abruptly she became aware that her hand was still covering his on the handle of the brush. Drawing it away, she struggled to remember her point. "You're not dressed for work now, and I was in the fashion business long enough to recognize quality. Those pants are linen, and you'll ruin them."

He was well aware of the sudden tension in her fingers and the look that had come into her eyes, but he only lifted a brow. "Are you saying I'm sloppy?"

"Only when you paint."

"Pot calling the kettle," he murmured, ignoring the way she jumped when he ran a finger down her cheek. He held it up to prove his point.

Laura wrinkled her nose at the smear of white paint on his fingertip—and tried to ignore the heat on her skin where his finger had brushed. "I'm not an artist." With a rag in one hand, she took his wrist in the other to clean the paint from his fingertip.

Such beautiful hands, she thought. She could imagine how it would feel to have them move over her, slowly, gently. To have them stroke and caress the way a man's might if he cared deeply about the woman beneath the skin he was touching. Her imagination had her moistening her lips as she lifted her gaze to his.

They knelt knee to knee on the drop cloth, with his hand caught in hers. It amazed her when she felt his pulse begin to thud. In his eyes she saw what he hadn't allowed her to see for days. Desire, pure and simple. Unnerved by it, drawn to it, she leaned toward him. The rag slipped out of her hand.

And the baby cried out.

They both jerked, like children caught raiding the cookie jar.

"He'll be hungry, and wet, too, I imagine," she said as she started to rise. Gabe shifted his hand until it captured hers.

"I'd like you to come back here after you've tended to him."

Longing and anxiety tangled, confusing her. "All right. Don't worry about the mess. I'll finish up later."

She was more than an hour with Michael, and she was a bit disappointed that Gabe didn't come in, as he often did, to hold the baby or play with him before he slept again. Those were the best times, those simple family times. Tucking the blankets around her son, she reminded herself that she couldn't expect Gabe to devote every free minute to her and the child.

Satisfied that the baby was dry and content, she left him to go into the adjoining bath and freshen up. After she'd washed the paint from her face, she studied herself in the mirrored wall across from the step-down tub. She didn't look seductive in baggy, masculine clothes, with her hair tugged back in a ponytail. Regardless of that, for an instant in the nursery, Gabe had been seduced.

Was that what she wanted?

How could she know what she wanted? She pressed her fingers to her eyes and tried to sort out her feelings. Confusion, and little else. One moment she imagined what it would be like, being with Gabe, making love with him. The next moment she was remembering the way it had been before, when love had had little to do with it.

It was wrong to continually let memories intrude. She told herself she was too sensible for that. Or wanted to be. She'd been in therapy, she'd talked to counselors and other women who had been in situations all too similar to her own. Because she'd had to stay on the move, she hadn't been able to remain with any one group for long, but they had helped her. Just learning that she wasn't alone in what had happened to her, seeing and talking with others who had turned their lives around again, had given her the strength to go on.

She knew—intellectually she knew—that what had happened to her was the result of a man's illness and her own insecurity. But it was one thing to know it and another to accept it and go on, to risk another relationship.

She wanted to be normal, was determined to be. That had been the communal cry from all the sessions in all the towns. Along with the fear and the anger and the self-disgust, there had been a desperate mutual need to be normal women again.

But that step, that enormous, frightening step from past to future, was so difficult to take. Only she could do it, Laura told herself as she continued to stare into her own eyes. With Gabe, and her feelings for him, she had a chance. If she was willing to take it.

How could she know how close they could be, how much they could mean to each other, if she didn't allow herself to want the intimacy?

Catching her lower lip between her teeth, she turned to study the lush bath. It was nearly as large as many of the rooms she'd lived in during her life. White on white on white, it gleamed and glistened and invited indulgence. She could sink into hot, deep water in the tub and soak until her skin was soft and pink. She still had most of a bottle of perfume, French and suggestive, that Geoffrey had bought her in Paris. She could dab it on her damp skin so that the scent seeped into her pores. Then she could…what?

She had nothing lovely or feminine to wear. The only clothes she hadn't taken to thrift shops or secondhand stores during her cross-country flight were maternity clothes. The two pairs of slacks and the cotton blouses didn't count.

In any case, what would it matter if she had a closetful of lace negligees? She wouldn't know what to do or say. It had been so long since she'd thought of herself strictly as a woman. Perhaps she never had. And surely it was better to try to reestablish that early friendship with Gabe before they attempted intimacy.

If that was what he wanted. What she wanted.

Turning away from the mirror, she went to find him.

She couldn't have been more surprised when she walked into the nursery and found the painting finished, the cans sealed and the brushes cleaned. As she stared, Gabe folded the drop cloth.

''You finished it,'' she managed.

''I seem to have struggled through without doing any damage.''

''It's beautiful. The way I'd always imagined.'' She stepped into the empty room and began arranging furniture in her head. ''There should be curtains, white ones, though I suppose dotted swiss is too feminine for a boy.''

''I couldn't say, but it sounds like it. It's warm enough, so I've left the windows open.'' He tossed the drop cloth over a stepladder. ''I don't want to put Michael in here until the smell of the paint's gone.''

''No,'' she agreed absently, wondering if the crib should go between the two windows.

''Now that this is out of the way, I have something for you. A belated Mother's Day present.''

''Oh, but you gave me the flowers already.''

He took a small box out of his pocket. ''There wasn't the time or the opportunity for much else then. We were living out of a suitcase and spending all of our time at the hospital. Besides, the flowers were from Michael. This is from me.''

That made it different. Intimate. Again she found herself drawn to him, and again she found herself pulled away. ''You don't have to give me anything.''

The familiar impatience shimmered. He barely suppressed it. ''You're going to have to learn how to take a gift more graciously.''

He was right. And it was wrong of her to continue to compare, but Tony had been so casual, so lavish, in his gifts. And they had meant so little. ''Thank you.'' She took the box, opened it and stared.

The ring looked like a circle of fire, with its channel-linked diamonds flashing against its gold band and nestled in velvet. Instinctively she ran a fingertip over it and was foolishly amazed that it was cool to the touch.

"It's beautiful. Absolutely beautiful. But—"

"There had to be one."

"It's just that it's a wedding ring, and I already have one."

He took her left hand to examine it. "I'm surprised your finger hasn't fallen off from wearing this thing."

"There's nothing wrong with it," she said, and nearly snatched her hand away.

"So sentimental, angel?" Though his voice had gentled, his hand was firm on hers. Now, perhaps, he would be able to dig a bit deeper into what she was feeling for him, about him. "Are you so attached to a little circle of metal?"

"It was good enough for us before. I don't need anything else."

"It was a temporary measure. I'm not asking you to toss it out the window, but be a little practical. If you weren't always curling your finger up, it would fall right off."

"I could have it sized."

"Suit yourself." He slipped it from her finger, then replaced it with the diamond circle. "Just consider that you have two wedding rings." When he offered her the plain band, Laura curled it into her fist. "The new one holds the same intentions."

"It is beautiful." Still, she pushed the old ring onto the index finger of her right hand, where it fit more snugly. "Thank you, Gabe."

"We did better than that before."

She didn't have to be reminded. Yet the memories flooded back when he slipped his arms around her. Emotions poured through with those memories the moment his mouth was on hers. His lips were firm and warm and hinted, just hinted, at his impatience as they slanted across hers. Though his arms remained gentle around her, his touch light and testing, she sensed a volcano in him, simmering and smoking.

As if to soothe, she leaned into him and lifted a hand to his cheek. Understanding. Acceptance.

Her touch triggered the need crawling inside him, and his arms tightened and his mouth crushed down on hers. She responded with a moan that he barely heard, with a shudder that he barely felt. Tense, hungry, he fell victim to her as much as to his own demands.

He had wanted before, casually and desperately and all the degrees in between. Why, then, did this seem like a completely new experience? He had held women before, known their softness, tasted their sweetness. But he had never known a softness, never experienced a sweetness, like Laura's.

He took his mouth on a slow, seeking journey over her face, along her jawline, down her throat, drinking in, then devouring. His hands, long and limber, slipped under her full shirt, then roamed upward. At first the slender line of her back was enough, the smooth skin and the quick tremors all he required. Then the need to touch, to possess, grew sharper. As his mouth came back to hers, he slid his hand around to cup, then claim, her breast.

The first touch made her catch her breath, pulling air in quickly, then letting it out again in a long, unsteady sigh.

How could she have known, even blinded by love and longings, how desperately she'd need to have his hands on her? This was what she wanted, to be his in every way, in all ways. The confusion, the doubts, the fears, drained away. No memories intruded when he held her like this. No whispers of the past taunted her. There was only him, and the promise of a new life and an enduring love.

Her knees were trembling so she braced her body against his, arching in an invitation so instinctive that only he recognized it.

The room smelled of paint and was bright with the sun that streamed through the uncurtained windows. It was empty and quiet. He could fantasize about pulling her to the floor, tugging at her clothes until they were skin-to-skin on the polished hardwood. He could imagine taking her in the sun-washed room until they were both exhausted and replete.

With another woman he might have done so without giving a thought to where or when, and little more to how. But not with Laura.

Churning, he drew her away from him. Her eyes were clouded. Her mouth was soft and full. With a restraint he hadn't known he possessed, Gabe swore only in his mind.

"I have work to do."

She was floating, drifting on a mist so fine it could only be felt, not seen. At his words, she began the quick, confused journey back to earth. "What?"

"I have work to do," he repeated, stepping carefully away from her. He detested himself for taking things so far when he knew she was physically unable to cope with his demands. "I'll be in the studio if you need me."

If she needed him? Laura thought dimly as his footsteps echoed down the hall. Hadn't she just shown him how much she needed him? It wasn't possible that he hadn't felt it, that he hadn't understood it. With an oath, she turned and walked to the window. There she huddled on the small, hard seat and stared down at the garden, which was just beginning to bloom.

What was there about her, she wondered, that made men look at her as a thing to be taken or rejected at will? Did she appear so weak, so malleable? She curled her hands into fists as frustration spread through her. She wasn't weak, not any longer, and a long time, in some ways a lifetime, had passed since she had been malleable. She wasn't a young girl caught up in fairy-tale lies now, she a woman, a mother, with responsibilities and ambitions.

Perhaps she loved, and perhaps this time would be as unwise a love as before. But she wouldn't be used, she wouldn't be ignored, and she wouldn't be molded.

Talk was cheap, Laura thought as she propped her chin on her knees. Doing something about it was a little costlier. She should go in to Gabe now and make herself clear. She cast a look at the door, then turned back to the window. She didn't have the courage.

That had always been her problem. She could say what she would or would not do, but when it came down to acting on it she found passivity easier than action. There had been a time in her life when she'd believed that the passive way was best for her. That had been until her marriage to Tony had fallen viciously apart. She'd done something then, Laura reminded herself, or had begun to do something, then had allowed herself to be pressured and persuaded to erase it.

It had been like that all her life. As a child she hadn't had a choice. She'd been told to live here or live there, and she had. Each house had had its own sets of rules and values, and she'd had to conform. Like one of those rubber dolls, she thought now, that you could bend and twist into any position you liked.

Too much of the child had remained with the woman, until the woman had been with child.

The only positive action she felt she'd ever taken in her life had been to protect the baby. And she had done it, Laura reminded herself. It had been terrifying and hard, but she hadn't backed down. Didn't that mean that buried beneath years of quiet compliance was the strength she'd always wanted to have? She had to believe that and, if she did, to act on it.

Loving Gabe didn't mean, couldn't mean, that she would sit quietly by while he made decisions for her. It was time to take a stand.

Rising, she walked out of the empty nursery and started down the hall. With each step her resolve wavered and had to be shored up again. At the door to his studio, she hesitated again, rubbing the heel of her hand on her chest, where the ache of uncertainty lodged. Taking one last breath, she opened the door and walked in.

He was by the long bank of windows, a brush in his hand, working on one of the paintings that had been stacked half-finished against the wall of the cabin. She remembered it. It was a snow scene, very stark and lonely and somehow appealing. The whites and cold blues and silvers gave a sense of challenge.

Laura was glad of it. A sense of challenge was precisely what she needed.

He hadn't heard her come in, so intent was he on his work. There was no sweeping strokes or bold slashes now, only a delicacy. He was adding details so minute, so exact, that she could almost hear the winter wind.

''Gabe?'' It was amazing how much courage it could take to say a name.

He stopped immediately, and when he turned the annoyance on his face was very apparent. Interruptions were never tolerated here. Living alone, he hadn't had to tolerate them.

''What is it?'' He clipped the words off, and he didn't set down his brush or move from the painting. It was obvious that he intended to continue exactly where he'd left off the moment he'd nudged her out of his way.

''I need to talk to you.''

''Can't it wait?''

She nearly said yes, but then she brought herself up short. ''No.'' She left the door open in case the baby should cry out and walked to the center of the room. Her stomach twisted, knotted. Her chin came up. ''Or, if it can, I don't want it to.''

He lifted a brow. He'd heard that tone in her voice only a handful of times in the weeks they'd been together. ''All right, but make it fast, will you? I want to finish this.''

Her temper flared too quickly to surprise her. ''Fine, then, I'll sum it up in one sentence. If I'm going to be your wife, I want you to treat me like one.''

"I beg your pardon?"

She was too angry to see that he was stunned, and too angry to recognize her own shock at her words. "No, you don't. You've never begged anyone's pardon in your life. You don't have to. You do exactly what suits you. If that means being kind, you can be the kindest man I've ever known. If it means being arrogant, you take that just as far."

With deliberate care, he set his brush down. "If there's a point to this, Laura, I'm missing it."

"Do you want me or don't you?"

He only stared at her. If she continued to stand in the pool of light, her eyes dark and defiant, her cheeks flushed with color, he might beg. "That's the point?" he said steadily.

"You tell me you want me, then you ignore me. You kiss me, then you walk away." She dragged a hand through her hair. When her fingers tangled with the ribbon that held it back, she tugged it out in annoyance. Pale and fragile, her hair fell around her shoulders. "I realize the main reason we're married is because of Michael, but I want to know where I stand. Am I to be a guest here who's alternately indulged and ignored, or am I to be your wife?"

"You are my wife." With his own temper rising, he pushed himself off his stool. "And it's not a matter of me ignoring you. I've simply got a lot of work to catch up on."

"You don't work twenty-four hours a day. At night—" Her courage began to fail. She thrust out the rest of the words. "Why won't you make love with me?"

It was fortunate that he'd set his brush down, or else he

might have snapped it in half. ''Do you expect performance on demand, Laura?''

Embarrassed color flooded her cheeks. That had once been expected of her, and it shamed her more than she could say to think she'd demanded it. ''No. I didn't mean it to sound that way. I only thought it was best that you know how I felt.'' She took a step back, then turned to go. ''I'll let you get back to work.''

''Laura.'' He preferred, much preferred, her anger to the humiliation he'd seen. And caused. ''Wait.'' He started after her when she whirled around.

''Don't apologize.''

''All right.'' There was still fire in her, he saw, and he wasn't entirely sure he should be relieved. ''I'll just give you a more honest explanation.''

''It isn't necessary.'' She started toward the door again, but he grabbed her arm and yanked her around. He saw it and cursed at it—the instant fear that leaped into her eyes.

''Damn it, don't look at me like that. Don't ever look at me like that.'' Without his realizing it, his fingers had tightened on her arm. When she winced, he released her, dropping his hands to his side. ''I can't make myself over for you, Laura. I'll yell when I need to yell and fight when I need to fight, but I told you once before, and I'll say it again. I don't hit women.''

The fear had risen, a bitter bile in her throat. It was detestable. She waited for it to pass before she spoke. ''I don't expect you to, but I can't make myself over for you, either. Even if I could, I don't know what you want. I know I should be grateful to you.''

''The hell with that.''

"I should be grateful," she continued, calm again. "And I am, but I've found out something about myself this past year. I'll never be anyone's doormat ever again. Not even yours."

"Do you think that's what I want?"

"I can't know what you want, Gabe, until you know yourself." She'd gone this far, Laura told herself, and she would finish. "Right from the beginning you expected me to trust you. But after everything we've been through you still haven't been able to make yourself trust me. If we're ever going to be able to make this marriage work you're going to have to stop looking at me as a good deed and start seeing me as a person."

"You have no idea how I see you."

"No, I probably don't." She managed a smile. "Maybe when I do it'll be easier for both of us." She heard the baby crying and glanced down the hall. "He doesn't seem to be able to settle today."

"I'll get him in a minute. He can't be hungry again. Wait." If she could be honest, he told himself, then so could he. He put a hand on her arm to hold her there. "It's easy enough to clear up one misunderstanding. I haven't made love with you, not because I haven't wanted to, but because it's too soon."

"Too soon?"

"For you."

She started to shake her head. Then his meaning became clear. "Gabe, Michael's over four weeks old."

"I know how old he is. I was there." He held up a hand before she could speak. "Damn it, Laura, I saw what you went through. How hard it was on you. However I feel, it simply isn't possible for me to act on it until I know you're fully recovered."

"I had a baby, not a terminal illness." She let out a huff of breath, but she found it wasn't annoyance or even amusement she felt. It was pleasure, the rare and wonderful pleasure of being cared for. "I feel fine. I am fine. In fact, I've probably never been better in my life."

"Regardless of how you feel, you've just had a baby. From what I've read—"

"You've read about this, too?"

That infuriated him—that wide-eyed wonder and the trace of humor in her eyes. "I don't intend to touch you," he said stiffly, "until I'm sure you're fully recovered."

"What do you want, a doctor's certificate?"

"More or less." He started to touch her cheek, then thought better of it. "I'll see to Michael."

He left her standing in the hall, unsure whether she was angry or amused or delighted. All that she was sure of was that she was feeling, and her feelings were all for Gabe.

Chapter 8

"I can't believe how fast he's growing." Feeling very grandmotherly but sporting a sleek new hairstyle, Amanda sat in the bentwood rocker in Michael's new nursery and cuddled the baby.

"He's making up for being premature." Still not quite certain how she felt about her mother-in-law, Laura continued to fold tiny clothes that were fresh from the laundry. "We had our checkup today, and the doctor said Michael was healthy as a horse." She pressed a sleeper to her cheek. It was soft, almost as soft as her son's skin. "I wanted to thank you for recommending Dr. Sloane. She's wonderful."

"Good. But I don't need a pediatrician to tell me this child's healthy. Look at this grip." Amanda chuckled as Michael curled his fingers around hers, but she stopped short of allowing him to suck on her sapphire ring. ''He has your eyes, you know.''

''Does he?'' Delighted, Laura moved to stand over them. The baby smelled of talc—Amanda of Paris. ''It's too early to tell, I know, but I'd hoped he did.''

''No doubt about it.'' Amanda continued to rock as she studied her daughter-in-law. ''And what about *your* checkup? How are you?''

''I'm fine.'' Laura thought about the slip of paper she'd tucked into the top drawer of her dresser.

''Looking a bit tired to me.'' There wasn't any sympathy in the voice; it was brusque and matter-of-fact. ''Haven't you done anything about getting some help?''

Laura's spine straightened automatically. ''I don't need any help.''

''That's absurd, of course. With a house this size, a demanding husband and a new baby, you can use all the help you can get, but suit yourself.'' Michael began to coo, pleasing Amanda. ''Talk to Gran, sweetheart. Tell Gran just how it is.'' The baby responded with more gurgles. ''Listen to that. Before long you'll have plenty to say for yourself. Just make sure 'My gran's beautiful' is one of the first. There's a sweet boy.'' She dropped a kiss on his brow before looking up at Laura. ''I'd say a change is in order here, and I'm more than happy to leave that to you.'' With what she considered a grandmother's privilege, Amanda handed the wet baby to Laura. She continued to sit as Laura took Michael to the changing table.

There was a great deal she'd have liked to say. Amanda was accustomed to voicing her opinions loud and clear—and, if necessary, beating anyone within reach over the head with it. It chafed a bit to hold back, but she'd learned enough in the past few weeks about the Eagletons and about Laura's life with them. Treading carefully, she tried a new tactic.

"Gabe's spending a lot of time at the gallery."

"Yes. I think he's nearly decided to go ahead with a new showing." Almost drowning in love, Laura leaned over to nuzzle Michael's neck.

"Have you been there?"

"The gallery? No, I haven't."

Amanda tapped a rounded, coral-tipped nail on the arm of the rocker. "I'd think you'd be interested in Gabe's work."

"Of course I am." She held Michael over her head, and he began to bubble and smile. "I just haven't thought it wise to take Michael in and interrupt."

It was on the tip of Amanda's tongue to remind Laura that Michael had grandparents who would delight in having him to themselves for a few hours. Again she bit the words back. "I'm sure Gabe wouldn't mind. He's devoted to the boy."

"Yes, he is." Laura retied the ribbons on Michael's pale blue booties. "But I also know he needs some time to organize his work, his career." She handed her son a small cloth bunny, and he stuck it happily in his mouth. "Do you know why Gabe is hesitating about a showing?"

"Have you asked him?"

"No, I—I didn't want to pressure him about it."

"A little pressure might be just what he needs."

Frowning, Laura turned. "Why?"

"It has to do with Michael, my son Michael. I'd prefer it if you asked Gabe the rest."

"They were close?"

"Yes." She smiled. She'd learned it hurt less to remember than to try to forget. "They were very close, though they were very different. He was devastated when Michael was killed. I believe the time in the mountains helped Gabe get back his art. And I believe you and the baby helped him get back his heart."

"If that's true, I'm glad. He's helped me more than I can ever repay."

Amanda gave Laura an even look. "Payments aren't necessary between a husband and wife."

"Perhaps not."

"Are you happy?"

Stalling, Laura laid the baby in the crib and wound the musical mobile so that he could shake his fists and kick at it. "Of course I am. Why wouldn't I be?"

"That was my next question."

"I'm very happy." She went back to folding and storing baby clothes. "It was nice of you to visit, Amanda. I know how busy your schedule is."

"Don't think you can politely show me out the door before I'm ready to go."

Laura turned and saw the faint, amused smile on Amanda's lips. Bad manners were enough out of character for her to make her flush. "I'm sorry."

"Don't be. I don't expect for you to be comfortable with me yet. I'm not entirely sure I'm comfortable with you, either."

A bit more relaxed, Laura smiled back. "I'm sure you're

always comfortable. I envy that about you. And I am sorry."

Amanda brushed aside the apology and rose to roam the room. She liked what her daughter-in-law had done here. It was a bright, cheerful place, not overly fussy, and just traditional enough to make her remember the nursery she had set up herself so many years before. There were the scents of powder and fresh linen.

A loving place, she thought. She knew she wouldn't have wanted any more for her son. It was very obvious to her that Laura had untapped stores of love.

"This is a charming room. I think so every time I step into it." Amanda patted the head of the four-foot lavender teddy bear. "But you can't hide here forever."

"I don't know what you mean." But she did.

"You said you'd never been to San Francisco, and now you're here. Have you gone to a museum, to the theater? Have you strolled down to Fisherman's Wharf, ridden a streetcar, explored Chinatown, any of the things a newcomer would surely do?"

Defensive now, Laura spoke coolly. "No, I haven't. But it's only been a few weeks."

It was time, Amanda decided, to stop circling and get to the point. "Let's deal woman-to-woman a moment, Laura. Forget the fact that I'm Gabe's mother. We're alone. Whatever is said here doesn't have to go any further."

Laura's palms were starting to sweat. She brushed them dry on the thighs of her slacks. "I don't know what you want me to say."

"Whatever needs to be said." When Laura remained silent, Amanda nodded. "All right, I'll begin. You've had some miserable spots in your life, some of them tragic. Gabe gave us the bare essentials, but I learned a good deal more by knowing who and what to ask.'' Amanda sat down again and crossed her legs. She didn't miss the flash in Laura's eyes. ''Wait until I've finished. Then you can be as offended as you like.''

''I'm not offended,'' Laura said stiffly. ''But I don't see the purpose in discussing what used to be.''

''Until you look what used to be square in the face, you won't be able to go on with what might be.'' She tried to keep her voice brisk, but even her solid composure wavered. ''I know that Tony Eagleton abused you, and that his parents overlooked what was monstrous, even criminal, behavior. My heart breaks for you.''

''Please.'' Her voice was strangled as she shook her head. ''Don't.''

''No sympathy allowed, Laura, even woman-to-woman?''

Again she shook her head, afraid to accept it and, more, to need it. ''I can't bear to think back on it. And I can't stand pity.''

''Sympathy and pity are entirely different things.''

''All that's behind me. I'm a different person than I was then.''

''I have no way of agreeing, as I didn't know you before. But I can say that anyone who stood on her own all these months must have great reserves of strength and determination. Isn't it time you used them, and fought back?''

''I have fought back.''

''You've taken sanctuary, a much-needed one. I won't

argue that running as you did took courage and stamina. But there comes a time to take a stand.''

Hadn't she said that to herself time and time again? Hadn't she hated herself for only saying it? She looked at her son, who gurgled and reached for the colorful birds circling over his head.

''And what? Go to court, to the press, drag the whole ugly mess out for everyone to gawk at?''

''If necessary.'' Her voice took on a tone of pride that carried to all corners of the room. ''The Bradleys aren't afraid of scandal.''

''I'm not a—''

''But you are,'' Amanda told her. ''You're a Bradley, and so is that child. It's Michael I'm thinking of in the long run, but I'm also thinking of you. What difference does it make what anyone thinks, what anyone knows? You have nothing to be ashamed of.''

''I let it happen,'' Laura said, with a kind of dull fury. ''I'll always be ashamed of that.''

''My dear child.'' Unable to prevent herself, Amanda rose to put her arms around Laura. After the first shock, Laura felt herself being drawn in. Perhaps it was because the comfort came from a woman, but it broke down her defences as nothing else ever had.

Amanda let her weep, even wept with her. The fact that she did, that she could, was more soothing than any words could have been. Cheek-to-cheek, woman-to-woman, they held each other until the storm passed. The bond that Laura had never expected to know was forged in tears. With her arm still around Laura, Amanda led her to the gaily striped daybed.

"That's been coming on for a while, I'd say," Amanda murmured. She drew a lace-edged handkerchief out of her breast pocket and unashamedly wiped her eyes.

"I don't know." Laura used the back of her wrist to smear away already-drying tears. "I suppose. Crying isn't something I should need, not anymore. It's only when I look back and remember."

"Now listen to me," Amanda said. All the softness had been erased from her voice. "You were young and alone, and you have nothing, nothing, to be ashamed of. One day you'll realize that for yourself, but for now it might be enough to know you're not alone anymore."

"Sometimes I'm so angry, just so angry that I was used as a convenience, or a punching bag, or a status symbol." It was amazing to her that fury could bring calm and wipe out pain. "When I am I know that no matter what it costs I'll never go back to that."

"Then stay angry."

"But…the anger for me, that's personal." She looked across the room at the crib. "It's when I think of Michael and I know they're going to try to take him…then I'm afraid."

"They don't just have to go through you now, do they?"

Laura looked back. Amanda's face was set. Her eyes glittered. So this was where Gabe got his warrior look, Laura thought, and felt a new kind of love stir. It was the most natural thing in the world for Laura to reach out and take her hand. "No, they don't."

They both heard the door open and close on the first floor. Immediately Laura began to brush her hands over her face. "That must be Gabe, home from the gallery. I don't want him to see me like this."

"I'll go down and keep him occupied." On impulse, she glanced at her watch. "Do you have plans for this afternoon?"

"No. Just to—"

"Good. Come down when your tidied up."

Ten minutes later, Laura came down to find Gabe cornered in the living room, scowling into a glass of club soda.

"Then it's all settled." Amanda fluffed a hand through her hair, well satisfied. "Laura. Good. Are you ready?"

"Ready?"

"Yes. I've explained to Gabe that we're going shopping. He's absolutely delighted with the reception I've planned for the two of you next week." The reception she'd only begun to plan on her way downstairs.

"Resigned," he corrected, but he had to smile at his mother. The smile faded when he glanced over at Laura. "What's wrong?"

"Nothing." It had been foolish to think that a quick wash and fresh makeup could hide anything from him. "Your mother and I were getting sentimental over Michael."

"What your wife needs is an afternoon out." Amanda rose, then leaned over to kiss Gabe. "I'd scold you for keeping her locked up this way, but I love you too much."

"I never—"

"Never once nudged her out of the house," his mother finished for him. "So it's up to me. Get your purse, dear. We have to find you something wonderful for the reception. Gabe, I imagine Laura needs your credit cards."

"My— Oh." Feeling like a tree blowing in a strong wind, he reached for his wallet.

"These should do." Amanda plucked two of them and handed them to Laura. "Ready?"

"Well, I... Yes," she said on impulse. "Michael's just been fed and changed. You shouldn't have any trouble."

"I can handle things," he told her, feeling more than a little put out. In the first place, he'd have taken her shopping himself if she'd asked. And in the second, though he didn't want to admit it, he wasn't totally sure of himself alone with the baby.

Reading her son perfectly, Amanda kissed him again. "Behave and we may bring you back a present."

He couldn't suppress the grin. "Out," he ordered. Then he caught Laura in turn and kissed her with the same light affection. It surprised him when she returned the embrace so ardently.

"Don't let her talk you into anything with bows," he murmured. "They wouldn't suit you. You should try to find something to match your eyes."

"If you don't let the girl go, we won't buy anything at all," Amanda said dryly, but she was pleased and a bit misty-eyed to see that her son was indeed in love with his wife.

It wasn't anyone's fault that Michael chose that particular afternoon to demand all the time and attention an infant could possibly demand. Gabe walked, rocked, changed, coddled and all but stood on his head. For his part, Michael gurgled, stared owlishly—and wept piteously whenever he was set down. He did everything but sleep.

In the end, Gabe gave up any idea of working for the rest of the day and carted Michael around with him. With the baby nestled in the crook of his arm, he ate a chicken leg and scanned the newspaper. Since no one was around to chuckle at him behind their hands, he discussed world politics and the major-league box scores with Michael while the baby shook a rattle and blew bubbles.

They took a walk in the garden once Gabe located one of the small knit hats Laura had bought to protect Michael from spring breezes. It gave him enormous pleasure to watch the baby's cheeks turn pink and his eyes look around, alert and interested.

He had Laura's eyes, Gabe thought as he studied them. The same shape, the same color, but without the shadows that made hers both sad and fascinating. Michael's eyes were clear and innocent of sorrow.

Michael whimpered at first, then decided to accept his fate, when Gabe slipped him into the little baby swing. After tucking his blankets in around him, Gabe sat cross-legged in front of him and began to stretch.

The daffodils were up in a glory of white and yellow trumpets. Baby irises poked through, purple and exotic. Lilacs, though still shy of their full bloom, offered their scent. For the first time since his own tragedy, Gabe felt at peace. In the mountains, all through the winter, he'd begun to heal. But here, at home, with spring all around, he could finally see and accept that life did go on.

The baby continued to rock, pink-cheeked and bright-eyed, his hands lifting and falling to the rhythm. His little face was already filling out, taking on his own personal look and shape. Gone was the terrifying fragility of the newborn. He was, Gabe supposed, already growing up.

"I love you, Michael."

And when he spoke he spoke both to the one who was gone and to the one who rocked contentedly in front of him.

She hadn't meant to be gone so long, but the chaotic few hours breezing through the shops had brought back the way she had felt during that brief period when she'd been on her own and eager to test life.

There had been a moment or two of guilt over using Gabe's credit cards so freely. Then it had been almost too easy, with Amanda lending support, to justify the purchases. She was Laura Bradley now.

She had an eye for color and line that came naturally and had been sharpened by her time as a model, so what she had chosen was neither extravagant nor fussy. It had given Laura a great deal of satisfaction to see Amanda nod with approval over her selections.

It was a step, Laura told herself as she carried her bags and boxes through the front door. It might be a step only a woman would understand, but it was definitely a step. She was taking her life in hand again, if only by acknowledging that she needed clothes—clothes that suited her own taste and style—to live it. She was humming when she walked upstairs.

It was there that she found them together, Gabe sprawled over the bed, with Michael snuggled in the curve of his arm. Her husband was sound asleep. Her son had kicked free of his light blanket and was shaking a rattle at the ceiling.

Quietly she set down her bags and crossed to them. It was a purely male scene, the man stretched across the bed, shoes still on, a spy thriller lying facedown on the coverlet, a glass of something that had once been cold leaving a ring on the antique nightstand.

The child, as if he understood that he was a part of this man's world, lay quietly and thought his own thoughts.

She wished she had even a portion of Gabe's skill. If she had, she would have drawn them together like this. Then the scene, the sweetness of it, would never be lost. For a while she sat on the edge of the bed and watched them.

It was so intimate, she thought, watching a man while he slept. She wanted to brush at the dark blond hair on his forehead, to trace the roughly hewn lines of his face, but she was afraid it would disturb him. Then the vulnerability would be gone, and this look at the private side of him would be over.

He was a beautiful man, though he didn't like to hear it. The compassion in him, which he often coated over with sarcasm or temper, ran deep. When she looked at him now, freely, without his being aware, she could see every reason why she'd fallen in love with him.

When Michael began to fret, she murmured and leaned over him, trying to pick him up without waking Gabe. At the first movement, Gabe's eyes opened. They were drowsy and very close to hers.

"I'm sorry. I didn't want to wake you."

He said nothing. Going with a dream she couldn't see

but was very much a part of, he cupped a hand at the back of her head and drew her lips to his. There was a tenderness there that she hadn't felt for a very long time, an offering, a promise.

It was a promise she wanted, if only he would give it. It was a promise she would believe in.

Michael, scenting his mother, decided it was time to eat.

Unsettled and wishing they'd had just a moment more, Laura eased back. When Michael began to root at her breast, she undid two buttons and let him have his way.

''Did he wear you out?''

''We were taking a short break.'' It never failed to fascinate him how perfectly beautiful she looked when she was nursing the baby. He'd already sketched her like this, but that was for himself. ''I didn't realize how much energy you need to handle someone so small.''

''It gets worse. When we were shopping I saw a woman with a toddler. She never stopped running. Your mother tells me she used to collapse every afternoon when you'd finally worn down enough to take a nap.''

''Lies.'' He shoved a couple of pillows behind his back and settled comfortably. ''I was a perfectly behaved child.''

''Then it was some other child who drew with crayon all over the silk wallpaper.''

''Artistic expression. I was a prodigy.''

''No doubt.''

He just lifted a brow. Then he spotted her bags across the room. ''I was going to ask if you had a good time with my mother, but the answer's obvious.''

She caught herself on the verge of an apology. That had to stop, she reminded herself. ''It was wonderful to buy shoes and actually see them when I stood up, and a dress that had a waist in it.''

''I suppose that's difficult for a woman, losing her figure during pregnancy.''

''I loved every minute of it. The first time I couldn't hook a pair of slacks I was ecstatic.'' She started to go on, then stopped. That was something he would never be a part of, she realized. The first joys and fears, the first movements. Looking down at Michael, she wished with all her heart that he was Gabe's child in every way. ''Still, I'm happy now not to look like an aircraft carrier.''

''It was more like a dirigible.''

''You give the most charming compliments.''

He waited until she shifted Michael to her other breast. There was an urge inside of him to trace his finger there, just above where the baby suckled. It wasn't sexual, or even romantic, it was more a wondering. Instead, he tucked his hands behind his head.

''I tossed some leftovers together. I've no idea if they're edible.''

Again there was the urge to apologize. Determined, Laura merely smiled. ''I'm hungry enough for marginally edible.''

''Good.'' Now he he did lean forward, but only to trace a fingertip over Michael's head. ''Come on down when he's settled. After this afternoon, I have a feeling he'll go out like a light when his belly's full.''

''I won't be long.'' She waited until she was alone, then closed her eyes, hoping she had the courage to carry out her plans for the rest of the evening.

* * *

She hadn't been just a woman in so long. Laura stood in front of the mirrored wall, fogged now from the steam of her bath. She looked like a woman. Her nightgown was the palest blue, nearly white. She'd chosen it because it had reminded her of the way the snow had looked on the mountains in Colorado. It fell down her body from thin straps and a lacy bodice. She ran her hand down it experimentally. The material was very thin and very soft.

Should she wear her hair up, or wear it down? Did it matter?

What would it be like to be Gabe's wife…really his wife? She pressed a hand to her stomach, waiting for the nerves to ebb. Memories threatened to surface, and she fought them back. Tonight she would take Amanda's advice. She would think not of what had been, but of what could be.

She loved him so much, but she didn't know how to tell him. Words were so difficult, so irrevocable. Worse, she was afraid that he would take her love with the same discomfort and disregard as he did her gratitude. But tonight…she hoped tonight she could begin to show him.

He was stripping off his shirt when she opened the door to the adjoining bedroom. For a moment the light coming from behind her fell over her hair and ran through the thin fabric of her gown. All movement stopped as though it were a play, just as the curtain rose. He felt the heat and the tightening in his stomach.

Then she switched off the bathroom light. He pulled off his shirt.

"I checked on Michael." Gabe was surprised he could

speak at all, but the words sounded normal enough. "He's sleeping. I thought I might work for an hour or two."

"Oh." She caught herself before she could twist her hands together. She was a grown woman. A grown woman should know how to seduce her husband. "I know you lost time this afternoon when I went out."

"I liked taking care of him." She was so slim, so beautifully frail, with her milky white skin and that blue-white gown. The angel again, with a fall of blond curls instead of a halo.

"You're a wonderful father, Gabe." She took a step toward him. She was already beginning to tremble.

"Michael makes it easy."

Should she have known it would be so difficult to simply cross a room? "Do I make it hard, to be a husband?"

"No." He lifted the back of his hand to her cheek. Her eyes were shades upon shades darker than the flow of silk she wore. He drew back, surprised by his own nerves. "You must be tired."

She bit off a sigh as she turned away. "It's obvious I'm not very good at this. Since seducing you isn't working, we'll try the more practical approach."

"Is that what you were doing?" He wanted to be amused, but his muscles were tight with tension. "Seducing me?"

"Badly." Opening her drawer, she drew out a small slip of paper. "This is my doctor's report. It says that I'm a normal, healthy woman. Would you care to read it?"

This time his lips twitched. "Covered all the bases, did you?"

"You said you wanted me." The paper crumpled in her hand. "I thought you meant it."

He had her arms before she could retreat. Her eyes were dry, but he could see, just by looking, her fractured pride. The burden he already felt grew heavier. What they had was still so tenuous. If he made a mistake it might vanish completely.

"I meant it, Laura, started meaning it from the first day you were with me. It hasn't been easy, being with you, needing you, and not being able to touch."

Gingerly she laid a hand on his chest and felt his muscles tighten. "There's no reason you can't now."

He slid his hands up to her shoulders so that his fingers brushed over the thin straps of her gown. If it was a mistake, he had no choice but to make it. "No physical one any longer. When I take you to bed, there can only be the two of us. No ghosts. No memories." When she dropped her gaze, he drew her closer, challenging her to lift it again. "You won't think of anyone but me."

Whether it was a threat or a promise, he lowered his mouth to hers. Her hands fluttered, then were trapped between their bodies.

It was only the press of lips upon lips, but her blood began to pound. The stirring he could cause so easily started in her stomach and spread, long before his hands moved over her, long before her lips parted.

Her hands were imprisoned, but she didn't feel vulnerable. His mouth wasn't gentle, but she didn't feel afraid. As the kiss deepened, as the intimacy grew, she didn't think of anyone but him.

She tasted as she had the very first time, ripe and fresh.

With his tongue he plundered her mouth, greedy for the flavor of her. There would be no turning back now, not when she was caught close in his arms and the lights were dim. He could hear her shuddering breath, and the steady ticking of the pendulum clock in the hallway. It was dark, it was quiet, they were alone. And tonight he would take a wife.

Her heart thudded against his bare chest, adding excitement. He ran his hands over her, feeling the smoothness of her skin, the slickness of her gown, feeling every tremble and every sigh his touch incited.

Greedy, he nipped his teeth into her lip as his hands moved lower. Passion sprung out, from him, from her, mixing together in a sudden, breath-stopping fury. Then he felt her body give against his in the ultimate gift of trust. The emotions that rose up in him tempered his desire. Tenderness, achingly sweet, more precious than diamonds, took its place.

Her hands were free. The paper still crumpled in her palm fluttered to the floor as she slipped her arms around him. Tentatively still. Her bones seemed to liquefy, degree by degree, until she wondered why she didn't simply slide out of his hands. Her mind, which had been swirling with needs, clouded with a pleasure that was softer, truer, than any she had ever imagined.

She stroked her hands over his back, feeling the muscle, the power. Wonder filled her at the discovery that anyone with such strength could be so gentle. His lips brushed over hers, testing, almost teasing, inviting her to set the pace. Or perhaps he was challenging her.

Hunger leaped inside her until she was locked against

him, her mouth seeking, avid, impatient. Then she was swept up into his arms. In the dim light she saw his eyes, only his eyes, their clear green darkened by need. Hers remained open and on his as he lowered her onto the bed.

She expected speed, a frenzy of greed and a drive for gratification. She wouldn't have thought less of him for it. Her love wouldn't have diminished. Against hers, his body was taut and straining. Circling her arms around him, she prepared to give him whatever he required.

But it wasn't speed he sought. And the greed was not only to take, but also to give.

When he ranged kisses over her throat, lingering, nibbling, she, too, went taut. She could only whisper his name as he continued the slow journey over her shoulders and down to the curve of her breasts, then up again, in teasing circles. Instinctively she turned her head, seeking his mouth, his jaw, his temple, as her body turned hot and cold with pleasure.

He needed to take care, for her. At the first touch, he'd been terrified. She had been with another man, she had had a child, but he knew the extent of her innocence. He'd seen it, hour after hour, when he'd painted her. He'd felt it each and every time he'd drawn her against him. If he was going to take that innocence, he was going to give her beauty in return.

She was so…responsive. Her body seemed to ebb and flow at the touch of his hands. Wherever he tasted, her skin grew warm. Yet even as she gave, and offered, there was a shyness about her, the slightest of hesitations. He wanted to take her beyond that.

Slowly, with movements that were little more than a

whisper along her skin, he drew the gown downward, following the trail of lace with his lips. At her first moan, his blood swam. He hadn't known that a sound, only a sound, could be so alluring. With light, openmouthed kisses he sensitized her skin until she began to shiver beneath him. In the lamplight she was exquisite, her skin like marble, her hair like silver. Her eyes were full of needs and uncertainties.

As he had once used his skill, his insight, to draw her emotions on canvas, he used it now to set them free.

She had never known there could be such sensitivity between a man and a woman. Even through the clouds of pleasure and the steadily rising tide of desire, she sensed his patience. She had never been so driven to touch a man before. With her fingertips and her palms, with her lips and her tongue, she discovered him. The urge came, strong, just to hold him, to wrap tight around him and hold on.

Then, without warning, he was taking her up, making her arch and gasp in shock and indescribable delight. Her mind and body were drained of everything but sensation. For an instant there was a terror of being totally out of control. His name burst out of her as she was carried away by a climax so strong, so intense, that she was left limp and dazed in the aftermath.

''Please, I can't...I've never...''

''I know.'' Strangely humbled, he lowered his lips to hers. He had wanted to give, had been driven to, but he hadn't known that in giving, so much would be returned to him. ''Just relax. There's no hurry.''

''But you haven't—''

He laughed against her throat. ''I intend to. There's time.

I want to touch you,'' he murmured, and began the slow, seductive journey again.

It wasn't possible. She would have said it couldn't be possible for her body to leap back in response to so gentle, so light, a touch. Yet within moments she was trembling again, aching again, wanting again. His tongue skimmed over her stomach, dipped to the curve of her thigh, until she was writhing, a victim now of her own desire and of the taste of heaven he'd already given her.

Then, impossibly, incredibly, she was tossed up and over again. This time, when she gasped and faltered, he slid into her.

Her moan merged with his.

Damp flesh pressed against damp flesh as they moved together. She'd never felt so strong, so utterly free, as she did now, joined as closely as was conceivable with Gabe.

She was everything he'd ever wanted, everything he'd ever dreamed of. Indeed, it was like a dream now, with the bursts and shudders of pleasure ripping through him. With his face pressed against her throat, he could smell her lightly provocative fragrance, mixed with the pungent, earthy scent of passion. He would go to the grave remembering that dizzying combination.

Her breath was fast and frenzied in his ear. Her body was just as fast and frenzied beneath his. He could feel her nails as she dug heedlessly into his back.

He would remember all of it.

Then he remembered nothing, and he let himself go.

Chapter 9

There had been a time, a brief time, when Laura had dressed in elegant clothes and gone to elegant parties. She had met people whose names were printed in slick magazines and flashed in bold headlines in tabloids. She'd danced with celebrities and dined with princes of fashion. However much it had seemed like a dream, it had been real.

It was true enough that she had enjoyed her time modeling for Geoffrey. The work might have been hard, but she'd been young enough, untried enough, to have been dazzled by the glamour—even after ten hours on her feet.

He had taught her how to stand, how to walk, even how to look interested when fatigue was all but pouring out of her ears. He'd shown her how to use makeup to enhance subtly or strikingly, how to use her hair to express a mood.

All the things he'd taught her had helped her maintain

an image during public events with the Eagletons. She'd been able to appear sophisticated and untroubled. At times, appearances were a great comfort.

She wasn't afraid she would embarrass herself or Gabe at the reception his parents were giving at their Nob Hill estate. But she wasn't certain she wanted to step back into that life again, either.

How might things have been if Gabe had been an ordinary man, a man of ordinary means? They might have found a little house with a little backyard and been swallowed up by anonymity. A part of her yearned for that, for the simplicity of it.

But that was wrong. Laura fastened the earrings she'd bought the week before, starbursts of blue stones. If Gabe had come from a different family and a different life, he wouldn't be the man she loved. The man she was almost ready to believe was beginning to love her.

There was nothing about him she wanted to change, not his looks, not his manner. She might wish occasionally that he would share with her a bit more of his thoughts and feelings, but she continued to hope that someday he would.

She wanted to be a full part of his life—lover, wife and partner. So far, she had come to be the first two.

When the door opened, she turned.

"If you're about ready, we'll—"

And he stopped and stared. This was the woman she'd only told him about, the one who had graced the covers of magazines and modeled silks and sables. Long-limbed and slender, she stood in front of the beveled mirror in a dress of midnight blue. It was very simple, leaving her shoulders and throat bare, then caught like a wish at her breasts to fall ruler-straight to her feet.

She'd wound her hair up, swept it back, so that only a few wheat-colored curls escaped to tease her temples.

She was beautiful, gloriously so, yet even as he was drawn to her, he felt as though he were looking at a stranger.

"You look wonderful." But he kept his hand on the knob and the room between them. "I'll have to paint you like this." *Beauty on Ice*, he thought, cool, aloof and unapproachable.

"I took your advice on the color." She picked up her purse, then clasped and unclasped it as she wondered why he was looking at her as though he'd never seen her before. "And I avoided bows."

"So I see." She should have sapphires, a collar of them, around her throat. "It's still a bit cool. Do you have a wrap?"

"Yes." Irked by his tone, she walked to the bed and snatched up a wide silk scarf in a riot of jewellike colors. It was then that he noticed that the back of the skirt was slit to the thigh.

"I imagine you'll create quite a stir in that little number."

She cringed inwardly, but, falling back on appearances, she managed to keep her face calm. "If you don't like the dress, why don't you just say so?" She swirled the scarf over her shoulders. "It's too late to change, but believe me, I won't wear it again."

"Just a minute." He grabbed her hand as she stared through the doorway. He could feel the smooth gold of her plain wedding ring on the index finger of her right hand. She was still his Laura, he thought as he linked his fingers with hers. He'd only had to look in her eyes to see it.

"I have to get Michael ready," she mumbled, and tried again to move past him.

"Do you expect an apology because I'm human enough to be jealous?"

Her face went still, her eyes blank. "I'm not wearing it to attract other men. I bought it because I liked it and I thought it suited me."

He brought a hand to her face and swore roundly when she jerked. "Look at me. No, damn it, not at him, at me." Her eyes lashed back up to him. "Remember who I am, Laura. And remember this—I won't tolerate having my every mood, my every word, compared with someone else's."

"I'm not trying to do that."

"Maybe you're not trying to, but you do."

"You expect me to turn my life around overnight. I can't."

"No." He ran his thumb over the ring again. "I don't suppose you can. But you can remember that I'm part of your new life, not your old one."

"You're nothing like him." It was becoming easier to let her hand relax in his. "I know that. I guess sometimes it's easier to expect the worst than to hope for the best."

"I can't promise you the best."

No, he wouldn't make promises he couldn't keep. That was the beauty of him. "You could hold me. That's as close as I need to get."

When his arms came around her, he pressed her cheek

against the shoulder of his black evening jacket. It smelled of him, and that made the last twists of tension dissolve.

"I suppose I was jealous, too."

"Oh?"

She smiled as she drew back enough to look into his face. "You look so good tonight."

"Really?" There was both discomfort and amusement in his tone.

"I've never seen you in evening clothes." She ran her finger down the dark lapel, which rested against a crisp white shirt. "Sort of like Heathcliff in a tux."

He laughed and cupped her face in his hands. "What a mind you have, angel. There's no hero in here."

"You're wrong." Her eyes were very solemn, very serious. "You're mine." He shrugged, but she kept him close. "Please, just this once, let me say it without you brushing it aside."

He just flicked a finger down her nose. "Don't expect me to walk around in armor too long. Let's get the baby. My mother knows how to make you miserable if you're late."

He wasn't a hero. He certainly wasn't comfortable being seen as one. Gabe was much more at ease discussing his work or speculating on the Giants' chances during the rest of the baseball season. He preferred arguments to good deeds.

When someone saw you as heroic, you invariably let them down. They expected you to have the right answers, the key to the lock, the light in the dark.

Michael had seen him as a hero. And, of course, he had let his brother down.

Michael had loved parties like this, Gabe thought as he sipped at the champagne that seemed to flow endlessly. He had loved the laughter, the people and the gossip. Michael had been unashamedly fond of rumors and whispers.

People had loved him moments after meeting him. He had been outgoing, funny, and as warm with strangers as with friends. It was Michael who had been the hero, doing favors without tallying the score, always willing to help or simply to be enthusiastic about a project.

Yet he'd had that streak of temper and toughness that had balanced him, prevented him from being overly… overly good, Gabe supposed.

God, he missed him still, at times unbearably.

There were people here who had known Michael, who had raised a glass with him or swapped stories with him. Perhaps that was what made it seem worse tonight, being in their parents' home, where they had grown up and shared so much and knowing that Michael would never walk into that room again.

Somehow you went on. One part of your life closed up, and another opened. Gabe looked across the room to where Laura stood talking to his father.

Sometime between the moment she'd rolled down the window of a wrecked car and the moment she'd placed a newborn child in his arms he'd fallen in love with her. It had come not with trumpets and flares but with quiet, soothing murmurs.

If there were such things as angels, one had sent Laura to him when he'd needed her most.

She was grateful to him, and open enough to give him love and affection in return for what he had given her. There were days when he believed that would be enough, for today, and for the tomorrows they would have together.

Then there were the other times.

He wanted to grab her, to demand again and again that she look at him, see who he was, what he felt. That she forget what had happened before and trust in what was happening now. He wanted to erase, the way he might have blanked out a canvas, what had gone on before, all the things that had put shadows in her eyes, all the things that made her hesitate just that split second before she smiled.

But he knew better than most that when you painted over part of someone's life you stole something. Bad experience or good, what had happened to Laura had made her what she was, the woman he loved.

But loving as he did, and being a selfish man, he wanted to be loved back, completely, without the strings of gratitude or the shadows of vulnerability. Wanting wouldn't make it so, but time might. He could give her a little more of that.

Someone laughed across the room. Glasses chinked. There was a scent of wine, flowers and women's fragrances. The night had cooperated with a full moon, and its glow shimmered just outside the open terrace doors. The room was ablaze with lamplight. Wanting a few moments away from the crowd and the noise, he slipped upstairs to check on his son.

''The boy looks more like you every time I see him,'' Cliff was saying.

''Do you think so?'' The thought had Laura lighting up. Perhaps she was vain after all.

"Absolutely. Though no one would believe you were a new mother, the way you're looking tonight." He patted her cheek in the way that always made her feel shy and delighted. "My Gabe has excellent taste."

"Shame on you, Cliff, flirting with a beautiful woman when your wife's not looking."

"Marion." Cliff bent down from his rangy height to give the newcomer a kiss. "Late as always."

"Amanda's already scolded me." She turned, sipping at her champagne, to give Laura a thorough study. "So this is the mysterious Laura."

"My new daughter." Cliff gave Laura a quick squeeze around the shoulders. "An old friend, Marion Trussalt. The Trussalt Gallery handles Gabe's paintings."

"Yes, I know. It's nice to meet you." She wasn't a beautiful woman, Laura thought, but she was oddly striking, with her sleek cap of black hair and her dark eyes. She wore a flowing rainbow-colored sheath that managed to be both arty and sophisticated.

"Yes, it is, since we have Gabe in common." Marion tapped a finger on the rim of her glass and smiled, but her eyes didn't warm. Laura recognized carefully polished disdain when she saw it. "You have his heart, and I his soul, you might say."

"Then it would seem we both want the best for him."

"Oh." Marion raised her glass. "Absolutely. Cliff, Amanda told me to remind you that hosts are supposed to mingle."

He grimaced. "Slave driver. Laura, be sure to work your

way over to the buffet. You're getting too thin already." With that he went to do his duty.

"Yes, you're amazingly slender for someone who had a child—what was it? A month ago?"

"Almost two." Laura shifted her glass of sparkling water to her other hand. She didn't deal well with subtle attacks.

"Time flies." Marion touched her tongue to her upper lip. "It's odd that in all that time you haven't stirred yourself to come down to the gallery."

"You're right. I'll have to come down and see Gabe's work in a proper setting." She steadied herself. Under no circumstances was she going to allow herself to be intimidated or to fall into the trap of reading between the lines. If Gabe had ever had any kind of romantic involvement with Marion, it had ended. "He relies on you, I know. And I hope you'll be able to persuade him to go through with a new showing."

"I haven't decided that's really a good idea for the time being." Marion turned to smile at someone across the room who had called her name.

"Why? The paintings are wonderful."

"That isn't the only issue." She turned back to give Laura a quick, glittering look. She hadn't been Gabe's lover, nor had there every been any urge on either side to make it so. Her feelings for Gabriel Bradley went far beyond the physical. Gabe was an artist, a great one, and she had been—and intended to go on being—the catalyst for his success.

If he had married within his circle, or chosen someone who could have enhanced or furthered his career, she would have been pleased. But for him to have wasted himself, and her ambitions, on a beautiful face and a smeared reputation was more than Marion could bear.

''Did I mention that I knew your first husband?''

If she had thrown her drink into Laura's face she would have been no less shocked. The cocoon that she had been able to draw around herself and Michael suffered its first crack.

''No. If you'll excuse me—''

''A fascinating man, I always thought. Certainly young, and a bit wild, but fascinating. A tragedy that he died so young, before he ever saw his child.'' She tilted her glass back until only a sheen of bubbles remained.

''Michael,'' Laura said evenly, ''is Gabe's child.''

''So I'm told.'' She smiled again. ''There were the oddest rumors just before and just after Tony died. Some said that he was on the verge of divorcing you, that he'd already removed you from the family home because you were, well, indiscreet.'' With a shrug, Marion set her glass aside. ''But that's all in the past now. Tell me, how are the Eagletons? I haven't spoke with Lorraine for ages.''

She was going to be ill, violently and humiliatingly ill, unless she succeeded in fighting back her rolling nausea. ''Why are you doing this?'' she whispered. ''Why should you care?''

''Oh, my dear, I care about anything that has to do with Gabe. I intend to see him reach the very top, and I don't intend to watch him be dragged down. That's a lovely dress,'' she added. Then she saw Amanda approaching and slipped away.

"Laura, are you all right? You're white as a sheet. Come, let me find you a chair."

"No, I need some air." Turning, she fled through the open glass doors and onto the smooth stone terrace beyond.

"Here, now." Coming up behind her, Amanda took her arm and steered her to a chair. "Sit a minute before Gabe comes along. He'll take one look at you and pounce on me for insisting you come out and socialize too soon."

"It's nothing to do with that."

"And something to do with Marion." Amanda took the water glass out of Laura's tightening grip. "If she led you to believe that there was something—personal—between herself and Gabe, I can only say its totally untrue."

"That wouldn't matter."

With a little laugh, Amanda cast a look back inside. "If you mean that, then you're a better woman than I. I've known one of my husband's former...interests for over thirty-five years. I'd still like to spit in her eye."

With a laugh of her own, Laura drew in the softly scented evening. "I know Gabe's faithful to me."

"And so you should. You should also know that Marion and Gabe were never lovers." She moved her shoulders a bit. "I can't say that I know about all of my son's affairs, but I do know that he and Marion only have art in common. Now, what did she say to upset you?"

"It was nothing." Laura brushed her fingers over her temples, as if to soothe away an ache. "Really, it was my own fault, overreacting. She only mentioned that she'd met my first husband."

"I see." Annoyed, Amanda turned her sharp-eyed glance into the drawing room again. "Well, I have to say

I find it very insensitive to bring up the subject at your wedding reception. One would have thought a woman like Marion would have more taste.''

''It's over and it's best forgotten.'' Straightening her shoulders, Laura prepared to go back in. ''I'd appreciate it if you wouldn't mention any of this to Gabe. There's no reason to annoy him.''

''No, I agree. I'll speak with Marion myself.''

''No.'' Laura picked up her glass again and sipped slowly. ''If there's anything that needs to be said, I'll say it myself.''

Amanda's smile spread and she said easily, ''If that's what you'd like.''

''Yes. Amanda...'' A decision made quickly, she thought, was sometimes the best. ''Could I leave Michael with you one day next week? I'd like to go into the gallery and see Gabe's paintings.''

Laura woke up out of breath and shivering. She struggled her way out of the nightmare to find herself in Gabe's arms.

''Just relax. You're all right.''

She drew in a big gulp of air, then let it out slowly. ''Sorry,'' she muttered, dragging a hand through her hair.

''Want anything? Some water?''

''No.'' As the fear passed, annoyance took its place. The glowing dial of the alarm clock read 4:15. They'd been in bed for only three hours, and now she was wide-awake and restless.

With his arm still around her, Gabe lay back on his pillow. ''You haven't had a nightmare since Michael was born. Did something happen at the party tonight?''

She thought of Marion and gritted her teeth. "Why do you ask?"

"I noticed that you seemed upset, and my mother annoyed."

"Did you think that I had an argument with your mother?" That made her smile and settle more comfortably against him. "No, in fact we get along very well."

"You sound surprised."

"I didn't expect to make friends with her. I kept waiting for her to bring out her broom and pointed hat."

He laughed and kissed her shoulder. "Just try criticizing my work."

"I wouldn't dare." Unconsciously she began to stroke her fingers through his hair. When she was here, like this, she believed she could handle anything that threatened her new family. "She showed me the mural in the parlor. The one with all the mythical creatures."

"I was twenty, and romantic." And he'd asked his mother a dozen times to have it painted over.

"I like it."

"No wonder you get along with her."

"I did like it." She shifted so that she could rest her arms on his chest. There was only a little moonlight, but she could see him. She didn't realize that it was her first completely unstudied move toward him, but he did. "What's wrong with unicorns and centaurs and fairies?"

"They have their place, I suppose." But all he was currently interested in was making love with her.

"Good. Then don't you think the side wall in Michael's room is the perfect place for a mural?"

He tugged at a curl that fell over her cheek. ''Are you offering me a commission?''

''Well, I've seen a few samples of your work, and it's not bad.''

He tugged harder. ''Not bad?''

''Shows promise.'' With a quick laugh, she ducked before he could pull her hair again. ''Why don't you submit some sample sketches for consideration?''

''And my fee?''

He was smiling; her skin was warming. Laura began to think the nightmare had been a blessing in disguise. ''Negotiable.''

''Tell you what. I'll do the mural on one condition.''

''Which is?''

''That you let me paint you again, nude.''

Her eyes widened. Then she laughed, sure he was joking. ''You should at least let me wear a beret.''

''You've been watching too many old movies, but you can wear a beret if you like—just nothing else.''

''I couldn't.''

''All right, then, scratch the beret.''

''Gabe, you're not serious.''

''Of course I am.'' To prove it, and to please himself, he ran a hand over her. ''You have a beautiful body...long dancer's limbs, smooth white skin, a narrow waist.''

''Gabe.'' She spoke to stop not his roaming hands but his conversation. She stopped neither.

''I've wanted to paint you nude since the first time we made love. I can still see the way you looked when I drew the nightgown away. Capturing that femininity, that subtle sexuality, would be a triumph.''

She laid her cheek on his heart. "I'd be embarrassed."

"Why? I know what you look like. Every inch of you." He cupped her breasts, scraping his thumbs lightly over her nipples. Her instant response rippled through him.

"No one else does." Her voice was husky now. Hardly realizing it, she began to run her hands over him. The journey was long, lazy, thorough.

There was something incredibly exciting about the idea. No one else knew the secrets of her body, the dips and curves. No one else knew how a touch here, a stroke there, could make her shyness melt into passion. He did want to capture that on canvas, the beauty of her, the sweetness of her inhibitions. The fire of passion just discovered. But he could wait.

"I suppose I could just hire a model."

Her head came up at that. "You—" The jealousy rose, so swift and powerful that it left her momentarily speechless.

"It's art, angel," he said, amused and not at all displeased. "Not a centerfold."

"You're trying to blackmail me."

"You're very sharp."

Her eyes narrowed. In deliberate seduction that surprised them both, she shifted so that her body rubbed tantalizingly over his. "Only if I get to choose the model."

His pulse was thudding. As she lowered her head to brush kisses over his chest, he closed his eyes. "Laura."

"No, Mrs. Drumberry. I met her tonight."

He opened his eyes. But when she used her teeth to tug on his nipple he arched beneath her. "Mabel Drumberry is a hundred and five."

''Exactly.'' She chuckled but continued her explorations, with a growing sense of power and discovery. ''I wouldn't trust you closed up in your studio with some sexy young redhead with lush curves.''

He started to laugh, but the sound became a moan as her hand ranged lower. ''Don't you think I can resist a sexy young redhead?''

''Of course, but she wouldn't be able to resist you.'' She rubbed her cheek along his jawline, which was already roughened with morning stubble. ''You're so beautiful, Gabe. If I could paint, I'd show you.''

''What you're doing is driving me crazy.''

''I hope so,'' she murmured, and lowered her mouth to his.

She'd never had the confidence to take charge, had never been sure enough of her skill or her appeal. Now it seemed right and wonderfully fulfilling to tease and taunt her man in passion.

His hands were in her hair, his fingers tangled and tense, as she dipped her tongue into his mouth and explored. Her moves were instinctive rather than experienced, and all the more seductive for it.

The power came to her not in a wild burst but with quiet certainty. She could be his partner here, his full partner. It was easy to show love, almost as easy as it was to feel it.

As she discovered him, she discovered herself. She wasn't as patient as he, not here. Strangely, in the daylight, the opposite was true. She saw him as a man who needed to move quickly, decisively, and if mistakes were made because of hurry they could be corrected or just as easily ignored. She was more cautious, more prone to think through alternatives before acting.

But in bed, in the role of the seductress, she found little patience in herself.

She was wild and wanton. Gabe found himself reaching for her, then being rocked helplessly by the sensations she brought to him. It was like having different woman in bed, one who felt like Laura, smelled like Laura, one he wanted as desperately as he wanted Laura.

When her mouth came down on his, it was Laura's taste, yet somehow darker, riper. And her body was like a furnace as she moved over him.

He tried to remember that this was his wife, his shy and still-innocent wife, who required infinite care and gentleness. He had yet to release his full range of passion with her. With Laura he had taken his time, used every drop of his sensitivity.

Now she was stripping him down to the nerve ends.

She could feel the power, and it was glorious. Despite her excitement, her mind was clear as a bell. She could make him weak, she could make him desperate. She could make him tremble. Breathlessly she pressed her lips to pulse points that she found by instinct. His heart was racing. For her. She could feel his body shudder at her touch. When he groaned, it was her own name she heard.

She heard herself laugh, and there was something sultry in the sound. A feminine triumph. The clock in the hallway struck five, and the echo went on and on in her head.

Then his arms were locked around her and the sound that was coming from his throat was long and primitive. His control snapped like a rubber band stretched too far.

Needs only half satisfied, so long held in check, flooded free. His mouth covered hers, bruisingly. But it wasn't a skip of fear she felt. It was a leap of victory.

Trapped in madness, they rolled across the bed, seeking, taking, demanding, with a kind of greed that made the mouth go dry and the soul shudder. The modest gown she wore was torn aside, seams ripping, lace shredding. His hands were everywhere, and they were far from gentle.

There was no shame. There was no shyness. This was freedom, a different kind from what he had already shown her. As desperate as he, she opened for him. When he plunged into her, the shock vibrated, wave after wave.

Fast and furious, they locked into their own rhythm, each driving the other.

Endless pleasure, sharp and edgy. Insatiable need spreading like wildfire. As she gave herself to him, as she asked and received more, Laura realized that, for the lucky, time could indeed stop.

Chapter 10

When the sky darkened, Laura was in the garden. It had become her habit to spend her mornings there while the baby slept or sat rocking in his swing in the sunlight. Since her arrival in Gabe's home, she'd found little to do indoors. The house almost took care of itself and, as she had once told him, Gabe was only sloppy when he painted.

More than that, there were too many rooms, too much space that she didn't yet feel a part of. In the nursery, which she'd decorated herself and where, through necessity, she spent many hours during the day and night, she felt at home. The rest of the house, with its heirlooms and its beautiful old rugs, its polished wood and its faded wallpaper, remained aloof to her.

But as spring had taken hold she had discovered an affinity and a talent for gardening, as well as a need for space and air. She liked the sunlight and the smells and the feel of the earth under her hands. She devoured books on plants, much as she had on childbirth, so that she could become familiar with flowers and shrubs and the care they required.

The tulips were beginning to bloom, and the azaleas were already ripe with blossoms. Someone else had planted them, but Laura had no trouble taking them to heart as her own. They flowered afresh every year. Nor did she feel awkward adding her own touches with moss roses and snapdragons.

Already she was planning to plant new bulbs in the fall, daylilies, windflowers, poppies. Then, over the winter, she would root her own spring flowers from seed, starting them in little peat pots that she would set in the sun room on the east side of the house.

''I'll teach you how to plant them next year,'' she told Michael. She could already imagine him toddling around the garden on short, sturdy legs, patting at the dirt, trying to snatch butterflies off blossoms.

He would laugh. There would be so much for him to laugh about. She would be able to catch him up in her arms and swing him around so that his eyes, which were still as stubbornly blue as hers, glowed and his laughter bounced on the air. Then Gabe would stick his head out of his studio window and demand to know what all the ruckus was about.

But he wouldn't really be annoyed. He'd come down, saying that if there was going to be so much noise he might as well forget about working for the morning. He'd sit on the ground with Michael in his lap and they'd laugh together about nothing anyone else would understand.

Sitting back on her heels, Laura wiped her brow with

the back of a gloved hand. Dreaming had always been her escape, her defense, her survival. Now it didn't seem like any of those things, because she was beginning to believe dreams could come true.

"I love your daddy," she told Michael, as she told him at least once every day. "I love him so much that it makes me believe in happy endings."

When the shadow fell over her, Laura glanced up and saw the first dark clouds roll over the sun. She was tempted to ignore them, and she might have if she hadn't known it took more than a quick minute to gather up all her gardening tools, Michael's supplies and the baby himself.

"Well, the rain's good for the flowers, isn't it, sweetie?" She stored the tools and bags of peat moss and fertilizers in the small shed near the back door, then drew Michael out of the swing. With the acquired coordination of motherhood, she carried the baby, his little cache of toys and the folded swing indoors.

She'd barely started upstairs when the first crack of thunder had both her and Michael jumping. As he began to wail, she fought back her own longstanding fear of storms and soothed him.

He calmed down much more quickly than she as she walked and rocked and murmured reassurances. Though the rain held off, she could watch the fury raging in the sky through Michael's windows. Lightning slashed, turning the light from gray to mauve, then back to gray, in the blink of an eye.

Eventually he began to doze, but she continued to hold him, as much for her own comfort as his.

"Silly, isn't it?" she murmured. "A grown woman more

afraid of thunder than a tiny baby.'' As the rain began to lash at the house, she made herself set the sleeping child in his crib so that she could close the windows.

At least that would keep her busy, Laura told herself as she moved from room to room to shut the windows against the pelting rain. Still, each time thunder boomed she jerked back. It wasn't until she started back into the nursery, telling herself she'd curl up on the daybed and read until the storm passed, that she remembered Gabe's studio. Thinking only of his work, she rushed down the hall.

She was grateful that the storm hadn't knocked out the power. The lights flared on at a touch. It seemed that her luck had held. The floor was wet by the ribbon of windows, but none of his paintings were stored there. Laura hurried down the line, shutting each one until the rain was muffled by the glass.

She started to do the practical thing and go for a mop, but then it struck her that this was the first time she had been in Gabe's studio alone. He'd never asked her not to go in, but the lack of privacy she'd lived with most of her life had made her fastidious about respecting that of others. Now, though, with the lights bright overhead and the thunder rolling in the distance, she felt comfortable there, as she did in the nursery. As she had in the cabin in the mountains.

The room smelled of him, she realized. It held that mixture of paint and turpentine, with the powdery addition of chalk, that often clung to his clothes and his hands. It was a scent that invariably put her at ease, even though it was also a scent that invariably aroused her. Like the man, she thought, the scent drew her emotions. She could love him and be comforted by him, just as she could be excited and confused by him.

What did he want from her? she wondered. And why? She thought she understood part of it. He wanted the solidity of family, an end to his own loneliness and passion in bed. He'd chosen her for those things because she'd been as anxious to give them as he was to take them.

It could be enough, or nearly enough. Her problem was, and continued to be, a quiet longing for more.

Shaking off the mood, she tried to picture him there in that room, alone, working, envisioning.

So much had been done here, she thought, so many hours creating, perfecting, experimenting. What made one man different from another in the way he saw and expressed what he saw? Crossing to his easel, she studied his work in progress.

A painting of Michael. The deep and simple pleasure of it had her hugging herself. There was a rough sketch tacked to the easel, and the portrait on canvas was just beginning to take shape. She could see that even since the sketch, which he'd drawn perhaps a week before, Michael had changed and grown. But because of this she would always be able to look back and see him exactly as he'd been in that one precious moment of time.

With her arms still crossed over her breasts, she turned to study the room. It was different without Gabe in it. Less...dramatic, she thought. Then she laughed a little, knowing he would hate that description.

Without him it was a wide, airy room, largely empty. On the floor were dried drops and smears of paint that could have been there for a week or a year. A small pedestal sink was built into one corner. She saw a towel tossed carelessly over its lip. There were shelves and a worktable with equipment scattered on them. Paints and bottles, jars crammed with brushes, pallet knives, hunks of charcoal and balled-up rags. Unframed canvases were stacked against the walls, much as they had been in Colorado. He hadn't hung anything here.

She wondered why she hadn't thought before to ask Gabe if he had anything she might hang in Michael's room. The posters she'd chosen were colorful, but one of Gabe's paintings would mean more. With that in mind, she knelt down and began to go through canvases.

How easily he drew out emotion. One of his pastel landscapes would make you dreamy. Next an edgy, too-realistic view of a slum would make you shudder. There were portraits, too—an impossibly old man leaning on a cane at a bus stop, three young girls giggling outside a boutique. There was a spectacular nude study of a brunette sprawled on white satin. Instead of jealousy, it raised a feeling of awe in Laura.

She went through more than a dozen, wondering why he'd stacked them so carelessly. Many were unframed, and all were facing the wall. Each one she held left her more astonished that she could be married to a man who could do so much with color and brush. More, each painting gave her a closer look at who he was. She could sense the mood that had held him as he'd worked. Rage for this, humor for that. Sorrow, impatience, desire, delight. Whatever he could feel, he could paint.

These didn't belong here, she thought, frustrated that he would close them up in a room where no one could see them or appreciate them or be touched by them. His signature was dashed in each corner, with the year just below. Everything she found had been painted no more than two years before, and no less than one year.

She turned the last canvas over and was caught immediately. It was another portrait, and this one had been painted with love.

The subject, a young man of no more than thirty, was grinning, a bit recklessly, as though he had all the time in the world to accomplish what he wanted to do. His hair was blond, a few shades lighter than Gabe's, and brushed back from a lean, good-looking face. It was a casual study, full-length, with the subject sprawled in a chair, legs spread out and crossed at the ankle. But, despite the relaxing pose, there was a sense of movement and energy.

She recognized the chair. It sat in the parlor of the Bradley mansion on Nob Hill. And she recognized the subject by the shape of the face, which was so much like her husband's. This was Gabe's brother. This was Michael.

For a long time she sat there, holding the painting in her lap, no longer hearing the storm. The lights flickered once, but she didn't notice.

It was possible, she discovered, to grieve for someone you hadn't even known, to feel the loss and the regret. That Gabe had loved his brother deeply was obvious in each brush stroke. Not only loved, she thought, but respected. Now more than ever she wished he trusted her enough to speak of this Michael, his life and his death. In the sketch of the baby Gabe had tacked on the easel she had seen this same kind of unconditional love.

If he was using the baby to help him get over the loss

of his brother, should she begrudge him that? It didn't mean he loved their Michael any less. Still, it made her sad to think of it. Until he talked to her, opened up his emotions to her as he did in his work, she would never really be his wife and Michael would never really be his son.

Gently she turned the canvas back to the wall and replaced the others.

When the rain stopped, Laura decided to call Amanda and follow through with her decision to visit the gallery. If she wanted Gabe to take another step toward her, she would have to take another toward him. She'd avoided going to the gallery, not for all the reasons she had given, but because she hadn't felt comfortable in her role as wife to the public person, the well-known artist. Insecurity, she knew, could only be overcome by taking a confident step forward, even if that step took all the courage you could muster.

She'd grown, Laura told herself. In the past year she'd learned not just to be strong but to be as strong as she needed to be. She might not have reached the peak, but she was no longer scrambling for a foothold at the bottom of the hill.

It was as easy as asking. After her thanks were brushed aside Laura hung up the phone and glanced at her watch. If Michael stuck to his usual schedule, he would wake within the hour and demand to be fed. She could take him to Amanda—the first big step—then drive to the gallery. She glanced down at the dirt—stained knees of her jeans. First she had to change.

The doorbell caught her halfway up the stairs. Feeling

too optimistic to be annoyed by the interruption, she went to answer it.

And the world crashed silently at her feet.

"Laura." Lorraine Eagleton gave a brisk nod, then strode into the hall. She stood and glanced idly around as she drew off her gloves. "My, my, you've certainly landed on your feet, haven't you?" She tucked her gloves tidily in a buff-colored alligator bag. "Where is the child?"

She couldn't speak. Both words and air were trapped in her lungs, crowding there so that her chest ached. Her hand, still gripping the doorknob, was ice-cold, though the panicked rhythm of her heart vibrated in each fingertip. She had a sudden, horrible flash of the last time she had seen this woman face-to-face. As if they had just been spoken, she remembered the threats, the demand and the humiliation. She found her voice.

"Michael's asleep."

"Just as well. We have business to discuss."

The rain had cooled the air and left its taste in it. Watery sunlight crept through the door, which Laura still hadn't closed. Birds were beginning to chirp optimistically again. Normal things. Such normal things. Life, she reminded herself, didn't bother to stop for personal crises.

Though she couldn't make her fingers relax on the doorknob, she did keep her eyes and her voice level. "You're in my home now, Mrs. Eagleton."

"Women like you always manage to find rich, gullible husbands." She arched a brow, pleased that Laura was still standing by the door, tense and pale. "That doesn't change who you are, what you are. Nor will your being clever enough to get Gabriel Bradley to marry you stop me from taking what's mine."

"I have nothing that belongs to you. I'd like you to leave."

"I'm sure you would," Lorraine said, smiling. She was a tall, striking woman with dark, sculpted hair and an unlined face. "Believe me, I have neither the desire nor the intention to stay long. I intend to have the child."

Laura had a vision of herself standing in the mist, holding an empty blanket. "No."

Lorraine brushed the refusal aside as she might have brushed a speck of lint from her lapel. "I'll simply get a court order."

The cold fear was replaced by heat, and she managed to move then, though it was only to stiffen. "Then do it. Until you do, leave us alone."

Still the same, Lorraine thought as she watched Laura's face. She spit a bit now when she was backed into a corner, but she was still easily maneuvered. It infuriated her now, as it always had, that her son had settled for so little when he could have had so much. Even in fury she never raised her voice. Lorraine had always considered derision a better weapon than volume.

"You should have taken the offer my husband and I made to you. It was generous, and it won't be made again."

"You can't buy my baby, any more than you can buy back Tony."

Pain flashed across Lorraine's face, pain that was real enough, sharp enough, to make Laura form words of sympathy. They could talk, had to be able to talk now, as one mother to another. "Mrs. Eagleton—"

"I won't speak of my son with you," Lorraine said, and the pain vanished into bitterness. "If you had been what he needed, he'd still be alive. I'll never forgive you for that."

There had been a time when she would have crumbled at those words, ready to take the blame. But Lorraine had been wrong. Laura was no longer the same. "Do you want to take my baby to punish me or to bind your wounds? Either reason is wrong. You have to know that."

"I know I can and will prove that you're unfit to care for the child. I'll produce documentation that you made yourself available to other men before and after your marriage to my son."

"You know that's not true."

Lorraine continued as if Laura hadn't spoken. "Added to that will be the record of your unstable family background. If the child proves to be Tony's, there'll be a custody hearing, and the outcome is without question."

"You won't take Michael, not with money, not with lies." Her voice rose, and she fought to bring it back down. Losing her temper would get her nowhere. Laura knew all too well how easily Lorraine could bat aside emotion with one cold, withering look. She believed, she had to believe, there was still a way of reasoning with her. "If you ever loved Tony, then you'll know just how far I'll go to keep my son."

"And you should know just how far I'll go to see to it that you have no part in raising an Eagleton."

"That's all he is to you, a name, just a symbol of immortality." Despite her efforts, her voice was growing desperate and her knees were beginning to shake. ''He's just a baby. You don't love him.''

''Feelings have nothing to do with it. I'm staying at the Fairmont. You have two days to decide whether or not you want a public scandal.'' Lorraine drew out her gloves again. The terror on Laura's face assured her that there was no risk of that. ''I'm sure the Bradleys would be displeased, at the least, to learn of your past indiscretions. Therefore, I have no doubt you'll be sensible, Laura, and not risk what you've so conveniently acquired.'' She walked out the door and down the steps to where a gray limo waited.

Without waiting for it to drive away, Laura slammed the door and bolted it. She was panting as though she'd been running. And it was running that occurred to her first. Dashing up the stairs, she raced into the nursery and began to toss Michael's things into his carryall.

They'd travel light. She'd only pack what was absolutely necessary. Before sundown they could be miles away. Headed north, she thought quickly. Maybe into Canada. There was still enough money left to help them get away, to buy them enough time to disappear. A rattle slipped out of her hand and landed with a clatter. Giving in to despair, she sunk onto the daybed and buried her face in her hands.

They couldn't run. Even if they had enough funds to keep them for a lifetime, they couldn't run. It was wrong, wrong for Michael, for Gabe, even for herself. They had a life here, the kind she'd always wanted, the kind she needed to give her son.

But what could she do to protect it?

Take a stand. Ride out the attack. Not cave in. But caving in was what she'd always done best. Lifting her head, she waited until her breathing had calmed. That was the old Laura's thinking, and that was exactly what Lorraine was counting on. The Eagletons knew how easily manipulated she had been. They expected her to run, and they would use that impulsive, erratic behavior to take her baby. They thought that if she was too tired to run she would sacrifice her child to protect her position with the Bradleys.

But they didn't know her. They had never taken the time or effort to really know her. She wouldn't cave in. She wouldn't run with her son. She was damn well going to fight for him.

The anger came then, and it felt wonderful. Anger was a hot, animate emotion, so unlike the icy numbness of fear. She'd stay angry, as Amanda had advised, because angry she would not only fight but fight rough and dirty. The Eagletons were in for a surprise.

By the time she reached the gallery she was in control again. Michael was safe with Amanda, and Laura was taking the first step of the route she'd already mapped out to see that he stayed safe.

The Trussalt Gallery was in a gracefully refurbished old building. Flowers, neatly trimmed and still wet from the recent rain, were grouped near the main entrance. Laura could smell roses and damp leaves as she pulled the door open.

Inside, skylights offered an open view of the still-cloudy sky, but the gallery itself was brilliant with recessed and track lighting. It was as quiet as a church. Indeed, as Laura paused to look, she could see that this was a place designed for the worship of art. Sculptures in marble and wood, in iron and bronze, were placed lovingly. Rather than competing with each other, they harmonized. As did the paintings aligned stylishly on the walls.

She recognized one of Gabe's, a particularly solemn view of a garden going to seed. It wasn't pretty; it certainly wasn't joyful. Looking at it, she thought of the mural he'd painted for his mother. The same man who believed enough in fantasies to bring them to life also saw reality, perhaps a bit too clearly. They had that in common, as well.

There were only a few patrons here on this rainy weekday afternoon. They had time to browse, Laura reminded herself. She didn't. Spotting a guard, she moved toward him.

"Excuse me, I'm looking for Gabriel Bradley."

"I'm sorry, miss. He wouldn't be available. If you have a question about one of his paintings, you may want to see Ms. Trussalt."

"No. You see, I'm—"

"Laura." Marion breezed out of an alcove. She was wearing pastels today, a long, slim skirt in baby blue that reached to her ankles, with a hip-skimming sweater in soft pink. The quiet colors only accentuated her exotic looks. "So you decided to pay us a visit after all."

"I'd like to see Gabe."

"What a pity." Without so much as a glance, Marion motioned the guard aside. "He's not here at the moment."

Laura curled her fingers tighter around the clasp of her purse. Intimidation from this quarter meant less than nothing now. "Do you expect him back?"

"As a matter of fact, he should be back before too long.

We're booked for drinks in, oh—'' she glanced at her watch ''—half an hour.''

Both the glance and the tone were designed to dismiss her, but Laura was far beyond worrying about games. ''Then I'll wait.''

''You're welcome to, of course, but I'm afraid Gabe and I have business to discuss. So boring for you.''

Weariness was a dull throb at the base of her skull. She had no desire to cross swords now. Her energy had to remain focused for a much more vital fight. ''I appreciate your concern, but nothing about Gabe's art is boring for me.''

''Spoken like a little Trojan.'' Marion tilted her head. There was a smile that had nothing to do with friendship in her eyes. ''You're looking a bit pale. Trouble in paradise?''

And she knew. As clearly as if Marion had said it out loud, she knew how Lorraine had found her. ''Nothing that can't be dealt with. Why did you call her, Marion?''

The smile remained in place, cool and confident. ''I beg your pardon?''

''She was already paying good money for detectives. I only had a week or two longer at most.''

Marion considered a moment, then turned to fuss with the alignment of a painting. ''I've always thought time was better saved than wasted. The sooner Lorraine deals with you, the sooner I can get Gabe back on track. Let me show you something.''

Marion moved across the gallery in a separate room, where the walls and floors were white. A sweeping spiral staircase, again in white, rose up in one corner. Above, balconies ran in a circle. A trio of ornamental trees grew under the staircase, fronted by a towering ebony sculpture of a man and a woman in a passionate, yet somehow despairing, embrace.

But it was the portrait that caught her attention, that drew it and demanded it. It was her own face that looked serenely back at Laura, from the portrait Gabe had painted during those long, quiet days in Colorado.

"Yes, it's stunning." Marion rubbed a finger over her lip as she studied it. She'd been tempted to take a knife to the canvas when Gabe had first unpacked it, but the temptation had faded quickly. She was too much a patron of the arts to let personal feelings interfere. "It's one of his best and most romantic pieces. It's been hanging only three weeks and I've already had six serious offers for it."

"I've already seen the painting, Marion."

"Yes, but I doubt you understand it. He calls it *Gabriel's Angel.* That should tell you something."

"Gabriel's Angel," Laura repeated in a murmur. The warmth spread through her as she took a step closer. "What should that tell me?"

"That he, like Pygmalion, fell a bit in love with his subject. That's expected now and again, even encouraged, as it often inspires great work such as this." She tapped a finger against the frame. "But Gabe's much too practical a man to string out the fantasy for long. The portrait's finished, Laura. He doesn't need you any longer."

Laura turned her head so that she could look directly at Marion. What was being said had run through her mind countless times. She told Marion what she had already told herself. "Then he'll have to tell me that."

"He's an honorable man. That's part of his charm. But once things come to a head, once he realizes his mistake, he'll cut his losses. A man only believes in an image," she said, with a gesture toward the portrait, "as long as the image is unsmeared. From what Lorraine tells me, you don't have much time."

Laura fought back the urge to turn and run. Oddly, she discovered it didn't take as much effort this time. "If you believe that, why are you taking so much trouble to move me along?"

"No trouble." She smiled again and let her hand fall away from the painting. "I consider it part of my job to encourage Gabe to concentrate on his career and avoid the kind of controversies that can only detract from it. As I've already explained, his involvement with you isn't acceptable. He'll realize that soon enough himself."

No wonder she had called Lorraine, Laura thought. They were two of a kind. "You're forgetting something, Marion. Michael. No matter what Gabe feels or doesn't feel for me, he loves Michael."

"It takes a particularly pitiful woman to use a child."

"You're right." Laura met her eyes levelly. "You couldn't be more right." When Laura saw that retort had hit home, she continued calmly, "I'll wait here for Gabe. I'd appreciate it if you'd tell him when he gets back."

"So you can run and hide behind him?"

"I can't see that Laura's reasons for coming to see me are your concern."

Gabe spoke from the entranceway. Both women turned toward him. He could read fury on Marion's face and distress on Laura's. Even as he watched, both women composed themselves in their own way. Marion lifted her brow and smiled. Laura folded her hands and raised her chin.

"Darling. You know it's part of my job to protect my artists from panicky spouses and lovers." Crossing to him, Marion laid a hand on his arm. "We're going to be meeting with the Bridgetons in a few minutes about the three paintings. I don't want you distracted and out of sorts."

He spared her only the briefest of glances, but in it Marion saw that he had heard too much. "I'll worry about my moods. If you'll excuse us now?"

"The Bridgetons—"

"Can buy the paintings or go to hell. Leave us alone, Marion."

She aimed a vicious glare at Laura, then stormed out of the room. Her heels echoed on the tile. "I'm sorry," Laura said after a long breath. "I didn't come here to make waves."

"Why, then? From the look of you, you didn't come to spend an afternoon in art appreciation." Before she could answer, he was striding to her. "Damn it, Laura, I don't like having the two of you standing here discussing me as though I were some prize to be awarded to the highest bidder. Marion's a business associate, you're my wife. The two of you are going to have to resolve that."

"I understand that completely." Her voice had changed, hardened to match his. "And you should understand that if I believed you were involved with her in any way I would already have left you."

Whatever he'd been about to say slipped completely away from him. Because he recognized the unshakable resolve in the statement, he could only stare at her. "Just like that?"

"Just like that. I've already lived through one marriage where fidelity meant nothing. I won't live through another."

"I see." Comparisons again, he thought. He wanted to shout at her. Instead, he spoke softly, too softly. "Then I've been warned."

She turned away so that she could close her eyes for a moment. Her head was pounding ruthlessly. If she didn't take the time to draw herself in, she would throw herself into his arms and beg for help. "I didn't come here to discuss the terms of our marriage."

"Maybe you should have. It might be time for us to go back to square one and spell it out."

She shook her head and made herself turn to face him again. "I wanted to tell you that I'm going to see a lawyer in the morning."

He felt the life drain out of him in one swift flood. She wanted a divorce. Then, as quickly as he'd been left limp, the fury came. Unlike Laura, he had never had to prime himself for a fight. "What the hell are you talking about?"

"It can't be put off any longer. I can't keep pretending it's not necessary." Again she wanted to step into his arms, to feel them close around her, make her safe. She kept an arm's length away and stood on her own. "I didn't want to start what will be a difficult and ugly period without letting you know."

"That's big of you." Spinning away, he dragged a hand through his hair. Above him, her portrait smiled gently down. As he stood between them, he felt as though he were caught between two women, between two needs. ‘‘What in the hell brought this on? Do you think you can kiss me goodbye at the door, then talk about lawyers a few hours later? If you haven’t been happy, why haven’t you said so?’’

‘‘I don’t know what you’re talking about, Gabe. We knew this would probably happen eventually. You were the one who told me there’d come a time when I’d have to face it. Now I’m ready to. I just want to give you the option of backing off before it’s too late to turn back.’’

He started to snap at her, then stopped himself. It occurred to him that what he had thought they were talking about, and what was actually being discussed were two different things. ‘‘Why do you need to see a lawyer in the morning?’’

‘‘Lorraine Eagleton came to the house this afternoon. She wants Michael.’’

No relief came at the realization that they weren’t speaking of divorce. There was no room for it. He recognized a flash of panic before fury replaced it. ‘‘She may as well want the moon, because she won’t have that, either.’’ He reached out to touch a hand to her cheek. ‘‘Are you all right?’’

She nodded. ‘‘I wasn’t, but I am now. She’s threatening a custody suit.’’

‘‘On what grounds?’’

She pressed her lips together, but her gaze didn’t waver. ‘‘On the grounds that I’m not fit to care for him. She told me she’ll prove that I was…that there were other men before and during my marriage to Tony.’’

‘‘How can she prove what isn’t true?’’

So he believed in her. It was just that easy. Laura reached for his hand. ''You can get people to do or say a great many things if you pay them enough. I've seen the Eagletons do that kind of thing before.''

''Did she tell you where she was staying?''

''Yes.''

''Then it's time I talked with her.''

''No.'' She had his hand before he could stride from the room. ''Please, I don't want you to see her yet. I need to talk with a lawyer first, make certain what can and can't be done. We can't afford the luxury of making a mistake in anger.''

''I don't need a lawyer to tell me she can't walk into my house and threaten to take Michael.''

''Gabe, please.'' Again she had to stop him. When her fingers curled around his arms, she felt the fury vibrating in him. ''Listen to me. You're angry. So was I, and frightened, too. My first impulse was to run again. I'd even started to pack.''

He thought of what it would have done to him to have come home to find the house empty. The score he had to settle with the Eagletons was getting bigger. ''Why didn't you?''

''Because it wouldn't have been right, not for Michael, not for you or for me. Because I love both of you too much.''

He stopped and cupped her face in his hands, trying to read what was behind her eyes. ''You wouldn't have gotten very far.''

The smile came slowly as she wrapped her fingers

around his wrists. ''I hope not. Gabe, I know what I have to do, and I also know that I can do it.''

He paused, taking it in. She spoke of love one moment, then of what she would do, not of what they would do. ''Alone?''

''If necessary. I know you've taken Michael as your own, but I want you to understand that if she pursues the suit it's going to get ugly, and what's said about me will affect you and your family.'' There was a moment's hesitation as she worked up the courage to give him a choice. ''If you'd rather not be involved in what's going to happen now, I understand.''

His choices had narrowed from the moment he'd seen her. They'd disappeared completely when she'd first put Michael in his arms. Because he didn't know how to explain, he cut through to the bottom line.

''Where's Michael?''

Relief made her giddy. ''He's with your mother.''

''Then let's pick him up and take him home.''

Chapter 11

She couldn't sleep. Both memory and imagination worked against Laura as her mind insisted on racing over what had happened, and what might happen the next day. It was almost a year since she had fled Boston. Now, thousands of miles away, she had chosen to take her stand. But she was no longer alone.

Gabe hadn't waited to make an appointment with his lawyer during regular business hours. He had made a phone call and requested—demanded—a meeting that evening.

Her life, her child, her marriage and her future had been discussed over coffee and crumb cake in the parlor while a low, wispy fog had rolled in from the bay. Her initial embarrassment about speaking with a stranger about her life, her first marriage and her mistakes had sharpened painfully, then vanished. It had seemed as though they were talking about someone else's experiences. The more openly it was discussed, with details meticulously examined and noted, the less shame she'd felt.

Matthew Quartermain had been the Bradleys' attorney for forty years. He was crusty and shrewd and, despite his stuffy exterior, not easily shocked. He'd nodded and made notes and asked questions until Laura's mouth had dried up from answering.

Because he hadn't sympathized or condemned, it had become easier to talk plainly. The truth, spoken in simple, unemotional terms, had been easier to face than it had to keep hidden. In the end she hadn't spared herself or Tony. And in the end she'd felt a powerful sense of having been cleansed.

At last she'd said it all, put all the misery and pain into words. She'd purged her heart and her mind in a way that her lingering sense of shame had never permitted before. Now that it was done, she understood what it was to wipe the slate clean and begin again.

Quartermain hadn't been happy with her final decision, but she'd been firm. Before papers of any kind were served or answered, she would see Lorraine again, face-to-face.

Beside Laura, Gabe lay sleepless. Like her, he was thinking back over the scene in the parlor. With every word that played back in his head his fury inched higher. She had spoken of things there that she had never told him, going into detail she had glossed over before. He'd thought he understood what she'd been through, and he'd thought his feelings about it had already peaked. He'd been wrong.

She hadn't told him about the black eye that had prevented her from leaving the house for nearly a week, or about Lorraine explaining away Laura's split lip by speaking of her daughter-in-law's clumsiness. She hadn't told him about the drunken attacks in the middle of the night, the jealous rages if she'd spoken with another man at a social function, the threats of revenge and violence when she'd finally found the courage to leave.

They'd come out tonight, in excruciating detail.

He hadn't touched her when they'd prepared for bed. He wondered how she could bear to be touched at all.

What she had been through was all too clear now. How could he expect her to put it aside, when he was no longer certain he could? No matter how gentle he was, how much care he took with her, the shadow of another man and another time was between them.

She'd said she loved him. As much as he wanted to believe it, he couldn't understand how anyone who had lived through that kind of hell could ever trust a man again, much less love him.

Gratitude, devotion, with Michael as the common ground. That he could understand. And that, Gabe thought as he lay in the dark, was more than many people were ever given.

He'd wanted more for them, had been on the verge of believing they could have more. That had been before all those words had been spoken downstairs while the quiet spring breeze had ruffled the curtains.

Then she turned toward him, her body brushing his. He stiffened.

"I'm sorry. Did I wake you?"

"No." He started to shift so that they were no longer touching, but she moved again until her head rested on his shoulder.

The gesture, the easy, uncomplicated movement toward him, tore him in two. The one who needed, and the one who was afraid to ask.

"I can't sleep, either. I feel as though I've run an obstacle course, and my body's exhausted from it. But my mind keeps circling."

"You should stop thinking about tomorrow."

"I know." Laura brushed her hair aside, then settled more comfortably. She felt the slight drawing away, the pulling back. With her eyes shut tight, she wondered if he thought less of her now that he knew everything.

"There's no need for you to worry. It's going to be all right."

Was it? Taking a chance, she reached through the dark for his hand. "The trouble is, different scenes keep popping into my head. What I'll say, what she'll say. If I don't..." Her words trailed off when the baby started crying. "Sounds like someone else is restless."

"I'll get him."

Though she'd already tossed the covers aside, Laura nodded. "All right. I'll nurse him in here if he's hungry."

She sat up and hugged her knees to her chest as Gabe tossed on a robe and strode to the nursery. A moment later the crying stopped, then started again. Under it, she could hear Gabe's voice, murmuring and soothing.

It was so easy for him, so natural. Sensitivity, tenderness, were as much a part of him as temper and arrogance. Wasn't that why she'd finally been able to admit that she loved him? There would be no cycle of despair, submission and terror with Gabe, as there had been with Tony. She could love him without giving up the pieces of herself that she'd so recently discovered.

No, he didn't think less of her. She couldn't be sure of all of his feelings, but she could be sure of that. It was just that he was as worried as she and felt obligated to pretend otherwise.

The light from the nursery slanted into the hallway. In it she could see Gabe's shadow as he moved. The crying became muffled, then rose in a wail. Recognizing the tone of the crying, Laura leaned back and shut her eyes. It was going to be a long night.

"Teething," she murmured when Gabe brought a sobbing Michael into the bedroom. Switching on the bedside lamp she smiled at him. All of them needed support tonight. "I'll nurse him and see if that helps any."

"There you go, old man. Best seat in the house." Gabe settled him in Laura's arms. The crying faded to a whimper, then disappeared completely as he suckled. "I'm going down for a brandy. Do you want anything?"

"No. Yes, some juice. Whatever's in there."

Alone, she held Michael with one arm and arranged her pillows behind her back with the other. It seemed so normal, so usual, just like any other night. Though there were nights when Michael was restless when her body craved sleep, there were others when she prized these hours in the middle of the night. These were the times she and Gabe would remember years down the road, when Michael took his first steps, when he started school, when he rode a two-wheeler for the first time. They'd look back and remember how they'd walked the floor, half dozing themselves. Nothing could change that.

They needed this, needed the normalcy of it. And, if only for a few hours, they would have it.

When Gabe came back in, he set her glass on the table beside her. Smiling, she lifted a hand to his arm. "Can I smell your brandy?"

Amused, he tilted the snifter for her and let her draw in the scent. "Enough?"

"Thanks. I always loved the taste of brandy late at night." Lifting her juice glass, she clinked it against his snifter. "Cheers." He didn't join her in bed, as she'd hoped he would, but turned to stand by the window. "Gabe?"

"Yes?"

"I'd like to make a deal with you. You tell me what's on your mind, ask any question you need to ask, and I'll tell you the absolute truth. Then, in return, I'll ask you and you'll do the same."

"Haven't you answered enough questions for one night?"

So that was it. Laura set her glass aside before she gently shifted Michael to her other breast. "You're upset because of the things I told Mr. Quartermain."

"Did you expect I would take them with a shrug?" When he whirled, the brandy sloshed dangerously close to the lip of the snifter. Laura said nothing as he tossed back half the contents and began to pace.

"I'm sorry it had to be brought up. I'd have preferred another way myself."

"It's not a matter of its being brought up." The words lashed out. He drank more brandy, but it did nothing to soothe him. "My God, it's killing me to think of it, to imagine it. I'm afraid to touch you, because it might bring it back."

"Gabe, you've been telling me all along that it's over, that things are different now. I know they are. You were right when you said I compared you with Tony, but maybe you don't understand that by doing that I helped myself realize that things could change."

He looked at her then, only for a moment, but long enough for her to see that her words weren't enough, not yet. "Things are different now, but I wonder why you don't hate any man who puts his hands on you."

"There was a time when I wouldn't have let any man within ten feet of me, but I was able to start putting things in perspective, through therapy, listening to other women who'd pulled themselves out of the spin." She watched him as he stood in the shadow, his hands thrust in the pockets of his robe and clenched into fists. "When you touch me, when you hold me, it doesn't bring any of that back. It makes me feel the way I've always wanted to feel about myself, about my husband."

"If he were alive," Gabe said evenly, "I'd want to kill him. I find myself resenting the fact that he's already dead."

"Don't do that to yourself." She reached out a hand to him, but he shook his head and walked back to the window. "He was ill. I didn't know that then, not really. And I prolonged it all by not walking away."

"You were afraid. You had nowhere to go."

"That's not enough. I could have gone to Geoffrey. I knew he would have helped me, but I didn't go, because I was pinned there by my own shame and insecurities. When

I finally did leave, it was because of the baby. That's when I began to get well myself. Finding you was the best medicine of all, because you made me feel like a woman again.''

He remained silent while she searched for the right words. ''Gabe, there's nothing either of us can do to change things that have already happened. Don't let it change what we have now.''

Calmer now, he swirled his brandy and continued to look out of the window. ''When you talked of lawyers in the gallery today, I thought you wanted a divorce. It scared me to death.''

''But I wouldn't have— Did it?''

''There you were, standing under the portrait, and I couldn't imagine what I would do if you walked away. I may have changed your life, angel, but no more than you've changed mine.''

Pygmalion, she thought. If he loved the image, he might eventually love the woman. ''I won't walk away. I love you, Gabe. You and Michael are my whole life.''

He came to her then, to sit on the edge of the bed and take her hand. ''I won't let anyone hurt either one of you.''

Her fingers tightened on his. ''I need to know that whatever we have to do we'll do it together.''

''We've been in this together right from the start.'' Leaning forward, he kissed her, while the baby dozed between them. ''I need you, Laura, maybe too much.''

''It can't be too much.''

''Let me go put him down,'' Gabe murmured. ''Then maybe we can continue that.''

He took the baby, but the moment he eased off the bed Michael began to cry.

They took turns walking, rocking, rubbing tender gums. Each time Michael was laid back in his crib he woke with a wail. Dizzy with fatigue, Laura leaned over the rail, patting and rubbing his back. Each time she moved her hand away he cried again.

"I guess we're spoiling him," she murmured.

Gabe sat heavy-eyed in the rocking chair and watched her. "We're entitled. Besides, he sleeps like a rock most of the time."

"I know. This teething's got him down. Why don't you go to bed? There's no sense in both of us being up."

"It's my shift." He rose and discovered that at 5:00 a.m. the body could feel decades older than it was. "You go on to bed."

"No—" Her own yawn cut her off. "We're in this together, remember?"

"Or until one of us passes out."

She would have laughed if she had had the energy. "Maybe I'll just sit down."

"You know, I've been known to watch the sun come up after a night of drinking, card playing or…other forms of entertainment." He began to pat Michael's back as Laura collapsed in the rocker. "And I can't remember ever feeling as though someone had run over me with a truck."

"This is one of the joys of parenting," she told him as she curled her legs under her and shut her eyes. "We're actually having the time of our lives."

"I'm glad you let me know. I think he's giving in."

"That's because you have such a wonderful touch," she murmured as she drifted off. "Such a wonderful touch."

Inch by cautious inch, Gabe drew his hand away. A man backing away from a tiger couldn't have taken more care. When he was a full two feet from the crib, he nearly let out a breath of relief. Afraid to push his luck, he held it and turned to Laura.

She was sound asleep, in an impossibly uncomfortable position. Hoping his energy held out for five minutes longer, Gabe walked over to pick her up. She shifted and cuddled against him instinctively. As he carried her from the room, she roused enough to murmur. "Michael?"

"Down for the count." He walked into their room, but rather than taking her to bed he moved to the window. "Look, the sun's coming up."

Laura stirred and opened her eyes. Through the window she could see the curve of the eastern sky. If she looked hard enough she could see the water of the bay, like a mist in the distance. The sun seemed to vibrate as it rose. And the echoes brought colors: pinks, mauves, golds. Softly at first, with the darker night sky still dominating above, the colors spread, then deepened. Pinks became reds, vibrant and glowing.

"Sometimes your paintings are like that," she thought aloud. "Changing, shifting angles, with the colors intensifying from the core to the edges." She nestled her head against his shoulder as they watched the new day dawn. "I don't think I've ever seen a more beautiful sunrise."

His skin was warm beneath her cheek, his arms strong, firm with muscle, as they held her to him. She could feel the light, steady beating of his heart. She turned her face toward his as the first birds woke and began to sing. When love was so easily reached, only a fool questioned it.

"I want you, Gabe." She laid her hand on his cheek, her lips on his lips. "I've never wanted anyone the way I want you."

There was a moment's hesitation. She felt it, understood it, then coaxed him past it. This wasn't the time to think of yesterdays or tomorrows. Her lips softened and parted against his and her hand slipped back to brush through his hair.

"You were right," she murmured.

"About what?"

"I don't think of anyone but you when we make love."

He hadn't meant to ask her for anything. He found there was nothing he couldn't ask.

She was so beautifully open. It made it possible, even easy, to put that part of her life that left him angry and bitter aside. That had nothing to do with where they could take each other. With his mouth still on hers, he moved to the bed. She wrapped her arms around him as he lay beside her. For a moment that was enough.

Morning embraces, sunrise kisses, after a long, sleepless night. Her face was pale with fatigue, but still she trembled for him. The sigh that passed from her lips to his was soft and drowsy. Her body arched, lazy, limber, at the stroke of his hands.

The dawn air was balmy as it fluttered through the window and over their skin. She parted his robe, pushed it back from his shoulders, so that she could warm his skin herself. Just as slowly, he drew off her nightgown. Naked, they lay on the rumpled sheets and made long, luxurious love.

Neither of them set the pace. It wasn't necessary. Here they were in tune, without words or requests. Demands were for other moments, night moments, when passion was hot and urgent. As the light turned gray with morning, desire was deliciously cool.

Perhaps the love she felt for him was best displayed this way, with ease and affection that lasted so much longer than the flare of a flame. She moved with him and he with her, and they brought pleasure to each other that came in sighs and murmurs instead of gasps and shudders.

She felt the roughness of his cheek when she stoked her hand there. This was real. Marriage was more than the band she wore on her finger or the coming together full of need and excitement in the dark. Marriage was holding on at daybreak.

He would have scaled mountains for her. Until now, somehow, the full extent of his feelings for her had escaped him. He'd recognized the need first, the love later, but now he understood the devotion. She was his in a way no other woman could ever be. For the first time in his life, he wanted to be a hero.

When they came together, full light was pouring over the bed. Later, still entwined, they slept.

''I know I'm doing the right thing.'' Still, Laura hesitated when they stepped off the elevator in Lorraine's hotel. ''And, no matter what happens, I'm not going to back down.'' She caught Gabe's hand in hers and held it tight. Lack of sleep had left her feeling light-headed and primed for action. ''I'm awfully glad you're here.''

''I told you before, I don't like the idea of you having

to see her again, to deal with her on any level. I can easily handle this on my own."

"I know you could. But I told you, I need to. Gabe..."

"What?"

"Please don't lose your temper." She laughed a little at the way his brows rose. The tension rising inside her eased. "There's no need to look like that. I'm only trying to say that shouting at Lorraine won't accomplish anything."

"I never shout. I do occasionally raise my voice to get a point across."

"Since we've gotten that straightened out, I guess the only thing left to do is knock." She felt the familiar flutter of panic and fought it back as she knocked on the door. Lorraine answered, looking regal and poised in a navy suit.

"Laura." After the briefest of nods, she turned to Gabe. "Mr. Bradley. It's nice to meet you. Laura didn't mention that you were coming with her this afternoon."

"Everything that concerns Laura and Michael concerns me, Mrs. Eagleton." He entered, as Laura could never have done, without an invitation.

"I'm sure that's very conscientious of you." Lorraine closed the door with a quick click. "However, some of the things Laura and I may discuss are private family matters. I'm sure you understand."

"I understand perfectly." He met her level gaze with one of his own. "My wife and son are my family."

The war of wills was silent and unpleasant. Lorraine ended it with another nod. "If you insist. Please, sit. I'll order coffee. The service here is tolerable."

"Don't bother on our account." Laura spoke with only

the slightest trace of nerves as she chose a seat. ''I don't think this should take very long.''

''As you like.'' Lorraine sat across from them. ''My husband would have been here, but business prevented him from making the trip. I do, however, speak for both of us.'' That said, she laid her hands on the arms of her chair. ''I'll simply repeat what has already been discussed. I intend to take Tony's son back to Boston and raise him properly.''

''And I'll repeat, you can't have him.'' She would try reason one last time, Laura thought, leaning forward. ''He's a baby, not an heirloom, Mrs. Eagleton. He has a good home and two parents who love him. He's a healthy, beautiful child. You should be grateful for that. If you want to discuss reasonable visitation rights—''

''We'll discuss visitation rights,'' Lorraine said, interrupting her. ''Yours. And if I have anything to say about it, they will be short and spare. Mr. Bradley,'' she continued, turning away from Laura. ''Surely you don't want to raise another man's child as your own. He hasn't your blood, and he only has your name because, for whatever reason, you married his mother.''

Gabe drew out a cigarette and lit it slowly. Laura had asked him not to lose his temper. Though he wouldn't be able to accommodate her, it wouldn't do to let it snap so quickly. ''You're very wrong'' was all he said.

She sighed, almost indulgently. ''I understand you have feelings for Laura. My son had them, too.''

The first chain on his temper broke clean in half. The rage could be seen in his eyes and heard in each precise, bitten-off word. ''Don't you ever compare my feelings for Laura with your son's.''

Lorraine paled a little, but went on evenly. "I have no idea what she may have been telling you—"

"I told him the truth." Before Gabe could speak, or move, Laura put a hand on his arm. "I told him what you know is the truth, that Tony was ill, emotionally unstable."

Now it was Lorraine who moved, rising deliberately from her chair. Her face was flushed and pinched, but her voice was held at the same even pitch. "I will not sit here and listen to you defame my son."

"You will listen." Laura's fingers dug hard into Gabe's arm, but she didn't give way. "You'll listen now the way you never listened when I was desperate for help. The way you never listened when Tony was screaming for it in the only way he knew. He was an alcoholic, an emotional wreck who abused someone weaker than he. You knew he hurt me, you saw the marks and ignored them or made excuses. You knew there were other women. By your silence, you gave him approval."

"What was between you and Tony was none of my concern."

"That's for you to live with. But I warn you, Lorraine, if you open the lid, you won't be able to handle what comes out."

Lorraine sat again, if for no other reason than the tone of Laura's voice and the fact that for the first time Laura had called her by her first name. That one change made them equals. This wasn't the same frightened, easily pressured woman she had known only a year before.

"Threats from someone like you don't worry me. The courts will decide if some loose-moraled young tramp will have custody of an Eagleton or if he'll be placed with those who can give him the proper upbringing."

"If you refer to my wife in that way again you'll have more than threats to deal with." Gabe blew out a long, narrow stream of smoke. "Mrs. Eagleton."

"It doesn't matter." Laura squeezed his hand. She knew he was on the verge of losing control. "You can't make me cringe anymore, Lorraine, and you won't make me beg. You know very well that I was faithful to Tony."

"I know that Tony didn't believe that."

"Then how do you know the child is his?"

Absolute silence fell the moment Gabe spoke. Laura started to speak but was held off by the look in Gabe's eyes. Color flooded into Lorraine's face again when she found her voice.

"She wouldn't have dared—"

"Wouldn't she? That's odd. You intend to prove that Laura was unfaithful to your son, and now you claim she wasn't. Either way, you have a problem. If she had had an affair with anyone. Me, for example." He smiled again as he crushed out his cigarette. "Or haven't you wondered why we were married so quickly, why, as you've already asked, I accept the child as my own?" He let that thought take hold before he continued. "If she had been unfaithful, the child could be anyone's. If she wasn't unfaithful, you haven't got a case."

Lorraine clenched and unclenched her fingers on the arm of the chair. "My husband and I have every intention of determining the child's paternity. I would hardly take someone's bastard into my home."

"Be careful," Laura said, so quietly that the words

seemed to vibrate in the air. ''Be very careful, Lorraine. I know you have no concern for Michael as a person.''

Fighting for control she so rarely lost, Lorraine settled again. ''I have nothing but the gravest concern for Tony's son.''

''You've never asked about him, what he looks like, if he's well. You've never demanded to see him, even a picture or a doctor's report. You've never once called him by name. If you had, if I'd seen in you one ounce of love or affection for the baby, I'd feel differently about what I'm about to say.'' The courage came without the need to muster it. ''You're free to draw up the papers and initiate a custody suit. Gabe and I have already notified our attorney. We'll fight you, and we'll win. And in the meantime, I'll go to the press with the story of what my life was like with the Eagletons of Boston.''

Lorraine's nails dug into the material on the arm of the chair. ''You wouldn't have the nerve.''

''I have that and more when it comes to protecting my son.''

She could see it, the calm, unshakable determination in Laura's eyes. ''Even if you did, no one would believe you.''

''But they would,'' Laura told her. ''People have a way of recognizing the truth.''

Lorraine's face was set when she turned to Gabe. ''Do you have any conception of what this kind of gossip could do to your family name? Do you want to risk your reputation, your parents' reputation, over this woman and a child who isn't even of your blood?''

''My reputation can handle it, and, to be frank, my parents are looking forward to a fight.'' There was a challenge in his voice now that didn't have to be feigned. ''Michael may not be of my blood, but he's mine.''

''Lorraine.'' Laura waited until they were face-to-face again. ''You lost your son, and I'm sorry for you, but you won't replace him with mine. Whatever the cost to protect Michael's welfare, I'll pay. And so will you.''

Putting a hand under her arm, Gabe rose, keeping Laura beside him. ''Your attorney can contact us once you've made your decision. Remember, Mrs. Eagleton, you're not pitting yourself against a lone pregnant woman. You're up against the Bradleys now.''

The moment they were in the hall, Gabe pulled Laura against him. He could feel the tremors coursing through her, so he held her a moment longer. ''You were wonderful.'' He kissed her hair before he drew her away from him. ''In fact, angel, you were amazing. Lorraine still doesn't know what hit her.''

The flush of pride was as warm and satisfying as anything she'd ever felt. ''It wasn't as bad as I thought,'' she said with a sigh, but she kept her hand in his as they walked to the elevator. ''I used to be so terrified of her, afraid to speak two words. Now I can see her for what she really is, a lonely woman trapped by her own strict sense of family honor.''

Gabe gave a quick, humorless laugh as the elevators doors opened. ''Honor has nothing to do with it.''

''No, but that's how she sees it.''

''Tell you what.'' He pressed the button for the lobby. ''We're going to forget about Lorraine Eagleton for the rest of the day. In fact, we're going to forget about her completely before long, but for now there's a little restaurant a few blocks away. Not too quiet, and very expensive."

"It's too early for dinner."

"Who said anything about dinner?" He slipped an arm around her waist as they walked out into the lobby. "We're going to sit at a table over the water, and I'm going to watch everyone stare at my gorgeous wife while we drink a bottle of champagne."

She loved him for that. Then her heart skipped a beat when he brought her fingers to his lips. "Don't you think we should wait to celebrate until Lorraine gives us her decision?"

"We'll celebrate then, too. Right now I want to celebrate being witness to an angel breathing fire."

She laughed and walked outside with him. "I could do it again. In fact..."

"What?"

She swept her gaze up to his. "I'd like to."

"Sounds as though I'm going to have to watch my step."

"Probably." She was giddy with success, but she was still practical. "I really shouldn't have champagne. Michael—"

"He'll love it," Gabe assured her, and signaled for his car.

Chapter 12

''You look exhausted.'' Amanda gave a quick shake of her head as she stepped into the house.

''Michael's teething.'' The excuse was valid enough, but more than a fretful baby was keeping Laura from sleeping at night. ''He's been down all of ten minutes. With luck, he might make an entire hour straight.''

''Then why aren't you napping?''

Since Amanda was already stepping into the parlor, Laura followed her in. ''Because you called and said you were coming over.''

''Oh.'' With a faint smile, Amanda took a seat, then tossed her purse on the table. ''So I did. Well, I won't keep you long. Gabe's not home?''

''No. He said he had something to see to.'' Laura sat in the chair facing her and let her head fall back. Sometimes small luxuries felt like heaven. "Can I get you some coffee, or something cold?"

"You don't look as though you can get yourself out of that chair. And, no, I don't need a thing. How is Gabe?"

"He hasn't been getting a great deal of rest, either."

"I'm not surprised. No word from Lorraine Eagleton or her attorney?"

"Nothing."

"I don't suppose that you're able to take the attitude that no news is good news?"

Laura managed a smile. "Afraid not. The longer this goes on, the easier it gets to imagine the worst."

"And if she takes this to court?"

"Then we'll fight." Despite her fatigue, her newly discovered power came through. "I meant everything I said to her."

"That's really all I wanted to hear." Sitting back, Amanda adjusted the pin on her lapel. A little too thin, a little too pale, she thought as she studied Laura. But, all in all, she thought her daughter-in-law was holding up well. "When this is over, you and Gabe should be able to tie up a few loose ends."

Laura caught herself before she dozed off. "Loose ends?"

"Yes, little things. Such as what you intend to do with the rest of your lives."

"I don't know what you mean."

"Gabe has his art, and you both have Michael, and however many other children you choose to bring into the world."

That was something that made Laura sit up straighter. More children. They'd never discussed the possibility of more. As she began to, she wondered if Gabe even wanted any. Did she? She passed a hand over her now flat stomach and imagined it filled with another child—Gabe's child this time, from the very first moment. Yes, she wanted that. Glancing over, she saw Amanda studying her quietly and with complete understanding.

"It's difficult to make decisions with so much hanging over us."

"Exactly. But it will pass. When it does, what are you going to look for? Since I spent more than two decades under the same roof as Gabe, I know that he can, when the muse in on him, lock himself in his studio for hours and days on end."

"I don't mind. How could I, when I see what he can accomplish?"

"A woman needs a solid sense of accomplishment, as well. Children can be the best of that, but..." She reached for her purse, opened it and took out a business card. "There's an abuse clinic downtown. It's rather small, and unfortunately not well funded. Yet." She intended to correct that. "They need volunteers, women who understand, who know there can be normal life after hell."

"I'm not a therapist."

"You don't need a degree to give support."

"No." She looked at the card on the table as the idea took root. "I don't know. I..."

"Just think about it."

"Amanda, did you go to the clinic?"

"Yes, Cliff and I went there yesterday. We were very impressed."

"Why did you go?"

Amanda lifted a brow in a gesture Laura knew Gabe had inherited. "Because there's someone we both care about who we wanted to understand better. Don't get up," she said as she rose. "I'll let myself out. Give Gabe my love and tell him his father wants to know if they're ever going to play poker again. The man thrives on losing money."

"Amanda." Laura pushed off her shoes before she curled her legs up in the chair. "I never had a mother, and the one I always imagined for myself was nothing like you." She smiled as her eyes began to close. "I'm not at all disappointed."

"You're coming along," Amanda said, and left Laura sleeping in the chair.

She was still there when Gabe came in. He tilted the bulky package against the wall. When she didn't stir at the rattle of the paper, he walked over to the couch. He didn't even have the energy to wish for his sketchpad as he stretched out his legs and almost instantly fell asleep.

The baby woke both of them. Gabe merely groaned and pulled a throw pillow over his face. Disoriented, Laura pulled herself up, blinked groggily at Gabe, then put one foot in front of the other to get upstairs.

A short time later, he went up after her.

"My timing's good," he decided when he saw that Laura was fastening a fresh diaper.

"I'm beginning to wonder about your timing." But she

was smiling as she lifted Michael over her head to make him laugh. "How long have you been home?"

"Long enough to see that my wife has nothing better to do than lounge around all day." He plucked Michael from her while she pretended to glare at him. "Do you think if we kept him awake and exhausted him with attention he'd sleep tonight?"

"I'm willing to try anything."

At that, Gabe sat on the floor and began to play nonsense games. Bouncing the Baby, Flying the Baby, Tickling the Baby.

"You're so good with him." Finding her second wind, Laura sat on the floor with them. "It's hard to believe you're new at this."

"I never thought about parenthood. It certainly has its compensations." He set Michael on his knee and jiggled him.

"Like walking the ten-minute mile at 2:00 a.m."

"That, too."

"Gabe, your mother came by."

"Should I be surprised?"

She smiled a little as she leaned over to let Michael tug at her hair. "She left a card—from an abuse clinic."

"I see." He reached over himself to untangle her hair from Michael's grip. "Do you want to go back into therapy?"

"No…at least I don't think so." She looked over at him. Michael was chewing madly at his chin. All the therapy she needed was sitting across from her. "She suggested I might like to volunteer there."

He frowned as he let Michael gnaw on his knuckle. "And be reminded day after day?"

"Yes—of what I was able to change."

"I thought you'd want to go back to modeling eventually."

"No, I haven't any desire to go back to modeling. I think I could do this, and I know I'd like to try."

"If you're asking for my approval, you don't need to."

"I'd still like to have it."

"Then you do, unless I see this wearing you down."

She had to smile. He still saw her as more fragile than she was or could ever have afforded to be. "You know, I've been thinking…with everything that's happened, and everything we've had to think and worry about, we haven't had much time to really get to know a lot about each other."

"I know you take entirely too long in the bathtub and like to sleep with the window open."

She took the stuffed rabbit Michael liked to chew on and passed it from hand to hand. "There are other things."

"Such as?"

"The other night, I said that you could ask me anything and I'd tell you the truth, and then I'd ask you something. Do you remember?"

"I remember."

"I never had my turn."

He shifted so that he could rest his back against the daybed. They were avoiding speaking of the phone call they were both waiting for. And they both knew it. Perhaps that was best, Gabe mused as the baby continued to rub his sore gums against his knuckles.

"Do you want to hear about my misspent youth?"

Though she was plucking nervously at the rabbit's ears, she smiled. "Is there time?"

"You flatter me."

"Actually, I'd like to ask you about something else. A few days ago, when it rained, I went into your studio to close the windows. I looked through some of your paintings. Perhaps I shouldn't have."

"It doesn't matter."

"There was one in particular. The one of Michael. Your brother. I'd like you to tell me about him."

He was silent for so long that she had to fight back the urge to tell him that it didn't matter. But it mattered too much. She was certain it was his brother's death that had sent him to Colorado, that was preventing him, even after all these months, from having a showing of his work.

"Gabe." She laid a tentative hand on his arm. "You asked me to marry you so that you could take on my problems. You wanted me to trust you, and I have. Until you can do the same, we're still strangers."

"We haven't been strangers since the first time we laid eyes on each other, Laura. I would have asked you to marry me with or without your problems."

Now she fell silent, as surprise ran through her, chased frantically by hope. "Do you mean that?"

He shifted the baby onto his shoulder. "I don't always say everything I mean, but I do mean what I say." When Michael began to whimper, Gabe stood to walk him. "You needed someone, I wanted to be that someone. And I, though I didn't know it until you were already part of my life, needed someone, too.''

She wanted to ask him how he needed her, and why, and if love—the kind she'd always hoped for—was somehow mixed up with that need. But they needed to go back further than that if they were ever to move forward.

''Please tell me about him.''

He wasn't certain he could, that he wouldn't trip over the pain, and then the words. It had been so long since he'd spoken of Michael. ''He was three years younger than I,'' he began. ''We got along fairly well growing up because Michael tended to be even-tempered unless backed into a corner. We didn't have many of the same interests. Baseball was about it. It used to infuriate me that I couldn't outhit him. As we grew older, I turned to art, and Michael to law. The law fascinated him.''

''I remember,'' she murmured, as some vague recollection stirred. ''There was something about him in an article I read about you. He was working in Washington.''

''As a public defender. He set a lot of tongues clucking over that decision. He wasn't interested in corporate law or big fees. Of course, a lot of people said he didn't need the money, anyway. What they didn't understand was that he would have done the same thing with or without his stock portfolio behind him. He wasn't a saint.'' Gabe set Michael in the crib and wound up the mobile. ''But he was the best of us. The best and the brightest, my father used to say.''

She had risen, but she wasn't certain he wanted her to

go to him. ''I could see that in the portrait. You must have loved him very much.''

''It's not something you think about, one brother loving another. Either it's there or it isn't. It isn't something you say, because you don't think it needs to be said. Then all you have is time to regret.''

''He had to know you loved him. He only had to see the portrait.''

With his hands in his pockets, Gabe walked to the window. It was easier than he could have imagined to talk to her about it. ''I'd badgered him to sit for me off and on for years. It became a family joke. I won five sittings from him in a poker game. A heart flush to his three of a kind.'' The pain clawed at him, no longer fresh, but still sharp. ''That was the last time we played.''

''What happened to him?''

''An accident. I've never believed in accidents. Luck, fate, destiny, but they called it an accident. He was researching a case in Virginia and took a small commuter plane to New York. Minutes after takeoff it went down. He was coming to New York because I was having a showing.''

Her heart broke for him. This time there was no hesitation as she went to him and put her arms around him. ''You've blamed yourself all this time. You can't.''

''He was coming to New York for me, to be there for me. I watched my mother fall apart for the first and only time in her life. I saw my father walk through his own home as if he'd never seen it before, and I didn't know what to say or do.''

She stroked his back, aching for him. There was no use telling him that being there was sometimes all that could be done. "I've never lost anyone I've loved, but having you and Michael now, I can imagine how devastating it would be. Sometimes things happen and there's no one to blame. Whether that's an accident or fate, I don't know."

He rested his cheek on her hair and looked out at the flowers she'd planted. "I went to Colorado to get away for a while, to be alone and see if I could paint again. I hadn't been able to here. When I found you, I'd begun to pull myself back. I could work again, I could think about coming home and picking up my life. But there was still something missing." He drew back and cupped her face in his hand. "You filled in those last pieces for me."

She curled her fingers around his wrist. "I'm glad."

When he held her, she closed her eyes. They would make it, Laura told herself. Whatever happened, they would make it. Sometimes need was enough.

"Gabe." She slid her hands down until they gripped his. "The paintings in your studio. They don't belong there." She squeezed his fingers with hers before he could speak or turn away. "It's wrong to keep them there, facing the wall and pretending they don't exist. If your brother was proud enough of you to want to be there for one of your showings, it's time you had one. Dedicate it to him. Maybe you didn't say the words, but there can't be any better way to show that you loved him."

He had started to brush it aside, to make excuses, but her last words hit home. "He would have liked you."

Her lips curved. "Will you do it?"

''Yes.'' He kissed her while she was still smiling. ''Yes, it's time. I've known that, but I haven't been able to take the last step. I'll have Marion start the arrangements.'' She stiffened, and though the change was only slight he drew her away to study her face. ''Problem?''

''No, of course not.''

''You do a lot of things well, angel. Lying isn't one of them.''

''Gabe, nothing could please me more than you going ahead with this. That's the truth.''

''But?''

''Nothing. All of this has really put me behind schedule. I need to give Michael his bath.''

''He'll hold a minute.'' He kept her with him by doing no more than running his hands down her arms. ''I know there's some tension between you and Marion. I've already told you there's nothing between us but business.''

''I understand that. I've told you what I would have done if I thought otherwise.''

''Yes, you did.'' Amusement moved over his face. She would have packed her bags and headed for the door, but she would have gotten no more than five feet. ''So what's the problem?''

''There is no problem.''

''I'd prefer not going to Marion with this.''

''So would I.'' Her chin came up. ''Don't push this, Gabe. And don't push me.''

''Well, well.'' He brought his hands to her shoulders as he nodded. ''It's a rare thing for you to get that look on your face. Whenever you do, I have this deep-seated urge to drag you down on the floor and let loose.'' When color flooded her face, he laughed and drew her closer.

''Don't laugh at me.'' She would have twisted away, but his hands were firm.

''Sorry. I wasn't, really, more at the situation.'' He thought that perhaps delicacy was called for, but then he rejected the idea. ''Want to fight?''

''Not at the moment.''

''If you can't lie better than that, we'll have to keep you out of poker games,'' he murmured, and watched her eyes cool. ''I overheard your discussion with Marion at the gallery.''

''Then you obviously don't need me to spell things out for you. She believes I'm going to hold you back, prevent you from reaching your full potential, and she took steps to stop it. I realize that the Eagletons would have found us, probably in a matter of days, but I won't forgive her for calling them. The fact that you're associated with her gallery means I have to be polite to her in public, but that's the extent of it.''

His hands had tightened on her shoulders, and all amusement had been wiped from his face. ''You're telling me that Marion called the Eagletons?''

''You just said you'd heard us, so—''

''I hadn't heard that much.'' Deliberately he relaxed his hands, then took a step back. ''Why didn't you explain this to me before so that we could have told her to go to hell?''

''I didn't think that you—'' She stopped and stared at him. ''Would you have?''

"Damn it, Laura, what more do I have to do to convince you that I'm committed totally to you and Michael?"

"But she said—"

"What difference does it make what she said? It's what I say, isn't it?"

"Yes." She folded her hands but didn't lower her gaze. It was what he said. And not once had he ever said he loved her. "I didn't want to interfere when it came to your work."

"And I won't tolerate Marion interfering in my life. I'll handle it."

"How?"

Exasperated, he tugged his hand through his hair. "One minute you talk of my work as though I had an obligation to mankind to share it, and the next you act as though I'd have to go begging to find another gallery."

"I didn't mean… You'll take your paintings out of Marion's gallery?"

"Good God," he muttered, and took another turn around the room. "Obviously we need to talk—or maybe talking's not what's called for." He took a step toward her, then swore when the phone rang. "Stay here." With that he turned on his heel and strode out.

Laura let out a long breath. He'd said something about dragging her to the floor and letting loose. That was what had been in his eyes a moment before. And what would that have proved?

She moved to the crib to hand a fretful Michael his favorite rabbit. It would only have proved that he wanted and needed her. She had no doubts about that. Why shouldn't she be surprised that he would cut himself off from Marion for her? But not for her, really, Laura thought as she leaned over to nuzzle the baby. For himself. Marion had made the mistake of interfering.

Reasons didn't matter, she told herself. Results did. A great deal had been accomplished here this afternoon. He'd finally trusted her with his feelings about his brother. She'd been able to say the right things to convince him to show his work, and Marion was out of their lives.

"That should be enough for one day," she murmured to Michael. But there was still an ache in her heart.

She wouldn't think about the Eagletons.

"He needs us, Michael." That, too, should have been enough. Perhaps they were a replacement for someone he had loved and lost, but he had already given the baby unconditional love. He had given her a promise of his fidelity. That was more than she'd ever had, more than she had come to believe she would ever have. And yet it wasn't enough.

"Laura."

She turned, annoyed because she was feeling weepy and dejected. "What is it?"

"That was Quartermain on the phone." He saw the fear come first, then saw it vanish to be replaced by determination. "It's over," he told her before she could ask. "The Eagletons' attorney contacted him a few minutes ago."

"Over?" She could only whisper. The strength she'd built up, layer by layer, began to slip.

"They've pulled back. There'll be no custody suit. Not

now, not ever. They don't want anything to do with the baby."

"Oh, God." She covered her face with her hands. The tears came, but she wasn't ashamed of them, not even when Gabe gathered her close. "Is he sure? If they change their minds—"

"He's sure. Listen to me." He drew her back, just a little. He wasn't entirely certain how she would feel about the rest. "They're going to file papers claiming that Tony wasn't Michael's biological father. They want him cut off legally from any future claim to the Eagleton estate."

"But she doesn't believe that."

"She wants to believe that."

She closed her eyes while relief and regret poured through her. "I would have tried to be fair, to let them see Michael. At least I want to believe I would have tried."

"He'll lose his heritage."

"The money?" When she opened her eyes, they were dark and damp. "I don't think that will matter to him. It doesn't to me. As far as family goes, he already has one. Gabe, I don't know how to thank you."

"Then don't. You were the one who stood up to her."

"I did." She brushed the tears away, and then there was laughter as she threw her arms around him. "Yes, I did. No one's ever going to take him away from us. I want to celebrate. To go dancing, have a party." She laughed again and squeezed him hard. "After I sleep for a week."

"It's a date." He found her lips with his, then held them there as she melted into him. Another beginning, he thought, and this time they'd take the first step properly. "I want to call my parents and let them know."

"Yes, right away." She pressed against him for a moment longer. "I'll give Michael his bath, and then we'll be down."

It was nearly an hour before she came downstairs, bringing a more contented Michael with her. The baby, fresh from his bath, was awake and ready to be entertained. Because her jeans had gotten wet, she'd changed into a pale lavender shirt and slacks. Her hair was loose around her shoulders, and both she and Michael smelled of soap and soft talc. Gabe met her at the foot of the stairs.

"Here, let me have him." He curled his arm around the baby and tickled his belly. "Looks like you're ready to go field a few grounders."

"So do you." Envious, Laura muffled a yawn. "You haven't had any more sleep than I have. How do you manage it?"

"Three decades of clean living—and a body accustomed to all-night poker games."

"Your father wants to play. Maybe Michael could sit in."

"Maybe." He tipped her chin up with his finger. "You really are ready to drop, aren't you?"

"I've never felt better in my life."

"And you can barely keep you eyes open."

"That's nothing five straight hours of sleep wouldn't fix."

"I've got something to show you. Afterward, why don't you go up and take a nap? Michael and I can entertain ourselves.'' His thumb traced along her jawline. Until Laura, he hadn't known that the scent of soap and powder could be arousing. ''Once you've rested, we can have our private celebration.''

''I'll go now.''

He laughed and caught her arm before she could start back up. ''Come see first.''

''Okay, I'm too weak to argue.''

''I'll keep that in mind for later.'' With the baby in one arm and the other around Laura, he walked into the parlor.

She'd seen the painting before, from the first brush strokes to the last. Yet it seemed different now, here, hung over the mantel. In the gallery, she had seen it as a beautiful piece of work, something to to be studied by art students and patrons, a thing to be commented on and discussed, dissected and critiqued. Here, in the parlor, in the late afternoon, it was a personal statement, a part of all three of them.

She hadn't realized just how much she resented seeing it in Marion's gallery. Nor had she known that seeing it here would make her feel, as nothing else had, that she had finally come home.

''It's beautiful,'' she murmured.

He understood. It wasn't vanity or self-importance. ''I've never done anything in my life that compares to this. I doubt I will again. Sit down, will you?''

Something in his tone had her glancing over at him before she settled on the couch. ''I didn't know you intended to bring it home. I know you've had offers.''

''I never had any intention of selling it. I always meant

it for here.'' Resting the baby on his hip, he walked over to the portrait. ''As long as I've lived here, I haven't done anything, or found anything, that I wanted to hang in that spot. It goes back to fate again. If I hadn't been in Colorado, if it hadn't been snowing, if you hadn't been running. It took what had happened to you, and what had happened to me, to bring us together and make this.''

''When you were painting it, I wondered why you seemed so driven. I understand now.''

''Do you?'' With a half smile, he turned back to her. ''I wonder just what you understand, angel. It wasn't until a little while ago that I realized you have no idea what I feel for you.''

''I know you need me, me and Michael. Because of what happened to all of us, we're able to make things better.''

''And that's it?'' He wondered if he was pushing too far, but he thought that if he didn't push now it might be too late. ''You said you loved me. I know gratitude's a big part of that, but I want to know if there's anything more.''

''I don't know what you want me to say.''

''I want you to look.'' He held out a hand. When she didn't move, he walked over to her and drew her to her feet. ''Look at the portrait and tell me what you see.''

''Myself.''

It seemed to be the day for showdowns, Gabe thought. He quickly carried the sleeping Michael upstairs to the nursery and put him in the crib. Going back down to Laura, he took her by the shoulders and, holding her in front of him, made her face the portrait. ''Tell me what you see.''

''I see myself as you saw me then.'' Why was her heart

hammering? ''I seem a little too vulnerable, a little too sad.''

Impatience had him giving her a quick shake. ''You don't see enough.''

''I want to see strength,'' she blurted out. ''I think I do. And I see a woman alone who's ready to protect what's hers.''

''When you look at her eyes. Look at them, Laura, and tell me what you see.''

''A woman falling in love.'' She shut her own. ''You must have known.''

''No.'' He didn't turn her toward him. Instead, he wrapped his arms around her so that they both continued to face the portrait. ''No, I didn't know, because I kept telling myself I was painting what I wanted to see. And what I was feeling myself.''

Her heart leaped into her throat and throbbed there. Whatever he could feel, he could paint. That had been her own conclusion. ''What are you feeling?''

''Can't you see it?''

''I don't want to see it there.'' She turned to grip the front of his shirt. ''I want to hear it.''

He wasn't sure he had the words. Words came so much less easily than emotion. He could paint his moods, and he could shout them, but it was difficult to speak them quietly when they mattered so much.

He touched her face, her hair, then her hand. ''Almost from the first you pulled at me in a way no one ever had before and no one ever will again. I thought I was crazy.

You were pregnant, totally dependent on me, grateful for my help."

"I was grateful. I'll always be grateful."

"Damn it" was all he could manage as he turned away.

"I'm sorry you feel that way." She was calm now, absolutely, beautifully calm, as he glared at her. She'd remember him like this always, she thought, with his hair tousled from his hands, a gray shirt with the sleeves shoved up to the elbows and his face full of impatience. "Because I intend to be grateful for the rest of my life. And that has nothing to do with my intending to love you for the rest of my life."

"I want to be sure of that."

"Be sure. You didn't paint what you wanted to see, you never do. You paint the truth." She took one step toward him, the most important step she'd ever taken. "I've given you the truth, Gabe. Now I have to ask for it. Are your feelings for me tied up in that portrait, in that image, are they an effect of your love for Michael, or are they for me?"

"Yes." He caught her hands in his. "I'm in love with the woman I painted, with the mother of my child, and with you. Separately and together. We could have met anywhere, under any circumstances, and I would still have fallen in love with you. Maybe it wouldn't have happened as quickly, maybe it wouldn't have been as complicated, but it would have happened." She started to move into his arms, but he held her back. "When I married you, it was for purely selfish reasons. I wasn't doing you any favors."

She smiled. "Then I won't be grateful."

''Thank you.'' He lifted her hands to his lips, the one that wore the old wedding band, then the one that wore the new. ''I want to paint you again.''

She was laughing as his lips came down to her. ''Now?''

''Soon.''

Then his hands were in her hair, and the kiss became urgent and seeking. It was met equally as her arms went around him. Love, fully opened, added its own desperation.

There was a murmur of pleasure, then a murmur of protest as he drew her to the floor. Her laugh turned to a moan when he unbuttoned her blouse.

''Michael—''

''Is asleep.'' He dragged her hair back, leaving her face unframed. Everything he'd wanted to see was there. ''Until he wakes up, you're mine. I love you, Laura. Every time you look at the painting, you'll see it. You were mine from the first moment I touched you.''

Yours, she thought as she drew him back to her. Gabriel's angel was more than a portrait. And she finally belonged.

* * * * *

NORA ROBERTS

Rules Of The Game

Harlequin Mills & Boon

First Published 1984
Second Australian Paperback Edition 2004
ISBN 0 733 55162 9

Published by
Harlequin Mills & Boon
3 Gibbes Street
CHATSWOOD NSW 2067
AUSTRALIA

Printed and bound in Australia by
McPherson's Printing Group

Chapter 1

"A jock. Terrific." Brooke took a long swallow of strong black coffee, tipped back in her glove-soft leather chair and scowled. "I love it."

"No need to be sarcastic," Claire returned mildly. "If de Marco wants to use an athlete for promotion, why should you object?" She gazed absently at the chunky gold ring on her right hand. "After all," Claire continued in her dry voice, "you'll be making quite a bit directing the commercials."

Brooke sent Claire a characteristic look. Direct, uncompromising gray eyes bored into the soft blue of the older woman's. One of Brooke's greatest talents, and her greatest weapons, was her ability to stare down anyone from a corporate president to a temperamental actor. She'd developed the knack early as a defense against her own insecurity and had since refined it to an art. It was an art, however, that didn't impress Claire Thorton. At forty-nine, she was the head of a multimillion-dollar company that she'd started with brains and guts. For nearly a quarter of a century, she had run things her way, and she intended to keep right on doing so.

She'd known Brooke for ten years—since Brooke had been an eighteen-year-old upstart who had wheedled her way into a job with Thorton Productions. Then she'd watched Brooke work her way up from gofer to gaffer, from gaffer to assistant cameraman and from there to director. Claire had never regretted the impulse that had led her to give Brooke her first fifteen-second commercial.

Intuition had been the basis for Claire's success with Thorton Productions, and intuitively she had sensed sharp talent in Brooke Gordon. In addition, Claire knew her, understood her, as few others did. Perhaps it was because they shared two basic traits—ambition and independence.

After a moment, Brooke gave up with a sigh. ''A jock,'' she muttered again as she gazed around her office.

It was one small room, the pale-amber walls lined with prints of stills from dozens of her commercials. There was a two-cushion sofa—reupholstered in chocolate-colored corduroy—not comfortable enough to encourage long visits. The chair with a tufted back had been picked up at a yard sale along with a coffee table that leaned slightly to the left.

Brooke sat behind an old, scarred desk that had a drawer that wouldn't quite close. On it were piles of papers, a gooseneck lamp and assorted disposable pens and broken pencils. The pens and pencils were jammed in a

Sevres vase. Behind her at the window, a dieffenbachia was slowly dying in an exquisitely worked pottery bowl.

''Damn, Claire, why can't they get an actor?'' Brooke tossed up her hands in her one theatrical gesture, then dropped her chin on them. ''Do you know what it's like to try to coax ball players and rock stars to say a line without freezing or hamming it up?'' With a disgusted mutter that gave no room for comment, she pushed the pile of papers into a semiordered heap. ''One call to a casting agent and I could have a hundred qualified actors parading through here itching for the job.''

Patiently, Claire brushed a speck of lint from the sleeve of her rose linen suit. ''You know it increases sales if a production's hyped by a recognizable name or familiar face.''

''Recognizable name?'' Brooke tossed back. ''Who's ever heard of Parks Jones? *Stupid* name,'' she muttered to herself.

''Every baseball fan in the country.'' The mild smile told Brooke it was useless to argue. Therefore, she prepared to argue further.

''We're selling clothes, not Louisville Sluggers.''

''Eight Golden Gloves,'' Claire went on. ''A lifetime batting average of three twenty-five. He's leading the league in RBIs this season. Jones has been at third base in the All-Star game for eight consecutive seasons.''

Brooke narrowed her eyes. ''How do you know so much? You don't follow baseball.''

''I do my homework.'' A cool smile touched Claire's round, pampered face. She'd never had a face-lift but was religious about her visits to Elizabeth Arden. ''That's why

I'm a successful producer. Now you'd better do yours." She rose languidly. "Don't make any plans, I've got tickets for the game tonight. Kings against the Valiants."

"Who?"

"Do your homework," Claire advised before she closed the office door behind her.

With an exasperated oath, Brooke swiveled her chair around so that she faced her view of Los Angeles—tall buildings, glittering glass and clogged traffic. She'd had other views of L.A. during the rise in her career, but they'd been closer to street level. Now, she looked out on the city from the twentieth floor. The distance meant success, but Brooke didn't dwell on it. To do that would have encouraged thinking of the past—something Brooke meticulously avoided.

Leaning back in the oversized chair, Brooke toyed with the end of her braid. Her hair was the warm soft red shot with gold that painters attempted to immortalize. It was long and thick and unruly. Brooke was feminine enough not to want it cut to a more manageable length and practical enough to subdue it into a fat braid during working hours. It hung down the back of a thin silk blouse past the waistband of overworked blue jeans.

Her eyes as she mulled over Claire's words were thoughtful. They had misty gray irises, long lids and were surrounded by lashes in the same fragile shade as her hair. She rarely thought to darken them. Her skin was the delicate ivory-rose her hair demanded but the frailty stopped there. Her nose was small and sharp, her mouth wide, her chin aggressive. It was an unsettling face—beautiful one moment, austere the next, but always demanding. She wore a hasty dab of rose lipstick, enameled dimestore earrings and a splash of two-hundred dollar-an-ounce perfume.

She thought about the de Marco account—designer jeans, exclusive sportswear and soft Italian leather. Since they'd decided to move their advertising beyond the glossy pages of fashion magazines and into television, they had come to Thorton Productions, and so to her. It was a fat two-year contract with a budget that would give Brooke all the artistic room she could want. She told herself she deserved it. There were three Clios on the corner shelf to her right.

Not bad, she mused, for a twenty-eight-year-old woman who had walked into Thorton Productions with a high school diploma, a glib tongue and sweaty palms. And twelve dollars and fifty-three cents in her pocket, Brooke remembered; then she pushed the thought aside. If she wanted the de Marco account—and she did—she would simply have to make the ball player work. Grimly, she swung her chair back to face her desk. Picking up the phone, Brooke punched two buttons.

''Get me everything we have on Parks Jones,'' she ordered as she shuffled papers out of her way. ''And ask Ms. Thorton what time I'm to pick her up tonight.''

Less than six blocks away, Parks Jones stuck his hands in his pockets and scowled at his agent. ''How did I ever let you talk me into this?''

Lee Dutton gave a smile that revealed slightly crooked teeth and a lot of charm. ''You trust me.''

''My first mistake.'' Parks studied Lee, a not quite

homely, avuncular figure with a receding hairline, puckish face and unnerving black eyes. Yes, he trusted him, Parks thought, he even liked the shrewd little devil, but… "I'm not a damn model, Lee. I'm a third baseman."

"You're not modeling," Lee countered. As he folded his hands, the sun glinted on the band of his thin Swiss watch. "You're endorsing. Ball players have been doing it since the first razor blade."

Parks snorted then walked around the tidy, Oriental-designed office. "This isn't a shaving commercial, and I'm not endorsing a mitt. It's clothes, for God's sake. I'm going to feel like an idiot."

But you won't look like one, Lee thought as he drew out a fragrant, slim cigar. Lighting it, he studied Parks over the flame. The long, lanky body was perfect for de Marco's—as was the blond, unmistakably California look. Parks's tanned lean face, navy-blue eyes and tousled curling hair had already made him a favorite with the female fans, while his friendly, laid-back charm had won over the men. He was talented, easy to look at and personable. In short, Lee concluded, he was a natural. The fact that he was intelligent was at times as much a disadvantage as an advantage.

"Parks, you're hot." Lee said it with a sigh that they both knew was calculated. "You're also thirty-three. How much longer are you going to play ball?"

Parks answered with a glare. Lee knew of his vow to retire at thirty-five. "What does that have to do with it?"

"There are a lot of ball players, exceptional ball players, who slip into oblivion when they walk off the diamond for the last time. You have to think of the future."

"I *have* thought of the future," Parks reminded him. "Maui—fishing, sleeping in the sun, ogling women."

That would last about six weeks, Lee calculated, but he wisely kept silent.

"Lee." Parks flopped into a Chinese-red chair and stretched out his legs. "I don't need the money. So why am I going to be working this winter instead of lying on the beach?"

"Because it's going to be good for you," Lee began. "It's good for the game. The campaign will enhance the image of baseball. And," he added with one of his puckish smiles, "because you signed a contract."

"I'm going to get in some extra batting practice," Parks muttered as he rose. When he reached the door, he turned back with a suspiciously friendly smile. "One thing. If I make a fool of myself, I'm going to break the legs on your Tang horse."

Brooke screeched through the electronically controlled gates then swerved up the rhododendron-lined drive that led to Claire's mansion. Privately, Brooke considered it a beautiful anachronism. It was huge, white, multileveled and pillared. Brooke liked to imagine two black-helmeted guards, rifles on shoulders, flanking the carved double doors. The estate had originally belonged to a silent movie idol who had supposedly decked out the rooms in pastel silks and satins. Fifteen years before, Claire had purchased it from a perfume baron and had proceeded to redecorate it with her own passion for Oriental art.

Brooke stomped on the brake of her Datsun, screaming to a halt in front of the white marble steps. She drove at two speeds: stop and go. Stepping out of the car, she breathed in the exotic garden scents of vanilla and jasmine before striding up the stairs in the loose-limbed gait that came from a combination of long legs and preoccupation. In a crowd, her walk would cause men's heads to turn but Brooke neither noticed nor cared.

She knocked briskly on the door, then impatiently turned the handle. Finding it unlocked, she walked into the spacious mint-green hall and shouted.

"Claire! Are you ready? I'm starving." A neat little woman in a tailored gray uniform came through a doorway to the left. "Hello, Billings." Brooke smiled at her and tossed her braid over her shoulder. "Where's Claire? I haven't the energy to search through this labyrinth for her."

"She's dressing, Ms. Gordon." The housekeeper spoke in modulated British tones, responding to Brooke's smile with a nod. "She'll be down shortly. Would you care for a drink?"

"Just some Perrier, it's muggy out." Brooke followed the housekeeper into the drawing room then slumped down on a divan. "Did she tell you where we're going?"

"To a baseball game, miss?" Billing set ice in a glass and added sparkling water. "Some lime?"

"Just a squirt. Come on, Billings." Brooke's smoky contralto became conspiratorial. "What do you think?"

Billings meticulously squeezed lime into the bubbly water. She'd been housekeeper for Lord and Lady Westbrook in Devon before being prized away by Claire Thorton. On accepting the position, she had vowed never to become Americanized. Edna Billings had her standards. But she'd never quite been able to resist responding to Brooke. A naughty young girl, she'd thought a decade before, and the opinion remained unchanged. Perhaps that was why Billings was so fond of her.

"I much prefer cricket," she said blandly. "A more civilized game." She handed Brooke the glass.

"Can you see Claire sitting in the bleachers?" Brooke demanded. "Surrounded by screaming, sweaty fans, watching a bunch of grown men swing at a little ball and run around in circles?"

"If I'm not mistaken," Billings said slowly, "there's a bit more to it than that."

"Sure, RBIs and ERAs and putouts and shutouts." Brooke heaved a long breath. "What the hell is a squeeze play?"

"I'm sure I have no idea."

"Doesn't matter." Brooke shrugged and gulped down some Perrier. "Claire has it in her head that watching this guy in action will give me some inspiration." She ran a fingertip down a shocking-orange ginger jar. "What I really need is a meal."

"You can get a hot dog and some beer in the park," Claire announced from the doorway.

Glancing up, Brooke gave a hoot of laughter. Claire was immaculately dressed in buff-colored linen slacks and tailored print blouse with low alligator pumps. "You're going to a ball game," Brooke reminded her, "not a museum. And I hate beer."

"A pity." Opening her alligator bag, Claire checked the contents before snapping it shut again. "Let's be on our way, then, we don't want to miss anything. Good night, Billings.''

Gulping down the rest of her drink, Brooke bolted to her feet and raced after Claire. ''Let's stop to eat on the way,'' she suggested. ''It's not like missing the first act of the opera, and I had to skip lunch.'' She tried her forlorn orphan's look. ''You know how cranky I get if I miss a meal.''

''We're going to have to start putting you in front of the camera, Brooke; you're getting better all the time.'' With a slight frown at the low-slung Datsun, Claire maneuvered herself inside. She also knew Brooke's obsession with regular meals sprang from her lean adolescence. ''Two hot dogs,'' she suggested, wisely buckling her seat belt. ''It takes forty-five minutes to get to the stadium.'' Claire fluffed her silver-frosted brunette hair. ''That means you should get us there in about twenty-five.''

Brooke swore and rammed the car into first. In just over thirty minutes, she was hunting for a parking space outside of Kings Stadium. ''...and the kid got it perfect on the first take,'' Brooke continued blithely, swerving around cars with a bullfighter's determination. ''The two adult actors messed up, and the table collapsed so that it took fourteen takes, but the kid had it cold every time.'' She gave a loud war whoop as she spotted an empty space, swung into it, barely nosing out another car, then stopped with a jaw-snapping jerk. ''I want you to take a look at the film before it's edited.''

''What have you got in mind?'' With some difficulty, Claire climbed out of the door, squeezing herself between the Datsun and the car parked inches beside it.

''You're casting for that TV movie, *Family in Decline.*'' Brooke slammed her door then leaned over the hood. ''I don't think you're going to want to look any further for the part of Buddy. The kid's good, really, really good.''

''I'll take a look.''

Together, they followed the crowd swarming toward the stadium. There was a scent of heated asphalt, heavy air and damp humanity—Los Angeles in August. Above them the sky was darkening so that the stadium lights sent up a white misty glow. Inside, they walked past the stands that hawked pennants and pictures and programs. Brooke could smell popcorn and grilled meat, the tang of beer. Her stomach responded accordingly.

''Do you know where you're going?'' she demanded.

''I always know where I'm going,'' Claire replied, turning into an aisle that sloped downward.

They emerged to find the stadium bright as daylight and crammed with bodies. There was the continual buzz of thousands of voices over piped-in, soft-rock music. Walking vendors carried trays of food and drink strapped over their shoulders. Excitement. Brooke could feel the electricity of it coming in waves. Instantly, her own apathy vanished to be replaced by an avid curiosity. People were her obsession, and here they were, thousands of them, packed together in a circle around a field of green grass and brown dirt.

Something other than hunger began to stir in her.

''Look at them all, Claire,'' she murmured. ''Is it always like this? I wonder.''

''The Kings are having a winning season. They're leading their division by three games, have two potential twenty-game-winning pitchers and a third baseman who's batting three seventy-eight for the year.'' She sent Brooke a lifted-brow look. ''I told you to do your homework.''

''Mm-hmm.'' But Brooke was too caught up in the people. Who were they? Where did they come from? Where did they go after the game was over?

There were two old men, perched on chairs, their hands between their knees as they argued over the game that hadn't yet started. Oh, for a cameraman, Brooke thought, spotting a five-year-old in a Kings fielder's cap gazing up at the two gnarled fans. She followed Claire down the steps slowly, letting her eyes record everything. She liked the size of it, the noise, the smell of damp, crowded bodies, the color. Navy-blue-and-white Kings pennants were waved; children crammed pink cotton candy into their mouths. A teenager was making a play for a cute little blonde in front of him who pretended she wasn't interested.

Abruptly Brooke stopped, dropping her hand on Claire's shoulder. ''Isn't that Brighton Boyd?''

Claire glanced to the left to see the Oscar-winning actor munching peanuts from a white paper bag. ''Yes. Let's see now, this is our box.'' She scooted in, then lifted a friendly hand to the actor before she sat. ''This should do very well,'' Claire observed with a satisfied nod. ''We're quite close to third base here.''

Still looking at everything at once, Brooke dropped into her chair. The Colosseum in Rome, she thought, must have had the same feel before the gladiators trooped out. If she were to do a commercial on baseball, it wouldn't be of the game, but of the crowd. A pan, with the sound low—then gradually increase it as the camera closed in. Then, *bamm!* Full volume, full effect. Clichéd or not, it was quintessentially American.

"Here you go, dear." Claire disrupted her thoughts by handing her a hot dog. "My treat."

"Thanks." After taking a healthy bite, Brooke continued with her mouth full. "Who does the advertising for the team, Claire?"

"Just concentrate on third base," Claire advised as she sipped at a beer.

"Yes, but—" The crowd roared as the home team took the field. Brooke watched the men move to their positions, dressed in dazzling white with navy-blue caps and baseball socks. They didn't look foolish, she mused as the fans continued to cheer. They looked rather heroic. She focused on the man on third.

Parks's back was to her as he kicked up a bit of dust around the base. But Brooke didn't strain to see his face. At the moment, she didn't need it—his build was enough. Six one, she estimated, a bit surprised by his height. No more than a hundred and sixty pounds—but not thin. She leaned her elbows on the rail, resting her chin on her hands.

He's lanky, she thought. He'll show off clothes well. Parks dipped for a grounder then returned it to short. For an instant, Brooke's thoughts scattered. Something intruded on her professional survey that she quickly brushed aside. The way he moved, she thought. Catlike? No. She shook her head. No, he was all man.

She waited, unconsciously holding her breath as he

fielded another grounder. He moved loosely, apparently effortlessly, but she sensed a tight control as he stepped, bent, pivoted. It was a fluid action—feet, legs, hips, arm. A dancer had the same sort of nonchalant perfection after practicing a basic routine for years. If she could keep him moving, Brooke mused, it wouldn't matter if the man couldn't say his own name on camera.

There was an unexpected sexuality in every gesture. It was there even when he stood, idly wanting to field another practice ball. It might just work after all, Brooke reflected as her eyes roamed up his body, brushing over the blond curls that sprang around the sides and back of his cap. It might just…

Then he turned. Brooke found herself staring full into his face. It was long and lean like his body, a bit reminiscent of the gladiators she'd been thinking about earlier. Because he was concentrating, his full, passionate mouth was unsmiling; the eyes, almost the same shade as the navy hat that shaded them, were brooding. He looked fierce, almost warlike, definitely dangerous. Whatever Brooke had been expecting, it hadn't been this tough, uncompromisingly sexy face or her own reaction to it.

Someone called out to him from the stands. Abruptly, he grinned, transforming into a friendly, approachable man with an aura of easy charm. Brooke's muscles relaxed.

''What do you think of him?''

A bit dazed, Brooke leaned back in her chair and absently munched on her hot dog. ''He might work,'' she murmured. ''He moves well.''

"From what I've been told," Claire said dryly, "you haven't seen anything yet."

As usual, Claire was right. In the first inning, Parks made a diving catch along the base line at third for the final out. He batted fourth, lining a long single to left field that he stretched into a double. He played, Brooke thought, with the enthusiasm of a kid and the diabolical determination of a veteran. She didn't have to know anything about the game to know the combination was unstoppable.

In motion, he was a pleasure to watch. Relaxed now, the first staggering impression behind her, Brooke began to consider the angles. If his voice was as good as the rest of him, she mused. Well…that was yet to be seen. After polishing off another hot dog, she resumed her position leaning against the rail. The Kings were ahead 2-1 in the fifth inning. The crowd was frantic. Brooke decided she would use some action shots of Parks in slow motion.

It was hot and still on the diamond. A fitful breeze fluttered the flag and cooled the spectators high up in the stands, but below, under the lights, the air was thick. Parks felt the sweat run down his back as he stood on the infield grass. Hernandez, the pitcher, was falling behind on the batter. Parks knew Rathers to be a power hitter who pulled to the left. He planted himself behind the bag and waited. He saw the pitch—a waist-high fast ball—heard the crack of the bat. In that one millisecond, he had two choices: catch the ball that was lined hard at him or end up with a hole in his chest. He caught it, and felt the vibration of power sing through his body before he heard the screams of the crowd.

A routine catch, most would say. Parks was surprised

the ball hadn't carried him out of the stadium. "Got any leather left on your glove?" the shortstop called to him as they headed back to the dugout. Parks shot him a grin before he let his eyes drift up to the stands. His eyes locked on Brooke's, surprising them both.

In reaction, Parks slowed a bit. Now there was a face, he thought, a man wouldn't see every day. She looked a bit like a ravished eighteenth-century aristocrat with her wild mane of hair and English rose skin. He felt an immediate tightening in his stomach. The face exuded cool, forbidden sex. But the eyes… His never left them as he approached the dugout. The eyes were soft-gray and direct as an arrow. She stared back at him without a blink or a blush, not smiling as most fans would do if they were bold, or looking away if they were shy. She just stared, Parks thought, as if she were dissecting him. With simultaneous twinges of annoyance and curiosity, he stepped into the dugout.

He thought about her as he sat on the bench. Here, the atmosphere was subdued and tense. Every game was important now if they were to maintain their lead and win the division pennant. Parks had the personal pressure of having a shot at a four hundred batting average for the year. It was something he struggled not to think about and was constantly reminded of by the press. He watched the leadoff batter ground out and thought of the redhead in the box behind third base.

Why had she looked at him like that? As if she wondered how he would look on a trophy case. With a soft oath, Parks rose and put on his batting helmet. He'd better get his mind off the little number in the stands and on the game. Hernandez was slowing down, and the Kings needed some insurance runs.

The second batter bounced one to shallow right and beat out the ball. Parks went to stand on deck. He stretched his arms over his head, one hand on the grip, the other on the barrel. He felt loose and warm and ready. Irresistibly, his eyes were drawn to his left. He couldn't see Brooke clearly from this distance, but he sensed she watched him still. Fresh annoyance broke through him. When the batter flied out, Parks approached the box.

What was her problem, anyway? he demanded as he took a testing swing. It would have been simpler if he could have characterized her as a typical Baseball Annie, but there was nothing typical about that face—or about those eyes. Planting his feet, he crouched into position and waited for the pitch. It came in high and sweet. Parks took a cut at it just before the ball dropped.

Coolly, he stepped out of the box and adjusted his helmet before he took his batting stance again. The next ball missed the corner and evened the count. Patience was the core of Parks's talent. He could wait, even when the pressure was on, for the pitch he wanted. So he waited, taking another ball and an inside strike. The crowd was screaming, begging for a hit, but he concentrated on the pitcher.

The ball came at him, at ninety miles an hour, but he had it judged. This was the one he wanted. Parks swung, getting the meat of the bat on the ball. He knew it was gone the moment he heard the crack. So did the pitcher, who watched his two-strike pitch sail out of the park.

Parks jogged around the bases while the crowd roared. He acknowledged the slap of the first base coach with a quick grin. He'd never lost his childlike pleasure in hitting the long ball. As he rounded second, he automatically looked over at Brooke. She was sitting, chin on the rail, while the crowd jumped and screamed around her. There was the same quiet intensity in her eyes—no light of congratulations, no pleasure. Irritated, Parks tried to outstare her as he rounded third. Her eyes never faltered as he turned for home. He crossed the plate, exhilarated by the homer and furious with an unknown woman.

"Isn't that marvelous?" Claire beamed over at Brooke. "That's his thirty-sixth home run this season. A very talented young man." She signaled a roving concessionaire for another drink. "He was staring at you."

"Mm-hmm." Brooke wasn't willing to admit that her pulse rate had soared with each eye contact. She knew his type—good-looking, successful and heartless. She met them every day. "He'll look good on camera."

Claire laughed with the comfortable pleasure of a woman approaching fifty. "He'd look good anywhere."

Brooke's answer was a shrug as the game went into its seventh inning. She paid no attention to the score or to the other players as she watched Parks steadily. She remained, arms over the rail, chin on hands, booted feet crossed. There was something about him, she mused, something beyond the obvious attraction, the basic sexuality. It was that looseness of movement overlying the discipline. That's what she wanted to capture. The combination would do more than sell de Marco's clothes, it would typify them. All she had to do was guide Parks Jones through the steps.

She'd have him swinging a bat in immaculately sophisticated sports clothes—maybe riding through the surf in de Marco jeans. Athletic shots—that's what he was built for. And if she could get any humor out of him, something with women. She didn't want the usual adoring stares or knowing looks, but something fanciful and funny. If the script writers could pull it off and Jones could take any sort of direction. Refusing to look at the ifs, Brooke told herself she would make it work. Within the year, every woman would want Parks Jones and every man would envy him.

The ball was hit high and was curving foul. Parks chased after it, racing all the way to the seats before it dropped into the crowd four rows back. Brooke found herself face-to-face with him, close enough to smell the faint muskiness of his sweat and to see it run down the side of his face. Their eyes met again, but she didn't move, partly because she was interested, partly because she was paralyzed. The only thing that showed in her eyes was mild curiosity. Behind them there were shouts of triumph as someone snagged the foul as a trophy.

Enraged, Parks stared back at her. ''Your name?'' he demanded in undertones.

He had that fierce, dangerous look on his face again. Brooke schooled her voice to calmness. ''Brooke.''

''All of it, damn it,'' Parks muttered, pressed for time and furious with himself. He watched one thin eyebrow lift and found himself wanting to yank her out of the stands.

''Gordon,'' Brooke told him smoothly. ''Is the game over?''

Parks narrowed his eyes before he moved away. Brooke heard him speak softly. ''It's just beginning.''

Chapter 2

Brooke had been expecting the call—after all, he had her name, and her name was in the book. But she hadn't been expecting it at six-fifteen on a Sunday morning.

Groggily, she groped for the phone as it shrilled, managing to grip the receiver as the cradle fell heavily to the floor. "'Lo," she mumbled without opening her eyes.

"Brooke Gordon?"

"Mmm." She snuggled back into the pillow. "Yeah."

"It's Parks Jones."

Instantly alert, Brooke opened her eyes. The light was soft and dim with dawn, early birds just beginning to chirp. She fumbled for the dented windup alarm beside her bed, then scowled at the time. Biting back a torrent of abuse, she kept her voice soft and sulky. "Who?"

Parks shifted the receiver to his other hand and scowled.

"Parks Jones, third base. The Kings game the other night."

Brooke yawned, taking her time about fluffing up her pillow. "Oh," was all she said, but a smile flashed wickedly.

"Look, I want to see you. We're flying back after the game in New York this afternoon. How about a late dinner?" Why was he doing this? he asked himself as he paced the small hotel room. And why, in God's name, wasn't he doing it with a bit more style?

"Dinner," Brooke repeated languidly while her mind worked fast. Wasn't it just like his type to expect a woman to have no plans that couldn't be altered to suit him? Her first instinct was to give him a cold refusal, then her sense of the ridiculous got the better of her. "Well..." She drew out the word. "Maybe. What time?"

"I'll pick you up at nine," Parks told her, ignoring the maybe. When he couldn't get a woman out of his head for three days, he was going to find out why. "I've got the address."

"All right, Sparks, nine o'clock."

"Parks," he corrected tersely and broke the connection.

Falling back on the pillow, Brooke started to laugh.

She was still in high good humor when she dressed that evening. Still, she thought it was too bad that the file she had read on Parks hadn't contained a bit more than all those baseball statistics. A few personal details would have given her more of an edge. What would Parks Jones have to say if he knew he was taking his future director to dinner? she wondered. Somehow Brooke didn't think he'd be too pleased when he learned she'd left out that little piece of information. But the whole scenario was too good to miss. And there was the fact that he'd touched off something in her that she wanted to get out of her system before they started to work together.

Wrapped in a bath towel, Brooke pondered her wardrobe. She didn't date often—her choice. Early experience had influenced her attitude toward men. If they were good-looking and charming, Brooke steered clear of them.

She'd been only seventeen when she'd met her first good-looking charmer. He'd been twenty-two and fresh out of college. When he'd come into the diner where she had worked, Clark had been quick with a joke and generous with a tip. It had started with a late movie once or twice a week, then an afternoon picnic in the park. It hadn't bothered Brooke that he wasn't working. He'd told her he was taking the summer off before he settled down to a job.

His family was well connected, genteel and Bostonian. The genteel, Clark had explained with an acerbic humor that had fascinated her, meant there were plenty of heirlooms and little ready cash. They had plans for him that he was consistently vague about with the carelessness of the young. He'd mentioned his family now and again—grandparents, sisters—with a humor that spoke of an intimacy she envied almost painfully. Clark could make fun of them, Brooke realized, because he *was* one of them.

He'd needed a bit of freedom, he'd claimed, a few months to flow after the regimentation of college. He wanted to be in touch with the *real* world before he chose the perfect career.

Young and starved for affection, Brooke had soaked up

everything he'd told her, believed every line. He had dazzled her with an education she had wished for but had never been able to have. He'd told her she was beautiful and sweet, then had kissed her as though he meant it. There had been afternoons at the beach with rented surfboards she'd hardly noticed that she'd paid for. And when she'd given him her innocence in a kind of panicked, shamed excitement, he had seemed pleased with her. He'd laughed at her naive embarrassments and had been gentle. Brooke had thought she'd never been happier.

When he'd suggested they live together, she'd agreed eagerly, wanting to cook and clean for him, longing to wake and sleep with him. The fact that her meager salary and tips now supported both of them had never crossed her mind. Clark had talked of marriage the same way he had talked of his work—vaguely. They were something for the future, something practical that people in love shouldn't dwell on. Brooke had agreed, rosily happy with what she'd thought was her first real home. One day they would have children, she had thought. Boys with Clark's handsome face, girls with his huge brown eyes. Children with grandparents in Boston who would always know who their parents were and where their home was.

For three months she'd worked like a Trojan, setting aside part of her small salary for the future Clark always talked of while he pursued what he called his studies and systematically rejected all the jobs in the want ads as unsuitable. Brooke could only agree. To her, Clark was much too smart for any manual labor, much too important for any ordinary position. When the right job came along, she knew he would simply stride into it then zoom to the top.

At times he'd seemed restless, moody. Because she had always had to steal her own privacy, Brooke had left him to his. And when he snapped out of it, he'd always been bursting with energy and plans. Let's go here, let's go there. Now, today. Tomorrow was always years away to Clark. To Brooke, for the first time in seventeen years, today was special. She had something—*someone*—who belonged to her.

In the meantime, she'd worked long hours, cooked his meals and hoarded her tips in a small apothecary jar on a shelf in the kitchen.

One night Brooke had come home from a late shift to find that Clark had gone, taking with him her small black-and-white television set, her record collection and her apothecary jar. A note was in its place.

Brooke,

Got a call from home. My parents are putting on the pressure—I didn't know it would start so soon. I should have told you before, but I guess I kept thinking it would just go away. An old family tradition—a merger with my third cousin, as in matrimony. Hell, it sounds archaic, but it's the way my people work. Shelley's a nice girl, her dad's a connection of my dad's. I've been more or less engaged to her for a couple of years, but she was still at Smith, so it didn't seem important. Anyway, I'll slip into her family's business. Junior executive with a shot at the V.P. in five years or so. I guess I hoped I'd tell them to take a leap when the time came, but I can't. I'm sorry.

There's no fighting a wall of family and old money

and stiff New England practicality, babe, especially when they keep reminding you that you're the heir apparent. I want you to know that these last couple of months I've had more breathing space than I've had in a long time, and I suppose than I'll have in an even longer time.

I'm sorry about the TV and stuff, but I didn't have the cash for the plane fare and the time wasn't right to tell my folks I'd already blown my savings. I'll pay you back as soon as I can.

I kept hoping it wouldn't have to be this way, but I'm backed into a corner. You've been great, Brooke, really great. Be happy.

Clark

Brooke had read the note twice before all the words registered. He'd gone. Her things hadn't mattered but he had. Clark was gone and she was alone—again—because she hadn't graduated from Smith or had a family in Boston or a father who could offer someone she loved a comfortable job so he'd choose her. No one had ever chosen her.

Brooke had wept until she was drained, unable to believe that her dreams, her trust and her future had been destroyed all in one instant.

Then she had grown up fast, pushing her idealism behind her. She wasn't going to be used ever again. She wasn't going to compete ever again with women who had all the advantages. And she wasn't going to slave in a steamy little diner for enough money to keep herself in a one-room apartment with dingy paint.

She had torn the note into tiny pieces, then had washed her face with icy water until all the traces of all the tears were gone.

Walking the pavement with all the money she had left in her pocket, she had found herself in front of Thorton Productions. She had gone in aggressively, belligerently, talking her way past the receptionist and into the personnel office. She'd come out with a new job, making hardly more than she had waiting tables, but with fresh ambition. She was going places. The one thing her betrayal by Clark had taught her was that she could depend on only one person: herself. No one was ever going to make her believe, or make her cry again.

Ten years later, Brooke drew a narrow black dress from her closet. It was a severely sophisticated outfit she had bought mainly for the cocktail circuit that went hand in hand with her profession. She fingered the silk, then nodded. It should do very well for her evening with Parks Jones.

As Parks drove through the hills above L.A. he considered his actions. For the first time in his career he had allowed a woman to distract him during a game—and this one hadn't even tried. For the first time, he had called a virtual stranger from three thousand miles away to make a date, and she didn't even know who the hell he was. For the first time, he was planning on taking out a woman who made him absolutely furious without having said more than a handful of words. And if it hadn't been for the road series that had followed that night game at Kings Stadium, he would have called her before this. He'd looked up her number at the airport on his way to catch a plane to New York.

He downshifted for the incline as he swung around a curve. All during the flight home, he had thought of Brooke Gordon, trying to pigeonhole her. A model or an actress, he had concluded. She had the face for it—not really beautiful, but certainly unique. Her voice was like something whispering through layers of smoke. And she hadn't sounded overly bright on the phone that morning, he reminded himself with a grimace as he stepped on the gas. There was no law that said brains had to go with intriguing looks, but something in her eyes that night... Parks shook off the feeling that he'd been studied, weighted and measured.

A rabbit darted out in front of him then stopped, hypnotized by his beams. Parks braked, swerved and swore as it raced back to the side of the road. He had a weakness for small animals that his father had never understood. Then, his father had understood little about a boy who chose to play ball rather than assume a lucrative position of power in Parkinson Chemicals.

Parks slowed to check his direction, then turned down the darkened back road that led to Brooke's tidy wooded property. He liked it instantly—the remoteness, the melodious sound of crickets. It was a small slice of country thirty-five minutes from L.A. Perhaps she wasn't so slow-witted after all. He pulled his MG behind her Datsun and looked around him.

Her grass needed trimming, but it only added to the rural charm of the house. It was a small, A-frame structure with lots of glass and a circular porch. He heard the tinkle of water from the narrow stream that ran behind the house. There was a scent of summer—hot, heavy blossoms he couldn't identify, and an inexplicable aura of peacefulness. He found himself wishing he didn't have to drive back down to a crowded restaurant and bright lights. In the distance a dog began to bark frantically, sending out echos to emphasize the openness. Parks climbed out of the car, wondering what sort of woman would choose a house so far from city comforts.

There was an old brass knocker in the shape of a hog's head at the right of the door. It made him grin as he let it bang. When she opened the door, Parks forgot all the doubts that had plagued him on his drive through the hills. This time he thought she looked like a seductive witch—fair skin against a black dress, a heavy silver amulet between her breasts. Her hair was pulled back at the temples with two combs, then left to fall wildly down to her hips. Her eyes were as misty as hell-smoke, the lids darkened by some subtle, glittering shadow. Her mouth was naked. He caught a drift of scent that brought him a picture of East Indian harems, white silk and dusky female laughter.

"Hello." Brooke extended her hand. It took every ounce of willpower to complete the casual gesture. How was she to have known her heart would start thudding at the sight of him? It was foolish, because she had already imagined what he would look like in sophisticated clothes. She'd had to if she was to plan how to film him. But somehow his body looked rangier, even more male in a suit coat and slacks—and somehow his face was even more attractive in the shadowed half-light of her front porch. Her plans to ask him in for a drink were aborted.

The sooner they were in a crowd the better. "I'm starving," she said as his fingers closed over hers. "Shall we go?" Without waiting for his answer, she shut the door at her back.

Parks led her to the car then turned. In heels, she was nearly eye level with him. "Want me to put the top up?"

"No." Brooke opened the door herself. "I like the air."

She leaned back and shut her eyes as he started back down toward the city. He drove fast, but with the studied control she had sensed in him from the beginning. Since speed was one of her weaknesses, she relaxed and enjoyed.

"What were you doing at the game the other night?"

Brooke felt the smile tug at her mouth but answered smoothly, "A friend had some tickets. She thought I might find it interesting."

"Interesting?" Parks shook his head at the word. "And did you?"

"Oh, yes, though I'd expected to be bored."

"I didn't notice any particular enthusiasm in you," Parks commented, remembering her calm, direct stare. "As I recall, you didn't move through nine innings."

"I didn't need to," she returned. "You did enough of that."

Parks shot her a quick look. "Why were you staring at me?"

Brooke considered for a moment, then opted for the truth. "I was admiring your build." She turned to him with a half smile. The wind blew the hair into her face, but she didn't bother to brush it aside. "It's a very good one."

"Thanks." She saw a flash of humor in his eyes that pleased her. "Is that why you agreed to have dinner with me?"

Brooke smiled more fully. "No. I just like to eat. Why did you ask me?"

"I liked your face. And it's not every day I have a woman stare at me as if she were going to frame me and hang me on her wall."

"Really?" She gave him an innocent blink. "I'd think that pretty typical in your profession."

"Maybe." He took his eyes off the road long enough to meet hers. "But then you're not typical, are you?"

Brooke lifted a brow. Did he know he'd given her what she considered the highest compliment? "Perhaps not," she murmured. "Why don't you think so?"

"Because, Brooke Gordon, I'm not typical either." He burst out of the woods and onto the highway. Brooke decided that she'd better tread carefully.

The restaurant was Greek, with pungent foods, spicy scents and violins. While Parks poured her a second glass of ouzo, Brooke listened to a waiter in a grease-splattered apron sing lustily as he served souvlaki. As always, atmosphere pulled at her. Caught up, she watched and absorbed while managing to put away a healthy meal.

"What are you thinking?" Parks demanded. Her eyes shifted to his, disconcerting in their directness, seducing in their softness.

"That this is a happy place," she told him. "The sort you imagine a big family running. Momma and Poppa in the kitchen fussing over sauces, a pregnant daughter chopping vegetables while her husband tends bar. Uncle Stefos waits tables.''

The image made him smile. ''Do you come from a large family?''

Immediately the light went out of her eyes. ''No.''

Sensing a boundary, Parks skirted around it. ''What happens when the daughter has her baby?''

''She pops it in a cradle in the corner and chops more vegetables.'' Brooke broke a hunk of bread in half and nibbled.

''Very efficient.''

''A successful woman has to be.''

Leaning back, Parks swirled his drink. ''Are you a successful woman?''

''Yes.''

He tilted his head, watching the candlelight play on her skin. ''At what?''

Brooke sipped, enjoying the game. ''At what I do. Are you a successful man?''

''At the moment.'' Parks flashed a grin—the one that gave his face a young, rather affable charm. ''Baseball's a fickle profession. A ball takes a bad hop—a pitcher blows a few by you. You can't predict when a slump will start or stop—or worse, why.''

It seemed a bit like life to her. ''And do you have many?''

''One's too many.'' With a shrug, he set his drink back on the table. ''I've had more than one.''

With her first genuine curiosity, Brooke leaned forward. ''What do you do to get out of one?''

''Change bats, change batting stances.'' He shrugged again. ''Change your diet, pray. Try celibacy.''

She laughed, a warm, liquid sound. ''What works best?''

''A good pitch.'' He, too, leaned forward. ''Wanna hear one?''

When her brow rose again, he lifted a finger to trace it. Brooke felt the jolt shiver down to her toes. ''I think I'll pass.''

''Where do you come from?'' he murmured. His fingertip drifted down her cheek, then traced her jawline. He'd known her skin would feel like that. Milkmaid soft.

''No place in particular.'' Brooke reached for her glass, but his hand closed over hers.

''Everyone comes from somewhere.''

''No,'' she disagreed. His palm was harder than she had imagined, his fingers stronger. And his touch was gentler. ''Not everyone.''

From her tone, Parks realized she was speaking the truth as she saw it. He brushed a thumb over her wrist, finding her pulse fast but steady. ''Tell me about yourself.''

''What do you want to know?''

''Everything.''

Brooke laughed but spoke with perfect truth. ''I don't tell anyone everything.''

''What do you do?''

''About what?''

He should have been exasperated, but found himself grinning. ''About a job, for starters.''

''Oh, I make commercials,'' she said lightly, knowing

he would conclude she worked in front of the cameras. The game had a certain mischievous appeal for her.

''I'll be doing that myself soon,'' he said with a quick grimace. ''Do you like it?''

''I wouldn't do it if I didn't.''

He sent her a narrowed look, then nodded. ''No, you wouldn't.''

''You don't sound as though you're looking forward to trying it,'' Brooke commented, slipping her hand from his. Prolonged contact with him, she discovered, made it difficult to concentrate, and concentration was vital to her.

''Not when I have to spout some silly lines and wear somebody else's clothes.'' Idly, he toyed with a lock of her hair, wrapping it around his finger while his eyes remained on hers. ''You've a fascinating face; more alluring than beautiful. When I saw you in the stands, I thought you looked like a woman out of the eighteenth century. The sort who had a string of anxious lovers.''

With a low sound of humor, Brooke leaned closer. ''Was that the first pitch, Mr. Jones?''

Her scent seemed intensified by the warmth of the candle. He wondered that every man in the room wasn't aware of it, and of her. ''No.'' His fingers tightened briefly, almost warningly, on her hair. ''When I make my first one, you won't have to ask.''

Instinctively, Brooke retreated, but her eyes remained calm, her voice smooth. ''Fair enough.'' She would definitely put him on film with women, she decided. Sultry brunettes for contrast. ''Do you ride?'' she asked abruptly.

''Ride?''

''Horses.''

''Yeah,'' he answered with a curious laugh. ''Why?''

''Just wondered. What about hang gliding?''

Parks's expression became more puzzled than amused. ''It's against my contract, like skiing or racing.'' He didn't trust the light of humor in her eyes. ''Should I know what game you're playing?''

''No. Can we have dessert?'' She flashed him a brilliant smile he trusted less.

''Sure.'' Watching her, Parks signaled the waiter.

Thirty minutes later, they walked across the parking lot to his car. ''Do you always eat like that?'' Parks demanded.

''Whenever I get the chance.'' Brooke dropped into the passenger seat then stretched her arms over her head in a lazy, unconsciously sensual movement. No one who hadn't worked in a restaurant could fully appreciate eating in one. She'd enjoyed the food…and the evening. Perhaps, she mused, she'd enjoyed being with Parks because they'd spent three hours together and still didn't know each other. The mystery added a touch of spice.

In a few months, they would know each other well. A director had no choice but to get to the inside of an actor—which is what Parks would be, whether he liked it or not. For now, Brooke chose to enjoy the moment, the mystery and the brief companionship of an attractive man.

When Parks sat beside her, he reached over to cup her chin in his hand. She met his eyes serenely and with that touch of humor that was beginning to frustrate him. ''Are you going to let me know who you are?''

Odd, Brooke mused, that he would have the same understanding of the evening she did. "I haven't decided," she said candidly.

"I'm going to see you again."

She gave him an enigmatic smile. "Yes."

Wary of the smile, and her easy agreement, Parks started the engine.

He didn't like knowing that she was playing him...any more than he liked knowing he'd have to come back for more. He'd known a variety of women—from icy sophisticates to bubbly groupies. There were infinite shadings in between, but Brooke Gordon seemed to fit none of them. She had both a haughty sexuality and a soft vulnerability. Though his first instinct had been to get her to bed, he now discovered he wanted more. He wanted to peel off the layers of her character and study each one until he understood the full woman. Making love to her would only be part of the discovery.

They drove in silence while an old, soft ballad crooned on the radio. Brooke had her head thrown back, face to the stars, knowing it was the first time in months she'd fully relaxed on a date and not wanting to analyze why. Parks didn't find it necessary to break a comfortable silence with conversation, nor had he found it necessary to slip in those predictable hints about how he'd like to end the evening. She knew there wouldn't be a wrestling match on the side of the road or an embarrassing, infuriating argument when they reached the front door. He was safe, Brooke decided, and closed her eyes. It seemed things were going to work very well after all. Her thoughts began to drift toward her schedule for the next day.

The motion of the car woke her, or rather the lack of

motion. Brooke opened her eyes to find the MG parked in her drive, the engine quiet. Turning her head, she saw Parks sprawled in his seat, watching her.

"You drive very well," she murmured. "I don't usually trust anyone enough to fall asleep in a car."

He'd enjoyed the moments of quiet while he'd watched her sleep. Her skin looked ethereal in the moonlight, ghostly pale with a hint of flush in her cheeks. The wind had tossed her hair so that Parks knew how it would look spread on a pillow after a wild night of loving. Sooner or later he'd see it that way, he determined. After his hands had tangled it.

"This time you're staring," Brooke pointed out.

And he smiled—not the quick grin she'd come to expect, but a slow, unsettling smile that left his eyes dark and dangerous. "I guess we'll both have to get used to it."

Leaning over, he opened her door. Brooke didn't stiffen or shift away from the brush of his body against hers; she simply watched. As if, Parks mused, she were considering his words very carefully. Good, he thought as he stepped from the car. This time she'd have something to think about.

"I like this place." He didn't touch her as they walked up the path to her house, though Brooke had expected him to take her hand or her arm. "I had a house in Malibu once."

"Not anymore?"

"Got too crowded." He shrugged as they walked up the porch steps. Their footsteps echoed into the night. "If

I'm going to live out of the city, I want a place where I'm not forever stumbling over my neighbor."

"I don't have that problem here." Around them the woods were dark and quiet. There was only the bubbling sound of the stream and the music of tireless crickets. "There's a couple who live about a quarter mile that way." Brooke gestured to the east. "Newlyweds who met on a television series that folded." Leaning back against the door, she smiled. "We don't have any trouble keeping out of each other's way." She sighed, comfortably sleepy and relaxed. "Thanks for dinner." When she offered her hand, she wondered if he would take it or ignore it and kiss her. Brooke expected the latter, even wondered with a drowsy curiosity what the pressure of his lips on hers would be like.

Parks knew what she expected, and her lips, as they had from the first, tempted him. But he thought it was time this woman had something unexpected. Taking her hand, Parks leaned toward her. He saw from her eyes that she would accept his kiss with her own sultry reserve. Instead, he touched his lips to her cheek.

At the brush of his open mouth on her skin, Brooke's fingers tightened in his. Usually she viewed a kiss or embrace distantly, as from behind a camera, wondering dispassionately how it would appear on film. Now she saw nothing, but felt. Low, turbulent waves of sensation swept through her, making her tense. Something seemed to ripple along her skin, though he never touched her—just his hand over hers, just his lips on her cheek.

Slowly, watching her stunned eyes, Parks journeyed to her other cheek, moving his lips with the same feather-lightness. Brooke felt the waves rise until there was an echoing in her head. She heard a soft moan, unaware that it was her own. As hunger swept over her, Brooke turned her mouth toward his, but he glided up her skin, whispering over her eyelids so that they fluttered down. Drugged, she allowed him to roam over her face, leaving her lips trembling with anticipation, and unfulfilled. She tasted his breath on them, felt the warm flutter as they passed close, but his mouth dropped to her chin to give her a teasing touch of his tongue.

Her fingers went limp in his. Surrender was unknown to her, so she didn't recognize it. Parks did as he caught the lobe of her ear between his teeth. His body was throbbing, aching to press against hers and feel the yielding softness that came only from woman. Against his cheek, her hair was as silky as her skin, and as fragrant. It took every ounce of control to prevent his hands from diving into it, to keep himself from plundering the mouth that waited, warm and naked, for his. He traced her ear with his tongue and felt her shudder. Slowly, he brushed kisses up her temple and over her brow on his way to her other ear. He nibbled gently, letting his tongue slide over her skin until he heard her moan again.

Still he avoided her mouth, pressing his lips to the pulse in her throat, fighting the urge to move lower, to feel, to taste the subtle sweep of her breast beneath the black silk. Her pulse was jerky, like the sound of her breathing. High up in the mountains, a coyote called to the moon.

A dizzying excitement raced through him. He could have her now—feel that long, willowy body beneath his, tangle himself in that wild mane of hair. But he wouldn't have all of her. He needed more time for that.

"Parks." His name came throatily through her lips, arousing him further. "Kiss me."

Gently, he pressed his lips to her shoulder. "I am."

Her mouth felt as though it were on fire. She had thought she understood hunger, having felt it too often in the past. But she'd never known a hunger like this. "Really kiss me."

He drew away far enough to see her eyes. There was no light in them now; they were opaque with desire. Her lips were parted in invitation, her breath shuddering through them. He bent close, but kept his lips an aching whisper from hers. "Next time," he said softly.

Turning, he left her stunned and wanting.

Chapter 3

"Okay, Linda, try to look like you're enjoying this." Brooke cast a look at her lighting director and got a nod. "E.J., sweep up, starting at her toes—take your time on the legs."

E.J. gave her a blinding white grin from his smooth mahogany face. "My pleasure," he said affably and focused his camera on the actress's pink painted toenails.

"It's so hot," Linda complained, fussing with the strap of her tiny bikini. She was stretched out on a towel in the sand—long, blond and beautiful, with a rich golden tan that would hawk a popular suntan lotion. All Linda had to do was to look lush and lazy and purr that she had an *Eden* tan. The bikini would do the rest.

"Don't sweat," Brooke ordered. "You're supposed to be glowing, not wet. When we roll, count to six, then bring up your right knee—slow. At twelve, take a deep breath, pass your right hand through your hair. Say your line looking straight at the camera and think sex."

"The hell with sex, I'm roasting."

"Then let's get it in one take. All right. Speed. Roll film, and...action."

E.J. moved up from the manicured toenails, up the long, slender legs, over a rounded hip, golden midriff and barely confined bosom. He closed in on Linda's face—sulky mouth, pearly teeth and baby blues—then went back for a full shot.

"I've got an *Eden* tan," Linda claimed.

"Cut." Brooke swiped a hand over her brow. Though it was still morning, the beach was baking. She thought she could feel the sand burning through the soles of her sneakers. "Let's pump a little life into it," she suggested. "We've got to sell this stuff on one line and your body."

"Why don't you try it?" Linda demanded, falling onto her back.

"Because you're getting paid to and I'm not," Brooke snapped, then clicked her teeth together. She knew better than to lose her temper, especially with this one. The trouble was that since her evening with Parks, she'd been on a perpetual short fuse. Taking a deep breath, Brooke reminded herself that her personal life, if that's what Parks Jones was, couldn't interfere with her work. She walked over and crouched beside the pouting model. "Linda, I know it's miserable out here today, but a job's a job. You're a pro or you wouldn't be here."

"Do you know how hard I worked on this tan to get this lousy thirty-second spot?"

Brooke patted her shoulder, conveying sympathy, understanding and authority all at once. "Well then, let's make it a classic."

It was past noon before they were able to load up their equipment. E.J. reached in the back of the station wagon he used and pulled two iced drinks out of a chest cooler. "Here ya go, boss."

"Thanks." Brooke pressed the cold bottle against her forehead before she twisted off the top. "What was with her today?" she demanded. "She can be a problem, but I've never had to drag one line out of her like that before."

"Broke up with her man last week," E.J. informed Brooke before he took a greedy swallow of grape soda.

Grinning, Brooke sat on the tailgate. "Anything you don't know, E.J.?"

"Not a thing." He propped himself beside her, one of the few on the Thorton staff who wasn't leery of the Tiger-lady, as Brooke had been dubbed. "You're going to that fancy de Marco party tonight."

"Yeah." Brooke gave a slow, narrow-eyed smile that had nothing to do with the brilliance of the sun. The party would be her chance to cut Parks Jones down a few pegs. She could still remember how she had stood shaking on her porch in the moonlight after the echo of his engine had died away.

"It's going to be a kick working with Parks Jones." E.J. downed the rest of his soda in one swallow. "The man's got the best glove in the league and a bat that won't quit smoking. Knocked in two more RBIs last night."

Brooke leaned against the door frame and scowled. "Good for him."

"Don't you like baseball?" E.J. grinned, tossing his empty bottle into the back of the wagon.

"No."

"Ought to have some team spirit," he mused and gave her knee a friendly squeeze. "The better he does, the more punch the campaign'll have. And if he gets into the series—"

"If he gets into the series," Brooke interrupted, "we have to wait until the end of October before we can start shooting."

"Well." E.J. stroked his chin. "That's show biz."

Brooke tried to glare, then chuckled. "Let's get back. I've got a shoot in the studio this afternoon. Want me to drive?"

"Naw." E.J. slammed the tailgate then headed for the driver's seat. "I like living."

"You're such a wimp, E.J."

"I know," he agreed cheerfully. "I've got this thing about traveling at the speed of light." After adjusting mirror-lensed sunglasses on his face he coaxed the station wagon's engine into life. It sputtered and groaned temperamentally while he crooned to it.

"Why don't you buy a new car?" Brooke demanded. "You get paid enough."

He patted the wagon's dash when the engine caught. "Loyalty. I've been cruising in this little darling for seven years. She'll be around when that flashy machine of yours is nuts and bolts."

Brooke shrugged, then tilted back her head to drain the bottle. E.J. was the only one who worked under her who dared any intimacy, which was probably the reason she not only allowed it but liked him for it. She also considered him one of the best men with a camera on the West Coast. He came from San Francisco where his father was a high school principal and his mother owned and operated a popular beauty salon. She had met them once and wondered how two such meticulous people could have produced a free-wheeling, loose-living man with a penchant for voluptuous women and B movies.

But then, Brooke mused, she'd never been able to understand families. Always she viewed them with perplexity and longing, as only one on the outside could fully understand. Settling back on the carefully patched seat, she began to plot out her strategy for her afternoon session.

"Heard you took in a Kings game the other night." E.J. caught her swift, piercing look and began to whistle tunelessly.

"So?"

"I saw Brighton Boyd at a party a couple of nights ago. Worked with him on a TV special last year. Nice guy."

Brooke remembered seeing the actor in the box next to hers and Claire's. She dropped her empty bottle on the already littered floor. "So?" she repeated coolly.

"Big Kings fan," E.J. went on, turning the radio up loud so that he had to shout over the top 40 rock. "Raved about Jones's homer—on a two-out, two-strike pitch. The man's a hell of a clutch hitter." While Brooke remained silent, E.J. tapped out the beat from the radio on the steering wheel. There was the glint of gold from a ring on his long dark fingers. "Brighton said Jones stared at you like a man who'd been hit with a blunt instrument. That Brighton, he sure does turn a phrase."

"Hmm." Brooke began to find the passing scenery fascinating.

"Said he came right over to your box chasing a foul. Had a few words to say."

Brooke turned her head and stared into E.J.'s mirrored glasses. "Are you pumping me, E.J.?"

"Hot damn! Can't pull anything over on you, Brooke; you're one sharp lady."

Despite herself she laughed. She knew a "no comment" would only cause speculation she'd like to avoid. Instead she stretched her legs out on the seat and treated it lightly. "He just wanted my name."

"And?"

"And nothing."

"Where'd you go with him?"

The faintest frown creased her brow. "I didn't say I went anywhere with him."

"He didn't ask your name because he was taking a census."

Brooke gave him a cool, haughty look that would have discouraged anyone else. "You're a gossipy old woman, E.J."

"Yep. You go to dinner with him?"

"Yes," she said on a sigh of surrender. "And that's all."

"Not as bright as he looks, then." He patted her sneakered foot. "Or maybe he felt funny about starting something up with the lady who'll be directing him."

''He didn't know,'' Brooke heard herself say before she could stop herself.

''Oh?''

''I didn't tell him.''

''Oh.'' This time the syllable was drawn out and knowing.

''I didn't think it was necessary,'' Brooke said heatedly. ''It was strictly a social meeting, and it gave me the opportunity to plan how best to film him.''

''Mm-hmm.''

She turned back in her seat and folded her arms. ''Shut up and drive, E.J.''

''Sure thing, boss.''

''As far as I'm concerned he can take his golden glove and smoking bat and sit on them.''

E.J. nodded wisely, enjoying himself. ''You know best.''

''He's conceited and cold and inconsiderate.''

''Must have been some evening,'' E.J. observed.

''I don't want to talk about it.'' Brooke kicked at the empty bottle on the floor.

''Okay,'' he said affably.

''He's the kind of man,'' she went on, ''who thinks a woman's just waiting to fall all over him just because he's moderately attractive and successful and has an average mind.''

''For a Rhodes scholar,'' E.J. mused as he slowed down for his exit.

''A what?''

''He's a Rhodes scholar.''

Brooke's mouth fell open, then shut with a bang. "He is not."

E.J. shrugged agreeably. "Well, that's what it said in *Sports View.* That was supposed to be the main reason he didn't start playing professional ball until he was twenty-two."

"Probably just a publicity hype," she muttered, but she knew better. She rode the rest of the way to the studio in frowning silence.

The de Marco California villa was an eyeful. Brooke decided that it had the dubious ability of making Claire's mansion look simple and discreet. It was huge, E-shaped and dazzling white with two inner courtyards. One held a grottolike pool complete with miniature waterfall, the other a sheltered garden rich with exotic scents.

When Brooke arrived, she could hear the high liquid sounds of harps and mixed conversation. People were ranged through the house, spilling outdoors and clustered in corners. Passing through the gold-toned parlor, she caught the mingling, heady scents of expensive perfumes and spiced food. There was the glitter of diamonds, swirl of silks and flash of tanned, pampered skin.

Brooke caught snatches of conversations as she strolled through, searching for the main buffet.

"But darling, he simply can't carry a series anymore. Did you see him at Ma Maison last week?"

"She'll sign. After that fiasco in England, she's itching to come back to Hollywood."

"Can't remember a line if you feed it to him intravenously."

''Left her for the wardrobe mistress.''

''My dear, have you ever seen *such* a dress!''

Hollywood, Brooke thought with halfhearted affection as she pounced on the remains of the pâté.

''I knew I'd find you here.''

Brooke turned her head as she speared a chunk of smoked beef. ''Hello, Claire,'' she managed over a mouthful of cracker. ''Nice party.''

''I suppose, as you always judge them by the menu.'' Claire gave her a long, appraising look. Brooke wore a buckskin jumpsuit, soft and smooth as cream, with a thick pewter belt cinched at her waist. She'd braided the hair at her temples and clipped it back over the flowing tousled mane, letting heavy pewter links dangle at her ears. Because she'd been distracted while applying it, she'd neglected her makeup and had only remembered to darken her eyes. As a result, they dominated her pale, sharp-featured face. ''Why is it you can wear the most outlandish outfits and still look marvelous?''

Brooke grinned and swallowed. ''I like yours, too,'' she said, noting that Claire was, as always, stylishly neat in pale-blue voile. ''What have they got to drink in this place?''

With a sigh, Claire motioned to a roving, red-suited waiter and chose two tulip glasses of champagne. ''Try to behave yourself. The de Marcos are very old-fashioned.''

''I'll be a credit to the company,'' Brooke promised and lifted her hand in acknowledgment of a wave from a stand-up comic she'd directed in a car commercial. ''Do you think I could get a plate?''

"Gorge later. Mr. Jones's agent is here, I want you to meet him."

"I hate talking to agents on an empty stomach. Oh, damn, there's Vera. I should have known she'd be here."

Brooke answered the icy smile from the slim honey-haired model who was the current embodiment of the American look. Their paths had crossed more than once, professionally and socially, and the women had taken an instant, lasting dislike to each other. "Keep your claws sheathed," Claire warned. "De Marco's going to be using her."

"Not with me," Brooke said instantly. "I'll take the ball player, Claire, but someone else is going to hold the leash on that one. I don't like my poison in small doses."

"We'll discuss it," Claire muttered then beamed a smile. "Lee, we were just looking for you. Lee Dutton, Brooke Gordon. She's going to be directing Parks." She placed a maternal hand on Brooke's arm. "My very best."

Brooke lifted an ironic brow. Claire was always lavish with praise in public and miserly with it behind closed doors. "Hello, Mr. Dutton."

Her hand was grabbed hard and pumped briskly. Discreetly, Brooke flexed her fingers while she made a swift survey. He was shorter than she was and rather round with thinning hair and startling black eyes. A creature of first impressions, she liked him on the spot.

"Here's to a long, successful relationship," he announced and banged his glass exuberantly against hers. "Parks is eager to begin."

"Is he?" Brooke smiled, remembering Parks's description of his venture into commercials. ''We're just as eager to have him.''

Claire sent her a brief warning look as she tucked her arm through Lee's. ''And where is he? Brooke and I are both anxious to meet him.''

''He has a hard time getting away from the ladies.'' Lee gave the proud, apologetic smile of a doting uncle. But the eyes on Brooke were shrewd.

''How awkward for him,'' she murmured into her glass. ''But I suppose he manages to live with it.''

''Brooke, you really must try the pâté.'' Claire sent her a teeth-clenched smile.

''I did,'' Brooke returned easily. ''Tell me more about Parks, Mr. Dutton. I can't tell you what a fan I am.''

''Oh, you follow baseball?''

Brooke tilted her glass again. ''Why, we were in the park only a few weeks ago, weren't we, Claire?''

''As a matter of fact.'' Claire didn't bother to try to outstare Brooke this time but turned to Lee. ''Do you get to many games?''

''Not enough,'' he admitted, knowing a game was afoot and willing to play. ''But I happen to have a few tickets for Sunday's game,'' he said, making a mental note to arrange for some. ''I'd love to escort both you ladies.''

Before Brooke could open her mouth, Claire doled out subtle punishment. ''There's nothing we'd like better.''

He caught Brooke's quick scowl before she smoothed her features. ''Well, there's Parks now.'' Lee bellowed for him, causing heads to turn before conversation buzzed again.

Parks's first reaction was surprise when he saw Brooke

standing beside his agent and the woman he knew was head of Thorton Productions. Then he experienced the same flare of reluctant desire he had felt on the other two occasions he'd seen her. He'd purposely let the days pass before he contacted her again, hoping the power of need would lessen. One glance at her told him it hadn't worked.

Apparently without hurry, he weaved through the crowd, stopping to exchange a few words when someone touched his arm, then gently disentangling himself. He'd learned, at an early age, how to keep from being cornered at a social occasion. In less than two minutes, Parks stood in front of Brooke.

Well done, Brooke thought. She answered Parks's smile cautiously, wondering what his reaction would be when they were introduced. She felt a jab of uneasiness then pushed it aside. After all, he'd been the one to wake her up at dawn and ask for a date.

"Parks, I want you to meet Claire Thorton, the lady who'll be producing your commercials." Lee laid his hand over Claire's in an unconsciously possessive gesture noticed only by Parks and Brooke. Parks was amused, Brooke annoyed.

"A pleasure, Ms. Thorton." He wanted to say he had expected a dragon from what he'd read of her professionally, not this soft-faced attractive woman with faded blue eyes. Instead, Parks smiled and accepted her hand.

"We're looking forward to working with you. I was just telling Mr. Dutton how much Brooke and I enjoyed your game against the Valiants a few weeks ago." Remembering his muttered demand for Brooke's name at the rail, Claire waited for the reaction.

''Oh?'' So this was her friend, he thought, turning to Brooke. With her face, he concluded she must be a regular for Thorton's commercials. ''Hello again.''

''Hello.'' Brooke found her hand claimed and held. Taking a hasty sip of champagne, she waited for the bomb to drop.

''Claire tells me Ms. Gordon is her best,'' Lee told Parks. ''Since you'll be working together closely, you'll want to get to know each other.''

''Will we?'' Parks ran his thumb along Brooke's palm.

''Only my best director for a project this important,'' Claire put in, watching them closely.

Brooke felt his thumb stop its casual caress, then his fingers tightened. There was no change in his face. To prevent a quick gasp of pain, she swallowed the rest of her champagne. ''So you direct commercials,'' he said smoothly.

''Yes.'' She tugged once to free her hand, but he only increased his grip.

''Fascinating.'' Casually, he plucked the empty glass from her other hand. ''Excuse us.'' Brooke found herself being dragged through the crowd of jewels and silks. Immediately, she quickened her pace so that it appeared she was walking with him rather than being led.

''Let go of me,'' she hissed, giving a nodding smile to another director. ''You're breaking my hand.''

''Consider it a preview of things to come.'' Parks pulled her through the open French doors, hoping to find a quiet spot. There was a three-piece band in the garden playing soft, dancing music. At least a dozen couples were taking advantage of it. Parks swore, but before he could maneuver her through the garden to a more private spot, he heard someone call her name. Immediately, he dragged her into his arms.

The hard contact with his chest stole her breath, the arm tight around her waist prevented her from finding any more. Ignoring the choking sound she made, Parks began to sway to the music. "Just wave to him," he ordered against her ear. "I'm not about to be interrupted with small talk."

Wanting to breathe again, Brooke obeyed. She was already planning revenge. When his grip lessened slightly, she drew in a sharp breath of air, letting it out on a string of abuse. "You overgrown bully, don't think you can drag me around just because you're this year's American hero. I'll only take it once, and I'll only warn you once. Don't you *ever* grab me again." Brooke stomped hard on his foot and was rewarded by having her air cut off again.

"You dance beautifully, Ms. Gordon," Parks whispered in her ear. He bit none too gently on the lobe. Between the fury and pain, Brooke felt a stir deep in her stomach. Oh, no, she thought, stiffening. Not again. The band switched to an up-tempo number but he continued to hold her close and sway.

"You're going to have a lot of explaining to do when I faint from lack of oxygen," she managed. Who would have thought that lanky body would be so hard, or the limber arms so strong?

"You won't faint," he muttered, slowly maneuvering her toward the edge of the garden. "And you're the one with the explaining to do."

She was released abruptly, but before Brooke could take

a breath, he was pulling her through a clump of azalea. "Look, you jerk..." Then she was back inside, dazed by bright lights and laughter. Without pausing, Parks dragged her through the center patio and into the adjoining courtyard.

There was no music here, except the liquid sound of the water falling into the grotto, and only a few couples more intent on themselves than on a man pulling a furious woman in his wake. Parks drew her close to the pool and into the shadows behind the high wall. Brooke was effectively sandwiched between him and the smooth rocks.

"So you like to play games," he murmured.

For the first time she was able to lift her face and stare into his. Her eyes glittered in the moonlight. "I don't know what you're talking about."

"No?"

She had expected him to be annoyed, but she hadn't expected this smoldering fury. It was in his eyes, in the hard lines of his face, in the poised readiness of his body. When she felt her heart begin to thud uncomfortably, she became only more defensive. "You made all the moves," she tossed out. "You *demanded* that I give you my name. You called *me* at six o'clock in the morning for a date. All I did was let Claire drag me to a ball game."

She made an attempt to push by him and found herself pressed back against the wall by a firm hand on her chest. "You were sizing me up," he said slowly. "At the game, at dinner. Tell me, how did I come out?"

Brooke put her hand to his wrist, but was surprised when he let her push his hand away. She began a careless recital she knew would infuriate him. "You move more like a dancer than an athlete—it'll be a plus on film. Your build is good, it'll sell clothes. You can be charming at times, and your face is attractive without being handsome. That could sell anything. You have a certain sexuality that should appeal to women who'd like their men to have it, too. They're the primary target, as women still do the bulk of buying in ready-to-wear."

Her tone had been schooled to annoy. Even so, Parks couldn't prevent his temper from rising. "Do I get a rating?"

"Naturally." The bitten-off words pleased her enormously. It was a small payment for the scene on her porch, but it was payment. "Your popularity quotient is fair at the moment. It should get higher after the first commercial is aired. Claire seems to think if you could get into the World Series and do something outstanding, it would help."

"I'll see what I can do," he said dryly. "Now, why didn't you tell me who you were?"

"I did."

He leaned closer. She caught a trace of sharp cologne over the smell of wet summer leaves. "No, you didn't."

"I told you I make commercials."

"Knowing I'd conclude you were an actress."

"Your conclusions are your own problem," Brooke told him with a shrug. "I never said I was an actress." She heard a woman's laugh muffled in the distance and the rush of water into the pool beside her. The odds, she mused, were not in her favor at the moment. "I don't see what difference it makes."

"I don't like games," Parks said precisely, "unless I know the players."

"Then we won't play," Brooke countered. "Your job is to do what I tell you—no more, no less."

Parks controlled a wave of fury and nodded. "On the set." He caught the hair at her waist, then let it slide through his hands. "And off?"

"And off, nothing." She'd put more emphasis on the last word than she had intended to. It showed a weakness she could only hope he didn't notice.

"No." Parks stepped closer so that she had to tilt back her head to keep her eyes level with his. "I don't think I like those rules. Let's try mine."

Brooke was ready this time for the sneak attack on her senses. He wouldn't be permitted to seduce her, make her tremble with those feather-light teasing kisses on her skin. With a cool, hard stare, she dared him to try.

He returned the look as seconds dragged on. She caught the glint of challenge in his eyes but didn't see the slow curve of his lips. No man had ever been able to meet her stare so directly or for so long. For the first time in years, Brooke felt a weakness in her primary defense.

Then he did what he had wanted to do from the first moment he had seen her. Parks dove his hands into the lushness of her hair, letting them sink into the softness before he dragged her against him. Their eyes clashed a moment longer, even as he lowered his lips and savaged hers.

Brooke's vision blurred. She struggled to bring it back into sharp focus, to concentrate on that one sense to prevent her others from being overpowered. She fought not to taste the hot, demanding flavor of his lips, to feel the quick, almost brutal nip of his teeth that would tempt her lips to part. She didn't want to hear her own helpless moan. Then his tongue was plundering, enticing hers to answer in a seduction totally different from the teasing gentleness of his first embrace. She struggled against him, but her movements only caused more heat to flare from the friction of her body on his.

Gradually, the kiss altered. The hard pressure became sweet. He nibbled at her mouth, as if savoring the flavor, sucking gently, though his arms kept her pinned tight. She lost even her blurred vision, and her will to resist went with it.

Parks felt the change, her sudden pliancy. Her surrender excited him. She wasn't a woman to relinquish control easily, yet both times he had held her, he'd prized it from her. With gentleness, he realized, suddenly aware that the anger had fled from his body and his mouth. It was gentleness that won her, whereas force would only be met with force. Now he didn't want to think—not for a moment. He wanted only to lose himself in the soft give of her body, the white-silk scent that poured from her and the dusky flavor of her mouth. They were all the seduction of woman, only intensified by her surrender.

Brooke felt the liquid weight in her limbs, the slow insistent tug in her thighs before the muscles went lax. Her mouth clung to his, yearning for more of the magic it could bring with the gentle play of tongue and teeth. His hands began a slow exploration of her body, kneading over the soft material. When she felt him loosen the narrow zipper that ran from her throat to her waist, she roused herself to protest.

"No." The words came on a gasp of breath as his fingers slid along her skin.

Parks gathered her hair in one hand, drawing her head back so that his eyes met hers again. "I have to touch you." Watching her, he glided his fingers over her breast, pausing briefly on the taut point before he roamed down to her flat, quivering stomach. "One day I'll touch all of you," he murmured. "Inch by inch. I'm going to feel your skin heat under my hands." His fingers trailed back to her breast, leaving a path of awakened flesh in their wake. "I'm going to watch your face when I make love to you."

Bending, he touched his lips to hers again, tasting her breath as it shuddered into his mouth. Very slowly, he drew up the zipper, letting his knuckles graze along her skin. Then he ran his hands up her back until their bodies fit together again.

"Kiss me, Brooke." He rubbed his nose lightly against hers. "Really kiss me."

Tingling from his touch, aroused by the whispered words, she pressed her open mouth to his. Her tongue sought his, hungry for the moist dark tastes that had already seeped inside of her. He waited for her demands, her aggressions, feeling them build as her body strained against his. With a groan of pleasure, Brooke tangled her fingers in his hair, wanting to drag him closer. When he knew his chain of control was on its last link, Parks drew her away. He'd learned more of her, but not enough. Not yet. And he wasn't going to forget that he had a small score to settle with her.

''When the camera's rolling, it's your game and your rules.'' He cupped her chin in his hand, wondering how many times he'd be able to walk away from her when his body was aching to have her. ''When it's not,'' he continued quietly, ''the rules are mine.''

Brooke took a shaky breath. ''I don't play games.''

Parks smiled, running a fingertip over her swollen mouth. ''Everyone does,'' he corrected. ''Some make a career out of it, and they aren't all on ball fields.'' Dropping his hand, he stepped back from her. ''We both have a job to do. Maybe we're not too thrilled about it at the moment, but I have a feeling that won't make any difference in how well you work.''

''No,'' Brooke agreed shortly. ''It won't. I can detest you and still make you look fantastic on the screen.''

He grinned. ''Or make me look like an idiot if it suited you.''

She couldn't prevent a small smile from forming. ''You're very perceptive.''

''But you won't, because you're a pro. Whatever happens between us personally won't make you direct any differently.''

''I'll do my job,'' Brooke stated as she stepped around him. ''And nothing's going to happen between us personally.'' She looked up sharply when a friendly arm was dropped over her shoulder.

''I guess we'll just wait and see about that.'' Parks sent her another amiable grin. ''Have you eaten?''

Brooke frowned at him dubiously. ''No.''

He gave her shoulder a fraternal pat. ''I'll get you a plate.''

Chapter 4

Brooke couldn't believe she was spending a perfectly beautiful Sunday afternoon at a ball game. What was more peculiar was that she was enjoying it. She was well aware that she was being punished for the few veiled sarcastic remarks she had tossed off at the de Marco party, but after the first few innings, she found that Billings was right. There was a bit more to it than swinging a bat and running around in circles.

During her first game, Brooke had been too caught up in the atmosphere, the people, then in her initial impressions of Parks. Now she opened her mind to the game itself and enjoyed. Being a survivor, whenever she was faced with doing something she didn't want to do, Brooke simply conditioned herself to *want* to do it. She had no patience with people who allowed themselves to be miserable when it was so simple to turn a situation around to your advantage. If it wasn't always possible to enjoy, she could learn. It pleased her to be doing both.

The game had more subtlety than she had first realized, and more strategy. Brooke never ceased to be intrigued by strategy. It became obvious that there were variables to the contest, dozens of ifs, slices of chance counterbalancing skill. In a game of inches, luck couldn't be overlooked. This had an appeal for her because she had always considered luck every bit as vital as talent in winning, no matter what the game.

And there were certain aspects of the afternoon, beyond the balls and strikes, that fanned her interest.

The crowd was no less enthusiastic or vocal than it had been on her first visit to Kings Stadium. If anything, Brooke reflected, the people were more enthusiastic—even slightly wild. She wondered if their chants and screams and whistles took on a tone of delirium because the score was tied 1-1, and had been since the first inning. Lee called it an example of a superior defensive game.

Lee Dutton was another aspect of the afternoon that intrigued her. He seemed—on the surface—a genial, rather unkempt sort of man with a faint Brooklyn accent that lingered from his youth. He wore a golf shirt and checked pants, which only accented his tubbiness. Brooke might have passed him off as a cute middle-aged man had it not been for the sharp black eyes. She liked him…with a minor reservation—he seemed inordinately attentive to Claire.

It occurred to Brooke that he found a great many occasions to touch—Claire's soft manicured hands, her round shoulder, even her gabardine-clad knee. What was more intriguing to Brooke was that Claire didn't, as was her habit, freeze Lee's tentative advances with an icy smile or a stingingly polite word. As far as Brooke could tell, Claire seemed to be enjoying them—or perhaps she was overlooking them because of the importance of the de Marco account and Parks Jones. In either case, Brooke determined to keep an eye on her friend, and the agent. It wasn't unheard-of for a woman approaching fifty to be naive of men and therefore susceptible.

If she were to be truthful, Brooke would have to admit she enjoyed watching Parks. There was no doubt he was in his element in the field, eyes shaded by a cap, glove in his hand. Just as he had been in his element, she remembered, at the glossy party at the de Marco villa. He hadn't seemed out of place in the midst of ostentatious wealth, sipping vintage champagne or handling cocktail party conversation. And why should he? she mused. After their last encounter, Brooke had made it her business to find out more about him.

He'd come from money. Big money. Parkinson Chemicals was a third-generation, multimillion-dollar conglomerate that dealt in everything from aspirin to rocket fuel. He'd been born with a silver spoon in one hand and a fat portfolio in the other. His two sisters had married well, one to a restauranteur who had been her business partner before he became her husband, the other to a vice president of Parkinson attached to the Dallas branch. But the heir to Parkinson, the man who carried the old family name in front of the less unique Jones, had had a love affair with baseball.

The love affair hadn't diminished during his studies at

Oxford under a Rhodes scholarship; it had simply been postponed. When Parks had graduated, he'd gone straight to the Kings' training camp—Brooke had to wonder how his family had felt about that—and there had been drafted. After less than a year on the Kings' farm team, he'd been brought up to the majors. There he had remained, for a decade.

So he didn't play for the money, Brooke mused, but because he enjoyed the game. Perhaps that was why he played with such style and steadiness.

She remembered, too, her impressions of him at the de Marcos'—charming, then ruthless, then casually friendly. And none of it, Brooke concluded, was an act. Above all else, Parks Jones was in complete control, on or off the diamond. Brooke respected that, related to it, while she couldn't help wondering how the two of them would juggle their need to be in charge when they began to work together. If nothing else, she mused as she crunched down on a piece of ice, it would be an interesting association.

Brooke watched him now as he stood on the bag at second while the opposing team brought out a relief pitcher. Parks had started off the seventh inning with a leadoff single, then had advanced to second when the next batter walked. Brooke could feel the adrenaline of the crowd pulsing while Parks talked idly with the second baseman.

"If they take this one," Lee was saying, "the Kings lock up the division." He slipped his hand over Claire's. "We need these runs."

"Why did they change pitchers?" Brooke demanded.

She thought of how furious she would be if someone pulled her off a job before it was finished.

''There's two on and nobody out.'' Lee gave her an easy paternal smile. ''Mitchell was slowing down—he'd walked two last inning and was only saved from having runs score by that rifle shot the center fielder sent home.'' Reaching in his shirt pocket, he brought out a cigar in a thin protective tube. ''I think you'll see the Kings going to the bullpen in the eighth.''

''I wouldn't switch cameramen in the middle of a shoot,'' Brooke mumbled.

''You would if he couldn't focus the lens anymore,'' Lee countered, grinning at her.

With a laugh, Brooke dove her hand into the bag of peanuts he offered her. ''Yeah, I guess I would.''

The strategy proved successful, as the relief man shut down the next three batters, leaving Parks and his teammate stranded on base. The crowds groaned, swore at the umpire and berated the batters.

''Now there's sportsmanship,'' Brooke observed, casting a look over her shoulder when someone called the batter, who struck out to end the inning, a bum—and other less kind names.

Lee gave a snort of laughter as he draped his arm casually over Claire's shoulders. ''You should hear them when we're losing, kid.''

The lifted-brow look Brooke gave Claire at the gesture was returned blandly. ''Enthusiasm comes in all forms,'' Claire observed. With a smile for Lee, she settled back against his arm to watch the top of the next inning.

Definitely an odd couple, Brooke mused; then she assumed her habitual position of elbows on rail. Parks didn't glance her way. He had only once—at the beginning of the game when he took the field. The look had been long and direct before he had turned away, and since then it was as though he wasn't even aware of her. She hated to admit it irked her, hated to admit that she would have liked to engage in that silent battle of eye to eye. He was the first man she *wanted* to spar with, though she had sparred with many since her first naive encounter ten years before. There was something exciting in the mind game, particularly since Parks had a mind she both envied and admired.

Lee was on target, as the Kings went to the bullpen when the starting pitcher walked two with one man out. Brooke shifted closer to the edge of her seat to watch Parks during the transition. What does he think about out there? she wondered.

God, what I wouldn't give for a cold shower and a gallon of beer, Parks thought as the sun beat down on the back of his neck. He'd been expecting the change of pitchers and was pleased with the choice. Ripley did well what a reliever was there to do—throw hard and fast. He gave a seemingly idle glance toward the runner at second. That could be trouble, he reflected, doing a quick mental recall of his opponent's statistics. The ability to retain and call out facts had always come naturally to Parks. And not just batting averages and stolen bases. Basically, he only forgot what he wanted to forget. The rest was stockpiled, waiting until he needed it. The trick had alternately fascinated and infuriated his family and friends, so that he generally kept it to himself. At the moment, he could remember Ripley's earned-run average, his win-loss ratio, the batting average of the man waiting to step into the batter's box and the scent of Brooke's perfume.

He hadn't forgotten that she was sitting a few yards away. The awareness of her kindled inside of him—a not quite pleasant sensation. It was more of an insistent pressure, like the heat of the sun on the back of his neck. It was another reason he longed for a cool shower. Watching Ripley throw his warm-up pitches to the catcher, Parks allowed himself to imagine what it would be like to undress her—slowly—in the daylight, just before her body went from limp surrender to throbbing excitement. Soon, he promised himself; then he forced Brooke to the back of his mind as the batter stepped up to the plate.

Ripley blew the first one by the batter—hard and straight. Parks knew that Ripley didn't throw any fancy pitches, just the fast ball and the curve. He was either going to overpower the hitters, or with the lineup of right-handers coming up, Parks was going to be very busy. He positioned himself another step back on the grass, going by instinct. He noted the base runner had a fat lead as the batter chipped the next pitch off. The runner was nearly at third before the foul was called. Ripley looked back over his shoulder at second, slid his eyes to first, then fired the next pitch.

It was hit hard, smashing into the dirt in front of third then bouncing high. There was never any opportunity to think, only to act. Parks leaped, just managing to snag the ball. The runner was coming into third in a headfirst slide. Parks didn't have the time to admire his guts before he tagged the base seconds before the runner's hand grabbed it. He heard the third base ump bellow, "Out!" as he vaulted over the runner and fired the ball at the first baseman.

While the crowd went into a frenzy, Brooke remained seated and watched. She didn't even notice that Lee had given Claire a resounding, exuberant kiss. The double play had taken only seconds—that impressed her. It also disconcerted her to discover that her pulse was racing. If she closed her eyes, she could still hear the cheers from the fans, smell the scent of sun-warmed beer and see, in slow motion, the strong, sweeping moves of Parks's body. She didn't need an instant replay to visualize the leap and stretch, the shifting of muscle. She knew a ball player had to be agile and quick, but how many of them had that dancerlike grace? Brooke caught herself making a mental note to bring a camera to the next game, then realized she had already decided to come back again. Was it Parks, she brooded, or baseball that was luring her back?

"He's something, isn't he?" Lee leaned over Claire to give Brooke a slap on the back.

"Something," Brooke murmured. She turned her head enough to look at him. "Was that a routine play?"

Lee snorted. "If you've got ice water for blood."

"Does he?"

As he drew on a cigar, Lee seemed to consider it. He gave Brooke a long, steady look. "On the field," he stated with a nod. "Parks is one of the most controlled, disciplined men I know. Of course"—the look broke with his quick smile—"I handle a lot of actors."

"Bless them," Claire said and crossed her short, slim legs. "I believe we all agree that we hope Parks takes to this, ah, alternate career with as much energy as he shows in his baseball.''

''If he has ten percent of this skill''—Brooke gestured toward the field—''in front of the camera, I'll be able to work with him.''

''I think you'll be surprised,'' Lee commented dryly, ''at just what Parks is capable of.''

With a shrug, Brooke leaned on the rail again. ''We'll see if he can take direction.''

Brooke waited, with the tension of the crowd seeping into her, as the game went into the bottom of the ninth inning. Still tied 1-1, neither team seemed able to break through the defensive skill of the other. It should have been boring, she mused, even tedious. But she was on the edge of her seat and her pulse was still humming. She wanted them to win. With a kind of guilty surprise, Brooke caught herself just before she shouted at the plate umpire for calling strike three on the leadoff batter. It's just the atmosphere, she told herself with a frown. She'd always been a sucker for atmosphere. But when the second batter came up, she found herself gripping the rail, willing him to get a hit.

''This might go into extra innings,'' Lee commented.

''There's only one out,'' Brooke snapped, not bothering to turn around. She didn't see the quick grin Lee cast at Claire.

On a three-and-two pitch, the batter hit a bloop single to center. Around Brooke, the fans went berserk. He might have hit a home run from the way they're reacting, she thought, trying to ignore the fast pumping of her own blood. This time Brooke said nothing as the pitcher was pulled. How do they stand the tension? she wondered, watching the apparently relaxed players as the new relief warmed up. Base runners talked idly with the opposition. She thought that if she were in competition, she wouldn't be so friendly with the enemy.

The crowd settled down to a hum that became a communal shout with every pitch thrown. The batter hit one deep, so deep Brooke was amazed at the speed with which the right fielder returned it to the infield.

The batter was content with a single, but the base runner had eaten up the distance to third with the kind of gritty speed Brooke admired.

Now the crowd didn't quiet, but kept up a continual howl that echoed and reverberated as Parks came to bat. The pressure, Brooke thought, must be almost unbearable. Yet nothing showed in his face but that dangerous kind of concentration she'd seen once or twice before. She swallowed, aware that her heart was hammering in her throat. Ridiculous, she told herself once, then surrendered.

"Come on, damn it," she muttered, "smack one out of here."

He took the first pitch, a slow curve that just missed the corner. The breath that she'd been holding trembled out. The next he cut at, fouling it back hard against the window of the press box. Brooke clamped down on her bottom lip and mentally uttered a stream of curses. Parks coolly held up a hand for time, then bent to tie his shoe. The stadium echoed with his name. As if deaf to the yells, he stepped back into the box to take up his stance.

He hit it high and deep. Brooke was certain it was a

repeat of his performance in her first game, then she saw the ball begin to drop just short of the fence.

"He's going to tag up. He'll tag up!" she heard Lee shouting as the center fielder caught Parks's fly at the warning track. Before Brooke could swear, the fans were shouting, not in fury but in delight. The moment the runner crossed the plate, players from the Kings' dugout swarmed out on the field.

"But Parks is out," Brooke said indignantly.

"The sacrifice fly scored the run," Lee explained.

Brooke gave him a haughty look. "I realize that"—only because she had crammed a few basic rules into her head—"but it hardly seems fair that Parks is out."

Chuckling, Lee patted her head. "He earned another RBI and the fleeting gratitude of a stadium full of Kings fans. He was one for three today, so his average won't suffer much."

"Brooke doesn't think much of rules," Claire put in, rising.

"Because they're usually made up by people who don't have the least idea what they're doing." A little annoyed with herself for becoming so involved, she stood, swinging her canvas bag over her shoulder.

"I don't know if Parks would agree with you," Lee told her. "He's lived by the rules for most of his life. Gets to be a habit."

"To each his own," she said casually. She wondered if Lee was aware that Parks was also a man who could seduce and half undress a woman behind the fragile covering of a rock wall in the middle of a crowded, glitzy

Hollywood party. It seemed to her Parks was more a man who made up his own rules.

''Why don't we go down to the locker room and congratulate him?'' Genially, he hooked his arms through Claire's and Brooke's, steamrolling them through the still cheering crowd.

Lee worked his way into the stadium's inner sanctum with a combination of panache and clout. Reporters were swarming, carrying microphones, cameras or notepads. Each one was badgering or flattering a sweaty athlete in the attempt to get a quote. In the closed-in area, Brooke considered the noise level to be every bit as high as it had been in the open stadium. Lockers slammed, shouts reverberated, laughter flowed in a kind of giddy relief. Each man knew the tension would return soon enough during the play-offs. They were going to enjoy the victory of the moment to its fullest.

''Yeah, if I hadn't saved Biggs from an error in the seventh inning,'' the first baseman told a reporter, deadpan, ''it might have been a whole different ball game.''

Biggs,the shortstop, retaliated by heaving a damp towel at his teammate. ''Snyder can't catch a ball unless it drops into his mitt. The rest of us make him look good.''

''I've saved Parks from fifty-three errors this season,'' Snyder went on blandly, drawing the sweaty towel from his face. ''Guess his arm must be going. Thing is, some of the hitters are so good they just keep smacking the ball right into Parks's mitt. If you watch the replay of today's game, you'll see what fantastic aim they have.'' Someone dumped a bucket of water on his head, but Snyder continued without breaking rhythm. ''You might notice how well I place the ball in the right fielder's mitt. That takes more practice.''

Brooke spotted Parks, surrounded by reporters. His uniform was filthy, streaked with dirt, while his face fared little better. The smudges of black under his eyes gave him a slightly wicked look. Without the cap his hair curled freely, darkened with sweat. But his face and body were relaxed. A smile lingered on his lips as he spoke. That battlefield intensity was gone from his eyes, she noted, as if it had never existed. If she hadn't seen it, hadn't experienced it from him, Brooke would have sworn the man wasn't capable of any form of ruthlessness. Yet he was, she reminded herself, and it wouldn't be smart to forget it.

''With only four games left in the regular season,'' Parks stated, ''I'll be satisfied to end up with a three eighty-seven average for the year.''

''If you bat five hundred in those last games—''

Parks shot the reporter a mild grin. ''We'll have to see about that.''

''A little wind out there today and that game-winning sacrifice fly would've been a game-winning home run.''

''That's the breaks.''

''What was the pitch?''

''Inside curve,'' he responded easily. ''A little high.''

''Were you trying for a four-bagger, Parks?''

He grinned again, his expression altering only slightly when he spotted Brooke. ''With one out and runners on the corners, I just wanted to keep the ball off the ground. Anything deep, and Kinjinsky scores...unless he wants the Lead Foot Award.''

"Lead Foot Award?"

"Ask Snyder," Parks suggested. "He's the current holder." With another smile, Parks effectively eased himself away. "Lee." He nodded to his agent while running a casual finger down Brooke's arm. She felt the shock waves race through her, and only barely managed not to jerk away. "Ms. Thorton. Nice to see you again." His only greeting to Brooke was a slow smile as he caught the tip of her hair between his thumb and forefinger. She thought again it was wise to remember he wasn't as safe as he appeared.

"Hell of a game, Parks," Lee announced. "You gave us an entertaining afternoon."

"We aim to please," he murmured, still looking at Brooke.

"Claire and I are going out to dinner. Perhaps you and Brooke would like to join us?"

Before Brooke could register surprise at Claire having a date with Lee Dutton, or formulate an excuse against making it a foursome, Parks spoke up. "Sorry, Brooke and I have plans."

Turning her head, she shot Parks a narrowed look. "I don't recall our making any plans."

Smiling, he gave her a brief tug. "You'll have to learn to write things down. Why don't you just wait in your box? I'll be out in half an hour." Without giving her a chance to protest, Parks strolled off toward the showers.

"What incredible nerve," Brooke grumbled, only to be given a sharp but discreet elbow in the ribs by Claire.

"Sorry you can't join us, dear," she said sweetly. "But

then you're not fond of Chinese food in any case. And Lee's going to show me his collection first.''

''Collection?'' Brooke repeated blankly as she was steered into the narrow corridor.

''We've a mutual passion.'' Claire gave Lee a quick and surprisingly flirtatious smile. ''For Oriental art. Can you find your way back to the seats?''

''I'm not a complete dolt,'' Brooke muttered, while giving Lee a skeptical stare.

''Well then.'' Casually, Claire tucked her hand into Lee's beefy arm. ''I'll see you Monday.''

''Have a good time, kid,'' Lee called over his shoulder as Claire propelled him away.

''Thanks a lot.'' Stuffing her hands in her pockets, Brooke worked her way up, then out to the lower level, third-base box. ''Thanks a hell of a lot,'' she repeated and stared out at the empty diamond.

There were a few maintenance workers scooping up the debris in the stands with humming heavy-duty cleaners, but other than that the huge open area was deserted. Finding it strangely appealing, Brooke discovered her annoyance waning. An hour before, the air had been alive, throbbing with the pulse of thousands. Now it was serene, with only the faintest trace of the crowd—the lingering odor of humanity, a whiff of salted popcorn, a few discarded cardboard containers. She leaned back against the rail, more interested in the empty stadium than the empty field.

When had it been built? she wondered. How many generations had crammed themselves into the seats and aisles to watch the games? How many thousands of gallons of beer had traveled along the rows of seats? She laughed a little, amused by her own whimsy. When a player stopped playing, did he come here to watch and remember? She thought Parks would. The game, she concluded, would get into your blood. Even she hadn't been immune to it…or, she thought wryly, to him.

Brooke tossed her head back, letting her hair fall behind her. The shadows were lengthening, but the heat still had the sticky, sweltering capacity of high afternoon. She didn't mind—she hated being cold. Habitually, she narrowed her eyes and let herself visualize how she would approach the stadium on film. Empty, she thought, with the echo of cheers, the sound of a ball cracking off a bat, a banner left behind to flutter in the breeze. She'd use the maintenance workers, sucking up the boxes and cups and bags. She might title it *Afterthought,* and there'd be no telling if the home team had left the field vanquished or victorious. What mattered would be the perpetuity of the game, the people who played it and the people who watched.

Brooke sensed him before she heard him—only an instant, but the instant was enough to scatter her thoughts and to bring her eyes swerving toward him. Immediately, all sense of the scene she had been setting vanished from her mind. No one else had ever had the power to do that to her. The fact that Parks did baffled her nearly as much as it infuriated her. For Brooke, her work was the one stability in her life—nothing and no one was allowed to tamper with it. Defensively, she straightened, meeting his stare head-on as he walked down to her in the loose, rangy stride that masked over a decade of training.

She expected him to greet her with some smart remark. Brooke was prepared for that. She considered he might greet her casually, as if his lie in the locker room had been perfect truth. She was prepared for that, too.

She wasn't prepared for him to walk directly to her, bury his hands in her hair and crush her against him in a long, hotly possessive kiss. Searing flashes of pleasure rocketed through her. Molten waves of desire overpowered surprise before it truly had time to register. His mouth pressed against hers in an absolute command that barely hid a trace of desperation. It was that desperation, more than the authority, that Brooke found herself responding to. The need to be needed was strong in her—she had always considered it her greatest weakness. And she was weak now, with the sharp scent of his skin in her senses, the dark taste of his mouth on her tongue, the feel of his shower-damp hair on her fingers.

Slowly, Parks drew away, waiting for her heavy lids to lift. Though his eyes never left hers, Brooke felt as though he looked at all of her once, thoroughly. "I want you." He said it calmly, though the fierce look was back on his face.

"I know."

Parks ran a hand through her hair again, from the crown to the tips. "I'm going to have you."

Steadying a bit, Brooke stepped out of his arms. "That I don't know."

Smiling, Parks continued to caress her hair. "Don't you?"

"No," Brooke returned with such firmness that Parks lifted a brow.

"Well," he considered, "I suppose it could be a very pleasant experience to convince you."

Brooke tossed her head to free her hair of his seeking fingers. "Why did you lie to Lee about our having plans tonight?"

"Because I'd spent nine long, hot innings thinking about making love to you."

Again he said it calmly, with just a hint of a smile on his lips, but Brooke realized he was quite serious. "Well, that's direct and to the point."

"You prefer things that way, don't you?"

"Yes," she agreed, settling back against the rail again. "So let me do the same for you. We're going to be working together for several months on a very big project that involves a number of people. I'm very good at my job and I intend to see that you're very good at yours."

"So?"

Her eyes flashed at his amused tone, but Brooke continued. "So personal involvements interfere with professional judgment. As your director, I have no intention of becoming your lover, however briefly."

"Briefly?" Parks repeated, studying her. "Do you always anticipate the length of your relationships beforehand? I think," he continued slowly, "you're more of a romantic than that."

"I don't care what you think," she snapped, "as long as you understand."

"I understand," Parks agreed, beginning to. "You're evading the issue."

"I certainly am not!" Temper flared, reflecting in her stance and her eyes as well as her voice. "I'm telling you straight out that I'm not interested. If that bruises your ego, too bad.''

Parks grabbed her arm when she would have swept by him. ''You know,'' he began in a careful tone that warned of simmering anger, ''you infuriate me. I can't remember the last time a woman affected me that way.''

''I'm not surprised.'' Brooke jerked her arm out of his hold. ''You've been too busy devastating them with your charm.''

''And you're too worried about being dumped to have any kind of a relationship.''

She made a quick, involuntary sound, as if she'd been struck. Cheeks pale, eyes dark, she stared at him before she shoved him aside to race up the stairs. Parks caught her before she'd made it halfway. Though he turned her back to face him firmly, his touch was gentle.

''Raw nerve?'' he murmured, feeling both sympathy and guilt. It wasn't often he lost control enough to say something he'd have to apologize for. Eyes dry and hurting, Brooke glared at him. ''I'm sorry.''

''Just let me go.''

''Brooke.'' He wanted to pull her into his arms and comfort, but knew she wouldn't accept it. ''I am sorry. I don't make a habit of punching women.''

It wasn't charm, but sincerity. After a moment, Brooke let out a long breath. ''All right. I usually take a punch better than that.''

''Can we take off the gloves—at least for the rest of the day?'' How deep was the hurt? Parks wondered. And how long would it take to win her trust?

''Maybe,'' Brooke returned cautiously.

"How about dinner?"

She responded to the smile before she realized it. "My weakness."

"We'll start there, then. How do you feel about tacos?"

She allowed him to take her hand. "Who's buying?"

They sat outdoors at a busy fast-food franchise with tiny metal tables and hard stools. Sounds of traffic and blaring car radios rolled over them. Brooke relaxed when she ate, Parks noted, wondering if she were consciously aware of the dropping of guards. He didn't think so. The relaxation was the same when she sat in an elegant restaurant with wine and exotic food as it was in a greasy little take-out with sloppy tacos and watered-down sodas in paper cups. After handing her another napkin, Parks decided to do some casual probing.

"Did you grow up in California?"

"No." Brooke drew more soda through her straw. "You did."

"More or less." Remembering how skilled she was in evading or changing the subject, Parks persisted. "Why did you move to L.A.?"

"It's warm," she said immediately. "It's crowded."

"But you live miles out of town in the middle of nowhere."

"I like my privacy. How did your family feel about you choosing baseball over Parkinson Chemicals?"

He smiled a little, enjoying the battle for control. "Stunned. Though I'd told them for years what I intended to do. My father thought, still thinks, it's a phase. What does your family think about you directing commercials?"

Brooke set down her cup. "I don't have any family."

Something in her tone warned him this was a tender area. "Where did you grow up?"

"Here and there." Quickly, she began to stuff used napkins into the empty cups. Parks caught her hand before she could rise.

"Foster homes?"

Eyes darkening with anger, Brooke stared at him. "Why are you pressing?"

"Because I want to know who you are," he said softly. "We could be friends before we're lovers."

"Let go of my hand."

Instead of obliging, Parks gave her a curious look. "Do I make you nervous?"

"You make me furious," she tossed back, evading one truth with another. "I can't be around you for more than ten minutes without getting mad."

Parks grinned. "I know the feeling. Still, it's stimulating."

"I don't want to be stimulated," Brooke said evenly. "I want to be comfortable."

With a half laugh, Parks turned her hand over, brushing his lips lightly over the palm. "I don't think so," he murmured, watching her reaction over their joined hands. "You're much too alive to settle for comfortable."

"You don't know me."

"Exactly my point." He leaned a bit closer. "Who are you?"

"What I've made myself."

Parks nodded. "I see a strong, independent woman with lots of drive and ambition. I also see a woman who chooses a quiet, isolated spot for her home, who knows how to laugh and mean it, who forgives just as quickly as she angers.'' As he spoke Parks watched her brows lower. She wasn't angry now, but thoughtful and wary. He felt a bit like a man trying to gain the confidence of a dove who might fly away at any time or choose to nestle in the palm of his hand. ''She interests me.''

After a moment, Brooke let out a long breath. Perhaps if she told him a little, she considered, he'd leave it at that. ''My mother wasn't married,'' she began briskly. ''I'm told that after six months she got tired of lugging a baby around and dumped me on her sister. I don't remember a great deal about my aunt, I was six when she turned me over to social services. What I do remember is being hungry and not very warm. I went into my first foster home.'' She shrugged then pushed away the debris that littered the table. ''It wasn't too bad. I was there for little more than a year before I got shuffled to the next one. I was in five altogether from the age of six to seventeen. Some were better than others, but I never belonged. A lot of that may have been my fault.''

Brooke sighed, not pleased to remember. ''Not all foster parents take in children for the money. Some of them—most of them,'' she amended, ''are very kind, loving people. I just never felt a part, because I always knew it would be temporary, that my sister or brother of the moment was real and I was...transient. As a result I was difficult. Maybe I challenged the people whose home I was placed in to want me—for me, not out of pity or social obligation or the extra dollars my living with them would bring in.

''My last two years in high school I lived on a farm in

Ohio with a nice couple who had an angelic son who would yank my hair when his mother's back was turned." A quick grimace. "I left as soon as I graduated from high school, worked my way cross-country waiting tables. It only took me four months to get to L.A." She met Parks's quiet, steady look and suddenly flared. "Don't feel sorry for me."

The ultimate insult, he mused, taking her rigid hand in his. "I wasn't. I was wondering how many people would have had the guts to try to make their own life at seventeen, and how many would have the strength to really do it. At the same age I wanted to head for the Florida training camps. Instead I was on a plane heading for college."

"Because you had an obligation," Brooke countered. "I didn't. If I had had the chance to go to college..." She trailed off. "In any case, we've both had a decade in our careers."

"And you can have several more if you like," Parks pointed out. "I can't. One more season."

"Why?" she demanded. "You'll only be..."

"Thirty-five," he finished with a wry smile. "I promised myself ten years ago that's when I'd stop. There aren't many of us who can play past forty like Mays."

"Yes, it's obvious you play like an old man," she returned dryly.

"I intend to stop before I do."

Taking a straw, she began to pleat it while she studied him. "Quit while you're ahead?"

"That's the idea."

That she could understand. "Does giving it up with half your life ahead of you bother you?"

''I intend to do something with the second half, but at times it does. Other times I think about all those summer evenings I'll have free. Do you like the beach?''

''I don't get there often, but yes.'' She thought about the long, hot commercial she'd just filmed. ''With occasional exceptions,'' she added.

''I have a place on Maui.'' Unexpectedly he leaned over, caressing her cheek with fingers that were whisper soft and undeniably possessive. ''I'm going to take you there one day.'' He shook his head as Brooke started to speak. ''Don't argue, we do that too much. Let's go for a drive.''

''Parks,'' Brooke began as they rose, ''I meant what I said about not getting involved.''

''Yeah, I know.'' Then he kissed her long and lingeringly while she stood with her hands filled with paper plates and cups.

Chapter 5

It was three days before Brooke heard from Parks. She was aware that the last four-game series in the regular season would be played out of town. She knew, too, from what she told herself was simply a casual glimpse at the sports section, that Parks had knocked in three more RBIs in the first two games. In the meantime, she was busy looking over the story board for his first block of commercials.

The word had come down that the first thirty-second spot would be filmed before the league play-offs, in order to capitalize on Parks's exposure in the competition. That left Brooke little time to prepare, with an already demanding schedule of studio and location shoots, editing and preproduction meetings. But challenge, like food, was vital to her.

Closed off in her office, with a half an hour's leeway

before she was due at the studio, Brooke ran over the final script for the initial de Marco commercial. Casually slick, she thought, approving. It had minimal dialogue and soft sell—Parks at the plate, swinging away while dressed in de Marco's elegant sports clothes, then a slow dissolve to the next scene with him dressed in the same suit, stepping out of a Rolls with a slinky brunette on his arm.

''Clothes for anytime—anywhere,'' Brooke muttered. The timing had been checked and rechecked. The audio, except for Parks's one-line voice-over, was already being recorded. All she had to do was to guide Parks through the paces. The salesmanship hinged on her skill and his charm. Fair enough, she thought and reached for her half cup of cold coffee as a knock sounded at her door. ''Yeah?'' Brooke turned the script back to page one, running through the camera angles.

''Delivery for you, Brooke.'' The receptionist dropped a long white florist's box on her cluttered desk. ''Jenkins said to let you know the Lardner job's been edited. You might want to check it out.''

''Okay, thanks.'' Curiously, Brooke frowned over the top of the script at the flower box. Occasionally, she received a grateful phone call or letter from a client when they were particularly pleased with a commercial—but not flowers. Then there'd been that actor in the car spot last year, Brooke remembered. The one who was on his third wife. He'd alternately amused and annoyed Brooke by sending her batches of red roses every week. But six months had passed since she had convinced him that he was wasting her time and his money.

More likely it was one of E.J.'s practical jokes, she

considered. She'd probably find a few dozen frog legs inside. Not one to spoil someone's fun, Brooke pulled off the ribbon and lifted the lid.

There were masses of hibiscus. Fragrant, dew-soft pink-and-white petals filled the box almost to overflowing. After the first gasp of surprise, Brooke dove her hands into them, captivated by their purely feminine scent and feel. Her office suddenly smelled like a tropical island: heady, exotic, richly romantic. With a sound of pleasure, she filled her hands with the blooms, bringing them up to her face to inhale. In contrast to the sultry scent, the petals seemed impossibly fragile. A small white card fluttered down to her littered desk.

Letting the flowers drift back into the box, Brooke reached for the envelope and tore it open.

I thought of your skin.

There was nothing else, but she knew. She shuddered, then chided herself for acting like a mooning teenager. But she read the line three times. No one had ever been able to affect her so deeply with such simplicity. Though Parks was a thousand miles away, she could all but feel those lean, strong fingers trace down her cheek. The flood of warmth, the flash of desire told her she wasn't going to escape him—had never truly wanted to. Without giving herself any time for doubts or fears, Brooke picked up the phone.

''Get me Parks Jones,'' she said quickly. ''Try Lee Dutton, he'll have the number.'' Before she could change her mind, Brooke hung up, burying her hands in the flowers again.

How was it he knew just what buttons to push? she wondered, then discovered at that moment she didn't care. It was enough to be romanced—and romanced in style. Lifting a single bloom, she trailed it down her cheek. It was smooth and moist against her skin—as Parks's first kiss had been. The ringing phone caught her dreaming.

"Yes?"

"Parks Jones on line two. You've got ten minutes before they need you in the studio."

"All right. Hunt me up a vase and some water, will you?" She glanced at the box again. "Make that two vases." Still standing with the blossom in her hand, Brooke punched the button for line two. "Parks?"

"Yes. Hello, Brooke."

"Thank you."

"You're welcome."

She hesitated, then let herself speak her first thought. "I feel like a teenager who just got her first corsage."

Dropping flat on his back on the bed, he laughed. "I'd like to see you with some of them in your hair."

Experimentally she held one up over her ear. Unprofessional, she thought with a sigh, and contented herself with the scent of them. "I've a shoot in the studio in a few minutes; I don't think the lights would do them much good."

"You have your practical side, don't you, Brooke?" Parks flexed the slight ache in his shoulder and closed his eyes.

"It's necessary," she muttered but couldn't quite bring

herself to drop the blossom back in the box. ''How are you? I wasn't sure you'd be in.''

''I got in about half an hour ago. They cut us down five to two. I went oh for three.''

''Oh.'' She frowned, not quite sure what she was supposed to say. ''I'm sorry.''

''I didn't seem to have any rhythm—it'll pass.'' Before the play-offs, he added silently. ''I thought of you, maybe too much.''

Brooke felt an odd twist of pleasure that was difficult to pass off. ''I wouldn't want to be responsible for a slump, particularly when I remember some of the remedies.'' His chuckle sounded faint and weary. ''Are you tired?''

''A bit. You'd think with the division wrapped up we'd glide through this last series. Last night we went eleven innings.''

''I know.'' She could have bitten off her tongue. ''I caught the highlights on the late news,'' she said breezily. ''I'll let you sleep, then. I just wanted to thank you.''

Her inadvertent admission had his lips twitching, but he didn't bother to open his eyes. With them closed, he had no trouble bringing her face into focus. ''Will I see you when I get back?''

''Of course. We'll be shooting the first segment on Friday, so—''

''Brooke,'' he interrupted firmly, quietly. ''Will I see you when I get back?''

She hesitated, then looked down at the mass of pink-and-white hibiscus on her desk. ''Yes,'' she heard herself saying. Pressing the flower to her cheek, she sighed. "I think I'm going to make a very big mistake."

"Good. I'll see you Friday."

The trick to being a good director, Brooke had always thought, was to be precise without being too technical, brisk without losing sympathy, then to split yourself up into several small parts so that you could be everywhere at once. It was a knack she had developed early on—on the job—without the formalized training of many of her colleagues. Perhaps because she had worked so many of the other aspects of filming, from timing a script to setting the lights to mixing sound, she was fiercely precise. Nothing escaped her eye. Because she knew actors were often overworked and insecure, she had never quite lost her sympathy for them even when she was ready to rage at a consistently flubbed line. Her early experience at waiting tables had taught her the trick of moving fast enough to all but be two places at once.

On a set or in a studio, she had complete self-confidence. Her control was usually unquestioned because it came naturally. She never thought about being in charge or felt the need to remind others of it; she simply *was* in charge.

With a copy of the script in one hand, she supervised the final adjustments on the lights and reflectors. The ball diamond, she had noted immediately, had an entirely different feel at home plate than it had from the stands. It was like being on an island, cupped amid the high mountain of seats, with the tall green wall skirting the back. The distance from plate to fence seemed even more formidable from this perspective. Brooke wondered how men with sticks in their hands could continually hit a moving ball over that last obstacle.

She could smell the grass, freshly trimmed, the dusty scent of dirt that had dried in the sun and a whiff of E.J.'s blatantly macho cologne. "Give me a reading," she ordered the lighting director as she glanced up at the thick clouds in the sky. "I want a sunny afternoon."

"You got it." The lights were focused as Brooke stepped behind camera one to check for shadows on the plate.

Parks loitered at the tunnel entrance a moment, watching her. This was a different woman from the one who he had treated to tacos—different still from the one he had held in his arms at the de Marco party. Her hair was trained back in one long braid, nothing like the flowing, gypsylike mane he was used to seeing. She wore jeans that were white at the stress points, a plain T-shirt the color of scrambled eggs, dusty tennis shoes and winking sapphires at her ears.

But it wasn't her hairstyle or the apparel that denoted the difference. It was the assurance. He'd seen it before, but each time it had been underlying. Now she sparked with it, gesturing, ordering while men and women set about giving her exactly what she demanded. No one questioned her. And, he considered, it was patently obvious that she wouldn't have permitted it.

Grimacing, he tugged at the sleeve of the thin silk shirt he wore. Who the hell would play ball in an outfit like this? he wondered with a glance at the creaseless cream slacks. The rules of this game were hers, he reminded himself, then stepped into the light.

"Bigelow, get these cables secure before somebody breaks a leg. Libby, see if you can scrounge up some ice water, we're going to need it. Okay, where's..." Turning at that moment, Brooke spotted Parks. "Oh, there you are." If she felt any personal pleasure at seeing him, she hid it well, Parks thought wryly as she turned to shout an order at her assistant. "I'm going to want you to stand at the plate so we can check the lighting and camera angles."

Without a word, Parks complied. You might as well get used to it, he told himself. You've got yourself locked into hawking somebody else's clothes for the next two years. He stuffed his hands in his pockets, cursed Lee briefly and stood in the batter's box. Someone stuck a light meter next to his face.

"You gonna wipe out the Valiants in the play-offs?" the technician demanded.

"That's the plan," Parks returned easily.

"I've got fifty bucks on it."

This time Parks grinned. "I'll try to keep that in mind."

"Detrick." Brooke gave the technician a jerk of her head to send him on his way as she approached Parks. "Okay, this is the easy part," she began. "No dialogue, and you're doing what you're best at."

"What's that?"

Brooke lifted a brow at the loaded question but continued smoothly. "Swinging a bat. Since the pitching coach has agreed to throw you a few, you should feel comfortable."

"Ever stood in the box without a helmet?" he countered.

"It wouldn't go with your outfit," she said mildly. She gave him a deliberately slow study—eyes sweeping up, then down, then back up again. "And it looks good."

"I like yours, too." His smile was quick and dangerous. "I'm going to like unbinding your hair."

"Makeup!" she called abruptly. "Give him a dusting, he's going to glow."

"Wait a minute," Parks began, deftly catching the wrist of the woman with the powder.

"No sweating on camera," Brooke drawled, pleased with his reaction. "All I want you to do is what you usually do when you're in uniform. Take your regular stance," she continued. "A couple of those test swings. After you hit the ball, I want one of those grins before you toss the bat aside."

"What grins?" Reluctantly, Parks released the makeup artist's wrist and suffered the powder.

With humor dancing in her eyes, Brooke gave him a singularly sweet smile. "One of those boy-on-the-beach grins. Quick, lots of teeth, crinkles at the corners of the eyes."

He narrowed them dangerously. "I'm going to get you for this."

"Try to keep the strikes to a minimum," she went on blithely. "Every strike's a take. You don't have to hit it out of the park, just *look* like you have. Got it?"

"Yeah, I got it." Annoyed, he nodded to the pitching coach as he walked by.

"You look real cute, Jones."

"Just try to get it near the plate," Parks retorted. "Do I get a bat?" he demanded of Brooke. "Or do I just pretend?"

For an answer, Brooke turned and shouted to her assistant. "Let's have the bat, E.J., are you set? Just roll the film—no sweeps, no pans, no close-ups. Remember, we're selling the clothes."

"This is aluminum."

Distracted, Brooke turned back to Parks. "What?"

"This bat is aluminum."

When he held it out, Brooke automatically took it from him. "Yes, it appears to be." As she started to pass it back to him, Parks shook his head.

"I use wood. A two seventy-seven A."

She started to come back with a curt remark, then stopped herself. If she was accustomed to anything, it was temperament. "Get Mr. Jones the bat he prefers," she told her assistant, tossing the first one to him. "Anything else?"

For a moment, he regarded her keenly. "Does everybody jump when you say?"

"Damn right. Keep that in mind for the next couple of hours, and we shouldn't have any problems."

His look sharpened fractionally. "While the cameras are on," he returned in a voice only she could hear.

Turning, she walked to stand behind the camera. Automatically, E.J. stepped back so that she could check the angle herself. Brows drawn together, Brooke stared at Parks through the lens as her assistant handed him another bat. "Okay, Parks, would you take your stance?" Her frown deepened as he leaned slightly over the plate, feet planted, knees bent, shoulders lined toward the mound. The frown vanished. ''Good,'' she decided, moving back so that E.J. could take her place.

''Ten bucks says he pulls one to left center.''

A brief nod was Brooke's acceptance of the bet. ''Parks, when I say action, I want you to take your stance again, then those testing swings. Keep your eye on the mound—*don't* look at the camera. Just forget we're here.'' With the first smile Parks had seen that morning, Brooke turned to the pitching coach. ''Are you all set, Mr. Friedman?''

''All set, sweetheart. I'll try not to blow it by you, Jones.''

Parks gave a snort of laughter. ''Just see if you can make it to the plate.'' He gestured to his uncovered head. ''And keep it low.''

Brooke took a last glance around, assuring herself everyone was in position. ''Let's do one for time. Set?'' She held up her hand, waiting for absolute silence. ''Roll film, and…action.''

She watched Parks crouch into position, then take two loose swings. The deep-blue silk of his shirt caught the light, accenting the play of muscles beneath. Hands on her hips, Brooke counted off the seconds and waited. Parks shifted his weight as the ball came toward him, tensed his muscles then checked his swing. The ball smashed into the pads behind him.

Just barely, Brooke controlled the need to swear. ''Cut.'' Battling her annoyance, she walked to him. ''Is there a problem, Parks?''

''Pitch was outside.''

''Like hell,'' Friedman called from the mound. ''It caught the corner.''

Immediately the crew split themselves up, arguing in favor of the batter or the pitcher. Ignoring them for the moment, Brooke gave her attention to Parks. ''This isn't the bottom of the ninth, you're just supposed to hit the ball. You'll notice,'' she continued, gesturing behind her, ''there aren't any fielders, no fans, no press.''

Parks set the bat, barrel down in the dirt, and leaned on the handle. ''You want me to swing at a bad pitch?''

Brooke met the amused blue eyes levelly. ''The quality of the pitch is immaterial,'' she countered as the argument raged behind them. ''Just hit the ball.''

With a shrug, he hefted the bat again. ''You're the boss…at the moment.''

The look held, long and challenging, before Brooke turned back to the crew. ''Take two,'' she announced, effectively cutting off the debate.

This time Parks didn't check his swing but drilled the ball up the foul line at third. Without looking at E.J., Brooke held out her hand. ''Time,'' she requested as a ten-dollar bill was stuffed in her palm.

Parks noticed a tiny brunette with a stop watch and clip board. ''Twelve and a half seconds, Brooke.''

''Good. All right, let's go for it.''

''This one's going over the fence,'' E.J. pronounced in an undertone to Brooke. ''Bet ten?''

''Take three,'' she called out with a nod of assent. ''Roll film, and…action!'' A satisfied smile touched her lips as she studied Parks. He was either getting into the spirit of things, or his own competitive spirit was driving him. Either way, it was working for her. The look on his face as he crouched over the plate was exactly what she wanted—the steady intensity that bordered on fierceness. A pity she couldn't work in a close-up, she mused, then lost the thought as Parks took a full swing at the pitch.

Power. The word rippled through her as he connected with the ball. She saw the instant the shirt strained over his shoulders, was aware of the bunching of muscles in his thighs beneath the soft, expensive material. It wasn't necessary to follow the path of the ball to know where it had gone. She knew the flash of grin on Parks's face had nothing to do with her direction. It was sheer pleasure. Brooke kept the film rolling as his eyes followed the ball out of the park. Still grinning, he turned to her, then gave a deprecatory shrug.

She should have been angry that he had looked at the camera against her directions, but the movement, the expression was perfect. Even as she dug in her pocket for E.J.'s ten dollars, she decided to keep it in.

''Cut.''

Spontaneous applause broke out, along with a few whistles. ''Nice pitch, Friedman,'' Parks commented.

The coach tossed another ball in the air. ''Just making you look good, Jones. The Valiants' pitchers won't be so friendly.''

Brooke swiped the back of her wrist across her damp brow. ''I'd like a couple more please. What was the time on that?''

''Fourteen seconds.''

''Okay. The light's shifting, check the reading. Mr. Friedman, I'd like to get a couple more.''

"Anything you say, sweetheart."

"Parks, I need a full swing like last time. No matter where the ball goes, look up and out—don't forget the grin."

Laying the bat on his shoulder, he drawled, "No, ma'am."

Brooke ignored him and turned away. "Lights?"

The technician finished the adjustments, then nodded. "Set."

Although she considered the third take close to perfect, Brooke ran through another three. Edited, this segment of the commercial would run twelve and a half seconds. That it took only three hours to set up and film showed that she ran a tight schedule.

"It's a wrap. Thanks," she added as she accepted the cup of ice water from her assistant. "We'll set up in front of the restaurant in..." She glanced at her watch. "Two hours, Fred, double-check on the Rolls and the actress. E.J., I'll take the film into editing myself." Even as she spoke, Brooke walked over to the mound. "Mr. Friedman." With a smile, she held out her hand. "Thank you."

He found her grip firm and her eyes soft. "My pleasure." With a chuckle, he tossed a spare ball into his mitt. "You know, in my day ball players plugged razor blades or beer. We endorsed bats and gloves." He cast a glance at Parks, who was signing a baseball for a technician. "No fancy designers would have asked us to sport his clothes."

Brooke shifted her eyes to Parks. He was laughing now, shaking his head at E.J. as the cameraman ticked off some point on his fingers. The casually elegant clothes suited him, as did the dark wood bat in his hand. "I'd hate to have him know I said it, Mr. Friedman,'' Brooke commented as she turned back to the coach, ''but Parks is a natural.''

With a shout of laughter, Friedman patted her on the back. ''He won't hear it from me, sweetheart. Last thing my pitchers need is a third baseman with a big head. One more thing,'' he added before Brooke turned away. ''I watched the way you run things.'' He gave her an expansive grin that revealed good dentures. ''You'd make a hell of a coach.''

''Thanks.'' Pleased with the compliment, Brooke made her way toward the plate, and Parks. ''You did very well.''

He regarded her extended hand with amusement, but accepted it. ''For a rookie?'' he countered.

When she started to remove her hand, Parks held it firmly, running a light fingertip over the inside of her wrist. He had the satisfaction of feeling her pulse jump then speed up. ''I didn't anticipate any problems, as you were simply playing yourself.'' Behind her, technicians were taking down lights and coiling cable. She heard E.J. describing the new lady he was seeing in glowing, if exaggerated, terms. Using all her willpower, Brooke concentrated on the background noises instead of the feel of Parks's finger tracing over her skin. ''The next scene should be fairly easy. We'll go over it on location this afternoon. If you have any questions—''

''Just one,'' Parks interrupted. ''Come here a minute.'' Without waiting for agreement, he drew her toward the dugout, stepped inside then just through the door that led to the locker rooms.

''What's the problem, Parks?'' Brooke demanded. ''I have to get into editing before the next shoot.''

''Are we finished here for now?''

With an impatient sigh, Brooke gestured to the equipment being packed. ''Obviously.''

''Fine.'' Pressing her back against the doorway, Parks covered her mouth with his.

It was a proprietary kiss with whispers of violence. The frustrations of the past hours seeped into it as he finally let them free. There was the annoyance of wanting her—of being too far away to touch for days, then being close enough, but not being permitted to. There was the exasperation of her cool professional treatment of him while he had fought an insistent growing desire. And there was the banked fury at being put in the position of taking orders from a woman who dominated his thoughts and denied his body.

Yet it was more agitating than soothing to press his body against the softness of hers. She filled him—the exotic scent, the ripe woman-taste of her mouth, the silken skin over the sharp, strong bones of her face. Almost desperately, he pressed closer, plunged deeper. He would *not* be filled. He would find that corner, that secret place that would open her for him so that he could have her at last—body and mind. To do that he needed the edge of control, over himself, and over Brooke. Her strength made it a challenge—his desire made it a necessity.

''Hey, Brooke, want a ride to the... Whoops.'' E.J. poked his head into the dugout then retreated. As Parks's lips freed hers, she could hear the cameraman whistling gleefully as he strolled away. Furious that she had completely lost track of time and place, Brooke shoved against Parks's chest.

"Let go of me!"

"Why?"

Apparently her ice-pick stare more amused than wounded him. "Don't you *ever* pull something like that when I'm working," she hissed, shoving a second time as Parks blocked her exit.

"I asked if we were finished," Parks reminded her, then backed her into the wall again.

"When we're on the job," Brooke said evenly, "I'm the director, you're the product." He narrowed his eyes at her choice of words, but she continued, full steam. "You'll do *exactly* what I tell you."

"The camera's not rolling, Brooke."

"I won't have my crew speculating, circulating gossip that can undermine my authority or my credibility."

His own temper rose in direct balance with need. She only aroused him more when she challenged. "Aren't you more afraid that you enjoy being touched by me? Doesn't it infuriate you that when I kiss you, you don't really give a damn who's in charge?" He bent his head so that his lips were only a breath from hers. "I took your orders all morning, Ms. Gordon. Now it's my turn."

Her lancelike stare didn't falter as the quiet words fluttered over her lips. With the tip of his tongue he traced them, enjoying their taste and her own suppressed passion. Merging desire stung the air—they both felt it, they both tried to rise above it in the struggle for dominance. Yet they both became aware that it was the desire that would win over each of them.

His lips rubbed over hers, without pressure or force, taunting her to demand he stop, daring her to resist her own needs. Their eyes remained open and fixed on each other. Both pairs of irises darkened as passion tempted each of them to surrender.

"We have another shoot this afternoon," Brooke managed as she fought to keep her voice steady.

"When we're filming, I'll do what you tell me." He kissed her once, hard and quick. "Tonight," he added, dealing with his own heated blood, "we'll see."

Chapter 6

Brooke chose to shoot during the late-afternoon lull using day-for-night filters, rather than compete with the evening traffic. It was a quick scene, relatively simple and very glossy. The champagne-colored Rolls would drive up in front of the posh restaurant, Parks would alight, in the same outfit, but wearing a jacket—already sponged and pressed from the morning—then offer his hand to the sleekly dressed brunette. She would step from the car, showing considerable leg, then flash Parks a look before linking her arm through his. The scene would then fade out, with Parks's voice-over dubbed in, stating the motto for the campaign.

"De Marco. For the man who's going places."

The visual would be another twelve seconds, so that combined with the stadium segment, the intro and the tag at the end, the commercial would round out at thirty seconds.

"I want a long shot of the rolls, E.J., then come in on Parks as he steps out. We don't want to lose the impact that he's wearing the same outfit he played ball in. Don't get hung up on the lady," she added dryly as she sent him a knowing look.

"Who me?" Pulling a Kings fielder's cap out of his back pocket, he offered it to Brooke. "Want to wear it? Team spirit?"

Placing one hand on her hip, Brooke stared at him without any change of expression. With a quick chuckle, E.J. fit the cap over his own modified Afro.

"Okay, boss, I'm ready when you are."

As was her habit, Brooke rechecked the camera angle and the lighting before she signaled the first take. The Rolls cruised sedately to the curb. Brooke played the background music over in her head, trying to judge how it would fit. On cue, Parks climbed out, turning to offer his hand to the brunette still inside. Frowning, Brooke let the scene play out. It wasn't right. She saw why immediately but took the few minutes until the cut to work out how to approach Parks.

With a gesture, Brooke indicated that she would speak to Parks while the driver backed up the Rolls for the next take. Putting a hand on his arm, she led him away from the technicians. "Parks, you have to relax." Because handling fidgety actors was second nature to her, Brooke's voice and manner were markedly different from the morning session. Parks noted it and bristled anyway.

"I don't know what you mean."

She steered him well away from where a few interested pedestrians were loitering by a barricade. "Number one," she began, "you're plugging a good product. Try to believe in it."

"If I didn't think it was a good product, I wouldn't be doing this," he retorted, frowning over her shoulder at the huddle of lights.

"But you're not comfortable." When Brooke gave his shoulder a reassuring pat, Parks scowled at her. "If you insist on feeling like an idiot, it's going to show. Wait," she ordered as he started to speak. "This morning, you felt more at ease—the stadium, a bat in your hand. After the first couple of minutes, you started to play the game. That's all I want you to do now."

"Look, Brooke, I'm not an actor—"

"Who's asking you to act?" she countered. "God spare me from that." She knew she'd insulted him, so she tempered the comment with a smile. "Listen, you're a winner, out on the town in a chauffeured Rolls with a gorgeous woman. All I want you to do is have a good time and look rather pleased with yourself. You can pull it off, Parks. Loosen up."

"I wonder how you'd feel if someone asked you to field a line drive with twenty thousand people watching."

Brooke smiled again and tried not to think about the minutes ticking away. "You do that routinely," she pointed out, "because you concentrate on your job and forget those thousands of people."

"This is different," he muttered.

"Only if you let it be. Just let me see that same self-satisfied look on your face that you had when you hit that homer this morning. Pretend, Parks.'' Brooke straightened the collar of his shirt. ''It's good for you.''

''Did you know that Nina has the IQ of a soft-boiled egg?''

''Nina?''

''My date.''

Brooke gave in to a sigh. ''Stop being so temperamental; nobody's asking you to marry her.''

Parks opened his mouth, then shut it again. No one had ever accused him of being temperamental. He'd never *been* temperamental. If his manager told him to take a three-and-one pitch, he took it. If the third base coach told him to steal home, he ran. Not because he was malleable, but because if he was signed with a team, he followed the rules. It didn't mean he always had to like them. With a quiet oath, he ran a hand through his hair and admitted that it wasn't so much what the orders were in this case, but who was laying them out. But then, the lights and cameras would eventually shut down.

''Fine, let's do it again.'' He gave Brooke the slow smile she'd learned not to trust before he walked toward the Rolls. Suspicious of his easy capitulation, Brooke turned back to stand beside E.J.

Parks gave her no more cause to complain, though they were more than two hours shooting the segment. Brooke found that she had more trouble with the professional actress—and a couple of fans who recognized Parks—than she had with him. It took three takes before she convinced Nina that she wasn't looking for glowing and adoring, but for sleek and aloof. Brooke wanted the contrast and ran everyone through the twelve seconds until she was certain she had it.

Then there was the matter of two fans who sneaked through the barricade to get Parks's autograph while the camera was still rolling. Parks obliged them, and though Brooke simmered at the interruption, she noted that he dispatched the fans with the charm of a seasoned diplomat. Grudgingly, she had to admit she couldn't have done better herself.

''That's a wrap,'' Brooke announced, arching her back. She'd been on her feet for over eight hours, bolting down a half a sandwich between segments. She felt pleased with the day's work, satisfied with Parks's progress and ravenous. ''You can break down,'' she told the crew. ''Good job. E.J., I've scheduled the editing and dubbing for tomorrow. If you want to see what we're going to do to your film, you can come in.''

''It's Saturday.''

''Yeah.'' She pulled the bill of the fielder's cap over his face. ''We'll start working at ten. Nina...'' Brooke took the actress's slim, smooth hand. ''You were lovely, thank you. Fred, make sure the Rolls gets back in one piece, or you'll have to face Claire. Bigelow, what's the new kid's name?'' Brooke jerked her head at a young technician who was busily packing up lights.

''Silbey?''

With a nod, Brooke made a mental note of it. ''He's good,'' she said briefly, then turned to Parks. ''Well, you made it through the first one. We'll dub in the voice-over tomorrow. Any scars?''

''None that show.''

"Maybe I shouldn't tell you that this one is the easiest on the schedule."

He met the humor in her eyes blandly. "Maybe you shouldn't."

"Where's your car?"

"Out at the stadium."

With a frown, Brooke checked her watch. "I'll give you a lift back there." She toyed with the idea of going by Thorton's first to take a quick look at the film, then discarded the idea. It would be better to look at it fresh in the morning. "I have to call Claire.... Well." Brooke shrugged. "That can wait. Any problems?" she asked to the crew in general."

"Tomorrow's Saturday," an aggrieved E.J. stated again as he packed up his equipment. "Woman, you just don't give a man a break."

"You don't have to come in," she reminded him, knowing he would. "Good night." With Parks beside her, Brooke started down the street.

"Do you make a habit of working weekends?" he asked, noting that after a long, hectic day she still moved as though she had urgent appointments to keep.

"When it's necessary. We're rushing this through to get it aired during the play-offs or, barring that, the series." She shot him a look. "You'd better be in it." Still walking, she began to dig in the purse slung over her shoulder.

"I'll try to accommodate you. Want me to drive?"

With the keys in one hand, Brooke looked up in surprise. "Have you been talking to E.J.?"

His brows drew together. "No. Why?"

''Nothing.'' Dismissing the thought, Brooke paused beside her car. ''Why do you want to drive?''

''It occurs to me that I may have had to stand in front of that stupid camera off and on all day, but you haven't stopped for over eight hours. It's a tough job.''

''I'm a tough lady,'' she responded with a trace of defensiveness in her voice.

''Yeah.'' He grazed his knuckles over her cheek. ''Iron.''

''Just get in the car,'' Brooke muttered. After rounding the hood, she climbed in, slamming the door only slightly. ''It'll take a little while to get across town in this traffic.''

''I'm not in a hurry.'' Parks settled comfortably beside her. ''Can you cook?''

In the act of starting the car, Brooke frowned at him. ''Can I what?''

''Cook. You know.'' Parks pantomimed the act of stirring a pan.

She laughed, shooting out of traffic with an exuberance that made Parks wince. ''Of course I can cook.''

''How about your place?''

Brooke zipped through a yellow light. ''What about my place?'' she asked cautiously.

''For dinner.'' Parks watched her shift into third as she scooted around a Porsche. ''It seems to me I'm entitled after feeding you a couple times myself.''

''You want me to cook for you?''

This time he laughed. She was going to fight him right down to the wire. ''Yeah. And then I'm going to make love to you.''

Brooke hit the brakes, stopping the car inches away from another bumper. "Oh, really?"

"Oh, really," he repeated, meeting her dagger-eyed stare equably. "We both just punched out on the time clock. New game." He fingered the end of her braid. "New rules."

"And if I have some objection?"

"Why don't we talk about it someplace quiet?" With his thumb, he traced her lips. "Not afraid, are you?"

The taunt was enough. When the light changed, Brooke hit the accelerator, weaving through Los Angeles traffic with grim determination.

"Did you know that you drive like a maniac?" Parks observed.

"Yes."

"Just a passing comment," he murmured, then settled back against the seat.

Despite the infuriated woman beside him, Parks had the same sensation of tranquility when Brooke zoomed up in her driveway, braking with a teeth-jarring jolt, that he had had the first time he had seen her house. There was a tang of fall in the air—that spicy, woodsy fragrance you never smelled in Los Angeles. Some of the leaves had turned so that splashes of red and amber and orange competed with the customary California green. The shadows of trees reflected in the glass of the windows as the sun dipped lower in the sky. Along the base of the house the flowers had been allowed to grow bushy and wild. Whether it had been by intent or lack of time, her unkempt garden was eye-catching and perfectly suited to the lonely mountain spot.

Without a word, Brooke slammed out of her side of the car. At a more leisurely pace, Parks followed suit. She was furious, Parks noted with a pleased grin. All the better. He didn't want an easy capitulation. From the first moment he had come into contact with her, he had looked forward to the struggle almost as much as he had looked forward to the outcome. He'd never had any doubt what that would be. When there was this much friction, and this much spark between a man and a woman, they became enemies or lovers. He had no intention of being Brooke's enemy.

Still keeping her stony silence, Brooke slipped the key into the lock and turned it. Walking inside, she left him to follow as he chose.

The fireplace caught his eye first. It was crafted from large stone, dominating one wall. The fire set was shiny brass, though dented and obviously old. Another wall was all glass, rising from either side of the door to the peak of the roof. Gazing at it, he felt not a loss of privacy but a basic sense of security. Rocking gently on his heels, he studied the rest of the main room.

A long armless sofa ranged in front of the fireplace, crowded with dozens of pillows. In lieu of a table a large, round hassock sat in front of it. Around this focal point a few chairs were scattered. All the colors were muted—ecrus, buffs, biscuits—set off by the surprising touches of huge, brilliant peacock feathers in a brass urn, a scarlet afghan tossed over the back of a chair, the vivid shades in the hooked rug on the planked floor.

A shelf had been built into the east wall. Ignoring Brooke's glare, Parks wandered to it. There was a small crystal butterfly that shivered in a rainbow of colors as the light struck it. There was a chipped demitasse set that had come from one of Brooke's yard sale jaunts along with a fat, grinning bear. Parks noted a piece of Wedgwood next to a pink monkey holding cymbals. It clapped them together gleefully when he flipped a switch. With a quick laugh, he flipped it off again. There were other treasures scattered haphazardly through the room, some priceless, some no more than department store whimsy.

Above his head, the second-floor balcony ran the length of the house. No closed-in spaces, he noted. He began to think the house itself would tell him more about Brooke than she would volunteer. The need for freedom of movement, the eclectic tastes, the combination of drab colors with the garish. It occurred to him that everything she owned would have been collected during the last ten years. But how much of the past had she brought with her?

Uncomfortable with Parks's silent, thorough survey, Brooke marched to a tiny corner cabinet to pull out a bottle. "You're free to take a tour," she said abruptly. "I'm going to have a drink."

"Whatever you're having's fine," Parks said with infuriating amiability. "You can show me around later." He proceeded to make himself at home on the low, spreading sofa. Leaning back, he glanced at the fireplace, observing by the ash that Brooke made good use of it. "Fire'd be nice," he said casually. "Got any wood?"

"Out back." Ungraciously, she stuck a glass under his nose.

"Thanks." After accepting it, Parks took her hand. "Sit

down,'' he invited with a pleasantness that put Brooke's teeth on edge. ''You've been on your feet all day.''

''I'm fine,'' she began, then let out a gasp of surprise as Parks yanked her down beside him. Realizing she should have been prepared for the move despite his outward mellowness only fanned her already strained temper. ''Who do you think you are,'' she began, ''barging in here, expecting me to whip up dinner then fall into bed with you? If you—''

''Hungry?'' Parks interrupted.

She sent him a searing look. ''No.''

With a shrug, he draped his arm behind her, propping his feet on the hassock. ''You're usually ill-tempered when you are,'' he commented.

''I am *not* ill-tempered,'' Brooke raged. ''And I am *not* hungry.''

''Want some music?''

Brooke drew in a deep breath. How dare he sit there acting as though she were *his* guest? ''No.''

''You should relax.'' With firm fingers, he began to knead the base of her neck.

''I'm perfectly relaxed.'' She pushed his hand aside, disturbed by the sensation of warmth creeping down her spine.

''Brooke.'' Parks set his glass on the floor, then turned to her. ''When you called me a few days ago, you accepted what you knew was going to happen between us.''

''I said I would see you,'' she corrected and started to rise. Parks hand came back to her neck and held her still.

''Knowing what *seeing* me meant,'' he murmured. His eyes met the fury in her gaze for a moment, then drifted down to focus on her mouth. "You might have refused to let me come here tonight...but you didn't." Slowly, he brought his eyes back to hers in a long, intense look that had her stomach muscles quivering. "Are you going to tell me that you don't want me?"

She couldn't remember the last time she had felt the need to break eye contact. It took all her strength of will to keep from faltering. "I...I don't have to tell you anything. You might remember that this is my time, my house. And—"

"What are you afraid of?"

As he watched, the confusion in her eyes turned back to fury. "I'm not afraid of anything."

"Of making love to me," he continued quietly. "Or to anyone?"

Angry color flooded her cheeks as she bolted up from the sofa. She felt a combination of rage and hurt and fear that she hadn't experienced in more than a decade. He had no right to bring the insecurity tumbling back over her, no right to make her doubt herself as a woman. Tossing her head, Brooke glared at him. "You want to make love?" she snapped. "Fine." She turned on her heel and marched to the stairs leading to the second floor. Halfway up, she threw an angry look over her shoulder. "Coming?" she demanded, then continued on without waiting for his reply.

The fury carried her across the balcony and into her bedroom, where she stood in the center of the room, seething. Her gaze landed on the bed, but she averted it quickly as she heard the sound of Parks's footsteps approaching. It was all very simple, she told herself. They would go to bed and work this attraction or animosity or whatever it was out of their systems. It would clear the air. She sent Parks another killing look as he walked into the room. Fear prodded at her again. In defense, Brooke hastily began to undress.

It was on the tip of his tongue to tell her to stop, then Parks calmly followed her example. She was trembling and didn't even know it, he observed. For the moment, they would play it her way. As with the first night he had taken her out, Parks knew what Brooke expected. Though the angry fear urged him to comfort, he was aware that it would be refused. He didn't even glance over when she dropped her T-shirt into a heap on the floor. But he noticed that she had kept a small clutch of his hibiscus on her dresser.

Naked, Brooke stomped over to the bed and pulled off the quilt. Head high, brows arched, she turned to him. "Well?"

He looked at her. The surge of sharp desire caused him to go rigid to control it. She was long and softly rounded with fragile, china-doll skin. The proud almost challenging stance was only accented by the overall frailty—until one looked at her eyes. Stormy, they dared him to make the next move.

Parks wondered if she knew just how vulnerable she was and vowed, even as he planned to conquer, to protect. Taking his time, he walked to her until they stood face-to-face. Though her eyes never faltered, he saw the quick nervous swallow before she turned toward the bed. Parks caught her braid in his hand, forcing her to turn back. The fury in her eyes might have cooled the desire of most men. Parks smiled, comfortable with it.

"This time," he murmured as he began to unbind the braid, "I'll direct."

Brooke stood stiffly as he slowly freed her hair. Her skin tingled, as if waiting for his touch—but he never touched her. Deliberately, Parks drew out the process, working his way leisurely up the confined hair until Brooke thought she would burst. When he had finished, he spread it over her shoulders as if it were the only task he would ever perform.

"It's fabulous," Parks murmured, absorbed in its texture, at the way the slanting sunlight brought out the hidden gold within the red. Lifting a strand from her shoulder, he buried his nose in it, wanting to absorb the fragrance. Brooke felt her knees weaken, her muscles go lax. Would he ever touch her?

She kept her eyes on his face, trying to avoid a dangerous fascination with the tawny skin of his chest, the mat of dark-gold hair and cords of muscles she had glimpsed in his bare shoulders. If she allowed herself to look, would she be able to prevent herself from touching? But when she noticed the thin gold chain around his neck, curiosity drove her to follow it down to the small gold circle that dangled from it. Because of this, she didn't see him shift ever so slightly to press his lips against the curve of her shoulder. The touch was a jolt, a branding shock that had her jerking back even as his hands spanned her waist.

"Relax." Fingers kneaded gently into flesh; warm lips nibbled it over his words. "I won't take you anywhere you don't want to go.'' Slowly, he ran the whisper-soft kisses over her shoulder, loitering at her throat. His fingertips ran down to her hips then back up in a rhythmic caress that could never soothe, but only arouse. He knew what he did to her—she knew her response was no secret. In a last attempt to hold her own, Brooke pressed her hands against his chest, arching back.

Parks still held her waist, but made no attempt to draw her back. Over the desire in his eyes, Brooke caught the light of humor. ''Want me to stop?'' he asked quietly. There was a trace of challenge in the question. She realized abruptly that whatever response she gave, she would still lose.

''Would you?'' she countered, fighting the urge to run her suddenly sensitive fingertips over his naked chest.

It was his slow, dangerous smile. ''Why don't you ask me and see?'' Even as she opened her mouth to form an answer, his fastened on it. The kiss was soft and deep, the sort she knew a woman could drown in. Brooke had only the vague realization that her hands had crept up his chest to link around his neck, only the faintest knowledge that her body was melting into his. Then she was falling—or perhaps she was drowning—until the cool sheets were under her back and his weight was on her.

She didn't question how her body seemed to have become liquid, only reveled in the unaccustomed freedom of motion and space. His hands were so sure, so unhurried, as if he wished and waited for her total fluidity. With a deft caress, a strategic brush of lips, he was unlocking every restriction she had placed on herself. This pleasure was thick, fluent. Brooke luxuriated in it, no longer caring what she gave up in order to receive. Weightless, helpless, she could only sigh as he took his mouth on a lazy journey down her body.

The flick of his tongue over her nipple brought a quick tug—not quite an ache—in her stomach. This pleasure was sharp, stunning. Then it was gone, leaving her dazed as he continued to range a moist trail over her.

His hands were never still, but moved so gently, almost magically, over her, that she could never pinpoint where the source of delight came from. It seemed to radiate through the whole of her, soothing, promising, luring. He caught the point of her breast between his teeth, causing a flash of heat to spring from her center out to her fingertips. But even as she gasped from it, arching, he moved on. He brushed his fingers over her inner thigh, almost absently, so that her skin was left heated then chilled. As fire and ice coursed through her, the sound of her own moan echoed in her head.

The quivering started—a drug wearing off. And the ache—unbearable, wonderful. She was no longer soothed, but throbbing and pleasure became exquisite torment. Suddenly her fingers were in his hair as she tried to press him closer. ''Make love to me,'' she demanded as her breath started to tremble.

He continued with the same mind-destroying caresses. ''Oh, I am,'' he murmured.

''Now.'' Brooke reached for him only to have him grip her wrists. His head lifted so that their eyes met. Even through a haze of passion she could see his intense concentration—that fierce warrior look.

''It's not so simple.'' He could feel her pulse hammering under his fingers, but he would give her no quick moment of pleasure. When he took her, she would never forget. Parks pressed his mouth to hers, not so gently. "I've only begun."

Still holding her wrists, he began a new journey over her, with his mouth only. As he captured her breast again, taking it into the heated moistness of his mouth, she could only writhe beneath him in a frenzy that had nothing to do with a desire to escape. The breezy patience had left him to be replaced by a demand that would accept only one answer. It seemed he would feed on her skin, nipping, suckling, licking until she was half-mad from need so long suppressed. It seemed he would taste, and taste only, for hours, assuaging a steady greed she was powerless to refuse.

The heat suffused her, enervated her. Her skin trembled and grew moist from it. Down the hollow between her breasts, over the lean line of ribs to the subtle curve of hip he traced kisses until he felt her hands go limp and her pulse rage.

When his tongue plunged into the warm core of her, she shuddered convulsively, crying out with the first delirious peak. But he was relentless. Even as she struggled for breath, his hands began a new journey of possession.

With hers free, Brooke gripped his shoulders, hardly aware of the tensing of his muscles. There was no part of her body he hadn't explored, exploited, in his quest to have all of her. Now her surrender became agility and drive. Neither of them knew that her true capitulation came when she began her own demands.

Her hands sped over him, touching all she could reach

while she twisted, wanting to taste—his mouth, his shoulder, the strong line of his jaw. Parks thought her scent intensified until it dominated all his senses—weakening and strengthening him at once. Her skin was moist and heated wherever his mouth nestled, bringing him another tantalizing image of white silk and forbidden passion. Husky murmurs and quick breathing broke the early-evening hush.

He was no longer thinking, nor was she. They had entered a place where thoughts were only sensations; sharp, aching, sweet and dark. Even as she fastened her mouth on his, Brooke trembled.

Then he was deep inside her, so swiftly that she dug her nails into his flesh in shock and pleasure. They merged, body to body, heart to heart, while all the sensations concentrated into one.

Chapter 7

Brooke luxuriated in the soft, warm security. As she hung between sleep and wakefulness she thought it was winter, and that she slept beneath a thick downy quilt. There was no need to get up, no need to face the cold. She could lie there for a whole lazy day and do nothing. She felt utterly peaceful, completely unburdened and pleasantly languid. Wanting to enjoy the sensations more, she struggled to shrug off sleep.

It wasn't winter, but early fall. There was no quilt, only a tangle of sheets that half covered her naked body as she curled into Parks. With sleep cleared from her mind, Brooke remembered everything—the first revelation of lovemaking, the surprise of having the secret door open without resistance, the hours of passion that had followed. There had been little talk, as the urgency to give and take had grown beyond the control of either of them. Time after time, fulfillment had led to rekindled desire, and desire to demand, until they had fallen asleep, wrapped tightly together.

Now, Brooke could remember her own insatiable thirst, the boundless energy and strength that had filled her. She remembered, too, Parks's ability to arouse her to desperation with patience…and that she had driven him beyond patience with a skill she had been unaware of possessing. But beyond the passion and pleasure, Brooke remembered one vital thing. She had needed him. This was something she had refused herself for years. To need meant dependence, dependence meant vulnerability. A woman who was vulnerable would always be hurt.

The night was behind her and dawn was breaking. In the misty gray light, Parks's face was relaxed, inches from hers, so that the warmth of his breath fluttered over her cheek. His arm was around her, his fingers curled into her hair, as if even in sleep he had to touch it. Her arm reached around to lock him close. They had slept, if only for a few hours, in a classic pose of possessing and possessed. But which one, Brooke thought hazily, was which?

With a sigh, Brooke closed her eyes. Not knowing was dangerous. The hours she had spent not caring put the independence she had taken for granted in jeopardy.

It was time to think again before it was too late, before emotions dominated her—those perilous emotions that urged her to burrow closer to Parks's warmth. If she were ever to stop the need for him from growing beyond her control, she had to do it now.

Brooke shifted in an attempt to separate her body from his. Parks tightened his hold and only brought her closer.

''No,'' he murmured without opening his eyes. With sleepy slowness he ran his hand down the length of her naked back. ''Too early to get up.''

Brooke felt her breasts yield against his chest, felt the warmth in her stomach begin to smolder to heat. His lips were close—too close. The need to stay in the security of his arms was so strong it frightened her. Again Brooke tried to shift, and again Parks brought her back.

''Parks,'' she said, then was silenced by his lips.

Brooke told herself to struggle against the deep, musky morning kiss, but she didn't. She told herself to resist the gentle play of fingertips on her spine, but she couldn't. The gray dawn suddenly took on a rosy hue. The air seemed to grow thick. Even as he touched her, her skin quivered to be touched again. Don't! her brain shouted. Don't let this happen. But she was already sinking, and sinking quickly. She made a sound of protest that became a groan of pleasure.

Parks shifted so that his body lay across hers. Burying his face in her hair, he took his hand down the length of her; the slight swell of the side of her breast, the firm line of ribs and narrow waist, a flare of hip and long smooth thigh. He could feel the struggle going on inside her, sense her desire to separate herself from what had begun to happen between them since that first meeting of eyes. His quick flash of anger was tinged with unexpected hurt.

''Regrets already?'' Lifting his head, he looked at her. Her eyes were dark, heavy with kindling passion. Her breathing was unsteady. But he knew she fought herself just as fiercely as she fought him. Her hands were on his shoulders, poised to push him away.

"This isn't smart," Brooke managed.

"No?" Controlling anger, ignoring the hurt, Parks brushed the hair from her cheek. "Why?"

Brooke met his eyes, because to look away would have admitted defeat. "It's not what I want."

"Let's be accurate." His voice was calm, his eyes steady. "It's not what you want to want."

"All right." Brooke shivered as his finger traced her ear. "It's not what I want to want. I have to be practical. We're going to be working together for quite a while. More technically, you'll be working for me. A solid professional relationship won't be possible if we're lovers."

"We are lovers," Parks pointed out, casually shifting so that the friction of his body on hers sent a shudder coursing through her.

"It won't be possible," Brooke continued, concentrating on keeping her voice steady, "if we go on being lovers."

Tilting his head, Parks smiled at her. "Why?"

"Because..." Brooke knew why. She knew dozens of logical reasons why, but no firm thought would form in her brain when he touched a light friendly kiss to her lips.

"Let me be practical a minute," Parks said after another quick kiss. "How often do you let yourself have fun?"

Brooke drew her brows together in annoyed confusion. "What do you mean?"

"You can work eight, twelve hours a day," Parks continued. "You can enjoy your job, be terrific at what you do, but you still need to throw a Frisbee now and again."

"Frisbee?" This brought on a baffled laugh that pleased

him. The hands on his shoulders relaxed. ''What are you talking about?''

''Fun, Brooke. A sense of the ridiculous, laziness, riding Ferris wheels. All those things that make working worthwhile.''

She had the uncomfortable feeling she was being expertly led away from the subject at hand. ''What does riding a Ferris wheel have to do with you and me making love?''

''Have you ever had a lover before?'' Parks felt her stiffen but continued. ''I don't mean someone you slept with, but someone you shared time with. I'm not asking you for any more than that.'' Even as he said it, Parks knew it wouldn't be true for long. He would ask for more, and she would fight him every step of the way. But then he had lived his life playing to win. ''Throw a few Frisbees with me, Brooke. Ride a few waves. Let's see where it takes us.''

Looking at him, she could feel her resistance melting. Before she could prevent it, her hand had lifted from his shoulder to brush at the hair that fell over his forehead. ''You make it sound so simple,'' she murmured.

''Not simple.'' He took her other hand and pressed his lips to the palm. ''Even fun isn't always simple. I want you…here.'' And his eyes came back to hers. ''Naked, warm, daring me to arouse you. I want to drive with you with the top down and the wind in your hair. I want to see you caught in the rain, laughing.'' He ran whispering kisses over her face, then paused at her lips to drink long and deep. ''I want to be with you, but I don't think it's going to be simple.''

Rolling over, Parks cradled her head on his chest, allowing her to rest and think while he brushed his hands through her hair. His words had touched her in tiny vulnerable places she couldn't defend. Was she strong enough, she wondered, to try things his way without losing control? Fun, she thought. Yes, they could give each other that. He challenged her. Brooke had to admit that she had come to enjoy even the friction. What had he said once? That they could be friends before they were lovers. Odd, she mused, that both had happened almost before she realized it. Only the niggling fear that she was already afraid of losing him kept her from relaxing completely.

"I can't afford to fall in love with you," she murmured.

An odd way to put it, Parks reflected as he continued to stroke her hair. "Rule one," he drawled. "Party A will not fall in love with Party B."

Making a fist, Brooke punched his shoulder. "Stop making me sound ridiculous."

"I'll try," he agreed amiably.

"Fun," she murmured, half to herself.

"A three-letter word meaning amusement, sport or recreation," Parks recited in a blandly didactic tone.

With a chuckle, Brooke lifted her head. "All right. I'll buy the Frisbee," she said before she pressed her mouth to his.

Parks cupped the back of her neck in his hand. "It's still too early to get up," he murmured.

Brooke's low laugh was muffled against his lips. "I'm not sleepy."

With a reluctant sigh, he closed his eyes. "Acting," he said thickly, "takes a lot out of you."

''Aw.'' Sympathetically, Brooke stroked his cheek. ''I guess you'd better conserve your strength.'' She pressed a kiss to his jaw, then his collarbone, before continuing down his chest. Her fingers tangled with the gold chain he wore. ''What's this for?''

Parks opened one eye to stare at the five-dollar gold piece that dangled from the chain Brooke held up. ''Luck.'' He shut his eyes again. ''My aunt gave it to me when I headed for the Florida training camp. She told my father he was a''—Parks reached back in his memory for the exact phrasing—''a stiff-necked old fool who thought in graphs and formulas, then gave me the gold piece and told me to go for it.''

Brooke turned the shiny circle over in her palm. So he carried a little piece of the past with him, too, she mused. ''Superstition?'' she asked as she dropped the chain and pressed her lips to his chest.

''Luck,'' Parks corrected, enjoying the feel of her mouth on his skin, ''has nothing to do with superstition.''

''I see.'' She scraped her nails lightly down his side and heard his quick inhalation of breath. ''Do you always wear it?''

''Mmm.'' She flicked her tongue over his nipple, bringing a low, involuntary groan from him. A sense of power whipped through her—light, freeing, tempting. His hands were buried in her hair again, seeking the flesh beneath. Brooke slid her body down, bringing them both a rippling slice of pleasure.

His scent was different, she discovered as she ran her lips over his skin. Different, she realized, because hers had mingled with it during the night. That was intimacy, as tangible as the act of love itself.

As the power stayed with her, she experimented. His body was strong and muscled beneath hers, tasting of man. He was taut and lean, his skin golden in the early-morning light. The palms that moved over her back were hard, calloused from his profession. Like the man, the body was disciplined, a product of that odd combination of pampering and outrageous demands any athlete subjects it to. She brushed her lips over the hard, flat stomach and felt the firm muscles quiver. Beneath her own smooth palms she could feel the sinewy strength of his thighs.

The knowledge of the pure physical strength he possessed excited her. With light touches and caresses, she could make this man breathe as though he had run to the point of collapse. With feathering kisses she could make this hardened athlete shudder with an inner weakness she alone was aware of. Though she didn't fully understand it, Brooke knew that she had given him something more than her body the night before, something more complex than surrender or passion. Without even knowing what the gift was, she wanted Parks to offer it in return.

Slowly, enjoying every movement of his body beneath hers, savoring each subtly different taste, she roamed up until her lips fastened greedily on his. How soft his mouth was. How nectarous, with a dark, secret cachet. Brooke savored it on her tongue, feeling it intensify until the draining, liquefying pleasure crept into her. Knowing she would lose that slim edge of control, she tore her mouth from his to bury it at his throat.

She felt the vibration of his groan against her lips, but

she couldn't hear it. Her heartbeat raged in her head until all of her senses were confused. If it was morning, how could she feel this sultry night pleasure? If she was seducing him, how was she so thoroughly seduced? Her body pressed against his, matching itself to the slow, tortuous rhythm he set even as she raced tormenting kisses along his flesh. The heat seeping into her only seemed to add to the delirium of power, yet it wasn't enough. She was still searching for something so nebulous she wasn't certain she would recognize it when it was found. And desire, sharp bolts of desire, were causing everything but the quest for fulfillment to fade.

Parks gripped her hair in one hand to pull her head up. She had only a brief glimpse of his face—the eyes half-shut but darker and more intense than she had ever seen them—before he brought her mouth down to his and devoured. All will, all sense was seeping out of her.

''Brooke...'' His hands were on her hips, urging her. ''Now.'' The demand was wrenched from him, hoarse and urgent. She resisted, struggling to breathe, fighting to hold some part of herself separate. ''I need you,'' he murmured before their lips met again. ''I need you.''

Then it was clear—for one breathless instant. She needed, and knew now she was needed in return. It was enough...perhaps everything. With a shuddering sound of relief and joy, she gave.

At nine fifty-five, Claire swept into the editing room. Neither the editors nor E.J. were surprised to see the head of Thorton Productions on the job on a Saturday morning. Anyone who had worked at Thorton more than a week knew that Claire wasn't a figurehead but an entity to be reckoned with. She wore one of her trim little suits, the color of crushed raspberries, and a trace of Parisian scent.

"Dave, Lila, E.J." Claire gave all three a quick nod before heading toward the coffeepot. A newer member of the staff might have scurried to serve the boss, but those lounging near the control board knew better.

"Made it myself, Ms. Thorton," E.J. told her as she poured. "It won't taste like the battery acid these two cook up."

"I appreciate that, E.J.," she said dryly. Just the scent of it revived her. Claire inhaled it, telling herself only an old fool thought she could dance until three and still function the next day. Ah, but how nice it was to feel like a fool again, she thought with a slow smile. "I'm told that the shoot went well, with no major problems."

"Smooth as silk," E.J. stated. "Wait till you get a load of Parks knocking that sucker over the fence." He grinned reminiscently. "I won ten bucks off Brooke with that hit." His selective memory allowed him to forget that it had been his ten dollars in the first place.

Claire settled into a chair with a quiet sigh. "Is Brooke in yet?"

"Haven't seen her." E.J. began to whistle as he recalled Brooke leaving the location with Parks. Accustomed to his habits, Claire only lifted a brow.

"Are you set up, Dave?"

"Ready to run through it, Ms. Thorton. Want to see it from the top?"

"In a moment." Even as Claire checked her watch, she heard Brooke's voice in the corridor.

''As long as you understand you have absolutely no say in what gets cut and what stays in.''

''I might have an intelligent comment to make.''

''Parks, I'm serious.''

His low chuckle rolled into the editing room just ahead of Brooke. ''Morning,'' she said to the group at large. ''Coffee hot?''

''E.J.'s special,'' Claire told her, watching Brooke over the rim of her mug as she sipped. She looked different, Claire thought, then slid her eyes to Parks. And there was the reason, she concluded with a small smile. ''Good morning, Parks.''

Her face remained bland and friendly, but he recognized her thoughts. With a slight nod, he acknowledged them. ''Hello, Claire,'' he said, abandoning formality as smoothly as he reached for a cup for himself. ''I hope you don't mind me sitting in on this.'' Taking the pot, he poured Brooke's coffee, then his own. ''Brooke has a few reservations.''

''Amateurs,'' Brooke said precisely as she reached for the powdered cream, ''have a tendency to be pains in the—''

''Yes, well I'm sure we're delighted to have Parks join us,'' Claire interrupted over E.J.'s chuckle. ''Run it through, Dave. Let's see what we've got.''

At her order, he flicked a series of buttons on the large control panel in front of him. Parks watched himself appear simultaneously on three monitors. He could hear Brooke's voice off camera, then the little man with the clapboard scooted in front of him announcing the scene and take.

"It's the third take that worked," Brooke announced as she settled on the arm of Claire's chair. "Casey at the bat didn't like the first pitch."

Her remark earned her a grin from Parks and a mild exclamation from Claire. "The lighting's very good." Claire studied the second take through narrowed eyes.

"The new boy, Silbey. He's got a nice touch. The clothes sell it." Brooke sipped while gesturing with her free hand. "Watch when he sets for the swing.... Yes." She gave a nod of approval. "Nice moves, no apparent restriction. He looks comfortable, efficient, sexy." Intent on the screen, Brooke didn't notice the look Parks tossed at her. "This is the one I want to use." She waited, silently, watching the replay of Parks's home run. The test swings, the concentration, the connection and follow-through, the satisfied grin and the shrug.

"I want to keep in the last bit," Brooke went on. "That gee-whiz shrug. It sells the whole business. That natural cockiness is its own appeal." Parks choked over his coffee, but Brooke ignored him. "As I see it, this segment is pretty clear-cut. The next I'm not so sure about. It's going to be effective...."

Cupping his mug in both hands, Parks sat down. For the next two hours he watched himself on the screens of the monitors, listened to himself being weighed, dissected, judged. Though the latter disconcerted him initially, he found that watching himself didn't bring on the feeling of idiocy he'd been certain it would. He began to think he might find some enjoyment out of his two-year stint after all.

Though he'd heard himself picked apart and put back

together countless times over the years—coaches, sports critics, other players—Parks couldn't find the same level of tolerance at hearing Brooke speak so matter-of-factly about his face and body, his gestures and expressions. All in all, he thought, it was as though he were the salable product, not the clothes he wore.

They ran the film back and forth, while Claire listened to input and made occasional comments. Yes, they would have to work in close-ups in the next shoot, his face was very good. It would be smart to fill another thirty-second spot with action to exploit the way he moved, showing the durability of the clothes as well as the versatility. They might try tennis shorts if his legs were any good.

At this Parks shot Brooke a deadly glance, half expecting her to offer her personal opinion. She caught it, then smothered a chuckle with a fit of coughing. Over Claire's head she gave him an innocent smile and an unexpectedly lewd wink. The quick response of his own body caused him to scowl at her. She was dressed like a waif, in baggy chinos and a sweater, her hair braided back and secured with a rubber band. From across the room he could smell the elusive, promising scent of her perfume.

''We taped his voice-over this morning,'' she told Claire. ''I think you'll find his voice is good, though how he'll handle real dialogue remains to be seen. Do we have the graphics for the tag-on, Lila?''

''Right here.'' She flipped a series of switches. On the monitor now was the de Marco logo of a black-maned lion against a cool-blue background. The signature line cartwheeled slowly onto the screen until it stopped below the cat. It held long enough for impact, then faded.

''Very classy,'' Brooke approved. ''then it's agreed? The third take from the first segment, the fifth from the second.''

''We saved you guys from a lot of splicing,'' E.J. commented as he toyed with an unlit cigarette. ''You should be able to put this together with your eyes closed.''

''I'd appreciate it if you'd keep them open,'' Claire said as she rose. ''Let me know when it's cut and dubbed. E.J., a splendid job, as always.''

''Thanks, Ms. Thorton.''

She handed him her empty mug. ''On the camera work, too,'' she added. The editors snickered as she turned toward the door. ''Parks, I hope you didn't find all this too boring.''

''On the contrary...'' He thought of the objective discussions on his anatomy. ''It's been an education.''

She gave him a mild smile of perfect understanding. ''Brooke, my office, ten minutes.'' As an afterthought she glanced at her watch. ''Oh, dear. Perhaps you'd like to join us for lunch, Parks.''

''I appreciate it, but I have a few things I have to do.''

''Well then.'' Patting his arm, she smiled again. ''Best of luck in the play-offs.'' She slipped away, leaving Brooke frowning after her.

''I probably won't get any lunch now,'' she muttered. ''If you'd said yes, she'd have made reservations at Ma Maison.''

''Sorry.'' Parks drew her out in the corridor. ''Did that wink mean you approve of my legs?''

''Wink?'' Brooke stared at him blankly. ''I don't know

what you're talking about. Winking during an editing session is very unprofessional.''

He glanced at the door she had closed behind her. ''The way you all talked in here, I felt that I was the product.''

With a half laugh, Brooke shook her head. ''Parks, you *are* the product.''

His eyes came back to hers, surprising Brooke with the flare of anger. ''No. I wear the product.''

She opened her mouth, then closed it again on a cautious sigh. ''It's really a matter of viewpoint,'' she said carefully. ''From yours, from de Marco's, even from the consumers', the clothes are the product. From the viewpoints of your producer, your director, your cinematographer and so forth, you're as much the product as the clothes you wear because we have to see that both of you are salable. If I can't make you look good, what you're wearing might as well be flea market special.''

He saw the logic but didn't care for it. ''I won't be a commodity.''

''Parks, you're a commodity every time you walk out on the diamond. This really isn't any different.'' Exasperated, she lifted her hands palms up. ''You sell tickets to Kings games, baseball cards and fielder's caps. Don't be so damned sanctimonious about this.''

''First it's temperamental, now it's sanctimonious,'' he muttered disgustedly. ''I suppose what it comes down to is we look at this little...venture from two different perspectives.''

Brooke felt a light flutter of fear inside her breast. ''I told you,'' she said quietly, ''that it would be difficult.''

His eyes came back to her, recognizing the shield she

was already prepared to bring down. Parks ran a finger down her cheek. ''And I told you it would be fun.'' Leaning closer, he brushed his lips over hers. ''We're both right. I have some things to do. Can I meet you back here later?''

Relaxing, Brooke told herself she had imagined the fear. ''If you like. I'll probably be tied up until around five.''

''Fine. You can cook me that dinner you promised me last night.''

Brooke lifted her chin. ''I never promised to cook you dinner,'' she corrected. ''But perhaps I will.''

''I'll buy the wine.'' Parks sent her a grin before he turned away.

''Wait.'' After a moment, Brooke went after him. ''You don't have your car.''

Parks shrugged. ''I'll take a cab.'' He saw her hesitate then struggle with a decision.

''No,'' she said abruptly, digging in her bag. ''You can use mine.''

Parks took the keys, and her hand. He knew enough about her to realize offering the use of her car, or anything else important to her, wasn't a casual gesture. ''Thank you.''

Her color rose—the first truly self-conscious thing he had noticed about her. ''You're welcome.'' Quickly, she drew her hand from his and turned away. ''See you at five,'' she called over her shoulder without stopping.

Brooke felt a bit foolish as she rode the elevator to Claire's office. How could she have blushed over a simple thank-you for the loan of a car? She glanced up at the numbers flashing over the elevator door. Oh, he knew her too well, she realized, knew her too well when she'd hardly told him anything.

He didn't know she still had the copy of *Little Women* her second foster mother had given her. He didn't know that she had adored those temporary parents and had been devastated when a broken marriage had caused her to be placed in another foster home. He didn't know about the horrid little girl she had shared a room with during what she still considered the worst year of her life. Or the Richardsons, who had treated her more like a hired hand than a foster child. Or Clark.

With a sigh, Brooke rubbed her fingers over her forehead. She didn't like to remember—didn't like knowing that her growing feelings for Parks seemed to force her to face the past again. Oh, the hell with it, Brooke thought with a shake of her head. It *was* the past. And she was going to have enough trouble dealing with the present to dwell on it.

Steadier, she stepped out into the wide, carpeted corridor of Claire's floor. The receptionist, a pretty girl with lots of large healthy teeth, straightened in her chair at Brooke's approach. She'd worked on the top floor for over two years and was still more in awe of Brooke than of Claire.

"Good afternoon, Ms. Gordon."

"Hello, Sheila. Ms. Thorton's expecting me."

"Yes, ma'am." Sheila wouldn't have contradicted her if her life had depended on it.

Unaware of the impression she made, Brooke strode easily down the corridor and through a set of wide glass doors. Here, two secretaries, known as the twins only because of identical desks, labored away on word processors. The outer office was huge, scrupulously modern and cathedral quiet.

"Ms. Gordon." The first twin beamed a smile while a second one reached for the button on her intercom.

"She's expecting me," Brooke said simply and breezed by them into Claire's office. The door opened silently. Brooke was halfway across the pewter-colored carpet before she realized Claire was sound asleep at her desk. Totally stunned, Brooke stopped dead in her tracks and stared.

The chair Claire sat in was high-backed pale-gray leather. Her desk was ebony, gleaming beneath stacks of neat papers. The glasses Claire wore for reading were held loosely in her hand. A Chinese "literary painting" in color wash and ink hung on the wall to her right, while behind her L.A. sunshine poured through a plate-glass window. Unsure what to do, Brooke considered leaving as quietly as she had come, then decided it was best to stay. Walking to the squashy leather chair facing the desk, she sat, then gently cleared her throat. Claire's eyes snapped open.

"Morning," Brooke said brightly and grinned at Claire's uncharacteristic confusion. "You'd do better on the sofa if you want a nap."

"Just resting my eyes."

"Mm-hmm."

Ignoring the comment, Claire reached for the papers she had been reading before fatigue had won. "I wanted you to have a look at the script for the next de Marco spot."

"Okay." Brooke accepted the script automatically. "Claire, are you all right?"

"Don't I look all right?"

Deciding to take her literally, Brooke studied her. Except for the heavy eyes, she decided, Claire looked better than ever. Almost, Brooke mused, glowing. "You look marvelous."

"Well then." Claire smoothed her hair before she folded her hands.

"Didn't you sleep well last night?" Brooke persisted.

"As it happens, I was out late. Now the script."

"With Lee Dutton?" The thought went through her mind and out her lips before she could stop it. Claire gave her a tolerant smile.

"As a matter of fact, yes."

Brooke set the script back on the desk. "Claire," she began, only to be interrupted by a knock on the door.

"Your lunch, Ms. Thorton." A tray was wheeled in by twin number one.

The scent of hot roast beef had Brooke rising. "Claire, I misjudged you." Lifting the cover from a hot plate, she inhaled. "Forgive me."

"Did you think I'd let you go hungry?" With a chuckle, Claire stood to move to the sofa. "Brooke, dear, I've known you too long. Bring me my salad and coffee like a good girl."

Nibbling on a potato wedge, Brooke obeyed. "Claire, I really want to talk with you about Lee Dutton."

"Of course." Claire speared a radish slice. "Sit down and eat, Brooke, pacing's bad for my digestion."

Plate in hand, Brooke approached the couch. She set it

on the low coffee table, picked up half a roast beef sandwich and began. ''Claire, are you actually dating Lee Dutton?''

''Does dating seem inappropriate to you for someone of my age, Brooke? Pass me that salt.''

''No!'' Flustered, Brooke looked down at Claire's outstretched hand. She gave her the salt shaker then took a defiant bite of her sandwich. ''Don't be ridiculous,'' she muttered over it. ''I can see you dating all manner of fabulous men. I have trouble seeing you out on the town with Lee Dutton.''

''Why?''

Brooke shifted her shoulders uncomfortably. This wasn't how she had intended it to go. ''Well, he's nice enough, and certainly sharp, but he seems sort of...well.'' Brooke sighed and tried again. ''Let's put it this way: I can see Lee Dutton in the neighborhood bowling alley. I can't picture you there.''

''No....'' Claire pursed her lips in thought. ''We haven't tried that yet.''

''Claire!'' Exasperated, Brooke rose and began to pace again. ''I'm not getting through to you. Look, I don't want to interfere with your life—''

''No?'' The mild smile had Brooke flopping back down on the couch.

''You matter to me.''

Claire reached over to squeeze her hand. ''I appreciate that, Brooke, I've been taking care of myself for a long time. I've even handled a few men.''

A bit reassured, Brooke began to eat again. ''I suppose if I thought you were really getting involved...''

''What makes you think I'm not?'' At Brooke's gaping stare, Claire laughed.

''Claire, are you—are you...'' She gestured, not quite certain she should put her thoughts into words.

''Sleeping with him?'' Claire finished in her calm, cultured voice. ''Not yet.''

''Not yet,'' Brooke echoed numbly.

''Well, he hasn't asked me to.'' Claire took another bite of salad and chewed thoughtfully. ''I thought he would by now, but he's quite conservative. Very sweet and old fashioned. That's part of his appeal for me. He makes me feel very feminine. You can lose that at times in this business.''

''Yes, I know.'' Brooke picked up her iced tea and stared into it. ''Do you—are you in love with him?''

''I think I am.'' Claire settled back against the gray-and-rose patterned sofa. ''I was only in love once before, really in love. I was your age, perhaps a bit younger.'' Her smile was soft for a moment, a girl's smile. ''In all the years in between, I've never met anyone I was attracted to enough, comfortable enough with, trusted enough, to think of marrying.''

Brooke took a long swallow of tea. She thought she understood Claire's phrasing all too well. ''You're thinking of marriage?''

''I'm thinking I'm almost fifty years old. I've built this up''—she gestured to indicate Thorton—''I have a comfortable home, a nice circle of friends and acquaintances, enough new challenges to keep me from dying of boredom, and suddenly I've found a man who makes me want to curl up in front of a fire after a long day.'' She smiled slowly and rather beautifully—not the girl's smile this time. "It's a good feeling." She let her eyes slide to Brooke, who was watching her closely. "I'd hate to see you have to wait twenty more years for it. Parks is a great deal more than mildly attracted to you."

For the third time, Brooke rose to pace the room. "We haven't known each other long," she began.

"You're a woman who knows her own mind, Brooke."

"Am I?" With a mordant smile, she turned back. "Perhaps I do know how I think, how I feel. I don't really know Parks, though. What if I give too much? What's to stop him from getting bored and moving on?"

Claire met her eyes steadily. "Don't compare him, Brooke. Don't make him pass tests for all those old hurts."

"Oh, Claire." Passing a hand through her hair, Brooke walked to stare out of the window. "That's the last thing I want to do."

"What's the first thing?"

"It's always been to have my own. To have my own so that nobody can come along and say, 'Whoops, you really only borrowed this, time to give it back.'" She laughed a little. "Silly, I suppose I've never really shaken that."

"And why should you?" Claire demanded. "We all want our own. And to get it, you and I both know there are a few basic risks involved."

"I'm afraid I'm falling in love with him," Brooke said quietly. "And the closer I get, the more afraid I am that it's all going to crumble under my feet. I have a feeling I need this defense…that if I fall in love with him, I need this edge of control, this little pocket of power, to keep myself from getting demolished. Is that crazy?''

''No. You're not the kind of woman who gives herself completely without asking for something back. You did that once, but you were a child. You're a woman who needs a strong man, Brooke. One strong enough to take, strong enough not to take all.'' She smiled as Brooke turned to face her. ''Give yourself a little time,'' she advised. ''Things have a way of falling into place.''

''Do they?''

Claire's smile widened. ''Sometimes it only takes twenty years.''

With a laugh, Brooke walked back to the sofa. ''Thanks a lot.''

Chapter 8

Brooke sat cross-legged on the softly faded Oriental rug in Claire's den. Sometime during the fourth inning she'd given up trying to sit in a chair. To her right, Lee and Claire sat on a two-cushioned brocade sofa. Billings had outdone herself by preparing her specialty, Beef Wellington, then had been mutely offended when Brooke had done little more than shift the food around on her plate. Though she chided herself for being nervous, Brooke had been able to do nothing but worry about the outcome of the play-offs since Parks had taken off for the Valiants' home stadium.

She'd been able to catch part of the first afternoon game on her car radio as she had driven to a location shoot. One of the production crew had thought ahead, bringing a portable radio with an earplug, and had kept up a running commentary between takes. Brooke had felt overwhelming relief when the Kings had taken the first game, then frustration and more nerves when they had lost the second. Now, she watched the third on the television set in Claire's small, elegant den.

"That man was out at second," Brooke fumed, wriggling impotently on the faded royal-blue rug. "Anyone with two working eyes could see that."

As she launched her personal attack, the Kings' manager, a squat man with the face of a dyspeptic elf, argued with the second base umpire. If she hadn't been quite so furious herself, Brooke might have admired the manager's theatrical gestures as he spun around, rolled his eyes to heaven and pointed an accusing finger in the umpire's face. The umpire remained unmoved and the call stood. With the Kings holding on to a thin one-run lead, a runner on second with one out boded ill.

When the next batter sent one sailing over the fence and the slim lead changed hands, Brooke groaned. "I can't stand it," she decided, pounding her fists on the rug. "I just can't stand it."

"Brooke's become involved in the game," Claire murmured to Lee.

"So I've noticed." He dropped a light kiss on her cheek. "You smell wonderful!"

The sensation of blood rising to her cheeks was pleasant. She had been romanced by suave masters of the game in the more than twenty-five years of her womanhood, but she couldn't remember one who had made her feel quite the way Lee Dutton could. If they had been alone, she would have snuggled closer, but remembering Brooke, she merely squeezed his hand. "Have some wine, dear," she said to Brooke as she reached for the iced bottle beside her. ''Good for the nerves.''

Because she was breathing a sigh of relief as the next batter struck out, Brooke didn't acknowledge the teasing tone. ''That's three out,'' she said as she took the cool glass from Claire.

''Two,'' Lee corrected.

''Only if you believe a nearsighted umpire,'' she countered, sipping. When he chuckled, she sent a grin over her shoulder. ''At least I didn't call him a bum.''

''Give yourself a little time,'' Lee advised, winking at Claire as she handed him a glass.

''You know, some of the players—'' Brooke began, then broke off with a gasp as a smoking line drive was hit toward third. Her stomach muscles knotted instantly. Parks dove sideways, stretching his arm out toward the speeding ball. He nabbed it in the tip of his glove just before the length of his body connected with the hard Astroturf. Brooke thought she could feel the bone-rattling jolt herself.

''He got it!'' Lee broke out of his casual pose with a jerk that nearly upset Claire's wine. ''Look at that, look at that! He got it!'' he repeated, pointing at the television image of Parks holding up the glove to show the catch while he still lay prone. ''That young sonofa—'' He caught himself, barely, and cleared his throat. ''Parks is the best with a glove in the league,'' he decided. ''In *both* leagues!'' He leaned forward to pound Brooke companionably on the back. ''Parks robbed him, kid. Stole a base hit from him as sure as God made little green apples.''

Because she watched Parks stand up and brush himself

off, Brooke relaxed. ''I want to see it on replay,'' she murmured. ''Slow motion.''

''You'll see that play a dozen times before the night's through,'' Lee predicted. ''And again on the eleven o'clock news. Hey, lookie here.'' Grinning, he gestured to the set. ''That's what I call classy timing.''

Brooke shifted her concentration to the de Marco commercial. Of course she'd seen it a dozen times in the editing room, and again on television, but each time she watched, she searched for flaws. She studied the graphics as Parks's cool clear voice spoke out to her. ''It's perfect,'' she said with a smile. ''Absolutely perfect.''

''How's the next one coming?'' Lee asked Claire.

''It's just waiting for Parks to be available. We hope to shoot next week.''

He settled back again, one arm around Claire. ''I'm going to enjoy seeing that one play during the series.''

''They still have two games to win,'' Brooke reminded him. ''They're a run behind in this one, and—''

''The opera's not over till the fat lady sings,'' Lee said mildly.

Brooke swiveled her head to look at him. Claire was snug beside him, a crystal glass in one hand. Lee's paunch strained against the buttons of his checked shirt. The ankle of one leg rested on the knee of the other while his foot bounced up and down to some personal tune. Abruptly, Brooke saw them as a perfect match. ''I like you, Lee,'' she said with a wide smile. ''I really like you.''

He blinked twice, then his lips curved hesitantly. ''Well, thanks, kid.''

She's just given us her blessing, Claire thought with an inward chuckle as she took Lee's hand in hers.

Brooke made her way through the airport crowd with steady determination. In addition to the usual flow of traffic at LAX, there were fans, mobs of fans, waiting to greet the incoming Kings team. Some carried handmade signs, others banners. There were, she noted with some amusement, a good number of truants in the Los Angeles school system that morning, not to mention a deficit in the work force. After the twelve-inning victory, Brooke thought the players deserved a bit of adulation. She also wondered if she'd ever be able to fight her way through so that Parks would see her. The impulse to surprise him, she realized, had not been practical. A truant father hoisted a truant second-grader onto his shoulders. Brooke grinned. Maybe not practical, but it was going to be fun.

Pushing her sunglasses atop her head, Brooke narrowed her eyes against the sun and waited for the plane to touch down. As it stopped being a dot in the sky and took on form, she began to experience the first flicker of nerves. She fidgeted nervously with her bag while she stood, crushed shoulder to shoulder, with excited fans.

He'll be tired, she thought as dozens of conversations buzzed around her. He's probably looking forward to going home and sleeping for twenty-four hours. Brooke ran a hand through her hair. I should have told him I was coming. She shifted her weight to the other foot, curled her fingers around the chain link in front of her and watched the plane glide to a stop.

The moment the door opened, the cheering started,

building, rising as the first men began to deplane. They waved back, looking tired and somehow vulnerable without their uniforms. Men, she thought. Simply men suffering from jet lag and perhaps a few hangovers. Then she smiled, deciding that the gladiators might have looked precisely the same the day after a bout.

As soon as she saw him, she felt warm. Beside Brooke, a teenager grabbed her companion and squealed.

"Oh, there's Parks Jones! He's bee-utiful."

Brooke swallowed a laugh as she thought of how Parks would react to the adjective.

"Every time I watch him, my knees get weak." The teenager pressed her lithe young body against the fence. "Did you see him in the commercial? When he smiled, it was like he was looking right *at* me. I nearly died."

Though she didn't take her eyes off Parks, Brooke smiled inwardly. My plan exactly, she thought, pleased with herself. Why do I feel like a woman watching her man come home from the wars?

Though her sharp director's eye had seen a group of tense and tired men, the fans saw heroes. They cheered them. Some of the players merely waved and moved on, but most came up to the fence to exchange words, jokes, a touch of hands. Brooke watched Parks walk toward the barrier with a man she recognized as Snyder, the first baseman. She wondered, by the intensity of their discussion, if they were outlining infield strategy.

"It would only take twenty-five or thirty cans of shaving cream to fill his locker," Snyder insisted.

"Takes too long and evaporates too fast," Parks commented. "You've got to be practical, George."

Snyder swore mildly and lifted his hand in acknowledgment to a shout in the crowd. ''Got a better idea?''

''Carbon dioxide.'' Parks scanned the crowd as they neared it. ''Quick and efficient.''

''Hey, yeah!'' Pleased, Snyder gave him a slap on the back. ''Knew your brains were good for something, Einstein.''

''And as long as I help you work out the mechanics,'' Parks added, ''my locker doesn't get filled with the thinking man's shaving cream.''

''There's that, too,'' Snyder agreed. ''Would you look at these people?'' His grin widened. ''Fantastic.''

Parks started to agree, then spotted a mass of red hair touched with gold in the sunlight. The fatigue drained as though someone had pulled a cork. ''Fantastic,'' he murmured and walked straight toward Brooke.

The teenager beside her made a moaning, melting sound and took a death grip on her friend's arm. ''He's coming over here,'' she managed in a choked whisper. ''Right over here. I know I'm going to die.''

Brooke tilted her chin up so that her eyes would stay level with his as he stopped on the other side of the fence. ''Hi.'' Parks's hand closed over hers on the metal wire. The simple contact was as intimate as anything she had ever known.

''Hi.'' Brooke smiled slowly, accepting the flare of desire and the sense of closeness without question.

''Can I get a lift?''

''Anytime.''

He pressed his lips to the fingers still curled around the wire. "Meet me inside? I have to get my baggage."

Out of the corner of her eye, Brooke saw the two teenage girls gawking. "Great catch last night."

He grinned before he stepped away. "Thanks."

Snyder caught him by the arm as Brooke melted back into the crowd. "Hey, I like that catch better."

"Off limits," Parks said simply, making his way down the line of fans and outstretched hands.

"Aw, come on, Parks, we're teammates. All for one and one for all."

"Forget it."

"The trouble with Parks," Snyder began to tell a grandfatherly type behind the fence, "is he's selfish. I make his throws look good. I bite the bullet when he lines a hospital pitch at me. And what thanks do I get?" He sent Parks a hopeful smile. "You could at least introduce me."

Parks grinned as he signed a snatch of paper a fan thrust through a hole in the fence. "Nope."

It took him nearly thirty minutes to get away from the crowd and through the terminal. Impatience was growing in him. The simple touch of fingers outside had whetted his appetite for a great deal more. He'd never been lonely on the road before. Even if there was a rain out or an off day away from home, you were surrounded by people you knew. You became as close as a family—close enough to spend endless evenings together or opt to spend one alone without bruising feelings. No, he'd never been lonely. Until this time.

Parks couldn't count the times he had thought of her over the last four days, but he knew that everything had suddenly slipped back into focus the moment he had seen her standing there. Now he saw her again.

Brooke leaned back against a pillar near the baggage belt, Parks's suitcase at her feet. She smiled but didn't straighten as she saw him. She'd hate to have him know just how crazily her pulse was racing. "You travel light," she commented.

He cupped her face in his hand and, oblivious to the people milling around them, brought her close for a long, hard kiss.

"I missed you," he murmured against her mouth, then kissed her again.

There were enough of his teammates still loitering around to start up a chorus of approval.

"Excuse me." Snyder tapped Parks on the shoulder and grinned engagingly at Brooke. "I believe you've made a mistake. *I'm* George Snyder. This is our aging bat boy." He gave Parks an affectionate pat.

"How do you do." Brooke extended her hand and had it enveloped in a huge, hard palm. "Too bad about those two strikeouts last night."

There were several jeers as Snyder winced. "Actually, I'm luring the Valiants into complacency."

"Oh." Amused, Brooke gave him a big smile. "You did very well."

"Sorry, Snyder, time for your shot." Parks signaled to two teammates, who agreeably hooked their arms through Snyder's to haul him away.

"Aw, come on, Jones, give me a break!" Good-naturedly, Snyder let himself be dragged away. "I just want to discuss my strategy with her."

"Goodbye, George." Brooke waved as Parks bent to retrieve his bag.

"Let's get out of here."

With her fingers laced through his, Brooke had no choice but to follow. "Parks, you might have introduced me to your friends."

"Dangerous men," he stated. "All dangerous men."

With a chuckle, she matched her pace to his. "Yes, I could see that. Especially the one holding a toddler on each hip."

"There are a few exceptions."

"Are you one?"

Parks caught her around the waist and drew her close against him. "Uh-uh."

"Oh, good. Want to come home with me and tell me your strategy?"

"That's the best offer I've had today." After tossing his bag in the rear of her car, Parks sprawled in the passenger seat. Accustomed to her driving pattern now, he relaxed and began to unwind by rambling about the previous day's game. Brooke said little, pleased to listen, glad that she had arranged to take the day off so that they could have a few hours together, alone.

"The commercial aired during each play-off game, you know," she commented as they headed out of town.

"How'd it look?" Parks laid his head back against the seat. God, it was good to know he didn't have to go anywhere or do anything for twenty-four hours.

"Fantastic." As the road opened up, so did the Datsun's throttle. "And I have it from the source that it plays very well."

''Hmm?''

''A teenager girl in that mob today.'' With near perfect mimicry, Brooke related the girl's comments. She caught Parks's automatic grimace at the term *bee-utiful* but swallowed a chuckle as she continued.

''Nice to know I devastate sixteen-year-old girls,'' he said dryly.

''You'd be surprised at the buying power of sixteen-year-old girls.'' With experienced ease, Brooke negotiated the curves on the narrowing road. ''Not so much directly, certainly, but indirectly through their parents. And since they'd like their teenage boyfriends to make their knees weaken, too, they'll push them toward de Marco jeans, shirts, belts, *ad infinitum.*'' Tossing her hair back, she slid her eyes to his. ''And you do have a great smile.''

''Yeah.'' He gave a modest sigh. ''I do.''

Brooke stopped in her driveway with a deliberate jerk that had him swearing. Wisely slipping from the car before he could retaliate, she headed up the path.

''Just for that,'' Parks began as he dragged his bag out of the back, ''I'm not going to give you the present I bought you.''

At the door, Brooke turned, her grin changing to a look of bewilderment. ''You bought me a present?''

Because she looked like a child who expected to be handed a brightly wrapped empty box, Parks treated it lightly. ''I did. But I'm seriously considering keeping it myself now.''

''What is it?''

''Are you going to open the door?''

Brooke shrugged, trying to pretend indifference as she

turned the key. ''There's a fire laid,'' she said as she breezed inside. ''Why don't you light it while I get us some coffee?''

''Okay.'' Setting his bag down, Parks stretched travel-cramped muscles. With a wince, he pressed his fingers to the ribs still sore from their contact with Astroturf.

She'd brought some of her garden inside, he noted, spotting the bowl of vibrant mums and zinnias on the side table across the room. The table, he observed, was Queen Anne; the bowl, dimestore special. Grinning, he went to the hearth. The combination suited her—the exquisite and the practical.

Parks struck a match and set it to the carefully rolled paper beneath the kindling. Dry wood caught with a crackle and a *whoosh.* He inhaled the smell that brought back flickering images of the past; evenings in the cozy parlor of his family home, camping trips with his uncle and cousins, weekends in England at the home of a college friend. He wanted to add to the pictures now with the memory of Brooke lying in his arms in front of the simmering fire while they made slow, endless love.

When he heard her returning, Parks stood, turning to face her as she entered with a tray holding a bottle and two glasses. ''I thought you might want wine instead.''

Smiling, Parks took the tray from her. ''Yes.'' After setting the tray on the hassock, Parks lifted the bottle, examining the label with a lifted brow. ''Is this a celebration?''

''A precelebration,'' Brooke countered. ''I expect you to win tomorrow.'' She picked up both glasses, holding them out. "And if you don't, we'll have had the wine in any case."

"Seems fair." Parks poured pale-gold liquid into the stemmed glasses. Taking one from her, he clinked the rims together. "To the game?" he asked with a slow smile.

Brooke felt the quick nervous flutter in her stomach and nodded. "To the game," she agreed and drank. Her eyes widened but remained steady when he reached out to take a handful of her hair.

"I saw this in the sunlight," he murmured. "Even in that mob of people at the airport, I'm not sure what I would have done if that fence hadn't been in the way." He let it sift through his fingers. "It was a long four days, Brooke."

She nodded, taking his hand to draw him onto the sofa beside her. The curves of her body seemed to fit naturally against the lines of his. "You're tense," she said quietly.

"Postseason games." He drew her closer, knowing the nerves would gradually drain before they built again the next day. "Maybe the lucky ones are the players raking leaves in their backyards in October."

"But you don't really think so."

Parks laughed. "No, I don't really think so. The playoffs pump you up until you're ready to explode, but the series..." He trailed off with a shake of his head. He didn't want to let his mind run that far ahead. The rules were three out of five—they weren't there yet. For now he didn't want to think of it, but of the woman beside him, the quiet afternoon and the long evening ahead. He thought that he'd remember her this way, a little pensive, with the smell of woodsmoke and fall flowers mixing with her own perfume. His mind drifted lazily, comfortably, as he sipped the iced wine and watched the flames dance.

"Have you been busy?"

Brooke tilted her head in absent agreement. She didn't want to think of work any more than Parks did. "The usual," she said vaguely. "E.J. talked me into seeing a perfectly dreadful movie where the cast pranced around in mythological costumes and shot lightning bolts."

"Olympian Revenge?"

"It had a talking three-head dragon."

"That's the one. I caught it in Philadelphia last month when we had a rain out."

"I saw the mike in the frame three times."

Parks chuckled at her professional disdain. "Nobody else did," he assured her. "They were all asleep."

"Gross ineptitude keeps me awake." She leaned her head against his shoulder. It occurred to her how empty her home had been for the last few days, and how cozy it felt again. Brooke had never felt the need to share it before. In fact, she had always had a strong proprietary feeling about what was hers. Now, sitting quietly on the sofa, she realized she had already begun to give up her privacy, willingly and with total unawareness. Turning her head, she studied Parks's profile. "I missed you," she said at length.

He turned his head as well so that their lips were close, not quite touching. "I'd hoped you would." Then he shifted so that his mouth grazed her cheek. She trembled. Not yet, he told himself as the heat flared inside him. Not quite yet. "Maybe I'll give you that present after all."

Brooke's lips curved against his throat. "I don't believe you bought me anything at all."

Recognizing the ploy but willing to play, Parks rose. "You'll have to apologize for that," he said soberly as he walked to his suitcase. He flipped open the case then rummaged inside. When he stood again, Parks had a white box in his hands. Brooke regarded it curiously but with some of the wariness he had noted outside.

"What is it?"

"Open it and find out," he suggested, dropping it into her lap.

Brooke turned it over, examining the plain white box, testing it for weight. She wasn't a woman accustomed to spontaneous gifts and in the short time he had known her, Parks had already given her two. "You didn't have to—"

"You *have* to give your sister a Christmas present," he said mildly, sitting beside her again. "You're not my sister and it isn't Christmas."

Brooke frowned. "I'm not sure I understand the logic in that," she murmured then opened the lid. Packed in wads of tissue paper was a fat pink ceramic hippo with heavily lashed eyes, a flirtatious grin and varicolored polka dots. With a laugh, Brooke drew it out. "She's gorgeous!"

"She reminded me of you," Parks commented, pleased with the laugh and the look of humor in her eyes when she turned them to him.

"Is that so?" She held the hippo up again. "Well, she does have rather fetching eyes." Touched, she stroked the wide ceramic flank. "She really is sweet, Parks. What made you think of it?"

"I thought she'd fit into your menagerie." Seeing the puzzled look on her face, he gestured toward the shelf that held her monkey and bear. "Then there's that pig on the front door, the little carving of a jack rabbit in your bedroom, the china owl on the windowsill in the kitchen."

Comprehension came slowly. There were animals of varying types and materials scattered all through the house. She'd been collecting them for years without having the slightest idea what she was doing. But Parks had seen. Without an instant of warning to either of them, Brooke burst into tears.

Stunned, then alarmed, Parks reached for her, not having a clue what he would offer comfort for. Still, he'd seen enough tears from his sisters to know that logic often had nothing to do with tears. Ashamed, and unable to stem the flow, Brooke evaded his arms and rose. "No, no, please. Give me a minute. I *hate* to do this."

Even as he told himself to respect her wishes, Parks was going to her. Despite her resistance, he pulled her against him. "I can't stand to *see* you do it," he muttered; then, with a hint of exasperation, "Why are you doing it?"

"You'll think I'm stupid. I hate being stupid."

"Brooke." Firmly, he cupped a hand under her chin and lifted it. Tears rolled freely down her cheeks. Knowing no other remedy, he kissed her—the soft lips, the wet cheeks, the damp eyelids. What began as a blind effort to comfort grew to smoldering passion.

He could feel it build in him as his mouth sought hers again. His hands moved through her hair like those of a man making his tentative way through bolts of silk. She trembled against him—sobs or desire Parks was no longer sure as the kiss went deeper and deeper. She opened for him, more giving than he could remember. Her defenses were down, he reminded himself, fighting the impatience to fill his own needs quickly. His murmurs were quiet-pitched to soothe, his hands gently stroking to arouse.

Even recognizing her own vulnerability, Brooke didn't resist. She wanted to drift into that smoky, weightless world where every movement seemed to be in slow motion. She wanted to feel that fire and flash that left you breathless. She wanted the down-soft contentment that would lull you to sleep and linger in the morning.

As he lowered her to the floor, the scent of woodsmoke grew stronger. Brooke could hear the pop and hiss of the logs as flames ate at them. His long patient kisses held her suspended—half in the reality of the wool rug beneath her back, the red flickers of firelight and sun on her closed lids, half in the world of dreams lovers understand. While her mind floated, flirting with each separate sensation, he undressed her.

Parks took infinite care with the tiny round buttons of her blouse, as if he could wait until the seasons changed outside the tall windows. There was no time here, no winter, no spring, only one everlasting moment. Brooke slipped her hands under his shirt, fingertips gliding over the warmth and the strength. As patient as he, she drew the material up, over his shoulders, then discarded it.

Flesh against flesh, they lay before the fire while the sun streamed through the massive windows and pooled over them. Kisses grew longer, interrupted only for sighs, for murmurs. She tasted the mellow warmth of wine on his tongue and was intoxicated.

Slowly, his mouth never leaving hers, Parks began to explore her body. Tiny, needlelike chills ran over her flesh, chasing the path of his hands. Feeling the light graze of his knuckles against the side of her breast, Brooke moaned, a liquid sound of pleasure. He took his tongue deeper into her mouth, gently exploiting this small weakness until the drug took full effect. She was limp, languid, utterly his. Then and only then did he give his lips the freedom to taste her skin again. It was as pungent as her scent, and somehow more erotic.

With moist, open-mouthed kisses he savored her, entranced her. Then the quick pressure of his teeth on some sensitive spot would bring her sharply aware, gasping with the change. His lips would soothe again, lulling her back into pliancy. Again and again he yanked her toward the flame, then guided her back to the clouds, until Brooke was no longer certain which she most desired.

She felt him draw her slacks down over her hips while he pressed those soul-wrenching kisses along her stomach. A mindless excitement filled her, rendering her helpless to do any more than move as he requested. His breath was warm on her intimate flesh so that the long muscles in her thighs trembled then went lax.

Still his mouth moved slowly. The hands that had already discovered every secret point of pleasure continued to caress and linger, keeping her trapped beneath a thin sheet of silken passion. The power she had experienced before moved through her, but her mind was too dazed to recognize it. She felt herself balanced on a slender edge—

desire's tightrope—and wanted to continue to walk it as much as she longed to fall headlong into the wild, churning sea below. Then he was above her again, his eyes looking down into hers for a long, long, moment before his lips descended. He was waiting, and she understood. Their mouths still clinging, Brooke guided him inside her.

Her moan melted into his mouth, hot and passionate. Though she was clinging to him now with a sudden, fierce strength, Parks moved slowly. Brooke felt herself fill, fill to the desperate point of explosion. Then the shudders, wracking, convulsive, until she seemed to slide back down some smooth cool path to the torrent again. Like a swimmer trapped in rushing white water, she was swept from peak to peak while he moved with tortuous slowness. She could feel the tight, tense control in him, hear it in the quick labored breaths that merged with hers as he prolonged the pleasure, and the agony. Then he murmured something—a prayer, a plea, an oath—and took them both tumbling off the tightrope.

He must have slept. Parks thought he had closed his eyes for only an instant, but when he opened them again, the slant of the sun was different. Brooke was beside him, her hair wrapping them to each other. Her eyes were wide and aware as she stared into his. She'd been watching him for nearly an hour. Parks smiled and pressed his mouth to her shoulder.

"Sorry. Did I fall asleep?"

"For a little while." She hid her face against his neck a moment. It was as though he had stripped off her flesh, exposing all her thoughts. She wasn't quite certain what she should do about it. "You must have been exhausted."

"Not anymore," he said truthfully. He felt alert, pumped with energy and...clean. The last made him give a quick shake of his head. He stroked a hand down her arm. "There was something I wanted to ask you before I got... distracted." Propping himself on his elbow, Parks looked down at her. "Why were you crying?"

Brooke moved her shoulders in a shrug and started to shift away. With a firm hand, Parks stopped her. He could feel the effort she was making to draw back from him, but he realized he could no longer permit it. Whether she knew it or not, she had given herself to him completely. He was going to hold her to it.

"Brooke, don't try to block me out," he said quietly. "It won't work anymore."

She started to protest, but the quiet, steady look in his eyes told her he spoke nothing less than the truth. That alone should have been a warning of where her heart was taking her. "It was a sweet thing to do," she said at length. "I'm not used to sweetness."

Parks lifted a brow. "That's part of it, perhaps. What's the rest?"

With a sigh, Brooke sat up. This time he let her. "I hadn't realized I'd been collecting." With both hands, she pushed her hair back, then wrapped her arms around her knees. "I overreacted when you pointed it out. I always wanted a dog, a cat, a bird, anything when I was growing up. It wasn't feasible the way I shifted around." She moved her shoulders again, causing her tumbled hair to shiver over her naked back. ‘‘It was kind of shattering to realize I was still compensating.’’

Parks felt a chord of sympathy and suppressed it. There was no quicker way to alienate her. ‘‘You’ve got your own home, your own life now. You could have anything you wanted.’’ Reaching around her, he poured more wine for both of them. ‘‘You don’t have to compensate.’’ He sipped, studying her profile.

‘‘No,’’ she agreed in a murmur. ‘‘No, I don’t.’’

‘‘What kind of dog do you want?’’

Brooke twirled the glass in her hand, then suddenly laughed. ‘‘Something homely,’’ she said, turning to grin at him. ‘‘Something down-to-the-ground homely.’’ She reached out, laying a hand on his cheek. ‘‘I didn’t even thank you.’’

Parks considered, nodding solemnly as he took the glass from her hand. ‘‘No, you didn’t.’’ In a quick move, he had her rolling on top of him. ‘‘Why don’t you thank me now?’’

Chapter 9

Claire came down to give the set her final approval. At the far end of the studio, serenely indifferent to the piles of equipment, lights and shades, was a cozy living room scene. A deep, cushy sofa in shades of masculine brown was spotlighted as technicians made adjustments. On a table beside it was a Tiffany lamp which would appear to give the soft, sexy lighting the crew was working to achieve. Claire worked her way around cable and cases to a new angle.

Tasteful, she decided. And effective. De Marco was pleased with the first spot. So pleased, Claire thought with a mild grimace, that he had insisted his current inamorata appear in this one. Well, that was show business, she decided as she checked her watch. Brooke had moaned and groaned at the casting, then had given in with the mutter that at least he hadn't insisted they write her any dialogue.

The studio segment was being filmed first, though it would appear at the end of the ad when aired. Judging Parks's temperament, Brooke had decided to go with what would probably be the most difficult portion for him first, then ease him into the rest. And, Claire mused as she checked her watch, their luck was holding. The Kings would compete in the World Series the following week, giving the commercials just that much more impact.

Outside the studio, a long buffet had been set up in the hall. E.J., the production coordinator and the assistant cameraman were already making the most of it. Brooke was in the studio, nibbling on a hunk of cheese as she supervised the finer details.

''Damn it, Bigelow, that light's flickering again. Change the bulb or get a new fixture in here. Silbey, let me see what kind of effect we get with that new gel.''

Obediently, he hit a switch so that the light filtered through the colored sheet and came out warm and sultry. ''Okay, not bad. Sound?''

The sound technician walked under the boom mike. With her face innocently bland, she began to recite a nursery rhyme with a few interesting variations. At the polite volley of applause, she curtsied.

''Any problems?'' Claire asked as she moved to stand beside Brooke.

''We've smoothed them out. Your end?''

''Everyone's accounted for. The talent's changing.'' Absently, she straightened the hem of her sleeve. ''I got a glimpse of de Marco's lady. She's gorgeous.''

''Thank God,'' Brooke said with feeling. ''Are we expecting him?''

''No.'' Claire smiled at the resigned tone of Brooke's voice. She heartily disliked relatives, friends or lovers hanging around a shoot. ''He tells me Gina claims he would make her nervous, but he left no doubt she's to be given the royal, kid-glove treatment.''

''I won't bite her,'' Brooke promised. ''I ran through Parks's lines with him. He has it cold…if he doesn't fumble it on camera.''

''He doesn't appear to be a fumbler.''

Brooke smiled. ''No. And I think he's starting to enjoy this whole business despite himself.''

''Good. I have a script I want him to read.'' Above their heads on a ladder, someone cursed pungently. Claire's smooth features never registered she had even heard. ''There's a part, a small one, I think he's perfect for.''

Brooke turned to give Claire her full attention. ''A feature?''

She nodded. ''For cable. We won't be casting for another month or two, so he's got plenty of time to think about it. I'd like you to read it, too,'' she added casually.

''Sure.'' Mulling over the idea of Parks as an actor, Brooke turned to call out another instruction.

''You might like to direct it.''

The order froze in her throat. ''What?''

''I know you're happy directing commercials,'' Claire went on as if Brooke weren't gaping at her. ''You've always said you enjoy creating the quick and intense, but this script might change your mind.''

''Claire''—Brooke might have laughed if she hadn't

been stunned—"I've never directed anything more complex than a sixty-second spot."

"Like the promo for the new fall shows you filmed last summer? Three major network stars told me you were one of the best they'd ever worked with." It was said dryly, hardly like a compliment. "I've wanted to ease you into something like this for a long time, but I didn't want to push." Claire patted her hand. "I'm still not pushing, just read the script."

After a moment, Brooke nodded. "All right, I'll read it."

"Good girl. Ah, there's Parks now." Her eyes ran over him with professional discrimination. "My, my," she murmured, "he does wear clothes well."

He looked as though he had chosen the pale-blue cashmere sweater and slate-gray jeans at random, shrugging into them without a thought. That they fit with tailored precision wasn't nearly as important as the sense of rightness—that careless style that comes not from money but from basic class.

That he had, Brooke thought. Beneath the attractive face and athletic body was a sense of class that one was born with or one was not. It could never be taught. He held a glass of ginger ale in his hand, looking over the rim as he studied the room.

He found it crowded and cluttered and apparently disorganized but for the small island of order that was a sofa, table and lamp. He wondered fleetingly how anyone could work sanely around the coiled snakes of cable, huge black cases and poles of light. Then he saw Brooke. She could, he thought with a smile. She would simply steamroll over the chaos until she got exactly what she wanted. She might have wept like a child in his arms only a few nights before, but when she was on the job she was as tough as they came.

Perhaps, he mused, that was why he'd fallen in love with her—and perhaps that was why he was going to keep that little bit of information to himself for a while. If he'd nearly panicked when he'd realized it, Brooke would undoubtedly do so. She wasn't quite ready to sit trustingly in the palm of his hand.

Brooke moved toward him, eyes narrowed. Parks thought uncomfortably that she could always make him feel like a department store dummy when she looked at him that way. It was her director's look, appraising, searching for flaws, mulling over the angles.

''Well?'' he said at length.

''You look marvelous.'' If she had noticed the faint irritation in his voice, she ignored it. Reaching up, she disheveled his hair a bit, then studied the effect. ''Yes, very good. Nervous?''

''No.''

Her face softened with a smile. ''Don't frown, Parks, it won't help you get into the mood. Now...'' Linking her arm in his, she began to lead him toward the set. ''You know your lines, but we'll have cue cards in case you draw a blank, so there's nothing to worry about. The main thing we want is that sort of laid-back, understated machismo. Remember this is the end of the segment; the first scene you're on the field in uniform, then there's the business in the locker room while you're changing, then this. Soft lights, a little brandy, a beautiful woman.''

''And I owe it all to de Marco,'' he said dryly.

''The woman in any case,'' she returned equably. ''It's simply a statement that clothes suit a man's image. Hopefully, men will be convinced that de Marco's right for theirs. You'll sit here.'' Brooke gestured toward the end of the couch. ''Give me that relaxed slouch of yours when you're unwinding. It's casual but not sloppy.''

He frowned again, helplessly annoyed that she could dissect his every gesture and put a label on it. ''Now?''

''Yes, please.'' Brooke stood back while Parks settled himself on the couch. ''Yes, good.... Bring your elbow back just a bit on the arm. Okay.'' She smiled again. ''That's what I want. You're getting very good at this, Parks.''

''Thanks.''

''You'll talk right into the camera this time,'' she told him, gesturing behind her to where the machine sat on a dolly. ''Easy, relaxed. The girl will come up behind you, leaning over as she hands you the brandy snifter. Don't look at her, just touch her hand and keep talking. And smile,'' she added, looking at her watch. ''Where is the girl?''

On cue, Gina entered, tall and voluptuous, followed by a stern-looking blonde and two men in business suits. Better than the photo de Marco sent over, Brooke noted, and that had been impressive. The woman was young, but not too young, a ripe twenty-five, Brooke estimated, with large sloe eyes and raven hair. Her body was curvy, shown to advantage in a clingy low-cut gown that stopped just short of censorship. She wouldn't get aloof from this one, Brooke mused, watching Gina make her way across the studio. Heat vibrated in every movement. This time she would go for pure sex—for the five and a half seconds Gina was on screen. For a thirty-second television ad, it would be more than enough.

Ignoring the appreciative mutters and elbowing of her crew, Brooke walked to meet de Marco's lady. "Hello." She extended her hand with a smile. "I'm Brooke Gordon, I'll be directing you."

"Gina Minianti," she purred in a voice that instantly made Brooke regret she'd have no lines.

"We're very pleased to have you, Ms. Minianti. Do you have any questions before we begin?"

Gina gave her a slight smile. *"Come?"*

"If there's anything you don't understand," Brooke began, only to have the blonde interrupt her.

"Signorina Minianti doesn't speak English, Ms. Gordon," she said briskly. "Weren't you informed?"

"Doesn't—" Breaking off, Brooke rolled her eyes to the ceiling. "Lovely."

"I'm Mr. de Marco's personal secretary. I'll be glad to translate."

Brooke gave the blonde a long hard look, then turned around. "Places," she called. "It's going to be a long day."

"A little stumbling block?" Parks murmured as she passed him.

"Shut up and sit down, Parks."

Controlling a grin, he stepped forward to take Gina's hand. "Signorina," he began, then caught Brooke's full attention when he continued in fluid Italian. Beaming,

Gina answered in a rapid spate, gesturing freely with her other hand.

"She's excited," Parks commented, knowing Brooke had stopped in her tracks behind him.

"So I gathered."

"She's always wanted to do an American movie." He spoke to Gina again, something that made her throw back her magnificent head and laugh throatily. Turning, she dismissed the blonde with a flick of the wrist and tucked her arm through Parks's. When they faced her, the tawny Californian, the raven Italian, Brooke was struck with the perfection of the contrast. That five and a half seconds of film, she thought, was going to crackle like a forest fire—and sell one hell of a lot of de Marco merchandise.

"You seem to speak Italian well enough to suit her," Brooke commented.

"Apparently." He grinned again, noting that Brooke wasn't the least jealous but appraising, as if he and Gina were already in a view screen. "She'd like me to interpret for her."

"All right, tell her we'll run through it once to show her what she needs to do. Let's have the lights!" Striding to the set, Brooke waited impatiently while Gina and Parks strolled behind her, heads close as he relayed Brooke's instructions. "Sit down, Parks, and tell her to watch closely. I'll run through it with you." Parks settled on the couch as she had instructed him. "Take it from the top, just as if the camera were rolling."

He began, talking easily, as if to a few friends on a visit. Perfect, Brooke thought as she picked up the prop brandy snifter and walked into camera range behind the couch. She leaned over, letting her cheek come close to his as she offered it. Without glancing from the camera, Parks accepted it, raising the fingers of his other hand to run down the back of Brooke's as it rested on his shoulder. She straightened slowly, moving out of camera range as he finished the dialogue.

"Now ask her if she understands what she's to do," Brooke ordered.

Gina lifted an elegant hand at Parks's question, silently communicating "of course."

"Let's try one." Brooke backed behind E.J. and the assistants who would dolly the camera platform forward for the close-ups. "Quiet on the set," she called, effectively cutting off a few discreet murmurs. "Roll film...." The clapper struck—Parks Jones for de Marco, scene three, take one. She narrowed her eyes at Parks. "Action."

He ran through it well enough for a first take, but Brooke decided he hadn't warmed to it yet. Gina followed instructions, bringing the snifter, leaning over him suggestively. Then she glanced up, startled, as the camera rolled in.

"Cut. Parks, explain to Gina not to look at the camera, please." She smiled at the woman, hoping she communicated patience and understanding. She needed a great deal of both by the fifth take. Instead of becoming more used to the camera, Gina seemed to be growing more unnerved. "Five minutes," Brooke announced. The hot lights switched off, and the crew began a pilgrimage toward the buffet. With another smile, Brooke gestured for Gina to join her and Parks on the sofa. "Parks, will you tell her she need only be natural. She's gorgeous, the few seconds she's going to be film will make a tremendous impact.''

Gina listened with brows knit, then tossed Brooke a smile. *''Grázie.''* Taking Parks's hand, she launched into a long, emotional torrent that turned out to be an apology for her clumsiness and a request for something cold to calm her nerves.

''Bring Signorina Minianti some orange juice,'' Brooke demanded. ''Tell her she's not clumsy at all,'' Brooke continued diplomatically. ''Ah, tell her to try to imagine you're lovers, and when the camera turns off—''

''I get the idea,'' Parks said with a grin. When he spoke to Gina again, she gave her throaty laugh then shook her head before she answered. ''She says she'll try to imagine it,'' Parks relayed to Brooke, ''but if she imagines it too well, Carlo will step on my face...or words to that effect.''

''We have to sacrifice for our art,'' Brooke told him dryly. ''Parks, it would help if you could put a little more steam into it.''

''Steam?'' he repeated, lifting a brow.

''A man who doesn't steam a bit with a woman like that hanging over his shoulder needs a transfusion.'' Rising, Brooke patted his shoulder. ''See what you can do?''

''Anything for art,'' he returned, sending her a wolfish grin.

As E.J. sat behind his camera again, Brooke walked to stand at his shoulder. ''Let's see if we can make one this time,'' she muttered.

''Boss, I can do this all day long.'' He focused his lens

on Gina and sighed. ''I think I've died and gone to heaven.''

''De Marco might arrange it if you don't watch your step. Places!''

Better, she mused. Yes, definitely better as they completed the sixth take. But not perfect. She told Parks to ask Gina to give the camera a languid look before she slid Parks an under-the-lashes smile. The direction lost something in the interpretation. ''Cut. Here, tell her to stand next to the camera and watch again.'' Brooke took Gina's place, moving behind him as he spoke, cupping the snifter of lukewarm tea. This time when Parks took it from her, he brought her other hand to his lips, pressing a soft kiss against it without breaking the rhythm of the dialogue. Brooke felt a jolt shoot up her arm and forgot to move away.

''Just seemed natural,'' Parks told her, linking his fingers through hers.

Brooke cleared her throat, aware that her crew was watching with avid interest. ''Give it a try that way, then,'' she said matter-of-factly. She walked back to E.J., but when she turned, Parks's eyes were still on her. Brooke gave a quick, frustrated shake of her head. She knew that look. Slowly, the meaning crystal-clear, Parks smiled.

''Places!'' Brooke called in her own defense.

It took three more takes before she got just what she wanted. A hot but self-satisfied Gina gave Parks two exuberant kisses, one on each cheek, then came over and chattered something at Brooke. Glancing up at Parks, Brooke saw that amused and all too innocent look on his face.

"Just say thank you," he advised.

"Thank you," Brooke said obediently as Gina took her hand and squeezed it. She swept off with her entourage. "What was I thanking her for?" Brooke used the sleeve of her shirt to dry the sweat on her forehead.

"She was complimenting your taste."

"Oh?"

"She said your lover was magnificent."

Dropping her arm, Brooke stared at him. "Really?" she said coolly.

Parks grinned, gave a deprecatory shrug then strolled off to see if anything was left at the buffet.

Hands on her hips, Brooke stared after him. She wouldn't give him the satisfaction of letting her own smile escape. "Location, one hour," she called out.

Brooke had been right in thinking that the third brief scene of the commercial would be the most difficult to film. She shot the second scene next, crowding lights, equipment and crew into the Kings locker room. Claire had arranged, with a little negotiating, to have a few of the better-known of Parks's teammates available for background or cameos. Once Brooke got them settled down so that they stopped waving at the camera or making fictitious announcements into the mike, it began to work. And work well.

Because of the relative ease with which the segment was progressing, Brooke found the headache growing at the base of her skull unexplainable. True, the locker room was noisy between takes, and after the first hour of many bodies under hot lights, it *smelled* like a locker room, but this headache was pure tension.

At first she simply ignored it; then, when that became impossible, she grew annoyed with herself. There was nothing to be tense about. Parks did what he was told, pulling the cashmere sweater over his naked chest for each take. And every time he smiled at her, Brooke felt the headache pulse.

By the time the crew was setting up for the scene on the diamond, Brooke had convinced herself she had it under control. It was just a nagging ache, something she would take care of with a couple of aspirin when she got home. As she watched the sound technician work on a mike, she felt a beefy arm slip over her shoulders.

''Hi.'' Snyder grinned down at her, drawing an automatic smile of response from Brooke. He was, she thought, about as dangerous as a cocker spaniel.

''Ready for the next scene, George? You did very well before. Of course, you won't be on camera this time.''

''Yeah, I wanted to mention that you're making a big mistake using Parks. Too skinny.'' He flexed a well-muscled arm.

Brooke gave his biceps a nod of approval. ''I'm afraid I don't have anything to do with the casting.''

''Too bad. Hey, now that I'm a star, are you going to pick me up at the airport?''

''Forget it, Snyder.'' Before Brooke could answer, Kinjinsky strolled over, a bat in one hand, a ball in the other. ''She's out of your league.'' He grinned at Brooke, jerking his head at his teammate. ''He specializes in belly dancers.''

''Lies.'' Snyder looked amazingly like an overgrown choirboy. ''All lies.''

''When my daughter grows up,'' Kinjinsky said mildly, ''I'm going to warn her about men like him.'' Walking to the plate, he tossed the ball up in the air then drilled it out to center field.

''Kinjinsky's the best fungo hitter on the team,'' Snyder told Brooke. ''Too bad he has such trouble with a pitched ball.''

''At least I can make it from first to second in under two and a half minutes,'' Kinjinsky tossed back.

Snyder, well used to ribbing about his base running, feigned an offended look. ''I have this genetic anatomical problem,'' he explained to Brooke.

''Oh.'' Playing along, she looked sympathetic. ''That's too bad.''

''It's called a lead foot,'' Parks commented as he came up behind them.

Hearing his voice had the headache she'd nearly forgotten drumming again. She turned to find him watching her and his teammates with a lazily amused smile. Parks wore full uniform, the blazing white that brought out the gold of his skin. The navy cap shaded his eyes, giving him a cocky, assured look. Quietly possessive, his eyes skimmed over her. This time Brooke felt a flutter in her stomach in addition to the throb at the base of her neck.

''Just keeping your woman entertained,'' Snyder said genially.

''Brooke's her own woman.'' But there was something unmistakably proprietary in the disclaimer.

Hearing it, Snyder realized there was something deeper

here than he had imagined. So the lightning's finally hit the Iceman, he thought. Snyder had the wit to rib unmercifully and the nature of a man who mends the broken wings of small birds. "When she sees how good I come across on camera, you're going to be out of a job."

"De Marco doesn't have a line for sumo wrestlers," Parks countered.

"Gentlemen," Brooke spoke, cutting them off. "The crew's ready. George, if you'd take your place at first to give Parks his target."

"Ouch." He winced. "Try not to take that literally, Jones. I don't want to be on the disabled list next week."

"Mike." Brooke stepped over to Kinjinsky. "If you'll just hit them to Parks—don't make it too easy for him, I want to see a little effort."

With a grin, Kinjinsky tossed up another ball. "I'll see what I can do."

Nodding, Brooke walked toward the crew. "Places. Parks, any questions?"

"I think I can handle this one." He stepped up to third, automatically kicking up a bit of dust with his spikes.

She looked through the lens, feeling another flutter in her stomach as she focused on Parks. Shifting his weight to one hip, he grinned at her, Brooke stepped back, gesturing to E.J.

"Hey, boss, you okay?"

"Yes, I'm fine. Roll film."

It went perfectly. Brooke knew she could have used the first take without a hitch, but opted for two more. They were equally smooth. Kinjinsky blasted the ball at Parks, enough to make him dive or leap before Parks in turn fired the ball at Snyder on first.

"Third take's the winner," E.J. announced when Brooke called the session a wrap.

"Yes." Unconsciously, she rubbed the back of her neck.

"He shouldn't have even caught it," E.J. went on, watching Brooke as he began to load his equipment.

"He seems to excel at doing the impossible," she murmured.

"Headache?"

"What?" Glancing down, she found E.J. watching her steadily. "It's nothing." Annoyed, she dropped her hand. Parks was already in a conference on the mound with his two teammates. He had his glove hand on his hip, grinning at Snyder's newest concept for a practical joke. "It's nothing," Brooke repeated in a mutter, reaching for one of the sodas in the ice chest.

It had to be nothing, she told herself as she tipped the bottle and drank deeply. Whatever was rolling around inside her was just a product of fatigue after a long day's work. She needed aspirin, a decent meal and eight hours' sleep. She needed to stay away from Parks.

The minute the thought entered her head, Brooke was infuriated. He has nothing to do with it, she told herself fiercely. I'm tired, I've been working too hard, I've— She caught E.J.'s speculative stare and bristled.

"Would you get out of here?"

His face cleared with a wide grin. "On my way. I'll drop off the film at editing."

With a curt nod, Brooke strode out to the mound to

thank Snyder and Kinjinsky. She heard the tail of Snyder's brainstorm, something about frogs in the bullpen, before Parks turned to her.

"How'd it go?"

"Very well." Heat was running along her skin now, too physical, too tangible. She gave her attention to his teammates. "I want to thank both of you. Without your help, it never would have gone so smoothly."

Snyder leaned his elbow on Kinjinsky's shoulder. "Just keep me in mind when you want something more than a pretty face in one of these commercials."

"I'll do that, George."

Parks waited through the rest of the small talk, adding comments easily though his concentration was all for Brooke. He waited until the ball players had wandered off toward the locker room before he took Brooke's chin in his hand. Closely, patiently, he examined her. "What's wrong?"

Brooke stepped away so that they were no longer touching. "Why should anything be wrong?" she countered. Her nerves had gone off like bells in her head at his touch. "It went very well. I think you'll be pleased with it when it's edited. With the two spots running throughout the series, we won't shoot another until November." Turning, she noted that most of the crew had gone. She found she wanted to be away before she and Parks were completely alone. "I have a few things to clear up back at the office, so—"

"Brooke." Parks cut her off cleanly. "Why are you upset?"

"I'm *not* upset!" Biting back fury, she whirled back to him. "It's been a long day, I'm tired. That's all."

Slowly, Parks shook his head. "Try again."

"Leave me alone," she said in a trembling undertone that told her, and him, just how close she was to the edge. "Just leave me alone."

Dropping his mitt to the ground, he took both her arms. "Not a chance. We can talk here, or we can go back to your place and hash it out. Your choice."

She shoved away from him. "There's nothing to hash out."

"Fine. Then let's go have dinner and see a movie."

"I told you I had work to do."

"Yeah." He nodded slowly. "You lied."

Sharp, bubbling anger filled her eyes. "I don't have to lie, all I have to do is tell you no."

"True enough," he agreed, holding on to his own temper. "Why are you angry with me?" His voice was calm, patient. His eyes weren't. The sun fell against his face, accenting that fierce sexuality.

"I'm not angry with you!" she nearly shouted.

"People usually shout when they're angry."

"I'm *not* shouting," she claimed as her voice rose.

Curiously, he tilted his head. "No? Then what are you doing?"

"I'm afraid I'm falling in love with you." Her expression became almost comically surprised after the words had tumbled out. She stared in simple disbelief, then covered her mouth with her hand as if to shove the words back inside.

"Oh, yeah?" He didn't smile as he took another step

toward her. Something was scrambling inside his stomach like a squirrel in a cage. ‘‘Is that so?’’

‘‘No, I...’’ In defense, she looked around, only to find that she was alone with him now. Alone in his territory. The stands rose up like walls to trap them inside the field of grass and dirt. Brooke backed off the mound. ‘‘I don’t want to stay here.’’

Parks merely matched his steps to hers. ‘‘Why afraid, Brooke?’’ He lifted his hand to her cheek, causing her to stop her retreat. ‘‘Why should a woman like you be afraid of being in love?’’

‘‘I know what happens!’’ she said suddenly with eyes that were dark and stormy in contrast to the trembling tone.

‘‘Okay, why don’t you tell me?’’

‘‘I’ll stop thinking. I’ll stop being careful.’’ She ran an agitated hand through her hair. ‘‘I’ll give until I lose the edge, then when it’s over I won’t have anything left. Every time,’’ she whispered, thinking of all the transient parents, thinking of Clark. ‘‘I won’t let it happen to me again. I can’t be involved with you for the fun of it, Parks. It just isn’t working.’’ Without being aware of the direction, Brooke had turned to pace to the third base bag. Parks felt the warmth of the gold piece against his chest and decided it was fate. Taking his time, he followed her. His percentage of errors at the corner was very small.

‘‘You are involved with me, whether you’re having fun at it or not.’’

She sent him a sharp glance. This wasn’t the easygoing man but the warrior. Brooke straightened her shoulders. ‘‘That can be remedied.’’

"Try it," he challenged, calmly gripping her shirt in his hand and pulling her toward him.

Brooke threw her head back, infuriated, and perhaps more frightened than she had ever been in her life. "I won't see you again. If you can't work with me, take it up with Claire."

"Oh, I can work with you," he said softly. "I can even manage to take your orders without too much of a problem because you're damn good at what you do. I told you once before I'd follow your rules while the camera was on." He glanced around, silently relaying that there was no camera this time. "It's tough to beat a man on his own ground, Brooke, especially a man who's used to winning."

"I'm not a pennant, Parks," she said with amazing steadiness.

"No." With one hand still gripping her shirt, he traced the other gently down her cheek. "Pennants are won through teamwork. A woman's a one-on-one proposition. Seventh-inning stretch, Brooke. Time to take a quick breath before the game starts again." The hand on her cheek moved up to cup her neck. She wondered that he couldn't feel the sledgehammers pounding there. Then he smiled, that slow dangerous smile that always drew her. "I'm in love with you."

He said it so calmly, so simply, that it took her a moment to understand. Every muscle in her body went rigid. "Don't."

He lifted a brow. "Don't love you or don't tell you?"

"Stop." She put both hands on his chest in an attempt to push him away. "It's not a joke."

"No, it's not. What are you more afraid of?" he asked, studying her pale face. "Loving or being loved?"

Brooke shook her head. She'd been so careful to keep from crossing that thin line—been just as careful to keep others from crossing from the other side. Claire had done it, and E.J., she realized. There was love there. But *in* love… How could a tiny, two-letter word petrify her?

"You could ask me when," Parks murmured, kneading the tense muscles in her neck, "and I couldn't tell you. There wasn't a bolt of lightning, no bells, no violins. I can't even say it snuck up on me because I saw it coming. I didn't try to step out of the way." He shook his head before he lowered his mouth to hers. "You can't wish it away, Brooke."

The kiss rocked her back on her heels. It was hard and strong and demanding without the slightest hint of urgency. It was as if he knew she could go nowhere. She could fight him, Brooke thought. She could still fight him. But the tension was seeping out of her, filling her with a sense of freedom she had thought she would never fully achieve. She was loved.

Feeling the change in her, Parks pulled back. He wouldn't win her with passion. His needs ran too deep to settle for that. Then her arms were around him, her cheek pressed against his chest in a gesture not of desire, but of trust. Perhaps the beginning of trust.

"Tell me again," she murmured. "Just tell me once more."

He held her close, stroking her hair while the breeze whispered through the empty stadium. "I love you."

With a sigh, Brooke stepped over the line. Lifting her head, she took his face in her hands. "I love you, Parks," she murmured before she urged his lips to take hers.

Chapter 10

Clubhouses have their own smell. Sweat, foot powder, the tang of liniments, the faint chemical aroma of whirlpools and the overlying fragrance of coffee. The mixture of odors was so much a part of his life, Parks never noticed it as he pulled on his sweat shirt. What he did notice was tension. That was inescapable. Even Snyder's determined foray of practical jokes couldn't break the curtain of nerves in the locker room that afternoon. When a team had spent months together—working, sweating, winning and losing—aiming toward one common goal, nothing could ease the nerves of facing the seventh game of the World Series.

If the momentum had been with them, the atmosphere would have been different. All the minor aches that plague the end of a season would barely have been noticed—the tired legs, the minor pulls. But the Kings had dropped the last two games to the Herons. A professional athlete knows that skill is not the only determining factor in winning. Momentum, luck, timing are all added for balance.

Even if the Kings could have claimed they'd fallen into a slump there might have been a little more cheer in the clubhouse. The simple fact was that they'd been outplayed. The number of hits between the opponents was almost even—but the Herons had made theirs count while the Kings had left their much needed runs stranded on base. Now it came down to the last chance for both teams. Then when it was over, they'd pick up their off-season lives.

Parks glanced at Snyder, who'd be on his charter boat in Florida the following week. Catching fish and swapping lies, he called it, Parks mused. Kinjinsky, getting heat applied to his ribs, would be playing winter ball in Puerto Rico. Maizor, the starting pitcher, would be getting ready to play daddy for the first time when his wife delivered in November. Some would go on the banquet circuit and the talk show circuit—depending on the outcome of today's game. Others would go back to quiet jobs until February and spring training.

And Parks Jones makes commercials, he reflected with a small grimace. But the idea didn't bring on the sense of foolishness it had only a few months before. It gave him a certain pleasure to act—though Brooke wouldn't call it that—in front of the camera. But he wasn't too thrilled with the poster deal Lee had cooked up.

He smiled a little as he drew on his spikes. Hype, Brooke had called it, saying simply it was part of the game. She was right, of course; she usually was about that aspect of things. But Parks didn't think he'd ever be completely comfortable with the way she could look him over with those calm eyes and sum him up with a few choice words. Wouldn't it disconcert any man to have fallen in love with a woman who could so accurately interpret his every expression, body move or careless word? Face it, Jones, he told himself, you could have picked an easier woman. Could have, he reflected, but didn't. And since Brooke Gordon was who and what he wanted, she was worth the effort it took to have her, and to keep her. He wasn't so complacent that he believed he had truly done either yet.

Yes, she loved him, but her trust was a very tenuous thing. He sensed that she waited for him to make a move so that she could make a countermove. And so the match continued. Fair enough, he decided; they were both programmed to compete. He didn't want to master her…did he? With a frown, Parks pulled a bat out of this locker and examined it carefully. If he had to answer the question honestly, he'd say he wasn't sure. She still challenged him—as she had from the very first moment. Now, mixed with the challenge were so many emotions it was difficult to separate them.

He'd been angry when Brooke wouldn't change her schedule and fly east during the games at the Herons' home stadium. And when he'd become angry, she'd become very cool. Her work, she had told him, couldn't be set aside to suit him or even herself…any more than his could. Even though he'd understood, Parks had been angry. He had simply wanted her there, wanted to know she was in the stands so that he could look up and see her.

He had wanted to know she was there when the long game was over. Pure selfishness, he admitted. They both had an ample share of that.

With a grim smile Parks ran a hand down the smooth barrel of the bat. She'd told him it wouldn't be easy. Brooke had been her own person long before he had pushed his way into her life. Circumstances had made her the person she was—though they were circumstances she had still not made completely clear to him. Still it was that person—the strong, the vulnerable, the practical and the private, whom he had fallen for. Yet he couldn't quite get over the urge he had at times to shake her and tell her they were going to do it his way.

He supposed what epitomized their situation at this point was their living arrangement. He had all but moved in with her, though neither one of them had discussed it. But he knew Brooke considered the house hers. Therefore, Parks was living with her, but they weren't living together. He wasn't certain his patience would last long enough to break through that final thin wall—without leaving the entrance hole a bit jagged.

With a quiet oath he reached into the locker and grabbed a batting glove, sticking it in his back pocket. If he had to use a bit of dynamite, he decided, he would.

''Hey, Jones, infield practice.''

''Yeah.'' He grabbed his mitt, sliding his hand into its familiar smoothness. He was going to handle Brooke, he told himself. But first there was a pennant to win.

Alternately cursing and drumming her fingers against the steering wheel, Brooke cruised the parking lot in search of a space. ''I knew we should've left earlier,'' she muttered. ''We'll be lucky to get anything within a mile of the stadium.''

Leaning back against the seat, E.J. interrupted his humming long enough to comment. ''Still fifteen minutes before game time.''

''When somebody gets you a free ticket,'' Brooke said precisely, ''the least you can do is be ready when they pick you up. There's one!'' Brooke gunned the motor and slipped between two parked cars with inches to spare. Hitting the brake, she glanced at her companion. ''You can open your eyes now, E.J.,'' she said dryly.

Cautiously, one at a time, he did so. ''Okay....'' He looked at the car beside him. ''Now how do we get out?''

''Open the door and inhale,'' she advised, wiggling out her side. ''And hurry up, will you? I don't want to miss them taking the field.''

''I've noticed your interest in baseball's increased over the summer, boss.'' Thankful for his thin frame, E.J. squeezed out of the Datsun.

''It's an interesting game.''

''Yeah?'' Joining her, he grinned.

''Careful, E.J., I still have your ticket. I could scalp it twenty times before we reach the door.''

''Aw, come on, Brooke, you can tell your friend what's already in the papers.''

She scowled at that, stuffing her hands in her pockets. There'd been pictures of her and Parks, tantalizing little articles and hints in every paper she'd looked at for more than a week. In L.A., gossip carried quickly—a hot ball player and his attractive director were definitely food for gossip.

"I even caught a bit in one of the trades," E.J. went on, blithely ignoring the storm clouds in Brooke's eyes. "Speculation is that Parks might take up, ah…show business," he said, giving her another grin, "seriously."

"Claire has a part for him if he wants it," Brooke returned, evading his obvious meaning. "It's small but meaty. I didn't want to go into it in depth with Parks until after the series. He has enough on his mind."

"Yeah, I'd say the man's had a few things on his mind for some time now."

"E.J.," Brooke began warningly as she passed over her tickets.

"You know," he continued when they fought their way through the inside crowd, "I've always wondered when somebody'd come along who'd shake that cool of yours a little."

"Is that so?" She didn't want to be amused, so she slipped her sunglasses down to conceal the humor in her eyes. "And you apparently think someone has?"

"Honey, you can't get within ten feet of the two of you and not feel the steam. I've been thinking…" He fussed with the front of his T-shirt as if straightening a tie. "As your close friend and associate, maybe I should ask Mr. Jones his intentions."

"Just try it, E.J., and I'll break all of your lenses." Caught between amusement and irritation, Brooke plopped down in her seat. "Sit down and buy me a hot dog."

He signaled. "What do you want on it?"

"All I can get."

"Come on, Brooke." He fished in his pocket for a couple of bills, exchanging them for hot dogs and cold drinks. "Buddy to buddy, how serious is it?"

"Not going to let up, are you?"

"I care."

Brooke glanced over at him. He was smiling, not the wisecracking grin she so often saw on his face, but a simple smile of friendship. It was, perhaps, the only weapon she had no defense against. "I'm in love with him," she said quietly. "I guess that's pretty damn serious."

"Grade-A serious," he agreed. "Congratulations."

"Am I supposed to feel like I'm walking on a cliff?" she demanded, only half-joking.

"Don't know." E.J. took a considering bite of his hot dog. "Never had the experience."

"Never been in love, E.J.?" Leaning back in her seat, Brooke grinned. "You?"

"Nope. That's why I spend so much time looking." He gave a heavy sigh. "It's a tough business, Brooke."

"Yeah." She took off his fielder's cap and swatted him with it. "I bet it is. Now shut up, they're going to announce the starting lineup."

A tough business, she thought again. Well, he wasn't far wrong, even if he had been joking. Looking for love was a lonely occupation, one she'd given up—or thought she'd given up—years before. Finding it—or having it tackle you from behind—was even tougher. Once it found you it clung, no matter how much you tried to shake it off. But she wasn't trying to shake it off, Brooke mused.

She was just trying to understand how it fit and make a few adjustments. The fabric kept changing.

''Playing third and batting fourth, number twenty-nine, Parks Jones.''

The already boisterous crowd went frantic as Parks jogged out on the field to take his place in the lineup. When he stood beside Snyder, he let his eyes drift over. They locked on Brooke's. With a smile, he gave the customary tip of his cap. It was a gesture for the crowd, but she knew it had been aimed at her personally. It was all the acknowledgment he would give her until it was over. It was all she expected.

''I'm going to outhit you today, Iceman,'' Snyder warned, grinning at the crowd. ''Then Brooke's going to realize her mistake.''

Parks never took his eyes off her. ''She's going to marry me.''

Snyder's jaw dropped. ''No kidding! Well, hey…''

''She just doesn't know it yet,'' Parks added in a murmur. He slapped hands with the right fielder, batting fifth. ''But she will.''

Brooke detected a change in Parks's smile, something subtle, but to her unmistakable. Narrowing her eyes, she tried to decipher it. ''He's up to something,'' she muttered.

E.J. perfected a shot with a small still camera. ''What?''

''Nothing.'' She swirled her drink so that ice chunks banged together. ''Nothing.''

A well-known blues singer stepped up to the mike to sing the national anthem. Two lines of athletes removed their caps. The crowd rose, silent for what would be the last time in more than two hours. The excitement was so tangible Brooke thought she could reach out into the warm October air and grab a handful of nerves. It built and built until it exploded with cheers and shouts and whistles as the last note of the song trembled. The Kings took the field.

Sportscasters are fond of saying that the seventh game of the World Series is the ultimate in sports events—the pinnacle test of teamwork and individual effort. This was no exception. In the first inning, Brooke saw the Kings' center fielder charge a ball, stretching forward to catch it on the run then holding on to it as the momentum carried him into a forward roll. She saw the Herons shortstop seem to throw heart and body after a ball to prevent it from going through the hole for a base hit. At the end of the fourth, the teams had one run apiece, each on solo home runs.

Brooke had seen Parks guard his position at third, stealing, as Lee would have put it, two certain base hits and starting the execution of a clutch double play. Watching him, Brooke realized he played this game just as he played every other—with total concentration, with steady determination. If he had nerves, if somewhere in his mind was the thought that this was *the* game, it didn't show. As he stepped up to bat, she leaned out on the rail.

Before he stepped into the box, Parks ran a hand up and down his bat as though checking for splinters. He was waiting for calm, not the calm of the shouting fans but inner calm. In his mind's eye he could see Brooke leaning on the rail, her hair tumbling over her shoulders, her eyes cool and direct. The knot of tension in his stomach eased.

When he stepped up to the plate his predominant thought was to advance the runner. With Snyder on first, he'd have to put it well out of the infield. And they'd be pitching him carefully. Both times he had come to bat, Parks had clipped a single through the hole between third and short.

Parks took his stance and looked directly into the pitcher's eyes. He watched the windup, saw the ball hurtling toward him, shifted his weight, then checked his swing. The slider missed the corner. Ball one.

Stepping out of the box, Parks knocked the bat against his spikes to clear them of dirt. Yeah, they were going to be careful what they gave him. But he could get Snyder to second just as easily on a walk as on a hit. The trouble was, second wasn't a sure scoring position for Snyder.

The second pitch missed, low and outside. Parks checked the signal from the third base coach. He didn't allow his eyes to drift over to where Brooke sat. Parks knew even that brief contact would destroy his concentration.

The next pitch came in on him, nearly catching him on the knuckles then bouncing foul. The crowd demanded a hit. Parks checked Snyder, who was keeping very cozy with the bag, before he stepped into the box again.

Hoping to even the count, the pitcher tried another fast curve. In that fraction of a second, Parks shifted his weight. Wrists square and unbroken, he connected, letting his hips bring the bat around. He had the satisfaction of hearing the ball crack off the bat before the crowd was on its feet, screaming.

The ball sailed over center field, and though three men gave chase, no one reached it before it smashed into the dirt of the warning track and bounced high over the wall. With the fans roaring on all sides, Parks settled for the ground-rule double. There was sweat trickling down his back, but he barely felt it. He thought once that if he'd pulled the ball a bit to the right, it would have gone over clean, scoring two. Then he forgot it.

With Snyder on third, he couldn't take a sizable lead, so he contented himself with putting only a couple of feet between himself and the bag. The odds that Farlo would sacrifice to score Snyder were slim. The outfielder could spray a ball to all fields, but he wasn't a power hitter. Parks crouched, shaking his arms to keep the muscles loose.

Farlo fell behind quickly, fouling off two pitches and frustrating the crowd. Parks simply refused to think of the possibility of being stranded on base again. The infield was playing them tight, looking for that ground ball that could be turned into a double play.

Parks saw the pitch, judged it to be a low curve and tensed. Farlo showed his teeth and smacked it to right field. Parks was running on instinct before he consciously told his feet to move. The third base coach was waving him on. Years of training had Parks rounding third at top speed and heading home without hesitation or question. He saw the catcher crouched, ready to receive the ball, shielding the plate like a human wall. It flashed through Parks's mind that the Herons' right fielder was known for his arm and his precision before he threw himself at the plate in a feet-first slide that had dirt billowing in the clouds. He felt the red flash of pain as his body connected with the catcher, heard his opponent's *whoosh* of air at the hit and saw the small white ball swallowed by the mitt.

They were a tangle of bodies and mutual pain as the umpire spread his arms. "Safe!"

The crowd went wild, stranger pounded on stranger, beer sloshed over cups. Brooke found that E.J. had grabbed her for a quick dance. His camera cut into her chest but it was several moments before she felt it.

"My man!" E.J. shouted, whirling her into the man on her right, who tossed his box of popcorn into the air.

No, she thought breathlessly. *My* man.

At the plate, Parks didn't concentrate on the adulation of the crowd, but on drawing enough breath into his lungs so he could stand again. The catcher's knee had slammed solidly into his ribs. Rising, he gave his uniform a perfunctory brush then headed to the dugout, where his teammates waited for him. This time, he allowed his eyes to find her. She was standing, her arms still around E.J. But her face softened with a smile that was only for him.

Touching his cap, he disappeared into the dugout. The trainer had the cold spray ready for his ribs.

Parks had forgotten his aches long before he had taken his defensive position in the top of the ninth. The Herons had whittled their lead down to one run with some blood and guts baserunning in the seventh. Since then, both teams had held like rocks. But now, Maizor was in trouble.

With only one out, he had a runner on second and a

power hitter coming to the plate. We could walk him and put him on, Parks considered as the catcher tipped back his mask on his way to the mound for a conference. But the Herons had more big bats in the lineup and a few pinch hitters who couldn't be underestimated. Parks sauntered over to the mound, noting as he did that Maizor was strung tight.

"Gonna go for him?" Parks asked as the catcher chewed on a wad of gum the size of a golf ball.

"Yeah, Maizor's gonna take care of him, aren't you, Slick?"

"Sure." He turned the ball over and over in his hand. "We all want a ride in Jones's new sports car."

Parks took the mention of the Most Valuable Player Award with a shrug. They were still two outs away, and all three men knew it. "One thing." He adjusted his cap. "Don't let him hit it toward me."

Maizor swore and grinned and visibly relaxed. "Let's play ball."

Over his shoulder, Maizor checked the runner on second. Satisfied that his lead wasn't too greedy, he fired the ball at the plate. Parks could almost hear the rush of the wind as the bat cut, just over the ball. Kinjinsky called out, telling him to bear down and do it again. He did, but this time the batter got a solid piece of it.

As if a button had been pushed, Parks went for it, lunging from his side as Kinjinsky dashed to cover him. He had only seconds to judge the speed and the height. Even as he let his body fall in the direction of the ball, he felt the runner pass him on his way to third. Landing on his knees, Parks caught in on the short bounce. Without taking the time to rise, he fired the ball toward third. Kinjinsky nabbed it and held his ground as the runner slid into him.

"Still trying to make the easy plays look hard," the shortstop commented as they passed each other. They were both coated with dirt and sweat. "One more, baby, just one more."

Parks let the long, mixed roar of the crowd wash over him as he crouched at third. His face was utterly impassive. The tying run was on first. By the time the count reached three and two, being on the diamond was like being in the eye of a hurricane. Noise and turbulence whirled around them from the stands. On the field, the tension was dead silent.

Maizor went inside, handcuffing the batter. The ball was hit, drifting foul. Parks gave chase as it drifted toward the seats, running at full speed as though the wall weren't looming up in front of him. He could get it, he knew he could get it—if an excited fan didn't reach over and make a grab.

With his free hand, he caught the rail and lifted his glove. He felt the impact of the ball as he closed his leather over it. While the crowd started to scream, he found he was looking directly into Brooke's eyes. The foul had all but fallen into her lap.

"Nice catch." Leaning over, she kissed him full on the mouth.

Then one of his teammates had him around the waist, and the rest was madness.

Parks had more champagne dumped on him than he could possibly have drunk. It mixed with sweat and washed some of the grime away. Snyder had positioned himself on top of a locker and from there emptied two bottles on anyone in sight—reporters and league brass included. Accused of showboating, Parks was tossed, fully dressed, into the whirlpool. Grateful, he stripped and remained where he was with half a bottle of champagne. From there he gave interviews while the water beat the aches from his body and bedlam raged around him.

The pitch on his double had been an outside fast ball. Yeah, his slide into home had been risky, considering the arm of the right fielder, but he'd had a good lead. He continued to answer questions as Snyder, in a champagne-drenched uniform, was not so gently assisted into the whirlpool with him. Parks slid down farther in the soothing water and drained the cold wine straight from the bottle. Yes, the redhead in the stands was Brooke Gordon, his director on the de Marco commercials. Parks smiled as Snyder wisecracked the reporters' attention to himself. Teammates might poke and prod into each other's business, but they protected their own.

Parks closed his eyes a moment, just a moment. He wanted to recapture that instant when she had leaned over and touched her lips to his. Everything had been heightened in that split second of victory. He had thought he could hear each individual shout from the crowd. He'd seen the sunlight glint on the chipped paint of the railing, felt the baking heat as his hand had wrapped around it. Then he'd seen her eyes, close, soft, beautiful. Her voice had been quiet, conveying excitement, humor and love all in two words. When they had touched his, her lips had been warm and smooth, and for an instant that had been all he had felt. Just the silky texture of her lips. He hadn't even heard the last out called. When he'd been dragged back on the field by his teammates, she had simply lowered her chin to the rail and smiled at him. *Later.* He had heard her thought as clearly as if she had spoken it.

It took two hours to urge the last reporter out of the clubhouse. The players were quieting. The first rush of victory was over, replaced by a mellowness that would very quickly become nostalgia. The year was over. There'd be no more infield practice, batting practice, night rides on planes with card games and snoring. They were in a business where today was over quickly and tomorrow took all their efforts. Now there wasn't a tomorrow, but next year.

Some were sitting, talking quietly on the benches in the midst of the locker room litter, as Parks dressed. He glanced at the second-string catcher, a boy of barely nineteen, completing his first year in the majors. He held his shin guards in his hands as if he couldn't bear to part with them. Parks put his mitt into his duffel bag and felt suddenly old.

''How're the ribs?'' Kinjinsky asked as he slung his own bag over his shoulder.

''Fine.'' Parks gestured to the boy on the bench. ''The kid's barely old enough to vote.''

''Yeah.'' Kinjinsky, a ripe thirty-two, grinned. ''It's hell, isn't it?'' They both laughed as Parks closed his locker for the last time that year. ''See you in the spring, Jones. My woman's waiting for me.''

Parks zipped up his bag while the thought warmed in

him. He, too, had a woman, and it would take him thirty minutes to drive to the mountains.

"Hey, Parks." Snyder caught him before he'd reached the door. "You really going to marry her?"

"As soon as I can talk her into it."

Snyder nodded, not questioning the phrasing of the answer. "Give me a call when you set it up. I'm the best man."

With a smile, Parks held out a hand and shook the beefy one. "Damned if you're not, George." He walked into the corridor, closing the door on the clubhouse and the season.

When he emerged outside, it was dusk. Only a few fans lingered, but he signed autographs for them and gave them the time they wanted. Parks thought idly about picking up another bottle of champagne for himself and Brooke as he signed his name to the bill of a twelve-year-old's battered hat. Champagne, a fire burning low, candles. It seemed like a good setting to propose marriage. It was going to be tonight, because tonight he didn't think he could lose.

The parking lot was all but deserted. The overhead lights were just flickering on as twilight deepened. Then he saw her. Brooke was sitting on the hood of his car, spotlighted in the flood of a security light, her hair like tongues of flame around her strong-boned, delicate-skinned face. Love welled up in him, a fierce possessive love that took his breath away. Except for the lips that curved, she didn't move. He realized then she had been watching him for some time. He struggled to regain some control over his muscles before he continued toward her.

"If I'd known you were waiting here, I'd have come out sooner." He felt the ache in his ribs again, but not from the bruise this time. This was from a need he was still not quite used to.

"I told E.J. to take my car. I didn't mind waiting." Reaching up, she put both hands on his shoulders. "Congratulations."

Very deliberately, Parks set his bag down on the asphalt then dove his hands into her hair. Their eyes held briefly, endlessly, before he lowered his mouth and took what he needed.

His emotions were more finely tuned than he had realized. All the pleasure of victory, the weariness that came from winning it, the dregs of excitement and tension surfaced, to be doubled then swept away by one all-encompassing need. Brooke. How was he to have known that she would grow to be everything—and all things? A bit unnerved by the intensity, Parks drew away. A man couldn't win when his knees were buckling. He ran his knuckles down her cheek, wanting to see that very faint, very arousing clouding of her eyes.

"I love you."

At his words, Brooke rested her head against his chest and breathed deeply. She could smell his shower on him, some subtle soap fragrance that spoke of gymnasiums and locker rooms that were inhabited only by men. For some reason, it made her feel acutely a woman. The light grew dimmer as they remained, held close and silent.

"Too tired to celebrate?" she murmured.

"Uh-uh." He kissed her hair.

"Good." Drawing away, she slid from the hood. "I'll buy you dinner to start it off." Brooke opened the passenger door and smiled. "Hungry?"

Until that moment, Parks hadn't realized that he was starving. What little he'd eaten before the game had been devoured by nerves. "Yeah. Do I get to pick the place?"

"Sky's the limit."

Fifteen minutes later, Brooke gazed around the garishly colored Hamburger Heaven. "You know," she mused, studying the overhead lights that were shaped like sesame seed rolls. "I'd forgotten your penchant for junk food."

"A hundred percent pure beef," Parks claimed, picking up an enormous double-decker sandwich.

"If you believe that, you believe anything."

Grinning, he offered her a French fry. "Cynic."

"If you call me names, I won't read you the sports page." She put her hand over the folded paper she'd just bought. "Then you won't hear the accolades the press have heaped on you." When he shrugged, unconcerned, she opened the paper. "Well, I want to hear them." With one hand on her milk shake, Brooke began to thumb her way through. "Here… Oh." She stopped dead and scowled.

"What is it?" Parks leaned over. On the front page were two pictures, side by side. The first was of his over-the-seats catch of the final out. The second was of Brooke's impulsive kiss. The caption read:

JONES SCORES…TWICE

"Cute," he decided, "considering I didn't score but snagged a pop fly." He twisted his head, skimming down the article which ran through the highlights of the game—

critiques and praise. ''Hmm.... 'And Jones ended it with a race to the rail, snagging Hennesey's long foul out of the seats in one of the finest plays of the afternoon. As usual, the MVP makes the impossible look routine. He got his reward from the luscious redhead'—here he shot Brooke a brief glance—'Brooke Gordon, a successful commercial director who's been seen with the third baseman on and off the set.'''

''I really hate that,'' Brooke said with such vehemence that Parks looked up in surprise.

''Hate what?''

''Having my picture splashed around that way. And this—this half-baked speculation. This, and that silly business in the *Times* a couple days ago.''

''The one that called you a willowy, titian-haired gypsy with smoky eyes?''

''It's not funny, Parks.'' Brooke shoved the paper aside.

''It's not tragic, either,'' he pointed out.

''They should mind their own business.''

Leaning back, Parks nibbled on a fry. ''You'd probably be the first to tell me that being in the public eye makes you public property.''

Brooke scowled at that, knowing they were precisely her words when they'd discussed the poster deal. ''*You're* in the public eye,'' she countered. ''It's the way you make your living. *I* don't. I work behind the camera, and I have a right to my privacy.''

''Ever heard of guilty by association?'' He smiled before she could retort. Instead of a curt remark, she let out a long sigh. ''At least they're accurate,'' he added. ''I've often thought of you as a gypsy myself.''

Brooke picked up her cheeseburger, frowned, then bit into it. ''I still don't like it,'' she muttered. ''I think...'' She shrugged, not certain how foolish she was going to sound. ''I've always been a little overly sensitive about my privacy, and now...what's happening between us is too important for me to want to share with anyone who has fifty cents for a paper.''

Parks leaned forward again and took her hand. ''That's nice,'' he said softly. ''That's very nice.''

The tone of his voice had fresh emotion rising in her. ''I don't want to hole up like a couple of hermits, Parks, but I don't want every move we make to be on the evening news, either.''

With a bit more nonchalance than he was feeling at the moment, he shrugged and began to eat again. ''Romance is news.... So's divorce, when it involves public people.''

''It's not going to ease up with the de Marco campaign, either, or if you decide to take that part in the film.'' She took another French fry out of its paper scoop and glared at it. ''The hotter you are, the more the press will buzz around. It's maddening.''

''I could break my contract,'' he suggested.

''Don't be ridiculous.''

''There's another solution,'' he considered, watching Brooke swallow the French fry and reach for another.

''What?''

''We could get married. Want some salt for those?''

Brooke stared at him, then found she had to search for her voice. ''What did you say?''

''I asked if you wanted some salt.'' Parks offered her

a tiny paper packet. "No?" he said when she neither answered nor moved. "I also said we could get married."

"Married?" Brooke echoed stupidly. "You and me?"

"The press would ease off after a while. Quietly married couples don't make news the same way lovers do. Human nature." He pushed his sandwich aside and leaned toward her. "What do you think?"

"I think you're crazy," Brooke managed in a whisper. "And I don't think this is funny."

Parks gripped her arm when she started to scoot out of the booth. "I'm not joking."

"You—you want to get married so we won't get our picture in the paper?"

"I don't give a damn if we get our picture in the paper or not, you do."

"So you want to get married to—to placate me." She stopped struggling against his hold on her arm, but her eyes filled with fury.

"I've never had any intention of placating you," he countered. "I couldn't placate you if I dedicated my life to it. I want to get married because I'm in love with you. I'm *going* to marry you," he corrected, suddenly angry, "if I have to drag you, kicking and screaming."

"Is that so?"

"Yes, that's exactly so. You might as well get used to it."

"Maybe I don't want to get married." Brooke shoved the food in front of them aside. "What about that?"

"Too bad." He leaned back, eyeing her with the same simmering temper with which she eyed him. "*I* want to get married."

''And that's supposed to be enough, huh?''

''It's enough for me.''

Brooke crossed her arms over her chest and glared at him. ''Kicking and screaming?''

''If that's the way you want it.''

''I can bite, too.''

''So can I.''

Her heart was thudding against her ribs, but Brooke realized it wasn't from anger. No, it had nothing to do with anger. He was sitting there, across a laminated table littered with food from a twelve-year-old's fantasy, telling her he was going to marry her whether she liked it or not. Brooke discovered, somewhat to her own amazement, that she liked it just fine. But she wasn't going to make it easy for him.

''Maybe winning the series went to your head, Parks. It's going to take more than a temper tantrum to get me to marry you.''

''What do you want?'' he demanded. ''Candlelight and soft music?'' Annoyed that he had scuttled his own plans, he leaned over again and grabbed her hands. ''You're not the kind of woman who needs scenery, Brooke. You know just how easy it is to come by and how little it means. What the hell do you want?''

''Take two,'' she said very calmly. ''You know your motivation,'' she began in her cool director's voice, ''but this time tone down the force and try for a little finesse. Ask,'' she suggested, looking into his eyes, ''don't tell.''

He felt the anger, or perhaps it had been fear, slide out of him. The hands that held hers gentled. ''Brooke''—he lifted a hand and pressed her fingers to his lips—"will you marry me?" Parks smiled over their joined hands. "How was that?"

Brooke laced the fingers with hers. "Perfect."

Chapter 11

What was she doing? In a sudden panic, Brooke stared at herself in the free standing long-length mirror. How could things be happening so fast and be so much out of her control? A year ago—no, even six months ago—she hadn't known Parks Jones existed. In something under an hour, she would be married to him. Committed. For life. Forever.

From somewhere deep inside her brain came a panicked call to run and run fast. Brooke hadn't realized she'd made a move until she was summarily jerked back into place.

''Be still, Ms. Gordon,'' Billings ordered firmly. ''There are two dozen of these little buttons if there's one.'' She used a complaining tone, though privately she thought Brooke's choice of an ivory satin gown with its snug bodice and flowing skirt was inspired. A good, traditional wedding dress, she decided, not one of those flighty trouser suits or miniskirted affairs in scarlet or fuchsia. Billings continued to fasten the range of tiny pearl buttons in back.

"Stand still now," she ordered again as Brooke fidgeted.

"Billings," Brooke said weakly, "I really think I'm going to be sick."

The housekeeper looked up at Brooke's reflection. Her face was pale, her eyes huge, made darker by the merest touch of slate-gray shadow. In Billings's staunch opinion, a bride was supposed to look ready to faint. "Nonsense," she said briskly. "Just a case of the flutters."

"Flutters," Brooke repeated, creasing her brow. "I never flutter. That's ridiculous."

The Englishwoman smiled fleetingly as Brooke straightened her shoulders. "Flutters, jitters, nerves—every woman born has them on her wedding day."

"Well, I don't," she claimed as her stomach muscles quivered.

Billings only sniffed as she finished her fastening. "There now, that's the last one."

"Thank God," Brooke muttered, heading for a chair before Billings caught her.

"No, you don't. You're not putting creases in that skirt."

"Billings, for heaven's sake—"

"A woman has to suffer now and again."

Brooke's opinion was a short four-letter word. Lifting a brow, Billings picked up a hairbrush from the vanity. "A fine way for a blushing bride to talk."

"I'm not a blushing bride." Brooke swept away before

Billings could apply the brush. ''I'm twenty-eight years old,'' she continued, pacing. ''I must be crazy, I must be absolutely crazy. No sane woman agrees to marry a man in a fast-food restaurant.''

''You're getting married in Ms. Thorton's garden,'' Billings corrected. ''And it's quite a lovely day for it.''

The practical tone caused Brooke to scowl. ''And I should never have let her talk me into that, either.''

''Hah!'' The exclamation had Brooke's brows lifting. Billings gestured threateningly with the hairbrush. ''Hah!'' she said again, effectively closing Brooke's mouth. ''No one talks you into anything. You're a hard-headed, stubborn, single-minded young woman, and you're shaking in your shoes because there's a hard-headed, stubborn, single-minded young man downstairs who's going to give you a run for your money.''

''I certainly am not shaking in my shoes,'' Brooke corrected, insulted. Billings saw the faint pink flush rise to the pale cheeks.

''Scared to death.''

Brooke stuck both fists on her hips. ''I am most certainly not afraid of Parks Jones.''

''Hah!'' Billings repeated as she pulled over a footstool. Climbing on it, she began to draw the brush through Brooke's hair. ''You'll probably stammer and quake when you take your vows, just like some silly girl who doesn't know her own mind.''

''I've never stammered in my life.'' Enunciating each word precisely, Brooke glared at their twin reflections in the mirror. ''And nothing makes me quake.''

''We'll just see about that, won't we?'' Rather pleased

with herself, Billings arranged Brooke's mane of hair into a cunningly tumbled mass. In this, she secured a delicate clip of pale-pink-and-white hibiscus. She had fussed that lily of the valley or rosebuds would have been more suitable, but secretly thought the exotic flowers were stunning.

"Now, where are those lovely pearl drops Ms. Thorton gave you?"

"Over there." Still fuming, Brooke pointed to the tiny jeweler's box that held Claire's gift.

They should have eloped as Parks had suggested, Brooke thought. What had made her think she wanted all this fuss and bother? What had made her think she wanted to get married in the first place? As her nerves started jumping again, she caught Billings's ironic stare. Brooke lifted her chin.

"Well, put them on," the housekeeper ordered, holding the pink-blushed pearls in her palm. "It was very clever of Mr. Jones to send you flowers to match them."

"If you like him so much, why don't you marry him?" Brooke muttered, fastening the earrings with fingers that refused to stop trembling.

"I suppose you'll do," Billings said briskly, swallowing a lump in her throat. "Even without a proper veil and train." She wanted badly to press a kiss to Brooke's cheek, but knew it would weaken both of them. "Come along, then," she said instead. "It's time."

I could still call it off, Brooke thought as she let Billings draw her down the hall. There's still time. No one can make me go through with this. The little skips of nerves in her stomach had increased to thumps. There's absolutely nothing that can make me walk out into that garden.

What was the phrase? she wondered. Marry in haste, repent at leisure? This was certainly haste.

It had only been four days since Parks had asked her. Four days. Maybe the big mistake had been in telling Claire. Good God, she'd never seen anyone move so fast once they'd gotten the bit between their teeth. Brooke decided she must have been in a state of shock to have let Claire sweep her along with plans and arrangements. An intimate ceremony in her terraced garden, a champagne reception. *Elope?* Claire had brushed that aside with a wave of her hand. Elopements were for silly teenagers. And wouldn't a three-piece ensemble be lovely? Brooke had found herself caught up. And now she was just caught.

But no, Brooke corrected as she and Billings reached the foot of the stairs. All she had to do was turn around and head for the door. She could get into her car and just drive away. That was the coward's way. Straightening her shoulders, Brooke rejected it. She wouldn't run, she would simply walk outside and explain very calmly she had changed her mind. Yes, that's all it would take. I'm very sorry, she practiced mentally, but I've decided not to get married after all. She'd be very calm and very firm.

"Oh, Brooke, you look lovely." And there was Claire, dressed in powder-blue silk with the sheen of tears in her eyes.

"Claire, I—"

"Absolutely lovely. I wish you'd let me have them play the wedding march."

"No, I—"

"It doesn't matter, as long as you're happy." Claire pressed her cheek to Brooke's. "Isn't it silly, I feel just like a mother. Imagine having your first pangs of motherhood at my age.''

''Oh, Claire.''

''No, no, I'm not going to get sloppy and sentimental and ruin my face.'' Sniffling, she drew away. ''It's not every day I'm maid of honor.''

''Claire, I want to—''

''They're waiting, Ms. Thorton.''

''Yes, yes, of course.'' Giving Brooke's hand a quick squeeze, she went out on the terrace.

''Now you, Ms. Gordon.'' Brooke stood where she was, wondering if the coward's way wasn't basically sound. Billings put a firm hand on her back and pushed. Brooke found herself out on the terrace facing Parks.

He took her hand. He was firm as he brought hers to his lips. She noticed his eyes, smiling, sure. He was in a pearl-gray suit, more formal than anything she had seen him wear. But his eyes held that complete intensity she knew they had when he waited for a pitch. She found herself walking with him to the center of the terrace that was surrounded by flowers and the ornamental trees Claire loved.

Still time, Brooke thought as the minister began to speak in a calm, clear voice. But she couldn't open her mouth to stop what was already happening.

She'd remember the scent always. Jasmine and vanilla, and the sweet drift of baby roses. But she didn't see the flowers because her eyes were locked on Parks's. He was repeating the words the minister spoke, the traditional words spoken countless times by countless couples. But she heard them as if they were uttered for the first time.

Love, honor, cherish.

She felt the ring slip onto her finger. Felt, but again didn't see because she couldn't take her eyes from his. From the branches of a weeping cherry, a bird began to trill.

She heard her own voice, strong and assured, repeat the same promises. And her hand, with no trembling, placed the symbol of the promise on Parks's finger.

A pledge, a promise, a gift. Then their lips moved together, sealing it.

I was going to run, she remembered.

''I'd have caught you,'' Parks murmured against her mouth.

Astonished and annoyed, Brooke drew back. He was grinning at her, his hands still caught in her hair. To the confusion of the others in the quiet, fragrant garden, Brooke cursed then threw her arms around his neck and laughed.

''Hey.'' Snyder gave Parks a firm shove. ''Give somebody else a chance.''

Claire's idea of a small gathering was the epitome of a producer's understatement. Though Brooke didn't bother to count heads, she knew there were well over a hundred ''absolutely essential guests.'' She found she didn't mind—the glitter was her gift to Claire. There was a bubbly fountain of champagne, a five-tiered pink-and-white cake and silver platters of food that for once Brooke had no interest in. Which turned out for the best, as she was swept from one person's arms to another, kissed, hugged and congratulated until it all became a blur of color and sound.

She met Parks's mother, a tiny, exquisite woman who kissed her cheek then burst into tears. His father crushed Brooke in a hug and murmured that now that Parks was married, he would stop the nonsense and come into the company. She found herself inheriting a family in a lump—a large, confusing family that didn't quite fit any of the imaginings of her youth. And through it all, she had barely more than glimpses of Parks as she was passed from cousin to cousin to be weighed, measured and discussed like a fascinating new acquisition.

''Leave the girl be a minute.'' A sturdy, pewter-haired woman swept the others aside with an imperious wave of her hand. ''These Joneses are a silly bunch.'' She sighed, then summed Brooke up with one long look. ''I'm your Aunt Lorraine,'' she said and extended her hand.

Brooke accepted the handshake, knowing instinctively the gesture was somehow more sincere and more intimate than all the kisses she had received. Then with a flash of insight, she knew. ''The gold piece.''

Lorraine smiled, pleased. ''Told you about that, did he? Well, he's a good boy…more or less.'' A straight, no-nonsense brow lifted. ''And he won't bully you, will he?''

With a grin, Brooke shook her head. ''No, ma'am, he won't.''

Lorraine nodded, giving Brooke's hand a quick pat. ''Good. I'll expect a visit in six months. It takes a couple that long to work out the first kinks. Now, if I were you, I'd get my husband and sneak out of this rabble.'' With this advice, she strode away. Brooke had her first twinge of genuine kinship.

Even so, it seemed like hours before they could slip away. Brooke had intended to steal back upstairs and change, but Parks had seen his opportunity and had pulled her outside, bundled her into his car and driven off. Now he stopped the car in the driveway of the A-frame and sighed.

''We made it.''

''It was rude,'' Brooke mused.

''Yeah.''

''And very smart.'' Leaning over, she kissed him. ''Especially since you managed to cop a bottle of champagne on the way.''

''Quick hands,'' he explained as he stepped from the car.

Brooke chuckled, but felt a fresh ripple of unease as they walked up the path. Parks's hand was closed over hers. She could feel the slight, unfamiliar pressure of her wedding ring against her skin. ''One problem,'' she began, pushing the feeling aside. ''You dragged me out of there without my purse.'' She glanced at the door, then back at Parks. ''No keys.''

Parks reached in his pocket and drew out his own. A faint frown creased her brow as she remembered he had a key to the door now. A key to her life. Though he noticed her reaction, Parks said nothing, only slipping the key into the lock. It opened silently. He swept her up into his arms, and with her laughter, the subtle disharmony was forgotten.

''I hadn't realized you were such a traditionalist,''

Brooke murmured, nuzzling at his neck, ''but...'' She trailed off at the sound of high, sharp yapping. Astonished, she looked down to see a small brown dog with a black muzzle racing around Parks's feet, making occasional dives for his ankles. ''What's that?'' she managed.

''Your wedding present.'' With his toe, he nudged the puppy, sending him rolling over on his back. ''Homely enough?''

Brooke stared down at the pushed-in mongrel face. ''Oh, Parks,'' she whispered, close to tears. ''You fool.''

''E.J. should've dropped him off about an hour ago, if he was on schedule. Guy at the pound thought I was crazy when I told him I wanted something down-to-the-ground homely.''

''Oh, I love you!'' Brooke squeezed his neck fiercely then wriggled out of his arms. In her satin wedding dress, she knelt on the floor to play with the puppy.

She looked young, Parks thought, too young, as she buried her face in the little dog's fur. Why would he constantly expose her vulnerabilities then be uncertain how to handle them? There was so much sweetness in her, and yet, was he somehow more comfortable with the vinegar she could serve him? It was the mix, Parks thought as he knelt to join her, the fascinating mix he couldn't resist.

''Our first child.'' Brooke chuckled when the puppy lay in exhausted slumber on the rug.

''He has your nose.''

''And your feet,'' she retorted. ''He's going to be enormous from the size of them.''

''Maybe you can cast him in a few dog food commercials,'' he commented as he drew Brooke to her feet.

Gently he kissed her cheek, then trailed his lips over her chin to the other one. He felt the sudden tremble of her breath on his skin. "Champagne's getting warm," he murmured.

"I'm not thirsty."

He was leading her slowly toward the stairs, still planting those soft, whispering kisses over her face on the journey, leaving her lips—her heating, seeking lips—subtly tormented. And they started to climb the stairs, without rush or hurry, while Parks began unfastening that long range of tiny buttons.

"How many are there?" he murmured against her mouth.

"Dozens," Brooke answered, loosening his tie as they reached the halfway point.

His fingers were nimble. Before they reached the door of the bedroom, he had the gown loosened to her waist. Brooke pushed the jacket from his shoulder, and with her teeth nipping at his neck, tugged his shirt from the waistband of his pants.

"Are you ever going to kiss me?" she demanded breathlessly.

"Mm-hmm." But he only drove her mad by running his lips over her shoulder as he nudged the satin aside. Then he drew it from her, running his hands slowly down her body until the material was only a pool of white at her feet. He toyed with the bits of lace she wore, tiny, filmy wisps designed to torment men. And even as they tormented him, Parks fought for control. There was always that last struggle for control before he found he was lost in her.

Her fingers slid down his naked ribs to brush over his stomach before she found the hook to his trousers. She heard his quick, indrawn breath before his hands became more demanding. Needing, wanting, she pulled him with her onto the bed.

Why should there be such desperation when they were now so securely bound to each other? Though neither of them understood it, they both felt it. The urgency to touch, taste. To possess. Gentleness was abandoned while hungry, primitive passion took its place. The teasing kisses stopped with a hard, burning pressure of mouth on mouth. Her hands sought, as skillfully as his, to find weaknesses. Every moan brought a fresh thrill of arousal, each sigh an increase of tortuous desire until neither knew if the sounds were from pleasure or desperation. And both refused to succumb to the fire.

He found her breast taut and firm. Greedily, his mouth sought it, sending a tearing thread of delight into the core of her. Even as she moaned in surrender, her hands pressed him closer, her body moving sinuously under his until he was lost in the taste of her.

Flesh heated against flesh. The pace quickened. Faster, faster until they were breathless and clinging but still not ready to yield. She ran her hands over his damp back, over the roping of muscles that accented his superior strength. But physical strength meant nothing in the inescapable quicksand of passion. They were both trapped in it, both equally incapable of freeing themselves.

With sudden strength, she shifted, so that they were tangled together, side by side. Her mouth fastened on his, devouring as eagerly as she was devoured, taking as mindlessly as she was taken. Her hair fell over them, curtaining their faces so that Parks couldn't breathe without breathing her. If he had been capable of thought, he might have imagined himself absorbed by her. But there was no thought for either of them, and the need had grown too great to be resisted.

She went willingly when he shifted her, drawing his mouth down to hers even as he entered her with something close to violence. Then there was only speed and heat, driving them beyond everything but each other.

''Should I need you more each time?'' Brooke wondered aloud.

''Mmm.'' Parks didn't want to move from the warm comfort of her body. It yielded under his, pressed deep into the mattress. ''Just don't stop.''

It was dusk. The light filtering through the windows was soft—and soon it would be night. Her wedding night. Yet she still felt only like a lover. How would it be to feel like a wife? Lifting her hand, she stared at the band on her finger. It was encrusted with diamonds and sapphires that glowed softly in the room's twilight. ''I don't want it to be different tomorrow,'' she thought aloud. ''I don't want it to change.''

Parks raised his head. ''Everything changes. You'll get mad if I use all the hot water for my shower. I'll get mad if you've drunk the last of the coffee.''

Brooke laughed. ''You have a way of simplifying things.''

''Those are the nuts and bolts of a relationship, Mrs. Jones,'' he claimed and kissed her.

The eyes that had begun to close for the kiss opened wide. ‘‘Jones,’’ she repeated. ‘‘I’d forgotten about that part of it.’’ She considered for a minute. ‘‘It makes me think of your mother…though of course she was very nice.’’

Parks gave a muffled chuckle. ‘‘Don’t worry. Just remember she lives three hundred miles away.’’

Brooke rolled over until she lay on top of him. ‘‘You have a very nice family.’’

‘‘Yeah, and we don’t want to get tangled up with them any more than we have to.’’

‘‘Well…’’ Brooke laid her head on his chest. ‘‘No. At least not too soon,’’ she added, thinking of his aunt. She relaxed again as he began to lazily stroke her hair. ‘‘Parks?’’

‘‘Hmm?’’

‘‘I’m glad we decided to come here instead of flying off somewhere.’’

‘‘We’ll go to Maui for a couple of weeks around Christmas. I want you to see my place there.’’

Brooke thought of her schedule if she decided to take Claire up on the feature for cable. Somehow or other, she’d managed to get the two weeks. ‘‘I love you.’’

His hand stopped a moment, then pressed her closer. They were three words she didn’t say often. ‘‘Did I tell you how beautiful you looked when Billings shoved you out on the terrace?’’

Brooke’s head shot up. ‘‘You saw that?’’

Grinning he traced her ear with his fingertip. ‘‘Funny, I didn’t expect you to be as terrified as I was.’’

Brooke regarded him a moment, then a smile curved on her lips. ''Were you really?''

''A half hour before the wedding, I'd run up a list of all the reasons why we should call it off.''

She lifted a brow. ''Were there many?''

''I lost count,'' he told her, ignoring the narrowing of her eyes. ''I could only think of one good reason to go through with it.''

''Oh, really?'' Her chin came up as she tossed her head. ''And what was that?''

''I love you.''

Brooke dropped her forehead onto his. ''That's it, huh?''

''The only one I could think of.'' He slid a hand down to her hip. ''Though one or two others are beginning to occur to me.''

''Mmm. Like it being good for the campaign.'' She began to nuzzle, just behind his ear.

''Oh, sure. That's top on my list.'' He groaned when the first shudder rippled through him. ''Right next to having somebody to sort my socks.''

''You can forget that one,'' Brooke murmured, moving down to his shoulder. ''But there's always having an in with the director when you do that part for cable.''

''Haven't decided to do it.'' His legs tangled with hers as they altered positions. ''Have you?''

''Not yet.'' Her thoughts began to drift as he cupped her breast. ''But you should.''

''Why?''

Lazily, her eyes opened to look into his. ''I shouldn't tell you.''

Intrigued, he propped himself on his elbow and toyed with her hair. "Why not?"

She sighed a little, while managing to convey a shrug. "The last thing you need is someone feeding your ego."

"Go ahead." He kissed her nose. "I can take it."

"Damn it, Parks, you're good."

He stopped in the action of twining her hair around his finger and stared at her. "What did you say?"

Brooke shifted again. "Well, I don't mean you can *act,*" she began. "Don't start getting delusions."

He grinned, enjoying her ironic lift of brow. "That's more like it."

"You have good camera presence," she went on. "Do you have any idea how many big stars stay big simply by playing themselves?" Parks grunted, more interested in the curve of her shoulder. "You know how to play yourself, Parks," Brooke persisted, drawing him back for a moment. "And if you were to stick to parts, at least for a while, that suited you…well, when you really are ready to retire from baseball you could walk right into a movie career."

He started to laugh, then stopped when he saw the look in her eyes. "You're not joking."

Brooke stared at him, then let out a long breath. "I'm really going to hate myself when I've got to deal with you as a director in a couple of weeks, but you're very, very good, and you should think about it. And if you get a star complex when I tell you to run through some business on camera a half a dozen times, I'll…"

"What?" he challenged.

''Something,'' Brooke said ominously. ''Something despicable.''

He gave her a wicked grin. ''Promise?''

Since she couldn't stop the laugh, she rolled him over forcibly so that she was lying across him again. ''Yeah. And now I'm going to make love to you until your bones dissolve.''

''Is this in my contract?'' he demanded.

''You better believe it.''

Chapter 12

Though it was November, Los Angeles was suffering from a heat wave that fried tempers and melted patience. Brooke's was no exception. She and Parks had had ten long, isolated days before she had begun work again—but they hadn't been trouble-free. Nothing's trouble-free, Brooke reminded herself as she knotted her blouse beneath her breasts. What fool thought a honeymoon would be? She had, she admitted ruefully as the camera crane was unloaded. But then how much thought had she really given to adjustments, to changes and, as Parks had termed it, the nuts and bolts business that made up a marriage?

She had accepted his name, and though she would keep her own professionally, it was Brooke Jones that she would sign to all legal documents. He had given up his apartment and moved into her house. She had his name, he had her key. Why did she feel she was tallying a balance sheet? Frustrated, Brooke wiped her forearm over her brow.

Was that what marriage was, she wondered, a series of checks and balances? With her marriage barely three weeks old, she should be blissfully happy, glowing. Instead, Brooke felt frustrated, annoyed and unsettled—perhaps more unsettled because she knew Parks was no more blissfully happy than she.

With a shake of her head, she told herself to put it aside. Bringing her personal problems to work wouldn't solve them—and more than likely it would make them worse, since she was directing Parks.

"Let's go up, E.J., I want to see the angle." Sitting in the basket beside him, she gave the crane operator a nod to take them up.

Below them, the beach spread gold. The surf kicked up, white and frothy, catching the glint of the sun and rainbowing through the lens. She thought she could feel the heat steam from the metal casing of the camera. "All right, I'll want a wide shot when he starts, then zoom in, but not too tight. At this angle, we'll get a good profile of the horse. The palomino's a nice contrast with the jeans. Set the speed. I want it slow enough so they see every muscle ripple."

"On Parks or the horse?" E.J. asked with a grin.

"On both," Brooke answered curtly, nodding to be brought down. Wiping her palms on the seat of her pants, she strode over to where Parks waited. He wore nothing but snug, low-slung de Marco jeans. "We're ready for you."

"All right." Parks gave her a long, steady look as he

hooked his thumbs in his front pockets. He wasn't sure why he was dissatisfied, or why he felt the need to annoy her. The friction had been growing between them for the past few days, building and shifting like some electric storm. But there'd been no boom of thunder, no slash of lightning to release the pressure. "What do you want?"

"You've seen the script," she reminded him.

"Aren't you going to give me my motivation?"

"Don't be a smart aleck, Parks," she snapped. "It's too damn hot."

"Just want to make sure I've got the right mood so you won't make me do it a half dozen times."

Temper flared in her eyes and was forcefully suppressed. She wouldn't let him taunt her into a public sniping. "You'll do it two dozen times if I feel it's necessary," she said as calmly as possible. "Now get on the horse, gallop straight down the beach in the shallows. And enjoy it."

"Is that an order?" he murmured, deceptively mild.

"It's a direction," he returned evenly. "I'm the director, you're the talent. Got it?"

"Yeah, I got it." Catching her close, he crushed her mouth with his. He felt the dampness of her blouse under his palm, the angry rigidity of her body and the yielding softness of her breasts. Why was he angry? he wondered even as his temper inched higher. Why did he feel he was dragging her close and shoving her away at the same time? "Got that?" he demanded as he turned and swung onto the horse.

She glared at him, a half-naked man astride a golden horse, as he smiled down at her with the cocky assurance she both loved and detested. Making him pay for that small victory would be a pleasure. Turning on her heel, Brooke strode back to her crew. "Take one," she ordered, then waited, turning ideas for vengeance over in her mind. She took the bullhorn her assistant handed her. "Places!" Parks led the palomino into the surf. Brooke stared at him, forcing herself to put her personal feelings on hold while she thought and felt and saw only as a director. "Roll film, and…action!"

He's magnificent, Brooke thought with a twin surge of pride and irritation. He took the horse into an easy, rolling gallop, kicking up the surf so that the streams of water rose high. Beads glistened on his skin, darkly tanned so that he and the palomino merged into one golden form. Parks's hair and the horse's mane lifted in the wind the motion caused. Strength, an elegance of movement and the simplicity of two beautiful animals. Brooke didn't need special effects to show her how it would look in slow motion.

"Cut. E.J.?"

"Fantastic," he called down. "Sales of de Marco jeans just went up ten percent."

"Let's make sure." Pulling her damp shirt away from her back, Brooke walked to where Parks waited, astride the horse. It had been fantastic, she mused, but not perfect. Spotting her, Parks broke off his conversation with the palomino's trainer.

"Well?"

"It looked pretty good. Let's do it again."

"Why?"

Ignoring the question, she absently patted the gelding's

smooth throat. ''I want you to look down the beach as you ride...all the way down.'' She didn't want that comfortable, free-wheeling sexuality this time, but a dash of aloofness, the solitary-man appeal flavored with the sensuality any female over twelve would recognize.

He shifted in the saddle, his eyes never leaving hers. ''Why?''

''Ride the horse, Parks,'' she countered. ''Let me sell the jeans.''

Very slowly, he dismounted. The trainer quickly remembered something he had to do somewhere else. Behind them, the crew became very busy. Parks held the reins in one hand while he and Brooke measured each other. ''Ever considered asking?'' he said quietly.

''Ever considered following directions?'' she tossed back.

He felt the salt spray drying on his skin. ''Too bad you've never been a team player, Brooke.''

''This isn't a ball game,'' she retorted, firing up. ''We all have our jobs to do. Yours is whatever I tell you it is.''

The flash of anger in his eyes suited her mood. She wanted a fight, a rip-roaring screamer that would tear through the tension of their last few days together. Planting her feet, Brooke prepared to attack and defend.

''No,'' he said with a sudden deadly calm that put her at a disadvantage, ''it's not. My job is to endorse de Marco.''

''And that's what I'm telling you to do.'' She forced herself to match his tone, though she badly wanted to shout. ''If you want to be a prima donna, wait until after we wrap. Take your complaints and talk to your agent.''

His hand snaked out to grab her arm before she could stalk away. ''I'm talking to my wife.''

Heart hammering in her throat, she looked down at the hand that held her. ''Your director,'' Brooke icily corrected, meeting his eyes. ''My crew's hot, Parks. I'd like to finish this before someone faints from heat exhaustion.''

His grip tightened. But he saw that her face was flushed from the heat and damp with sweat. ''We're not finished with this,'' he told her as he released her arm. ''This time, you're going to take a good hard look at the rules.'' Swinging onto the horse, Parks rode away before she could think of an appropriate comment.

Brooke frowned after him as she stalked back to the crane. ''Take two.''

He could have given no logical, succinct explanation for his anger. Parks only knew he was furious. He had only one motivation as he stalked down the corridors to Brooke's office—to have it out with her. He wasn't certain what *it* was, but he would have had it out with her on location if she hadn't been gone before he'd realized it. Though he wasn't thrilled about coming to terms with her in her office, he'd had plenty of experience in meeting a challenge on the opposition's home field. All it meant was that he would take the offensive first.

Brushing by her secretary without a word, Parks pushed open the door to Brooke's office. Empty.

''I'm sorry, Mr. Jones.'' The secretary hurried up to him, warned by the dangerous light in his eye. ''Ms. Gordon…Mrs. Jones isn't in.''

"Where?" Parks demanded curtly.

"I— Perhaps Ms. Thorton's office. If you'll wait, I'll check for you...." But he was already heading out with a long, determined stride that had her chewing on the nail of her forefinger. It looked like Brooke was in trouble. And some people have all the luck, the secretary mused before she went back to her desk.

In less than five minutes, Parks walked by the twins in Claire's outer office and opened her door without knocking. "Where's Brooke?" he demanded, not bothering to greet Claire or his agent.

"Good afternoon, Parks," Claire said easily. "Tea?" She continued to pour Lee's cup as if a furious man weren't at that moment glaring at her.

Parks gave the classic little tea service a brief glance. "I'm looking for Brooke."

"You've missed her, I'm afraid." Claire sipped her tea, then offered Lee a plate of macaroons. "She was in and out a half an hour ago. Would you like a cookie, Parks?"

"No...." He managed to get a tenuous hold on his manners. "Thanks. Where did she go?"

Claire nibbled on a macaroon, then dusted her fingers on a pink linen napkin. "Didn't she say she was going home, Lee?"

"Yep. And she wasn't in any better mood than Parks is." He sent his client a bland smile before he wolfed down a cookie.

"No, she wasn't, was she?" Claire folded her hands on her lap. "Tell me, dear, are you two having a tiff?"

"No, we're not having a tiff," Parks muttered, not certain what they were having. It occurred to him suddenly how cozy his agent and his producer were on the small two-cushioned sofa. "What are you two having?" he countered.

"Tea." Claire smiled her dry smile.

"Why don't you have a seat and cool off," Lee invited. "You look like you've just played nine full innings."

"We were shooting on the beach," Parks murmured. Did Lee Dutton have his arm around Claire Thorton, or was he seeing things?

"It went well?" Claire asked, noting his expression, amused by the reason for it.

"Apparently Brooke was satisfied."

"Apparently," Claire murmured, then shot him a level stare. "When are you and Brooke going to relax and enjoy yourselves?"

Parks's speculative look changed to a frown. "What do you mean?"

"I mean I've never in my life seen two people spend so much time poking at each other."

"Is that what you call it?" Parks muttered, stuffing his hands in his pockets.

"For want of a better term." Claire set her teacup carefully in its saucer. "I realize, of course, that the power game is a founding part of your relationship, and provides its own stimulation, but don't you think it's time you became a family as well as opponents?" Keeping her eyes level, Claire settled into the crook of Lee's arm.

Parks stared at her for nearly a full minute. Power game, he repeated silently. Well yes, it was an intricate part of what they were to each other. They had both looked for strength, challenge, and would have walked the other way if they hadn't found the combination. But as for the rest—a family… Was that what was niggling at the back of his mind?

Wasn't it true that he couldn't resolve himself to the fact that they were living in *her* house, surrounded by *her* things? He still felt uncomfortably like a guest. Even as fresh annoyance grew, he remembered their discussing a trip to Maui. He had told Brooke he wanted her to see *his* place. But… Even as he searched for an excuse, he knew he wouldn't find one.

Turning, Parks paced to the window and scowled out. "I don't think Brooke's ready for a family relationship." The brief, undignified answer Claire gave him had Parks turning back, half-amused. Lee merely reached forward and snatched another cookie.

"She's looked for one all of her life. If you know anything about her, you know that." Suddenly angry, Claire rose. "Is it possible for two people to live together and not understand the other's needs, the other's hurts? How much has she told you about how she grew up?"

"Barely anything," Parks began. "She—"

"How much did you ask?" Claire demanded. "Don't tell me you didn't want to pry," she said quickly, cutting him off. "You're her husband, it's your business to pry. You can be civilized enough to respect her privacy and never touch on what she really needs from you."

"I know that she needs to know she can make her own place," he tossed back. "I know that it doesn't matter if it's a chipped cup or a Hepplewhite table, as long as it's hers."

"Things!" Claire raged. "Yes, she needs things. God

knows she never had them as a child, and the child in her still hurts because of it. But they're only a symbol of what she really wants. Brooke walked in here, an eighteen-year-old adult with nothing more than a few dollars in her pocket and a lot of guts. Someone she thought she loved had taken everything from her, and she wasn't ever going to let that happen again.'' Her mouth tightened, her eyes frosting over at the memory. ''It's your job to show her that it won't.''

''I don't want to *take* anything from her,'' Parks retorted heatedly.

''But you want her to give,'' Claire shot back.

''Of course I do, damn it. I love her.''

''Then listen to me. Brooke's struggled all her life to have something of her own, to have some*one* of her own. She has the things. She's earned them. If you want to share them with her, share her life, you'd better have something pretty special to offer in return. Love isn't enough.''

''What is?'' Parks tossed back, furious at being lectured by someone half his size.

''You'd better figure it out.''

Parks measured her another moment. ''All right,'' he said coolly and left without another word.

Lee rose from the sofa to stand beside Claire. Her pampered skin was flushed with temper, her faded blue eyes icy. ''You know,'' he mused as he studied her, ''I've never seen you in full gear before.''

''I don't often lose my temper.'' Claire fluffed at her hair. ''Young people,'' she stated, as if the two words explained everything.

"Yeah." Taking her shoulders, he turned her to face him. "They don't know a good thing when they've got it." His puckish round face creased with a grin. "How'd you like to spend the rest of your life with an overweight theatrical agent?"

The ice melted from Claire's eyes, but the flush remained. "Lee, I thought you'd never ask."

Parks was fighting his way through L.A. traffic when he heard the first report of the fire. His anger at Claire, his frustration that she had spoken no more than the truth, was switched off instantly as he caught the tail end of a news broadcast reporting brush fires in Liberty Canyon—less than an hour away from Brooke's isolated A-frame. No, there wasn't anger now, but a sick sense of fear that had his palms slipping damply on the wheel.

Had she gone home? he wondered frantically as he sped around a cruising Ferrari. Would she have the television set on, the radio, or would she be in one of her solitary moods? After a hot, enervating day on location, she would often simply shower and sleep for an hour. Recharging, he had called it jokingly. Now the idea terrified him.

As he drove higher, he began to scent the fragrance of dry leaves burning. A faint haze of smoke rose into the sky to the east. Thirty minutes, Parks estimated as he pressed his foot on the accelerator. Forty, if they were lucky. It would take him nearly half that to get there.

There was no wind to hurry the fire along, he reminded himself, fighting to keep calm. They weren't calling it a firestorm…not yet. Brooke was probably already packing up her most important things—he might even meet her on the road on her way down. Any minute she could come zipping around one of the curves in the road leading back down the mountain. They'd get a hotel, talk this business out. Claire was right, he hadn't dug deep enough. Once he had promised himself he would learn the whole woman. It was long past time to make good on the promise.

Parks could almost taste the smoke now, the thick black smoke that led the way for the fire. He saw a pack of small animals—rabbits, raccoons, a fox—race down the road on the other side in their migration to lower elevation. It was close, then, he thought, too close. Why in God's name wasn't she speeding down the road toward safety? He drove the last fifteen miles in a blur of speed and fear.

Parks only took the time to register that Brooke's car was in the driveway before he was out of his own and racing toward the house. She had to be asleep, he decided, not to know the fire was closing in. Even without the radio on, the haze of smoke and smell of burning brought the news. He burst through the front door, calling her name.

The house was silent. There was no sound of hurried movement, of drawers slamming, nothing to indicate frantic packing. Parks was racing up the stairs two at a time when he heard the dog barking. He swore, but kept going. He'd forgotten the dog completely in his fear for Brooke. And the fear grew again when he saw the bed was empty. He was racing through the second floor, still calling, when a movement outside the window caught his eye.

Rain? he thought, pausing long enough to stare. No, water—but not rain. Going to the window, he saw her.

Relief was immediately overlapped by irritation, and irritation by fury. What the hell was she doing standing in the backyard watering the lawn when the smoke was thick enough to block out the trees to the east?

With a quick jerk, he pulled up the window and shouted through the screen. ''Brooke, what the hell are you doing?''

She jolted, then looked up. ''Oh, Parks, thank God! Come down and help, there isn't much time. Close the window!'' she shouted. ''The sparks could get inside. *Hurry!*''

He moved, and moved quickly, intending on shaking her until she rattled then dragging her to the car. Halfway down the stairs, he leaped over the banister and headed to the back door. ''What the hell are you doing?'' he demanded again. Then, instead of shaking her, he found he was holding her tight enough to make her bones crack. If he hadn't heard the radio, if she'd been sleeping… *If.* A thousand ifs ran through his mind as his mouth came down frantically on hers.

It was the sudden howl of wind that brought him back. A sudden ripple of terror ran down his spine. The wind would speed the fire and feed the flames. Brush fire became firestorm. ''We've got to get out of here.''

He had dragged her nearly two feet before he realized she was fighting him. ''No!'' With a show of pure strength, Brooke broke away from him then picked up the hose she had dropped.

''Damn it, Brooke, we can't have more than fifteen minutes.''

He took her arm again and again she broke away. ''I

know how much time there is.'' She aimed the spray of water toward the house again, soaking the wood. The sound drummed in the air over the growing fierceness of the wind.

For the first time, Parks noticed that she was wet and filthy and wearing only a bathrobe. She'd just been stepping from the shower when the special report on the radio had warned her of the approaching fire. He looked at the dirt and grass stains on the silk of her robe and realized what she'd been doing. The land around the house had been cleared. She'd done it with her hands. He saw the scratches and dried blood on them and on her legs and ankles. Now, with the puppy barking frantically around her, she was wetting down the house.

''Are you crazy!'' he demanded as the first flash of admiration was drowned in fresh fury. Parks grabbed her arm again, ripping the shoulder seam of her robe. ''Do you know what a firestorm is?''

''I know what it is.'' Her elbow connected with his ribs as she struggled away. ''If you won't help, stay out of my way; half the house hasn't been wetted down yet.''

''You're getting out of here.'' Parks pulled the hose out of her hand and started dragging her. ''If I have to knock you unconscious.''

Brooke shocked them both by planting her fist solidly on his jaw. The blow was enough to free her so that she stumbled back, losing her balance and landing on all fours.

''I said stay out of my way,'' she hissed, then choked as the smoke clogged her lungs.

Parks dragged her to her feet. His eyes were as wild with fear and fury as hers. ''You idiot, are you going to fight a firestorm with a garden hose? It's wood and glass!" he shouted as he shook her. "Wood and glass," he repeated, coughing as he threw a hand toward the house. "Is it worth dying for?"

"It's worth fighting for!" she shouted back against smoke and wind as the tears started to flow. "I won't give in to the fire, I *won't!*" She began fighting him again, more desperately than before.

"Damn it, Brooke, stop!" He took her shoulders until his fingers bit into her flesh. "There isn't time."

"The fire won't have it. Not our home, don't you understand?" Her voice rose, not in hysteria but in fierce determination. "Not *our* home."

Parks stopped shaking her, again finding that his arms had wrapped around to hold her close. Understanding flooded through him, and in its wake came every emotion he'd ever experienced. Is that what Claire had meant, he wondered, when she'd said love wasn't enough? Love was enough for beginning, but sustaining took every feeling a human being was capable of. *Our home,* she had said. And with the two words Brooke had cemented everything.

He drew her away. The tears were streaming, her breath was labored. Her eyes were rimmed with red but steady. He knew he had never felt more for another, and never would. And suddenly he knew that questions and answers weren't necessary for him to know the whole woman. Without speaking, he let her go and picked up the hose himself. Brooke stayed where she was while he turned the water onto the house. With the back of her wrist, she wiped the stinging tears from her face.

"Parks…"

He turned, smiling the grim gladiator smile. ''It's worth fighting for.'' Brooke let out a shuddering sigh as she closed her hand over his. ''We'll need towels to breathe through, a couple of blankets. Get them while I hose down the rest of the house.''

It seemed like hours passed while they worked together, soaking the wood and each other, the dog, again and again while the smoke grew thicker. The wind screamed, threatening to rip the blanket Parks had tossed over her out of her hands. The heat, Brooke thought. She wouldn't be able to bear the heat. But the flames still held off. There were moments she almost believed the fire would veer away, then she would be choking on the smoke and taking her turn with the hose until she couldn't think at all. There was only one goal—to save the house she'd shared with Parks—the symbol of everything she had ever needed. Home, family, love.

With the towels pressed to their faces, they worked their way around and around the house, soaking the roof, the sides, all the surfaces the heat seemed to dry again so quickly. They no longer spoke, but worked systematically. Two pairs of arms, two sets of legs, working with one mind—to protect what was theirs.

Parks saw the flames first, and was almost too awed to move. It wasn't a furnace, he thought, or an oven. It was hell. And it was racing toward them. Great, greedy towers of fire belched out of the main body like spears. And in the midst of unbearable heat, he felt the icy sweat of human fear.

''No more.'' In a quick move, he grabbed Brooke's arm and scooped up the puppy.

''What are you doing? We can't leave now.'' Stumbling and choking, Brooke fought to free herself.

''If we don't leave now, we could be dead.'' He pushed Brooke into his car and shoved the puppy into her arms. ''Damn it, Brooke, we've done all we can.'' His hands were slick with sweat as he turned the key. ''Nothing you can buy is worth dying for.''

''You don't understand!'' With the back of her hand she smeared grime and tears together on her face. ''Everything—everything I have is back there. I can't let the fire take it all—everything that means anything to me.''

''Everything,'' he repeated in a murmur. Parks stopped the car to stare at her with red-rimmed, stinging eyes. ''All right, if that's how you feel, I'll go back and do what I can.'' His voice was curiously flat and emotionless. ''but, by God, you stay here. I won't risk you.''

Before she could take in what he'd said or what he was doing, he was gone. For a moment, the hysteria had complete control. She trembled with it, unable to move or think. The fire was going to take her home, all her possessions. She'd be left with nothing, just as she had been so many times before. How could she face it again after all the years of struggling, of work, of wanting?

The puppy squirmed in her arms and whimpered. Blankly, Brooke stared down at him. What was she doing sitting there when her house was in danger? She had to go back, go back and save…Parks.

Fear froze her, then had her springing from the car and racing through the smoke. She'd sent him back—he'd gone back for her. For what? she thought desperately. What was she trying to save? Wood and glass—that's what he'd called it. It was nothing more. He was her home, the real home she'd searched for all her life. She shouted for him, sobbing as the smoke blocked everything from view.

She could hear the fire—or the wind. Brooke was no longer certain one was separate from the other. All that was clear now was that if she lost him now, she truly lost everything. So she shouted his name again and again, fighting her way through the smoke to get to him.

For an instant she could no longer breathe, no longer be certain where she was or where to run. An image flashed through her mind, one of herself as a young girl approaching a small two-story house where she would spend a year of her life. She couldn't remember the names of the people who would be her parents for those twelve months, only that sense of disorientation and loneliness. She'd always felt as lonely going in as she had coming out. She'd always been separate, always an outsider, until she'd met Parks.

She saw him racing back to her, misted through the curtain of smoke. Before she could separate one image from another, she was in his arms.

''What happened?'' he demanded. ''I heard you shouting, I thought—'' He buried his face against her neck a moment as the fear ebbed. ''Damn it, Brooke, I told you to stay in the car.''

''Not without you. Please, let's go.'' She was dragging on his arm, pulling him back down the road toward the car.

''The house—''

''Means nothing,'' she said fiercely. ''Nothing does

without you.'' Before he could react, Brooke was climbing into the driver's seat herself. The moment Parks was beside her, she started down the twisting road.

After nearly a mile, the smoke thinned. It was then Brooke felt the reaction set in with shudders and fresh tears. Pulling off the road, she laid her head on the steering wheel and wept.

''Brooke.'' Gently, he brushed a hand over her wet, tangled hair. ''I'm sorry. I know the house was important to you. We don't know yet that it's gone or beyond repair. We can—''

''Damn the house!'' Lifting her head, she looked at him with eyes that were both angry and desolate. ''I must've been crazy to act that way. To send you back there when…'' Trailing off, she swore and slammed out of the car. Slowly, Parks got out and followed her.

''Brooke.''

''You're the most important thing in my life.'' She turned to him then, taking deep breaths to keep the tears back. ''I don't expect you to believe that after the way I behaved, but it's true. I couldn't let go of the house, the things, because I'd waited so long to have them. I needed the identity they gave me.'' Because the words were painful, she swallowed. ''For so long everything I had was only mine on loan. All I could think of was that if I didn't keep that house, those things, I'd be lost again. I don't expect you to understand—''

''I will understand.'' He took her face in his hands. ''If you'll let me.''

She let out a long, shuddering breath. ''I never belonged anywhere, to anyone. Ever. It makes you afraid to trust. I always told myself that there'd be a day when I'd have my own things, my own place—I wouldn't have to share them, I wouldn't have to ask. It was something I promised myself because I couldn't have survived without that one hope. I forgot to let go of that when I didn't need it anymore."

"Maybe." He stroked a thumb over her cheek. "Or maybe you had without realizing it. Back there, you called it *our* home."

"Parks." She reached up to place her hands on him. "I don't care if the house is gone, if everything in it's gone. I have everything I need, everything I love, right here in my hands."

They were wet, filthy, exhausted. Alive. Parks looked at her blackened face and matted hair, the red-rimmed eyes. She'd never looked more beautiful to him. Throats raw from smoke, eyes stinging, he reached for her. Together, they fell to the grass.

Brooke was laughing and weeping as he kissed her. Her face was streaked with soot and tears, but his lips raced wildly over it. Passion met passion. Bruises were unfelt as they touched each other while a need, as volatile as the fire they had challenged, raged through them. When the tatters of her robe were gone, his sodden clothes joined it, they lay tangled, naked on the grass. Again and again, their mouths clung, drawing the strength and victory of the moment from each other, climbing beyond the smoke and stench of the fire left behind to a clean, bright world.

She knew she had never been so aware, so stunningly alive. Her body seemed to hum from a thousand pulses that grew more erratic as he touched her. With her arms tight around him, his body pressed against hers, she felt the sensation of absolute trust. He would protect, she would defend, against any outside forces that threatened. During the fire, they had ceased to be a man and a woman. They had become a unit. Somewhere beneath the swirling passion, Brooke felt peace. She had found her own.

They made love while the smoke broke into mists above their heads. And when they were spent, they clung still, unwilling to break the unity so newly discovered.

''You've hurt yourself,'' Parks murmured, touching a bruise on her shoulder.

''I don't feel hurt.'' She buried her lips at his throat and knew she would never forget the smell of smoke and ash and loving. ''I hit you.''

''Yeah, I noticed.''

Hearing the grin in his voice, she closed her eyes. ''You were only thinking of me. I'm sorry.''

''Now you're thinking of us.'' He pressed his lips to her temple. ''I'm glad.''

''We won,'' she whispered.

Parks lifted his head to look down at her. Taking his thumb, he rubbed a streak of soot from her skin. It was the color of her eyes, he thought, seeing it on his own flesh. ''We won, Brooke.''

''Everything.''

His lips curved before he brought them down to hers. ''Everything.''

She cradled his head on her shoulder, gently stroking his hair. Tiny pieces of ash continued to float above her like memories. ''I said once I didn't want anything to change.... I was afraid to let it change. I was wrong.''

Closing her eyes, she let herself absorb his closeness. ''It's not quite the same now.''

''Better,'' he murmured. ''It makes a difference. It'll always make a difference.''

She sighed, knowing the contentment she had always searched for was irrevocably bound up in one man, one love. ''But we'll still play the game, won't we?''

This time when he lifted his head, he grinned. Brooke's lips curved in response. ''By our own rules.''

* * * * *